THE WOODEN WOLF

In the last quarter of 1944, in England, there was a story about an American pilot who flew de Havilland Mosquitoes. This pilot, it was said, was the tactical equivalent of ten divisions on the ground. General H. H. "Hap" Arnold, commander of the U.S. Army Air Force, said you could "introduce one lone airplane into the fifteen decisive battles of the world, and the course of history would have been changed."

This pilot, a specialist in trains and bridges, was called the Wooden Wolf.

To understand what the name meant, you have to start around D-Day, June 6, 1944 . . .

"I quite understand why ninety percent of the historic assassinations have been successful. The only preventive measure . . . is to live irregularly—to walk, to drive and to travel at irregular times and unexpectedly . . . whenever I go anywhere . . . I go off unexpectedly and without warning to the police . . . [I] could be eliminated at any time by an idiot or a criminal."

Adolf Hitler

THE WOODEN WOLF

JOHN KELLY

GOLDEN APPLE PUBLISHERS

THE WOODEN WOLF

*A Golden Apple Publication / published by arrangement with
E. P. Dutton & Co., Inc.*

Golden Apple edition / January 1984

Golden Apple is a trademark of Golden Apple Publishers

Acknowledgment is made to the following:
Air Ministry Pamphlet 165, Oxygen Sense, *1944.*
Atheneum, for an excerpt from Room 39, *copyright © 1969
by Donald McLachlen.*
Ballantine Books, for an excerpt from The Conspirators: 20th
July. 1944, *copyright © 1971 by Roger Manvell.*
Francis, Day and Hunter, for an excerpt from Albert, 'Arold
and Others *by Marriott Edgar and Stanley Holloway.*
*Houghton Mifflin Co., for permission to quote from the fol-
lowing volumes of* The Second World War *by Winston Chur-
chill: II, Their Finest Hour; V, Closing the Ring, and VI,
Triumph and Tragedy, copyright 1950, 1951, and 1953 re-
spectively by Houghton Mifflin Co.*
William Morrow & Co., Inc., for an excerpt from The War
in the Air, *copyright © 1968 by Gavin Lyall.*
A. D. Peters & Co., Ltd., for an excerpt from Nightfighter
by C. F. Rawnsley and Robert Wright.
Royal Air Force Pamphlet 2019C, Pilot's Notes for Mos-
quito T-111, *1943.*
The Saturday Evening Post, *March 3, 1945.*
Simon and Schuster, Inc., for an excerpt from The Rise and
Fall of the Third Reich, *copyright © 1959, 1960 by William
L. Shirer.*
Warner Paperback Library, for an excerpt from Spymaster
*by Ladislas Farago, copyright © 1954 by Funk and Wagnalls
Co.*

ISBN 0-553-19761-4

Published simultaneously in the United States and Canada

PRINTED IN THE UNITED STATES OF AMERICA

for Joan

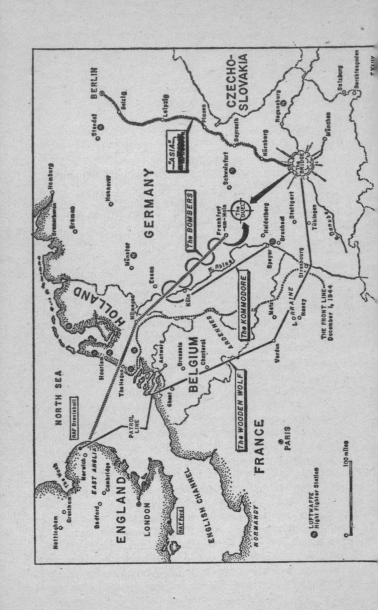

Foreword

by Rear Admiral Matthew B. Dampier,
USN (Ret.)

Beginning in Chapter Three of this book, you will learn that I was, according to the author, the "central figure" of his story. That is an opinion, typical of the many that I will not confirm or deny or even discuss. My function in writing the foreword to a fictional story is different from what it would be for nonfiction. That may appear to be obvious until it is understood that this *was* originally intended to be a work of nonfiction. It took some years for the naïve author to be educated in the ways of the Navy and, more importantly, in certain American and British laws. Now, having strongly opposed the original intention, why have I accepted the long-standing invitation to contribute something to another man's story?

I have accepted because now the story is mainly about people I once cared for very much. For more than thirty years, I was unable to find out what happened to some of these people. The author has constructed a model—that is what I prefer to call this story—of what might reasonably have happened. I felt I owed him something, if not blanket approval. If I have done the job properly, it will be clear that approval was not my function at all. My function seemed to be that of giving a point of view, my own, on several matters already public but perhaps not widely known or properly appreciated. Then I thought I might add a few personal remarks on private matters, the only small revelations that I felt I could make.

First, I should say something about attachés, for I was a naval air attaché in London during the time spanned by this book. What does an attaché do? Let me quote from a Foreign Office Letter of Appointment to a Naval Attaché in His Majesty's Service (it will serve as well for American practice).

> The King has been graciously pleased to approve your appointment as Naval Attaché to His Majesty's Legation at —————. You should bear in mind that you ... do not hold an independent post ... you should take the greatest care to avoid any action liable to create the suspicion that you are attempting to procure secret information by illicit means. You must have no relations or communications with persons acting, or professing willingness to act, as spies or secret agents. ...

In my time, the naval attaché had a dual allegiance. He was primarily accredited to the embassy and served the ambassador, who was Joseph P. Kennedy, Sr., when I arrived in London. But the attaché also reported to the Director of Naval Intelligence and this, for many reasons, was the more basic and important allegiance. I was an *air* attaché. Many embassies have naval attachés, but London was a busy and important center of war and the NA had to have help. And Britain, of course, had a remarkable air force.

In general, any attaché was one of the freest of government officers. This official freedom, however, could bleed away all personal freedom. Holidays and leaves were never taken without purpose; no town was visited for its famous cuisine or great museums; no operation site, planned or actual, could be seen for trivial reasons. And the official freedom always bore the danger of a short career. It is no secret that I was under threat of court-martial from 1945 to 1947, that

I was reduced in numbers and therefore out of the running for Navy command circles during the Cold War, that I was retired early, and that there was then a hotly debated retirement promotion to rear admiral. The details are off the track of what I want to say, but they were such as to permit no other way of handling my case. In all honesty, I would have had to recommend the same procedure.

Now let us consider those private channels I was supposed to have into high and powerful minds on both sides of the Atlantic Ocean and out into the Pacific Ocean. Closely related, of course, are all those things I "saw," those documents I "read" and those verbal orders and permissions I "heard." Let us go right to the top, to Winston Churchill.

Yes, I met Churchill on several occasions, all in my role as air attaché. But I met King George once, too. I knew personally many of the highest officers in the Royal Air Force, including members of the all-powerful Air Council. And my big boss in England was Admiral Harold R. Stark, who commanded all U.S. naval forces in Europe. Until shortly after Pearl Harbor, Stark had been Chief of Naval Operations. Naturally, as the air attaché in London from 1940 through 1945, I met and worked with a large number of influential persons.

Practically all you have to know about Churchill, really, is what he has written about himself. Others have only added footnotes. But this must be said about Churchill's great history of World War II, to keep things in perspective: he was able to discuss, in those six volumes, no more than the tip of the iceberg. Intelligence, for example; under him were no less than 30,000 professionals dealing with all aspects of intelligence. He often became his own intelligence officer, demanding the raw data for his own eyes, and that may have been a mistake.

No one who reads this book can fail to ask, Did the prime minister in fact have cognizance, motive and even personal action with respect to the main event described? On this important point, the author suggests that documents exist—we can hardly entertain seriously the *memory* of conversations—which bear the overpowering imprint of Churchill. My own memory and files on this subject must remain silent. In fairness, I must say that I have seen the author's files and will certify that they were obtained in a proper manner and are totally accurate, to the best of my knowledge.

When Churchill became prime minister in 1940, he immediately issued a philosophical statement and a related directive. He wrote that he was a "strong believer in transacting official business by *The Written Word* . . . to express opinions and wishes rather than orders." To make sure that his "name was not used loosely," he gave out this directive on 19 July 1940:

> Let it be very clearly understood that all directions emanating from me are made in writing, or should be immediately afterwards confirmed in writing, and that I do not accept responsibility for matters relating to national defence on which I am alleged to have given decisions, unless they are recorded in writing.

I think this is interesting because it raises the question of how much of any man's power is actually exerted through written channels. From what Churchill *did* write, we know that his immense command of great issues was matched only by his greed for microsocopic details. He was personally concerned and even acquainted with, so it seems, the very molecules of the British Empire. His "prayers," those exquisite and often harsh memos, dealt with every imaginable Allied interest of importance and also with ration cards, the shape of helmets, bombed-out glass in London, pig farming, the ape colony on Gibraltar, Cuban cigars, ringing of church bells on Christmas Day, and so forth.

The reader must decide whether such a man as Churchill could possibly manage his affairs through writing alone.

Now, between the general question of Churchill and the special question of my men in England, I find myself happy to endorse some technical claims of the author which are important and rightly told.

About aircraft. The de Havilland Mosquito you will soon meet was surely one of aviation's more remarkable developments. But the de Havillands were a remarkable family. I never met Sir Geoffrey, but I did know young Geoffrey, who was his father's chief test pilot, killed in 1946 while testing a Vampire jet at world record speeds over the Thames. Young Geoffrey's cousins, Olivia and her sister Joan Fontaine, are actresses. I have never seen their films but I have seen a Canadian Mosquito called *Joan* and christened by the actress. In my opinion, the Mosquito was the most beautiful machine that ever flew and the deadliest. It was used by the Royal Air Force for "pinpoint missions," what we today call (ironically) surgical operations. When the author says that Mosquito crews can place a bomb through a window on the *right* side of a certain door in a building, believe him. Six Mosquitoes did such things at Gestapo Central in The Hague on 11 April 1944, destroying the Dutch Central Registry which listed thousands of names marked for persecution, torture and death. Göring finally said that he wished the *Luftwaffe* had developed such a wooden aircraft for him; they had tried but the German glue came unstuck. In 1944 and 1945, the fast Mosquito was a greater problem for the Germans, we now know, than were the heavy bombers.

About trains. One of the prerequisites to the successful landing and extension of the Normandy invasion was the disruption of communications, including transportation by such means as trains. Our own Arthur J. Goldberg was in charge of the OSS ground sabotage of trains, which was an outstanding success. But eventually the major destruction of trains came from the air, especially from Mosquitoes. Squadron Leader Peter Panitz of the Royal Canadian Air Force, a Mosquito pilot, once destroyed six whole trains in as many minutes. Alfried Krupp von Bohlen und Halbach said that the disruption of rail transport was the end of Germany. Albert Speer, who initially thought that six more heavy bombings like that of Hamburg in 1943 would end the war, finally said that Germany could carry on with every city in ruins if he could transport materiel between the ruins.

And now *people*—the heart of this foreword. Even after thirty-odd years, I cannot fully express my innermost feelings about a disaster that loomed before my eyes in November of 1944. Six American naval officers reporting to me were killed or lost. Two more were incapacitated as a team when one of them, the pilot, was injured. Finally, two Czechs and the last of my ten men were lost on December 1. You will read about these things and hear the men talking. What more can I say?

I can say something about the author, which might interest a reader. He was more than irrepressible, he was relentless. He was at first an enemy that I had to take seriously. He bombarded me with notes, often Xerox copies of 3 × 5 cards that were meant to intimidate me by suggesting the power of his files. One of these notes cracked my defense:

fable   Web. N 20th
1. A fictitious narrative intended to teach some truth or precept . . .
2. A story or legend invented and developed by imagination or superstition and at one time quite generally believed, but now known to be imaginative; a myth.
3. A story that is not true.
Syn.—allegory, apologue, legend, myth.

allegory
1. A story in which people, things, and happenings have another meaning, as in a fable or parable; allegories are used for teaching or explaining.

I was asked to write the foreword on this basis. *Legend* and *myth* bothered me and *apologue* I had to look up. *Fable* was beneath me but allegories were, at one time, my profession: At that point, I wrote this foreword.

There is a final statement to make on one of my

people, who I would designate as the "central figure" of the story. He is called John Croft, and I am told that he is properly the "main character." You will find that the author calls me many things, including The Holy Ghost. I would deny this ridiculous nickname if John Croft had not given it to me. Here is how it happened.

Croft was not particularly eloquent on the ground. Secondhandedly, I learned that he was the Churchill *and* the Roosevelt of the English tactical airwaves. One night, when he was on an exercise over the Irish Sea, a French pilot in the Royal Air Force—remember that there were Frenchmen, Poles, Czechs and even a few Russians and Germans flying for England —a French pilot was in trouble and was telling about this trouble on the wrong channel, in French. (The French chaps, on training in Mosquitoes by the way, flew that night into Mount Snowdon, which is the only mountain you have to worry about in Great Britain.)

Apparently, the French pilot kept saying, *"Mon Dieu, mon Dieu."* Croft said finally, "This *is* God, so for Christ's sake, will you speak English or get off this channel? My son and I are working over here." It was a rule that English had to be used to the ground stations. It was also understandable that pilots often talked to each other in their native tongues.

When Croft came up to London shortly after this episode, he told me that his Son was William McLaughlin, his radar officer-navigator. "And who is the Holy Ghost?" I asked. "You are," said Croft.

That is how it was in our group in England in 1944.

Huddersfield
Lancs., England

THE
WOODEN
WOLF

PART ONE

Training

TAKE CAT IN NIGHT FIGHTER, AIM
GUNS WHERE CAT IS LOOKING. Sugges-
tion sent to Fighter Command, late 1940.

Gavin Lyall
The War in the Air

1

Midnight

In medieval charts, Britain's southeast quadrant was the savage head of a ragged sea serpent menacing the lowlands of the Continent. The brow above was the bulge of East Anglia. Below, the narrow jaw was Kent. Deep in the throat of the Thames was precious London.

East Anglia. First landhold of British Romans, earldom of the Saxons. A melancholy flatland, lashed by wild North Sea storms washing deep into ancient soil the blood of warriors who founded the peaceful shires of Essex, Suffolk, Cambridge and Norfolk.

In the last quarter of 1944, the communications traffic between London and Norfolk was heavy. In the midst of all this, there was an especially secure connection, a double one, between the Air Ministry, Adastral House, London, and a certain RAF air station in Norfolk. On the evening of November 30, an air vice-marshal in London called a wing commander in Norfolk to say that something important was about to happen. The conversation was in clear, but the two men knew each other and a sort of jargon code had developed between them. "Confirmation will come," said the AVM, "by Telex within fifteen minutes." In thirteen minutes the wing commander's teletype was clattering by London's direction a nonsense of five-letter "words." After translation by the station intelligence officer, the message led to action. The whole action of this story.

December 1 came to Norfolk on the trailing crescent of a vast polar front, a silver lid of cloud, a film wheeling westward over the coast toward the city of Norwich to expose a dark and sodden shire. Neither Norwich nor the night fighter station close by at RAF Brevishall seemed to mark the passing of the week-long storm.

There was no moon.

Two closely guarded de Havilland Mosquitoes were parked remotely from others dispersed widely around the Brevishall perimeter. But all the sleek aircraft of No. 68 Squadron (N/F) wore on the sides of their slim fuselages the same squadron identity letters, WM, light gray, about two feet high. Each aircraft also had its own letter: A-Able, F-Freddie . . . twenty-two in all. Between WM and the Mossie's own letter was the familiar British roundel, a yard-in-diameter bull's-eye, red in the center, then white, then blue, with a thin border of yellow.

In the dimly lighted cockpit of K-for-King, a young woman's head bobbed about in the process of shutting down her Mosquito's twin Rolls Royce Merlins. The woman raced each engine briefly to clear it, then quickly cut the switch. It was like hearing, twice, from out in the forest somewhere, a large animal in great peril. Dying with a last roar, a final shriek, strangled, its throat in the teeth of the victor. Brevishall's civilian neighbors hardly noticed the steady thunder of engines coming out of the mysterious fighter station. What shattered the nights for these people and angered them was that roar, that shriek, that sharp decay of sound, the weird echoes, and most of all that sudden silence.

As the airscrews of K-King whined and wind-milled to a stop, the cockpit light went out and a hatch below the Mosquito's chin popped open. A fleshy WAAF wobbled backward down a flimsy ladder. The cold wind took the woman's breath away. Stabbing frozen hands into the pockets of her oily slate-colored coverall, Leading Aircraftwoman Heather Stampford listened with experience and understanding to the complaints of her cooling engines. Their tortured hot innards spoke to her a whispered tongue of metallic groans and pings. Heather understood what the metal said.

"Stand easy, old girl," said Heather, "they'll be along straightaway."

The metal spoke but the wood of the Mosquito's shark-shaped body, wings and elliptical tail surfaces was silent except for faint drumming sounds made by the wind on a smooth fabric skin. That skin helped to make the craft very fast. With a cabinetmaker's finish, drag was greatly reduced; no seams, no rivets to catch the wind. So the wind played only lightly upon Heather's Wooden Wonder. That's what they called it now around the world, yes, but at first it had been ridiculed as de Havilland's Folly. How the transformation came about is easily learned, but it will take a little time.

To warm her feet and liven the dead muscles of her legs, Heather danced a snappy hornpipe on the soaked turf near the starboard tire of the Mossie, a wheel which stood as high as her chest. The wing stub between the fuselage and the right-hand engine was a sort of roof for her, and looking up from her shelter, Heather saw that the raw drizzle had stopped while she'd been up in the cockpit. Stepping out in front of the Mosquito, she watched a thinning veil of cloud directly overhead sweep slowly to the northwest. For the first time in a week, she saw a bright star pulsing in the black velvet sky. The star evoked a secret, pagan wish regarding the navigator of her wooden kite. Kissing the numb fingertips of her right hand, she traced a cross on the fuselage, on Bill McLaughlin's side. It was for her American lieutenant commander, Bill, and indirectly for Lieutenant Croft too, although Heather hated the bad-tempered sod of a pilot. She turned and walked back toward the tail, where the fuselage bore the serial number MM609/G. The G was for high security around special-mission or experimental machines. *That silly GI,* thought Heather, *how it mucks up a girl's life . . . the twenty-four-hour guard . . . all the modifications. . . .*

She flashed her small torch on the beautiful watch McLaughlin had given her. Fifty feet back of the Mossie, the invisible sentry was attracted by the glow.

"What time, Miss?"

"Ten past twelve."

"Taa. Gettin' set for a prang, are they?"

"Might do."

To the new sentry, who was very young, Heather sounded a little unfriendly. He had hoped she'd come back and talk to him. He didn't know how friendly Heather really was, for she was right now dreadfully worried and preoccupied.

They should be coming along the perimeter road any minute now. The Bedford lorry would stop down at L-Love's spot first, to drop off Adeš and Miloslav, those no-nonsense Czechs. Then they'd bring the Americans to her. She would say to the lieutenant, and her life would be on it, "Sir, the aircraft is ready."

Down the road by L-Love, Heather saw someone playing the weak beam of a handtorch around the undercarriage and up into the wheel wells. Just the ground crew, all men. Those Czechs, especially Adeš, didn't like women working on their aircraft. Those fellows must be nervous too. Lots of legs moving around.

Delay always made Heather very nervous. She adjusted her necktie, smoothed down her jumper with several quick tugs.

Prang, the sentry had said. A crash, sometimes a dirty word. The WAAF began to whistle, slowly, almost inaudibly, the plaintive tune of *Waltzing Matilda.* In her head, she heard only the new words:

> *Ops in a Mossie,*
> *Ops in a Mossie,*
> *Who'll go on Ops in a Mossie with me?*
> *O, he sang*
> *As he swang*
> *And he pranged it on the hangar roof!*
> *Who'll go on Ops in a Mossie with me?*

Behind Heather, K-for-King faced dumbly east into the bitter wind blowing out of Germany. In the dark, with its engines dead, the Mosquito could have been one of those many balsa models that its pilot had built as a boy. Like the models, the Mosquito sat exactly where it was placed, never moving, waiting for the boys, the men, to come back and play. To take K out and play again. To kill something.

Five hundred miles east of Brevishall, twenty miles south of Berlin, a deluxe Federal Railways train drove through wet sleet at the lower edge of the city's anti-aircraft web. Approaching open country, the engine-driver opened his throttle to build up his speed. Eight cars snaked obediently behind the powerful black-and-red Pacific loko pulling them down to Munich. A flash of lightning revealed stylized silver eagles of the *Luftwaffe* along the wet, green, gleaming sides of one coach. This train was *Reichsmarschall* Göring's *Asia,* one of his mobile headquarters.

Behind the locomotive's tender was a dull gray, coffin-shaped flakwagon, with cramped housing for the crew of its 88-millimeter gun.

The *Reichsmarschall'*s private coach followed the flakwagon. It had two bedrooms and a small study, with service galleys. This coach was empty.

In the next coach was a large salon and a film projection room. Here three *Luftwaffe* officers were reviewing the latest secret releases from the Rechlin proving center on the modified Messerschmitt 262 jet fighter.

The third car, a crowded operations room, was the scene of a conference of fourteen men, including three of general rank. Cognac and schnapps were available from *Luftwaffe Gemeiner,* who moved among the high-ranking officers with the ease and skill of long service in a swaying, mobile headquarters. The forward end of the car was a signals center, closed off by large panes of frosted glass. Radio equipment was manned and active. A telephone switchboard and a bank of teleprinters were temporarily dead, while *Asia* was underway.

Fine foods and wines were served in the fourth

car, a dining room paneled in rosewood. Crested china and silverware, with fresh flowers, were set out at eight tables. At the late hour, only a *Luftwaffe* general, an executive from the Ruhr and an assistant finance minister of the Reich were being served.

The fifth car bore a long, polished conference table with sixteen chairs and had a lounge area toward the rear. This was the coach whose sides carried the handsome eagles. Five men were clustered at the table's forward end, closely engaged in noisy conversation and drink. At the head of the table a grossly fat man in a striking pale blue marshal's uniform wore *Luftwaffe* pilot wings, many medals on the left breast, and the rare *Ordre pour le mérite,* the Blue Max of the Great War, suspended by a ribbon at the throat.

In the next to last car—a second flakwagon brought up *Asia's* rear—the décor was Victorian in deep brown mahogany and festooned drapes of gray velvet. Two guards with Schmeisser submachine guns stood in the forward vestibule. Anyone allowed to pass by them would walk back along a side aisle serving three bedrooms. Opposite the door of the first bedroom, a small bouquet of flowers wilted down around the neck of a hanging cut-glass jardinière. In the nameplate on the door was a card on which, in a feminine hand, someone had scrawled the name Eva Braun.

Through the half-glass door that separated the aisle from a large after-parlor, one could see a small conference table with eight chairs. The greenish light from an old-fashioned umbrella chandelier fell onto many large maps and lit the faces of three men poring over them, but left the rest of the parlor in darkness. One of the men, wearing a plain uniform jacket with no markings but a Party armband, was pounding his fist on the maps—*bang*! and *bang!* and *bang!* and *bang!*—right under the nose of a silent, white-haired full general of the Army. An Alsatian bitch, a wolfhound, lay asleep near the twitching foot of the violent man, who was her master. The third man at the table —round-faced, stocky, unmemorable—said nothing but made occasional notes in a black leather journal.

A kilometer ahead of *Asia,* pacing it, was the drab and almost empty pilot train. All over the countryside through which the trains came up to full speed, the low and weeping clouds were charged with inner lightning and resonant with the drumbeat of continuous thunder.

From a blacked-out railroad tower north of Belzig, the passage of two trains was noted and entered into the log of Herr Anton Scheubel, an elderly *Flugwachtmann.* He wrote by the light of a taped handtorch. Scheubel had been expecting the trains. On one of the tower telephones, the old man called a Berlin number . . . heard seven rings . . . listened for a few seconds . . . and said only "Ah, I was calling Belzig," and hung up. One minute later, Scheubel repeated the procedure precisely, except that he called a Belzig number and said he meant to call Berlin.

Long retired from the Federal Railways System, Anton Scheubel served the Reich in two capacities. As a *Flugwachtmann,* his main job, he was simply an airraid warden. Since he was in an unused railroad tower anyway, he also logged trains for the System free of charge and it was helpful to them. But out of the second, simple job came Anton Scheubel's real reason, at age seventy-six, for staying young, sharp and very careful. He was, in Allied lingo, a "train-watcher": indeed, he worked for the Allies. He saw trains move past only one spot in Germany—his tower; he told people in Berlin and Belzig about his trains. His small reports moved pins on maps in London and Washington. Scheubel was content with his anonymous, dangerous work. He had lost two grandsons in Russia and these fine lads would be proud of *Grossvati,*

Five hundred miles apart, Heather Stampford looked at her new watch and Anton Scheubel saw his trains, and these events were related.

There was something else, in England, one hour earlier. Lieutenant (junior grade) John Croft, USNR, arrived at Brevishall in a delapidated little Morris and he had with him a fine-looking woman in a black naval

uniform. It was the woman's car and its sad state was
only partly a result of wartime autocar attrition in
England; the woman was a reckless driver. It terrified
John Croft to ride with her but she wouldn't let him
drive without a proper permit. The woman was a sublieutenant in the Women's Royal Naval Service, a
WREN.

The car, the little car, stopped briefly at the
Brevishall sentry box, where there was mild flap. The
station had come under special security two weeks ago
and the guards were wary. Croft showed his face and
card. The car was passed. It wound its way among
the roads of Brevishall and scraped the curb in front
of the Ops building, a one-story structure in the middle
of the Brevishall complex.

The left-hand door of the Morris opened. Croft
got out and looked up at the sky. (Only pilots and
children look up at the sky.) It was still raining, the
cloud was ten-tenths, total. Croft went round to the
driver's side, where the window was rolled down. There
was a brief conversation. Croft bent down and kissed
the woman. Then he turned and walked into the Ops
building. And she spun the wheel and drove viciously
out of Brevishall.

She would talk to Croft later in the night.

Croft was not all that he seemed to be, even to
the WREN, perhaps especially to her. He was a man
whom she loved, true. In a way, he loved her, too. But
Croft was not really *liked* by many, women or men,
although he was respected and admired by all of them,
even his enemies—literally, his enemies on the Continent, who knew far more about the man's work, its
results, than anyone in England could possibly know.
In England there were a few, six or seven men, all of
them older than Croft, who worshiped the ground he
walked on. There was a joke there. When the pilot
walked on the ground, he was not at home and was
sometimes clumsy. Even Heather Stampford saw how
things changed when Croft climbed her ladder and put
on the gloves she always left for him, tucked behind
the electrical gunsight. His gloves, but she liked to
wear them when she worked on K-King.

In the last quarter of 1944, in England, there was a story about an American pilot who flew de Havilland Mosquitoes. This pilot, it was said at the Supreme Commander's headquarters, was the tactical equivalent of ten divisions on the ground. General H. H. "Hap" Arnold, commander of the U. S. Army Air Force, said you could "introduce one lone airplane into the fifteen decisive battles of the world, and the course of history would have been changed." This pilot, a specialist in trains and bridges, was called the Wooden Wolf. To understand how that name came about, you have to go back about six months. To understand what the name meant, you have to start around D-Day, June 6, 1944.

2

Op-33-H

The manufacture of a government assassin began at ten thirty on the morning of 7 June 1944, when a deeply tanned lieutenant (junior grade) came into the Navy Department main building in Washington and asked for Room 4802. That was Op-33-H, the night fighter desk, one of the deepest "desks" under the Chief of Naval Operations. There was a holiday atmosphere upon the immense building, whose miles of corridors were briefly alive with extra visiting, with excited conversations, even with laughter. CNO would have to wink at a lot of long lunches this day, leading to an afternoon of happy underproduction. The invasion of France was underway and seemed to be working. Any newcomer to the gray mausoleum on Constitution Avenue could hardly know that its atmosphere was rarely so happy, but like Washington and all the world, he would have to know about D-Day.

Eighth wing, fourth deck, they told the visitor with the wrinkled khakis.

The jg did not seem to know about D-Day. He was irritated when the enlisted WAVE at the information desk called him back to sign the visitor log. She was annoyed because he hardly noticed her. Tuned-out, he was. Then the next visitor came in and the WAVE forgot forever the man who violated her book. He had written:

NAME	RANK	FILE NO.	STATION	VISITING?	PURPOSE?
Croft, J.	Lt(jg)	158179	CNO	Op-33-H	VISIT!

A naval message from this very building had brought John Croft to Washington from a famous carrier in the Pacific. Translated by a cipher machine at sea, the message was converted into the following orders:

From:	The Commanding Officer
To:	LT(jg) John (n) Croft, A-V(N), USNR
Via:	The Commander, Fighting Squadron (NIGHT) ONE
Subject:	Change of duty.

1. When directed by your commanding officer, duty completed. Detached.

2. Report to the Senior Officer Present Ashore at Island 6, for first available government air/surface transportation to a port whose name you will provide orally.

There was more. Island 6 was the atoll of Majuro in the Marshall Islands, captured as a fleet anchorage for the first major task force that finally would threaten Japan itself. From this unknown atoll, Croft's journey to Washington had been a nightmare of Navy confusion. Like a lost book in the Library of Congress, the night fighter pilot had wandered in the Pacific Ocean with a chance of recovery entirely acceptable to drafters of orders.

Captain Carlton L. I. Parmenter, USN, was in his office early (for him) at nine thirty to do a little homework on his late arrival from the Pacific. The Op-33-H administrative officer had called the captain's apartment two hours earlier to say that the pilot was in town. The duty officer's memo said: "Croft reported in circa midnight, mad as hell no one here. Told report back 1030 sharp. Tough customer, Captain!"

There had been a D-Day party lasting twelve hours; the captain was a little shaky. His imaginary ulcer was muttering and one of his WAVE yeomen had just given him three more aspirins for the headache. Op-33-H, a crowded hive of three rooms, was rich in women only because its commanding officer had to have a lot of sympathy. The only thing Clip Parmenter liked better than young women was to worry about the whole night fighter program and to battle with all its enemies in the Navy. The tougher they were, the better!

So this Croft, a jg, is tough? Gently coupling an English cigarette with a silver holder, Parmenter's soft eyes scanned the memo again. His WAVEs, perhaps for reasons of their own, called the skipper "old cat eyes" even though the eyes were almost black and had long, feminine lashes. One of the legends was that the big pupils went down to slits just before Parmenter struck, or when someone surprised him with a sudden light for his cigarette. He took the gold lighter from the desk and lit the cigarette in the holder. *A jg is a gnat, really!*

He started through Croft's jacket and office file, as he had done so casually a month ago. His memory was excellent but too full of the high-powered people he controlled, too jammed with complex events he had set into motion. All that nagged Parmenter was that now he was supposed to know all about Croft, who had been one of the first ensigns in old Project X-Ray, the captain's original brainchild in radar night fighting. He certainly couldn't picture Croft. The files soon showed him that he didn't remember much of what he'd seen there, either. They'd even slipped in a couple of entirely new items.

Clip Parmenter was the human analogue of an outrageously expensive cut diamond. He was abrasive, hard; nothing scratched him. He was always cool and could be cold, yet the inner fires that drove him could flash out suddenly along certain tangents. No one had yet found in Parmenter just that cleavage plane along which the finest, the perfect diamond can be shattered by a proper blow. He was unlikely to be bought, since he already owned everyone important to him, everything he coveted. All his uniforms, even the whites and khaki shirts, were made in London and fitted in New York (not Washington!). The Royal Navy touch was hard to put your finger on but it was there. The gold naval aviator wings were *solid* gold; the eagles on the collar points were *solid* platinum. That these trinkets were discarded with the laundry and replaced from a vault in Parmenter's apartment was not true, of course, but people knew that it was possible.

What Captain Parmenter did remember about Croft was pretty well known in classified circles. The pilot had gone out with the first part of Gus Horn's Night Fighting One—Parmenter's first product under old X-Ray—suddenly ordered to Guadalcanal and Munda in the Solomon Islands, in the middle of 1943. There, one miserable night over Munda, Croft became the first radar night fighter in the world to shoot down an enemy plane from a single-engine, single-seat fighter.

Then Croft had gone over to the carrier-based echelon of VF(N)-1, whose real problems were admirals, not enemy. Once again the pilot intercepted a twilight "lamplighter" that was dropping yellow-green phosphorus flares down over the whole fleet—a ghastly scene—to light the way in for a torpedo plane attack coming in low over the water. Croft splashed the flare snooper in flames a few hundred yards away from the top admiral's bridge. The Munda trick again, this time from a carrier. That was the real beginning of night operations in the fleet. Croft was followed by others but he would always be remembered as the first. Parmenter was grateful to Croft but he did not really know who Croft was.

The first shock to come out of Croft's file was a copy of an old request that a serious ensign had writ-

ten by himself and brought one morning into the
X-Ray office at NAS, Quonset Point, Rhode Island:

From: Ens. John (n) Croft, A-V(N), USNR
To: The Commanding Officer, Project
           X-Ray
Subject: Escort of civilian into restricted areas.

1.   Permission is hereby granted to Ensign
           Croft to escort his father, Arthur B.
           Croft, a civilian advertising account
           executive, into the following areas:
           a) Project X-Ray offices.
           b) VF(N)-1 ready room.
           c) VF(N)-1 line.
2.   The subject civilian will not be shown
           anything of restricted, confidential or
           secret nature during this tour.

Croft began coming back a little to Parmenter. The
captain remembered the amateur Navy-style request,
but it was the father's occupation that did it, mainly.
What ensign would think that an advertising man was
somehow a preferred security risk? The request had
been granted over the most famous initials in the Navy
night fighter world—C.L.I.P.

The real surprises, for Parmenter, were these:

For the action at Munda, Gus Horn, commanding VF(N)-1, had recommended Croft for the Distinguished Flying Cross. Upgrading recommended.

For the action at sea, the fleet admiral had recommended Croft for the Silver Star. Upgrading supported.

Croft had guided back to the carrier a day fighter
pilot with a 20-millimeter shell in the back of his
brain. In the course of this guidance, Croft had shot
down two of three Japanese fighter planes, using the
wounded pilot as a foil. The fleet admiral recommended the Navy Cross for this feat and would support a Congressional Medal of Honor.

In his travels to Washington, Croft had shuttled
between Majuro in the Marshalls and Tarawa in the
Gilbert Islands. At Tarawa one night, while waiting

for transportation, Croft had borrowed a Marine Corsair fighter, *without radar,* and on a practice flight had found and shot down the largest flying boat in the world, called an *Emily.* From the Tarawa island commander to the skipper of the Marine day fighter squadron, there was unanimous agreement that Croft should have a Navy Cross. In the words of Major Trilling, commanding VMF-201 at Tarawa: ". . . This pilot, a transient, used our aircraft, familiar to him but *without radar,* to find and destroy a Kawanishi H8K flying boat that, we have reason to believe, was shadowing the next move of Task Force 58 out of Majuro." (Croft would remember. When the flying boat went down, he flew station over it until two torpedo boats arrived. All ten crew members of this giant flying boat were killed by his guns, for the landing on the water had been too gentle to kill anyone.)

For the first time in his life, Parmenter did not know what to do. In minutes, he was to face a junior officer he did not really know. At that moment, Lieutenant March, the administrative officer, came to the captain's door with a lieutenant (junior grade) of average build who wore no wings. It was therefore a surprise to hear March say, "This is Mr. Croft." Parmenter thought March was bringing in a new office replacement. One look at the officer brought that Ensign Croft back to Parmenter. The eyes, the eyes! Neutral eyes, narrow chips of gray porcelain, triangular mirrors glinting at the world—triangular windows looking at a world of Parmenters.

"Croft!" Parmenter cried, "Croft, at last!" Around the big desk the captain came, his arms wide, suggesting the breakup to a carrier landing. "Where have you been?"

"In the Pacific, Captain."

It was the same Parmenter of X-Ray. A commander then. Silver cigarette holder, English cigarettes, never smoked past the first inch—symmetry. The uniforms: those khakis, with creases in the shirts matching like railroad tracks the creases in the trousers. Like a Marine DI, he was. Ninety degrees, humid as hell in Washington—Parmenter never sweated, no dark spots, just like a Marine. Croft shook the captain's dry, manicured hand.

"My God, Croft," said Parmenter, "what's kept you?"

"Sorry, Captain Parmenter," said Croft, "but a Priority Two is no good west of California." The pilot glanced sidewise at March. "Could someone check, sir, on this? I've wasted a month of my life. Sir!"

"Please," said the captain, "sit down." *God, how he loved to talk to these fellows from the action!* By an indescribable glance, March was dismissed. Parmenter said, "Tell me what happened. Everything! I am in charge of night fighting for this Navy, Mr. Croft, and it will prosper, I assure you! What's wrong out there, tell me! Be frank."

Croft looked at Parmenter for a full minute. He looked at the man. He looked at the dress. He saw the expensive gadgets on the desk and the framed mementos on the wall.

"Okay, Captain," said Croft, "here you are. It's your Navy, sir. I'm temporary. I think your admirals are old. I think your admirals don't know what radar is. Your admirals waste everybody you train. *Sir.*" Croft was taking an inch-thick stack of papers from his briefcase, mostly with handwriting on odd-sized Navy blanks. He placed about thirty neatly typed sheets on top.

"I've had a lot of time lately, Captain, to think. Everything I have to say is here. Not too well organized, a lot of sketches. But the typed report is a good summary, I think. I was going to address it to Captain Hamilton out at NOCTU"—that was Night Operations & Combat Training Unit (Pacific)—"until I met him. May I address it to you? It's important."

"Oh, oh, Croft, love to have it, love it! One of my women can—"

"Now, Captain," said Croft, laying the stack on the big desk, "can you tell me why I'm here? I'd like to talk about *that.*"

Slash. Parmenter's usual big buildup was destroyed before it ever got airborne, and the captain saw that right away.

"How thoughtless of me," said Parmenter, "but surely Eric, Captain Hamilton, told you what's going on."

Parmenter knew damn well that NOCTU's powerful chief, the toughest bastard in Hawaii, had said nothing to Croft. The reason was that Clip Parmenter had said nothing to Eric Hamilton in the first place.

"Captain Hamilton said I was coming back here to check out in the Tigercat." The Grumman F7F Tigercat was the Navy's great new hope as a twin-engine, two-man night fighter for the carriers. "He got me checked out in twin-engine, while I was at Barber's Point. *Is* it the F7?"

"Partly true, Croft, partly true—if there's time. But tell me this. Wasn't it Captain Hamilton who really held you up out there?"

"Only half of it. The other half was *before* I got to Hawaii. Between the Big E and Pearl Harbor, I bummed around most of that ocean in ships you wouldn't believe. They flew me down from Majuro to Tarawa. It all began at Tarawa. . . ."

In the pilot's briefcase was a collection of orders, endorsements, permissions, meal chits and mess receipts that could stoke the Navy Department furnaces for half a day. Mostly it was a record of aimless touring and occasional sightseeing in the Gilbert Islands and the Marshalls. There was nothing written down about the *Emily* at Tarawa nor did Croft say anything about it.

"Well," said Parmenter jovially, "we never thought you'd be hijacked at NOCTU, believe me. But it didn't take long to get you out of there, did it now?"

"A month, sir, exactly. I didn't know until a week ago that I was coming here. I didn't know I was late for anything. What *am* I late for, Captain?"

"So you think it's the Tigercat, eh?" Parmenter had to salvage just a little drama from his wrecked buildup. He symbolized confidentiality by rolling the big leather chair closer to the end of the desk where Croft sat.

"That's what Captain Hamilton told me."

"Yes, you'll fly the F7F here at Anacostia or at Patuxent River, if there's time. But there may not be time, because you, Croft, are going to England."

"England!"

That reaction, at least, pleased Parmenter. "Yes," he said, "you are the last of five pilots we've been sending to the Royal Air Force to go through their regular night fighter training course. You may remember, perhaps, that I spent some time with the RAF."

"Yes sir." Some might not remember but no one could forget.

"Five radar officers, fighter-directors actually, are in England, too, and each of them will be teamed with a pilot. Lieutenant Commander William McLaughlin, I think, will fly with you. You may know him. Captain Hamilton sent him on from NOCTU. But"—the pause was more for Eric Hamilton than for Croft— "neither you nor McLaughlin will go back to Captain Hamilton. I have to tell you, Croft, how things have changed in our training program back here since you went out with VF(N)-1. We have a NOCTU(Lant) now, to start with"—*Lant* meant Atlantic—"which came from the training part of my old Project X-Ray. The technical part of X-Ray came down here to the Patuxent River air station. There's simply no comparison anymore with the small operation we had going up there in Rhode Island."

Before continuing, Parmenter's childish curiosity finally forced him to ask about Croft's wings. The pilot was not wearing the wings on his khaki blouse, which made Parmenter ill at ease. It was bad enough that the khakis themselves were so badly wrinkled and mussed.

"Croft, did you, ah—were you aware your wings are missing?" Parmenter could have said more about the casual dress and bearing but he did not.

"Yes sir, they must have fallen off. I haven't had a chance to get new ones."

The old wings belonged now to a TWA stewardess who had done a big favor for Croft. After the flight from San Francisco, the stewardess had borrowed a typewriter in the TWA airport office. It had taken her almost all night to do the thirty pages that Croft had given to Captain Parmenter. The stuff was impossible to understand (Croft knew that) and that made slow going. The pilot hovered over her every minute, not only to make corrections as errors came off the keys, but to put every scrap of paper they handled (and at the end the typewriter ribbon) into his briefcase. Just before dawn they finished, when the pilot was still chipper but the woman was beat. So beat, and with an afternoon flight. He took her to her hotel and said goodbye in the lobby. Many strange things she had seen in her job but nothing like this—nothing like this man. Croft went twice around in the hotel's revolving door and came back on the lobby side. He got an envelope from the clerk, put his wings in it, and wrote her name. She didn't need a note from him.

"It was rough enough, Croft," said Parmenter, "putting all of you together, and the sorting-out when you come back will be worse. I make few friends here, let me tell you." Sympathy, even a little from Croft. "But that's not your problem. You'll be in England at least three months. You'll fly Beaufighters mainly, with a little time at the finish in the Mosquito. Do you know this airplane?"

"I've read about it. I saw one at the Quonset line the day we shipped out for Guadalcanal. It had Canadian markings."

"Yes, I borrowed that one for Project X-Ray. Flew it myself. It is a delightful machine." Unlike Captain Hamilton, Parmenter these days talked flying more than he flew.

Parmenter was not through weaving a delicate caul of mystery around the assignment to England.

"We've booked passage for you on one of the New York Clippers. Military flights to the British Isles have been suppressed, quite unreliable, since well before D-Day. You will go through Ireland or Lisbon, so of course you will have to wear civilian clothes. March will tell you about all these things. He is at the State Department now, I imagine, arranging a special passport for you. Now, you have been at sea for a year. May I—what I hate to ask—can you possibly manage, as a leave, the few odd days it will take to package you up here and in New York?"

"No problem, Captain. No one knows I'm here. A few phone calls."

"Our phones are yours. Call anywhere. Aren't you from New York?" Parmenter suddenly made the connection between New York and the old request to escort an "advertising" father through X-Ray and VF(N)-1 working spaces. "You fly out of New York. Will that help?"

"Yes."

There was an awkward pause, at least for Parmenter, who had a sense of conversational logic and rhythm that was suddenly not working with this distant man. He began scribbling rapidly on a pad, with the gold pen that had castrated so many proposals, raised so many hopes only to erase them, drawn lines through a few careers. As he wrote, he said, "I want you to see as many of these men, some of them out in the Arlington and Potomac annexes, as you can before you leave Washington. . . ."

On June 10, at 0800, a speedboat raced up and down the takeoff lane of the Pan-American Marine Basin, LaGuardia Field, checking the choppy waters for debris. A deep-bellied Boeing 314 waited for the clearance signal from the shore tower, like a racing yacht trying to stay behind the starting line. The four engines were balanced against a stiff wind from Long Island Sound. With a terse radio message from the tower and a green light, the majestic Clipper under full power gained speed on the water, broke away from its boiling wake, skated briefly on its step, tapped the small waves as if to wipe water from its keel, then rose into the low, bright sun far down the Sound.

In spite of the Clipper's interior elegance, John Croft was depressed. He sat alone in one of the five smaller lounges, going through the contents of his precious briefcase. The special passport, No. 38356, said that "the bearer is a Government official proceeding abroad on classified official business." Signed Cordell Hull, Secretary of State. Irish Legation and British Consulate visas were stamped "official gratis courtesy." But there was no Portuguese visa. This had been the signal to Croft that the BOAC reservation, Shannon via Lisbon, should be canceled. This signal had meant "LaGuardia, not Port Washington; no Lisbon."

The orders said: "On or about 10 June 1944 you will proceed to the British Isles and upon arrival proceed and report to the Commander, U. S. Naval Forces in Europe, and to such other places as may be necessary for temporary duty under instruction involving flying." These were not thrilling orders. Instruction. The orders *were* copied to the Director of Naval Intelligence, which was something, but there had been no opportunity to visit Op 16 (Intelligence). No personal visit with Admiral Radford. No checkout in the Tigercat. No time at all.

A rain the night before had swept out all the sky over the New England coast. There was not a single cloud over the sparkling Atlantic; the smooth air and the water were so clean as to seem sterile. Croft made a tour of the Clipper's lower deck, which was for passengers. There were nine connecting compartments. In addition to the five lounges, there was a main lounge doubling as a dining room, served by a large galley. Two deluxe sleeping compartments were private when the flying boat was made up for luxury peacetime trips; these were open now. Croft had counted only fourteen passengers. The Clipper could accommodate twenty-five to forty passengers, depending upon the sleeping arrangements. With all the space, including nearly four feet of headroom, the big boat seemed to be the first-class part of a compact ocean liner.

They were a dull lot, these men in civvies, all of them older than Croft. Probably most of them were military. From the ages alone—and from the air priorities, which did not match his One—Croft guessed these men were of very high rank or important civilians. They were all on Two or Three priorities; Croft told no one he had a One.

At lunch, Croft joined the two he had privately nicknamed "The Twins" because they were inseparable and even looked alike. They had haircuts ordinarily found only in a Marine boot camp. One of them had come aboard with a leather envelope that looked like a squashed loaf of bread. Croft saw later that this envelope was tied to the man's waist with a tube of leather. Inside the tube was a chain.

It was the twins who invited Croft to have lunch with them in one of the small lounges. A steward had covered one of the low tables with linen. The man chained to the pouch was a State Department courier, a Marine, Second Lieutenant Buck. His companion was a Marine guard, First Sergeant "Semper" Schlegel. Neither Marine tried to hide the Colt .45 that was under his arm. These men, Croft learned, made an average of six Atlantic crossings a month.

The twins had figured out most of the passengers. There were only three civilians, traveling together, probably aircraft engineers. "Boeing," Schlegel said, "because I heard them talking about cutting out some of the airframes of this boat."

"We figure that you," said Buck with a disarming grin, "are either Air Force or Navy, probably Intelligence."

With grim memories of the Marine DI's in his early training, Croft was tempted to flake these two right out. *Air Force!* "No, not Air Force, not Navy," was all Croft said.

Late in the afternoon, the Clipper made a frustrating overnight stop in Newfoundland, at the Botwood seadrome near Gander. Croft had heard that Pan-American was still leery about night flying, but he had not calculated the route timing. To land in Ireland around dawn of 12 June, they would have to use up half of the eleventh and all of the night, losing five hours on the way.

The stewards began waking their passengers at dawn of the twelfth, as the Clipper descended through

thick cloud off Kerry Head at the broad mouth of the
River Shannon. (Croft was wide awake, his forehead
pressed against the window.) Ireland, as it rose out of
the gray mists, was a forbidding sight. Only when the
silver flying boat skimmed a hundred feet over the
cliffs, as the flat rays of the sun brushed the hilltops,
was it clear that Ireland was a land of wet, wet green.

At the Foynes landing on the river, customs officials waited under a portable canopy to collect passports and find out whose luggage would be examined. Croft's bag was immune. His passport was taken
and he was told that they would bring it back to him
in the port restaurant, if the gentleman would care to
go there. The Irish put on a soft, friendly face, Croft
thought, but they were hard people.

For breakfast that morning, the Navy pilot enjoyed one of the finest steaks he'd ever had. Just before the steak was served, he had the shock of seeing
several airport laborers coming on duty, stopping by
the massive bar, mirrored and oaken, tossing off shots
of straight whiskey. For the first time, Croft understood what a "belt" of liquor meant. His stomach
turned over at the sight.

The Marine twins joined Croft and ordered bacon
and eggs, as they would do at any port in the world.

"One thing sure," said Lieutenant Buck, "you're
a pilot. That was a lousy landing we just had and you
were working the hell out of your rudder pedals."

"Probably Navy," said Schlegel. "The Clipper
you called a *boat*. It had a *hull*. Port, starboard, deck
—you know what I mean."

Croft was embarrassed but faithful to what he'd
been told in Washington. "I'm not saying. Maybe I'm a
Marine."

"Never," said Buck. "Even if you looked like a
Marine, they're as scarce in England as snakes in Ireland. Marines in Europe are either State couriers or
embassy guards. Take my word."

A customs man came into the restaurant, with
passports in his hand. He came first to Croft and the
Marines, and gave back their passports. "Mr. Croft,"
he said, "from your passbook, it seems that New York

is a bit careless these days. You might have a look."

Flipping through his passport, Croft was perplexed.

"The picture, Mr. Croft, the photo. A borrowed jacket, was it?" In New York, the photographer had several jackets to lend his uniformed customers. "That's fine, a little loose perhaps, but the jacket's fine. That does leave the shirt, though, doesn't it? Is it not a uniform shirt? Now, sir, see the wee holes in the shirt collars." Croft had taken off his collar bars; the photographer had reminded him to do that. The customs man went on: "Them holes bein' so close together, says I, they wasn't the big Army or Air Force bars the man had taken off his shirt. It's the Navy or Marines for him, I says." The other two at the table were grinning at Croft, but the customs man was solemn. "And then there's that black tie. Aha! says I, surely it's the Navy for Mr. Croft."

Croft arrived in Paddington Station, London, at six thirty in the evening. Counting the long day's journey from Foynes—a very casual bus ride to the Limerick airport, a BOAC flight over to Bristol, England, and the Bristol Express to London—the pilot had traveled more than twelve thousand miles from his carrier in the Pacific. Five transport planes, two ships, two trains and a bus at an average speed, Croft calculated, of eight knots counting delays. He almost took a taxi at Paddington directly to the American Embassy before remembering that, even though London was closer to the war than Washington, the sun was setting slowly and it was probably after hours for warriors who fought out of office buildings. He called the number in his notebook, Regent 8484; the duty desk was extension 14. After some confusion, Croft was directed to the Park Lane Hotel and told to report back at 0900 next morning, 20 Grosvenor Square.

The hotel entrance was shielded by a thick sandbag barrier with plywood baffles at either side, through which you came into the lobby. Not until later did Croft realize that these baffles were light locks for the blackout. He had not yet seen a real blackout—they were a joke in American cities—for it was summer, when the English night takes hours to fall.

In his big room on the top floor, Croft spread out a map of London he'd bought at the station. From his windows, he identified Green Park right across Piccadilly and St. James's Park just beyond, with Buckingham Palace between the two. He could see where the Thames curves closest to the parks; he could not see the river itself. South of the Thames, a toy train chuffed slowly out of a large station, probably Waterloo. London was at rest.

After a luxurious bath in the swimming pool of a tub, Croft put on his greens (no khakis or whites in the United Kingdom) and walked down Piccadilly toward the Circus. There was light enough to make out color but no one even glanced at the uniform, rare in England. Croft saw the shoulder badges of Norway and Poland on Royal Air Force blue-gray uniforms, Free French fliers, Coldstream Guard officers, one Scot in kilts, lots of American types, and two drab Russians (who were generals). In a restaurant called Oddenino's, busy with vaguely American-style service and male-female maneuvering and very noisy, Croft ordered mushrooms on toast and studied this first active interior of wartime London he'd seen.

At nine o'clock, after dinner, which was supper, he followed for the first time what someone would later call his "walking beat." It was a rhomboid around Mayfair; up Regent Street he went, from Piccadilly Circus, then west along the shopping thoroughfare of Oxford Street, down Park Lane to Hyde Park corner, and east again to the hotel, which was halfway down Piccadilly.

Around ten thirty, Croft was in bed reading a book called *England, Their England* by A. G. MacDonell. Through the wide-open windows came a sound like that of an outboard motor, more accurately a motorcycle running under water. Croft had heard many sounds that carried the threat of death but never a sound like this one. It was the most raucous, the most *evil* sound he had ever heard. From the window, he saw that a yellow-orange star south of St. James's Park seemed to detach from its orbit and approach the earth. Somewhere over the Thames the strange light was seen to be pulsing; it traced a dotted line toward the hotel. Suddenly the light went out, the sound stopped. There was the muffled roar of an explosion not far from the hotel, Croft thought. Eeriest was the pronounced pause between the simultaneous extinction of the light and the rattling sound and the explosion.

By midnight, four more of the phantoms had dotted the dark sky—*this* was a blackout!—gone silent, and Croft heard two of them strike somewhere close by. One of the explosions could be felt faintly in the hotel. At one o'clock, the pilot dressed, went out into the hall, pressed the lift button. There was no answer. He walked down nine flights to the lobby. There was only a desk clerk there, who pointed to a door leading to a subground floor. There, in a large ballroom, a party was in progress. Several hundred people were milling around, a third of them dancing to a Glenn Miller record.

"What's going on?" Croft asked an army sergeant who was clapping his hands in time to the music.

" 'String of Pearls,' I'd say, mate." The man was half drunk.

"No, no, I mean those things outside. Have you had these things before."

"P'raps it's ruddy blitz again, 'oo knows? Remember blitz? This 'ere is just like a gathering under the old blitz."

The ballroom was jumping, the noise deafening. Croft had to conclude by himself that he had witnessed the arrival in London of the world's first unmanned aircraft missiles. There was no other logical explanation.

3

The Air Attache

Commander Matthew Dampier, U. S. Naval Attaché for Air, returned from Normandy at dawn on June 13 to a London once more under attack. In the taxi from Victoria Station to the embassy, his newspapers told the attaché that at least four "pilotless aircraft" had crossed the coast during the night; one of these had killed six Londoners and injured nine. The stories were obviously written with little hard fact behind them, indicating that details of the flying bombs (as Dampier knew them) had not been officially released. The press seemed anxious again to provide all evidence of damage, including the obituaries giving casualty numbers and street addresses, to interested observers. Dampier knew that those who sent the flying bombs over would be desperate to know where their blind weapons of revenge were striking. He suspected that this sort of information would have to be suppressed.

After five years in this mammoth target city which so obsessed the enemy, Dampier had grown to love London with an almost childlike devotion. He identified with these stubborn Londoners, whose pride now sadly embraced even the ugly wounds and wreckage that had become the most prominent landmarks in a town that had been centuries building its glorious structures. Dampier even liked the damnable weather; the streets he rode over this morning were slick under a drizzle-mist. As he entered Grosvenor Square, an odd thought struck the commander: only in London could you hear that strange muffled *whirr* of the small tires on damp pavement.

The taxi stopped at the American Embassy. As the driver watched the three-striper's broad back disappear into the handsome Georgian building, the Marine sentry in dress blues was going through a marvelous evolution with his rifle, a salute known to be one of the more impressive sights in Grosvenor Square. The rifle clatter died; the trim little taxi hummed off. Once more the square was quiet. Until the colors were run up at the embassy an hour after sunrise, only the catatonic Marine marked this place as American territory.

In his second-floor office at the front of the empty building, Dampier set a pot of water on the hotplate for his tea. He was still euphoric from his meeting with the prime minister. A week's worth of mail on his desk and the list of classified mail in the communications vault would have to wait. Only two of the memos were of any personal interest: Rothschild was back in London and would drop by later in the morning; Croft was at the Park Lane Hotel. These two messages pleased Dampier, for they fit what he had to think about before his day began. The day would be busy and extra long, as it always was after one of his trips. Almost no one knew, of course, that he'd left for Normandy this time; probably all guessed correctly when he was gone and the invasion was announced. (Stark knew, and Dampier wrote himself a reminder to see the admiral before noon. He'd see Rothschild and Croft first. There might be a personal touch he could pass on to the old man.)

Through an unlikely contact, a Lady Saxe-Rowland, the attaché had received an invitation to observe the Normandy landing operation, a legitimate activity for him, from an unusual vantage point. From the afternoon of June 5, he was a guest in HMS *Kelvin,* destroyer flagship of the admiral commanding all surface vessels in the Arromanches harbor. Back in Portsmouth again in the early hours of June 10, *Kelvin* took on an important party headed by the prime minister.

More than anything else, it was the prime minister's personality that encouraged Dampier. They had spoken only casually and, from the attaché's side, guardedly about all kinds of things that were happening and that could happen. Churchill's easy rambling made it less difficult to touch lightly on several very delicate matters. It was the typical discourse of embassy and state receptions and banquets, or better, parties. Indeed, the mere presence of the PM in *Kelvin* created a holiday atmosphere for everyone. To Admiral Vian, Churchill had said, "Since we are so near, why shouldn't we have a plug at them ourselves before we go home?" By God! If they hadn't then closed in to 7000 yards off the beach and opened fire with all guns on a totally silent coast. The Prime was like a small boy; he even asked to pull one of the gun lanyards himself. Everyone laughed when he suggested that perhaps they should turn tail and depart "at the highest speed."

The prime minister. Having now met him informally, Dampier saw that the stories were weak watercolors of the man. There was only one concrete souvenir of the meeting. The PM said to call his office in about a week. "You must say, Commander, that you were Mr. P's shipmate in His Majesty's ship *Kelvin,* and I think they will put you through directly to me. Mr. P. is a little code I use quite sparingly. And *Kelvin* will serve to remind *me,* although I have an astonishing memory."

Dampier noticed Parmenter's name in the classified mail list. In the vault, he sat down to read what was mainly a summary of Parmenter's views on the latecomer, Croft. ". . . I'm sending some of these things to you, Matt," Parmenter wrote, "for you have the greatest need while Croft is there . . . Perhaps you could arrange to have Stark make one or more of the awards recommended for Croft, if they come through in time . . . I'll expedite from this end. . . ."

That, thought the grinning Dampier, was just the personal touch he'd bring, not necessarily today, to Admiral Stark.

While Dampier was reading about him, Croft waited for his breakfast in the Park Lane dining room. He had ordered bloaters, powdered eggs, powdered milk. The bloaters he had seen ordered at the table of a brigadier, sixtyish, stout, too pink in the face, and his frail wife. These two were the only other ones in the dining room when Croft had come in; his usual instinct would be to keep his distance. But the women had smiled at him in a compelling, sad way that made it seem rude to go across the large room. All through the meal the woman fought tears; the brigadier was embarrassed but gentle with her. Based only on whispers, it was Croft's theory that the woman's black dress, the general's black sleeveband, were for the recent death of a son. They were in London for the funeral—no, a posthumous ceremony. *The King himself* . . . Croft could not hear what the brigadier said about the king.

The bloaters *were* kippers, which Croft had tasted once in Quebec before the war. (Spring, 1941 . . . underage, twenty, parental consent . . . Croft, Sr., isolationist . . . Royal Canadian Air Force, escape to Canada! . . . Croft, Sr., business connections, radio station CHRC, Quebec City . . . RCAF enlistment *denied.*)

As the English couple were leaving the dining room, the brigadier came over to offer his newspaper to the American. He smiled stiffly, shyly, an awkward version of his wife's wistful smile. "The—those damn things last night," he said, "they're calling them robots, flying bombs. Th-thought you might like to read about them."

One of the bombs, the paper said, had killed six people in Bethnal Green. The waiter told Croft that was about three miles east of the hotel.

When Croft left the hotel, he was sure he had fixed the embassy's location on the map in his mind, but he kept turning corners out of short streets without finding Grosvenor Square. Berkeley Square he found by accident and that was interesting. There a barrage balloon squadron was inflating its ugly beast from helium tanks. The olive drab balloon took shape slowly, rising like a festered blister out of the earth. Croft, always comfortable with technicians, spent a fascinating ten minutes in Berkeley Square, learning how balloons worked and how deadly they had been in the night blitz. Early this morning, the balloons had been ordered back into the city, to see if their cables would not slice down this new threat, the flying bomb. As this fat slug took on final shape, the huge sergeant-in-charge, who had hands like a welder's gloves, walked the American two streets over to the southeast corner of Grosvenor Square. "There she is, sir," the sergeant said, waving one of those hands proudly, "your bloomin' U. S. of A." Yew-Ess-uv-Eye, actually, is what he said.

Croft's first meeting in the embassy with Commander Dampier was technically more satisfying, if less dramatic, than the one he'd had six days ago with Captain Parmenter in Washington, To begin with, Dampier was real; he was not fancy, affected or effusive. His dignified, cool manner suggested power that might be far greater than Parmenter's. This meeting was technically satisfying for Croft because of Commander Dampier's stripped-down style, which was evident in the brief greeting and in the first statement Matthew Dampier ever made to John Croft.

"I've been waiting for you, Croft, and I am extremely happy to have you here." There was a quick handshake, no courtly gestures, no frills at all. "Now, I'm sure the main thing on your mind is the temporary duty assignment in England, which I will tell you all about before you leave this office. But last night something happened. I was out of London until just a couple of hours ago and have yet to see a flying bomb. Did you?"

"I'm sure I saw four of them," said Croft, "and I heard two explosions. But even from the newspaper story, I can't connect everything up."

"Well, anyway, you've seen history made," said

Dampier, "and now we have to wait to find out how important this new problem will be. Only one of the sketches in the papers came close to the real thing. Here, look at this."

The attaché quickly drew on a pad something resembling an airplane, except that it had very stubby wings on a bomb-shaped body and a large stovepipe affair sticking out behind above the tail. Croft, who liked to draw, sensed that this was an accurate sketch.

"This thing," said Dampier, "has close to a two-thousand-pound warhead and it *is* a bomb. But the heart of the matter is that piggyback pipe. That's an extremely simple type of engine, a pulsejet or ramjet. The ones you saw were launched from ramps across the Channel. Then they were self-guiding on a compass and a gyro, aimed for London. Timing was preset by the number of turns a small propeller made through the air. When the right number of turns for London were counted, the fuel was cut off and this little airplane turned into a bomb."

"How big are they, Commander?"

"Roughly half the size of a fighter plane. The British have been expecting them for about a year and they've got a plan for defense against them. I guess you saw the antiaircraft gun they're setting up out there in the square."

When Croft arrived at the embassy, he had seen a gun crew in Grosvenor Square, but there wasn't time to watch them. "Yes," he said, "and over in Berkeley Square I saw a balloon going up. It seems to me, sir, that bringing them down when they're right over London may be a mistake. Guns, maybe, if the bomb is blown up in the air, but not balloons."

"You're right, Croft. A bomb already over London *may* fly right past before cutting out. It was different in the blitz when the game was to bring down a *manned* airplane at any cost. Airplanes and trained crews are not expendable. Flying bombs are. No, the defense plan will depend mainly on fighter planes over the Channel and coast, then a wide gun belt, and close to London a balloon barrage. Personally, I think it won't be long before they close down the guns and balloons inside the city."

"One thing that occurs to me," Croft said, "is that these flying bombs won't care at all whether it's night or day. Bad weather or good. That's a tough one for our side."

"It is. Listen, I can see—if this kind of attack can't be handled properly and is carried out on a big scale, I can see many ways it could be worse than the regular bombing raids several years back. Psychologically, for example. Isn't there something scary about pilotless aircraft? No offense, of course."

Croft barely smiled, enough to indicate that he liked Dampier. The attaché was not an aviator. In a complex way, his mention of pilotless aircraft to a pilot, a near-stranger, was like Croft's smile.

"I'll go you one better, Commander," said Croft. "Maybe, even before this war is over, maybe we'll have one guided missile chasing another."

Dampier grinned. "It could happen," he said, "after you night fighters teach the chaser-robot how to do it."

Long ago, Dampier had wanted to be a pilot. More than that, he had wanted most of all to be a Navy fighter pilot, a *carrier* fighter pilot. In training, at Pensacola, one "ride" in the decompression chamber showed that he had marginal compensation for low oxygen tension. He was washed out. Why did they wait until a man had flown a hundred hours before giving him the chamber test?

"Okay, Croft," said Dampier, "the training. Forgive me if I repeat what Captain Parmenter told you."

"He was vague, sir."

"Yes, the captain can be vague, that's his way, but he's one of our genuine articles. I have just read some pretty fine things he said about you. His letter, I imagine, came over with you in the Clipper, in a courier's pouch."

Lieutenant Buck, thought Croft. *Sergeant Schlegel.*

"All right, Croft, here it is. You're late, no fault

of yours. Four pilots are up at RAF Spitalgate, a station near Nottingham. They are all multi-engine pilots and they are learning the British way of flying. Parmenter tells me that you have been checked out on two engines."

"Yes. Sir, what is Spitalgate?"

"Everyone asks. There are two answers, Croft. First, RAF Spitalgate is an advanced flying unit. Second—and this is what I think you are asking—'spital' means two things. Originally it was a loathsome place, a hospital, you see. Then it came to mean a resting place on the way to better things."

"I like the last one," said Croft. "Is that what you like, Commander?"

"Definitely." For a split second, Dampier thought this young jg was reading his mind. "You'll have to go some to catch up with your friends. They've been there about three weeks and they're due back in London in the next few days. Meanwhile, your radar officers have been converting to British ways, too, at a radar school called Ouston, way up near the Scottish border. Did Captain Parmenter tell you that Lieutenant Commander William McLaughlin will be flying with you?"

"He did. I've heard of McLaughlin."

"He left NOCTU(Pac) before you arrived there. Bill McLaughlin was one of the first shipboard fighter-directors in the fleet. He says he doesn't particularly miss the Pacific. When he was out there, on the other hand, he said it was hard to imagine a war without vast fetches of ocean between some pinpoint atolls."

"It's true. It's also hard to imagine dropping bombs on civilians."

Dampier nodded slowly. "Well, to continue, there's a deadline coming up soon that we should try to meet and that is June nineteenth. That's next Monday. We've arranged to have all of you put into a regular night operational training course which starts that day at another station, Cranfield, near Bedford. Now, that pushes you."

Croft shrugged.

"Three things will help," continued Dampier. "I've

arranged with Spitalgate to speed you through. Then, at Cranfield, most of the first month is ground school and day flying. And most important, I think, is that you are the only one in our group with night fighter background. In fact, it's my understanding that none of the Britishers in the night OTU course have that background, either. Other experience but not night fighting."

"I'll do my best, Commander."

"I haven't the slightest doubt. Now, do you have—"

The phone rang, a *buzzbuzz—buzzbuzz* that sounded quaint to Croft. It was the first English phone he'd heard.

"Seth!" Dampier exclaimed, "welcome back! . . . yes, I got your message . . . sure, come over right away . . . Croft is here . . . he'll probably take the one o'clock to Grantham . . . right, see you."

"That was Lieutenant Commander Seth Roth-schild," Dampier told Croft, "the senior officer of your group. He got back from Ouston last night and so did his pilot, from Spitalgate, Archie Tarbox. Archie is also a lieutenant commander, a former airlines pilot. They'll be here in fifteen minutes. This is quite a pair, and you'll see what I mean." Dampier shook his head and chuckled, saying, "I hope the rest of the day goes this way—but it won't. Listen, I forgot to tell you that there's a one o'clock train from King's Cross Station that would get you to Spitalgate by tea-time. Could you make that?" It was ten o'clock.

"I've made everything else so far, Commander. When should I leave here?"

"Eleven would be fine. I'm going to try and see Admiral Stark about that time anyway, and you'd have half an hour or so with Rothschild and Tarbox. They can tell you things that I can't. I listen to them a lot."

At ten twenty, a pair of lieutenant commanders in blues appeared at Dampier's door. A pair, Croft thought, in the sense of *two* and only in that sense. In every other way, these two were hopelessly mismatched, or so it seemed. The attaché went quickly through the introductions. Seth Rothschild, the radar officer, had the slight stoop of some very tall men—Rothschild was six and a half feet tall—and the gentle, elklike face that often came out of generations of aristocracy. Such a face was the hallmark of the Windsors, rulers of Britain, of King George VI himself. Such a face was Seth's, of the Jewish family Rothschild, which bought kings and sold emperors and traded prime ministers for gold and diamonds.

"Pleased to meet you, John," Rothschild said. "We were beginning to think that Bill McLaughlin might have to learn to fly himself."

Tarbox was from Tennessee. Not tall to begin with, the shy Archibald Tarbox was diminished by his preference for half hiding behind Rothschild's left arm. Croft later learned that Tarbox always did this. Rothschild's pilot was the younger of the two but he had a vinegar face that made him older and a growling voice that spoke in monosyllables or not at all. When he was introduced to John Croft, all he said was a flat *"Angh!"* It was Croft's impression that Archibald Tarbox was barely alive, walking around partly in his sleep. That first impression may have been the worst judgment that Croft ever pronounced over another human.

Dampier asked Rothschild about Ouston, about new British radar methods, about the four other American radar officers who were still in the north. Seth Rothschild had a low, even way of speaking, highly organized and unhesitating, absolutely eloquent. Croft was fascinated; it almost sounded to him as if Rothschild were reading aloud from a book, a book of quality that he had just written himself. The few hesitations occurred when Tarbox shook his head and mumbled, or simply shifted his loose-jointed body noisily. Rothschild seemed to understand every time for he would pause, glance solemnly at his pilot and then continue as if nothing had happened. Mostly, Tarbox just slouched in his chair, his eyes closed, nodding constantly, yawning occasionally. Croft was not sure, at this time, that Rothschild and Tarbox were entirely happy with each other. This was an important point because Croft, who was hearing more and more about McLaughlin, his own prechosen radar officer, was just beginning to think seriously about always having another man in the cockpit. He was still thinking cockpit but it would be a cabin.

When Croft excused himself at eleven o'clock, it was also time for Dampier to find out about his meeting with Admiral Stark. Rothschild found that John Croft planned to have lunch early at the Park Lane, if possible, and pack his stuff.

"I'm staying at Claridge's," Rothschild said, "and I was going to invite you for lunch there, but you wouldn't have time. Will I be in the way if I join you at your hotel?"

"Not at all," answered Croft. "Maybe you could teach me about London. You could start with the English money, maybe."

"Glad to," said Rothschild. "Archie, can you come with us?"

Tarbox had put on his old, salty cap, which had a rubber raincover on it; he looked like an American policeman. The hat was much too big for him and he had large ears, which the heavy hat rested on and turned into a pair of front mudguards on a car. He considered Rothschild's invitation and the decision seemed painful for him. Finally, he said, "Aw-w . . . nah, Seth. Got some things to do."

In front of the embassy, Tarbox may have said goodbye, but if he did, Croft missed it. The pilot jammed his hands into his raincoat pockets and shuffled away, up North Audley Street, opposite to the direction Croft and Rothschild took to the Park Lane.

"Is he mad at something?" Croft asked.

"No, not at all," said Rothschild, "he's always that way. Whenever we come to London, which is often, he rarely eats with us and he's never gone to the theater. But he calls me several times a day to find out what's going on. He'll probably call Claridge's at tea-time this afternoon. If I'm not there, I'll find a note in my box. The notes just say 'Mr. Tarbox called,' there's never a message."

On their way to the hotel, Rothschild pointed out

many sights to Croft, including the rubble of places that were still called by their famous names, even though they were now only ghosts. In most cases, their remains were simply too much to clean up with limited manpower. And too numerous. Rothschild also took Croft by the Navy canteen, which was important to know about for its cheap necessities of life, everything from soap to sweaters. Croft stocked up on some things he'd forgotten and some things Rothschild said would be useful.

At the Park Lane, Seth selected John's lunch, without seeming to, and went on to tell about the good and the bad of English wartime food: "The sausages are mealy . . . you should really get to like tea, for the coffee is bad, burned and mostly chicory . . . but always drink coffee after dinner with your RAF associates, for it is done and they don't like it either. . . ." Seth would have made a superb teacher; he had ways of making things easy to remember.

While waiting for lunch, they got out all their money, the bills and the change, and Croft had a lesson in English currency. The currency was difficult and irrational. The lesson was remarkable because, when it was over, it was irrelevant to ask why the English didn't change the clumsy money. They didn't change, Seth taught, because it wasn't at all difficult for them, you see, and besides it was part of their history that they could hold in their hands. Croft saw that it would be a mistake to lose this tangible symbol of history.

Commander Dampier was with Admiral Harold R. Stark until twelve thirty. "Betty" Stark was one of Dampier's two bosses in England; the other boss was the ambassador, formerly Joseph P. Kennedy and now John G. Winant. The admiral was more important to Dampier, whose career was after all the Navy and whose main function was to be the eyes and ears in England of the director of Naval Intelligence.

What Dampier told Stark had to do with Normandy mainly, although he planted a few seeds in the admiral's shrewd mind. When he told Stark about the

naval officers in the RAF night fighting program, he
merely indicated that the most recent arrival was a
pilot who had really distinguished himself in the Pacific. He also mentioned obliquely that he'd given some
thought, just idle thought, to the possibility of putting
these men into operational squadrons with the RAF.
If Stark even focused on that, he didn't say anything
for or against.

Just before John Croft left London for Grantham, as
he carried the green issue Valpack and the gray parachute bag packed with everything he owned into King's
Cross Station, he heard again the evil rattle of a flying
bomb. This one bore straight across the center of the
city through muddy cloud, unseen, the satanic clatter
momentarily paralyzing a million hearts. As it crossed
the zenith above the station, Croft's eyes were locked
for a full minute with the unwavering eyes of an im-
passive bobby. They and all the people around them
were wax figures, all coming to life slowly and at the
same time, as the harsh roar above their heads diminished and the bomb scuttled on to play roulette
with other Londoners. Croft would always find it this
way in the crowds: the people who had been spared
would listen on, relieved but guilty, passing their fear
on and on to others across the city. No one heard this
bomb above King's Cross Station stop; its idiot voice
faded out of range.

The train to Grantham gave Croft a few hours to
think. He had many things to think about, based more
on what three men had *not* said to him than on what
they had said. Parmenter, Dampier, Rothschild. A captain, a commander and a lieutenant commander. The
descending progression of rank was so normal, on the
face of it, that Croft had given it no thought. Until he
had met Seth Rothschild.

Captain Parmenter, in Washington, had done his
best to make the most of a straightforward training assignment. But he was known to be not just an anglo-
phile, but an anglomaniac. Croft had discounted much
of Parmenter's romantic superstructure on the basic
orders—but not all. The captain was foolish but by

no means a fraud. He was the head of Navy night fighting and Dampier said he was a "genuine article."

And then Dampier. The air attaché gave Croft details of the training assignment that were not even known to Parmenter, but Dampier could not conceal from Croft a vague impatience, an emotional momentum that had something to do with the attaché's long residence in London. Croft knew, was absolutely certain, that whatever was about to happen, he was caught up in Dampier's momentum. Matthew Dampier had won Croft's trust in a very short time and the pilot was irrevocably committed to him.

Finally, Seth Rothschild. This man, the gentlest of men, was the most mysterious that Croft had ever met. As Seth had taught Croft about the workaday life of wartime England and London, never suggesting the autocrat, never hinting sovereign knowledge, he had somehow given to the suggestions of Parmenter and the instructions of Dampier an imprimatur that was hard to define. Power, Croft finally decided, was the answer. It was power that Seth Rothschild suggested, a type of power that the pilot could not imagine, a transcendental force that was illustrated but not explained by the ocean tides or by a comet that humans watched without understanding for a week of nights.

There were also important personal questions in Croft's mind. *Why am I here?* was the first, naturally. They had grabbed him out of the Pacific, when he had been on the way to success. Now what? Croft was on his way in the Pacific but in England he might fail. He hated failure.

And what has become of me? Croft thought. To understand this more important question, it should be known that John Croft was twenty-four years old. Like all the young, Croft had been a *strategist* in his early years: the young always said that they would have to control, manipulate, improve this insane world. It had to be so! But then—then time passed more quickly, the young aged, the failures accumulated. What remained for the young to do was *tactics*. Strategy was what took place before the battle, tactics was what remained to do after the battle began. Croft, at twenty-four, had given up his ideals of strategy; he was not in that class. But he was in a subclass of tactics. He was a technician, only a technician, but even in his own mind he had come to believe that he was perhaps the best of his kind in the entire world. It was a frightening thought, not an encouraging one, for when an ordinary man is thrust into an extraordinary position, there are questions in the soul not easily answered.

In the last half hour of his trip to Grantham, John Croft wrestled alone with these unanswerable questions.

4

RAF Spitalgate

The Grantham afternoon express brought John Croft into Robin Hood's territory at four thirty P.M. The town of Grantham in Lincolnshire was only twenty miles from Nottingham, whose dark Sherwood Forest had menaced the king's authority hundreds of years ago, thrilling a ten-year-old American who could not sleep for thinking about Robin Hood, Friar Tuck, Little John, Alan-a-Dale—and the Lady Marian, too, although she had been an annoyance to the boy and a great trouble to Robin.

In front of the Grantham station, Croft asked a taxi driver about a ride to RAF Spitalgate. The New Yorker was hardly prepared for such an answer.

"Love to do it, guv," said the driver, "but 'ave to tell you, honor bound, there's a service bus over there at the stop right now fillin' up for Spitalgate. Costs you less than 'arf, too. Costs you exactly nuffin'."

Croft thanked the unusual man—who said, "Just show 'em your commission, captain, or what 'ave you" —and hefted the bags to cross the street toward the bus. At that moment, a small, dusty car angled out of the traffic and shot over to the sidewalk in front of the taxi.

"I say there," said the driver, "you *are* Lieutenant Croft, aren't you?" His voice was unnaturally loud, as if he had just dismounted a horse he'd ridden through the wind. "I'm Flight Lieutenant Pugh and I've come to take you out to Spitalgate."

"Yes, I'm Croft. But I wasn't expecting anyone to meet me. I appreciate this."

"It's not all charity, Croft, since I get some of me petrol this way. But seriously, I am in charge of you and your American colleagues and I see no reason why you chaps should start off with a dim view of old Albion. Besides"—Pugh lightly stroked both sides of a tan-blond cavalier's mustache—"I will undoubtedly visit the colonies postwar and would want to have many friends feathered away for the occasion."

"All right," said Croft, "I'm your man in New York." Pugh's exuberant frankness was charming, childlike, but Croft also had the impression that the pilot, behind his façade of the loud imperative, was like himself a thinker. Unlike himself, Croft knew, Pugh was easy to like. "Lieutenant Pugh, much as I hate the idea, I would be happy to take you up into the Statue of Liberty and have a look at her lamp. Now, tell me, how fast can I get out of this Spitalgate place?"

Pugh grinned as he waited to tack his little car onto the highway traffic out of Grantham. There was a delay because of a long military convoy.

"Haven't started yet," said Pugh, "and you want to get out. Well, I don't blame you. But here's what they told us. You fellows, they said, had to learn the British cockpit, all the lingo, and the British way of flying. Sorry, but it *is* that much different, you know. So here I am, Brian Manford Pugh, charged by my service to see that you are bloody well one of us before you leave this little hell called Spitalgate. By the way, what do your friends call you?

"John. And you're Brian?"

"Only to me mum and a few favored popsies, from time to time. I'm Sandy to most, the color of the hair. But the name could suggest sand, shifting sands, not shifty but adaptable. At the mercy of a good, stiff breeze, perhaps." Pugh's strong voice softened to a conspiratorial level. "And just how is it, John, that you wish to blow me about?"

It was an invitation. Croft realized that the shrewd Englishman had quickly sized him up as one who could not deal in small talk. Pugh was open to a proposition.

"Here's the problem, Sandy. Next Monday I'm supposed to report to the night OTU at Cranfield, but—"

"Yes, you may know that one of your fellow pilots, Tarbox, finished up yesterday. Perhaps you saw him in London? Two more of them taped it up this afternoon, but I think they're not leaving until tomorrow, so you'll see them at tea." Pugh hesitated and his words became faintly clipped. "Lieutenant Murdock has—he had some problems adjusting to us here and that did delay him early on, although I'm sure he'll wind up in good form over the next few days."

Murdock was only a name to Croft, yet it acquired from Pugh's carefully chiseled manner an aura that was disturbing. Rather, it was disturbing that Croft had already figured Sandy Pugh to be an exceptional judge of human nature, and on that basis alone, the stranger Mudrock's reputation was already lightly tarnished.

"They told me in London," Croft continued, "that you were giving our pilots fifteen hours or so, and I'm wondering if you can do the same for me in about four days."

"It depends," said Pugh. He flipped the switch that signaled a left turn, and the car shot off the highway, bouncing wildly onto a country road. "It depends partly on you, of course, and I only say that as an incorruptible instructor, one who will not tolerate incompetence that tends, personally, to kill me. It depends on the weather, which has lately been fairly good hereabouts. It depends on aircraft availability. Somehow, John, I think you will manage. The RAF is a ponderous wonder, I'll admit, fortunately shot through with charming defects like me."

Pugh turned, not looking directly at his passenger, to deliver a self-satisfied smile. He was not just an instructor, he was in charge of all flight instruction at the Advanced Flying Unit (Pilot), Spitalgate. *In charge,* no question.

The late afternoon sun was brilliant, almost painfully blinding because of its low position—Pugh was driving mainly to the west—until the light was abruptly cut off when the car plunged into miles of dense forest. As in a tunnel, the narrow road seemed to be carved out of a solid mass of yew and ash under a lofty cover of oak. It was so dark that Pugh switched on his headlamps. If there had been such roads in the days of Robin Hood, one could imagine the ease and delight of a highwayman's life in old Lincolnshire.

They came out into a large, natural clearing, where the winding road was lined by a dozen houses. It was a sort of disconnected village. At the far end of this sudden hamlet in the forest was the sentry post to RAF Spitalgate. The air station spread out for nearly two miles beyond the gate, its main cluster of buildings sending long shadows across the landing field. A grass field! Croft had the impression of a 1914 aerodrome, an impression that was reinforced by the variety of structures he saw as Pugh drove on to the officers' mess. The work area buildings along the edge of the flying field were an assortment of plain brick sheds with big windows boarded over or painted black, odd shacks made of wood, galvanized steel and even tarpaper, and the ugly Nissen huts. The officers' mess, a mile farther on, was the only substantial building and a handsome one that appeared to be of the eighteenth century, a lord's manor house. A row of eight small brick cottages started near one corner of the mess and curved back toward the wood behind it.

"They'll be putting you up in one of those cottages," said Pugh, as he turned the car into a tree-shaded gravel loop that led up to the mess veranda. "What say we have a spot of tea, John?" asked Pugh, "You can leave your luggage and we'll check you in later. Tiffin-time, tea, is specially sacred in the RAF, sort of reminds us we're civilized after all. I should like the honor of introducing you to it."

Croft followed Pugh. They bypassed the main

entrance hall of the mess, going directly into a large
drawing room by way of one of its French windows,
wide open to the first cool breezes of early evening.
There were about twenty men in the room, all but two
of them in the blue uniform of the RAF. No matter
how warm it was, Croft would never see a gathering of
the RAF in shirtsleeves.

Pugh led Croft over to the two naval aviators who
wore the forest greens.

"Dickie, Peter," said Pugh, "I feel ridiculous introducing fellow Americans to one another, but here is
your lost John Croft." Pugh folded his arms grandly
and stood back, beaming as if he had found what
everyone was looking for. The officers shook John's
hand.

"I'm Dick Priest," said the taller, bulky lieutenant
with the round, pleasant face, the jowls. He had the
strong accent of the deep South. "And this is Peter
Garland, who writes poetry and has never worked
a day in his life." Garland was pale, hospital pale, with
vaguely haunted eyes in a pinched face, with deep and
permanent creases between the thin eyebrows. He
smiled wanly but said nothing. He wore the Navy
Cross blue and white ribbon under his wings.

"Dickie, where is Murdock?" asked Pugh.

"I have no idea," said Priest. "He may be in
Grantham. I think he said something about going into
town after his last hop."

Pugh said he would get tea for Croft and he went
over to the serving table where an enlisted rank pre-
sided over the sweets and savories. He was clearly in-
tent on socializing. He introduced Croft to several
RAF types, who would be his instructors. Croft took
the first opportunity to draw Pugh aside and lay out the
plan that they would follow.

"I enjoy meeting your staff, Sandy," said Croft,
"but I'm not here to meet people. The Navy sent me
here to fly. Can we finish the tea, Sandy, and go fly?"

Pugh's cup was at his lip. His eyes met Croft's
cold, gray, unblinking, relentless gaze. Pugh smiled
and lowered his cup. "I believe you are serious," he
said, "and you want to start right away, is that it?"

"Yes."

Pugh gulped his tea, which was not his way.

"All right, my Yankee friend, let us get cracking. I will begin now, this very minute, to fly your ruddy arse off. Is that what you want?"

"Yes."

Pugh drove Croft down to the dispersal area. "You will hardly find our ancient crates exciting, but that's not the point of your Spitalgate exercise. The point is, John, that we can give you some tips about the English airspace. This airspace is not quite like any other, for it lies over a nervous island that is practically one great aerodrome. Listen to me carefully when we fly together, for I will be speaking of things that will ease the burden for you when you go on the night OTU at Cranfield. I will occasionally speak of little things that will keep you alive."

In the sudden role of the instructor, Pugh was awesome. He cared not at all what transient pilots, whoever they were, thought of him when he was teaching them. Sandy Pugh of the officers' mess was not the same Pugh who parked his car at the instructors' dispersal hut.

There was an undistinguished twin-engine airplane squatting on the grass in front of the hut, a worn-looking machine not much larger than Croft's Corsair fighter. Pugh shouted at a sergeant mechanic in black coveralls, who was pitching horseshoes solitaire not far from the small bomber.

"Ho there, Chiefy!" said Pugh, "git me kerridge hitched up, will you? We'll be riding off in ten minutes or so."

Pugh had a small office in the hut, where the station instructors had their lockers and waited or got ready for their flights. Croft stripped down to his skivvies and put on his regular summerweight, birdcloth flying coverall, while Sandy called Control to arrange flight clearance.

"You chaps do have the costumes, don't you," said the amused Pugh, when he came out of the office. "I'll have to lend you one of our helmets temporarily, though, so you'll have the proper earphones to plug into the R/T and intercom. You can draw your own helmet from stores in the morning. By the way, you should take a mae west, too, unless you have one in that great sack of yours. We'll be taking a turn over some water this evening."

Croft reached into the parachute bag and brought out his flat Navy mae west, a more compact preserver than the bulky RAF vest that made Pugh look like a pouter pigeon. The American's preserver had an ugly hunting knife dangling at one side; it was the size of a small machete.

"What a ferocious pig-sticker you carry!" said Pugh. "That's the form now in the Pacific, eh, going after the Nips with the old cutlery?"

"No, we just use these on headhunters in the hills of Borneo." Croft's knife and all the remarks about it were something he had to live with; he could not fly without the knife. Neither could he hide it. It had to be right out front where he could get at it when the fire came again, as it would sooner or later. Croft would have a knife to cut himself out of The Second Fire. There had been no knife in The First Fire.

As Pugh and Croft strapped themselves into the ancient Bristol Blenheim, the American tried to focus on the slow, old bomber's respected history rather than on its cramped crew quarters and its unlovely outlines. This was the interim night fighter of 1940, even then a virtual discard but one that had served as the first platform for the successful use of airborne search radar against an enemy aircraft. Pugh wisecracked about the creaking and groaning and the spitting of the engines as his "tinful of nuts and bolts" rumbled and rattled over the uneven ground toward the takeoff caravan.

Croft sat beside Pugh's right shoulder on a seat something like a little barstool. This Blenheim was not a trainer; it only had the pilot's controls on the left side. Although the Navy pilot had not flown often in the second seat of any airplane, he could not remember anyone whose ease in a cockpit was as impressive as Pugh's. In all the business of getting them airborne—"unstuck" as Pugh called it—the Englishman's fluid mastery of his machine seemed all the more impressive by contrast with his attire. The heavy helmet he wore, of course, for the earphones—no American ever wore a helmet in a multi-engine cabin, only a headset and maybe a baseball cap. Sandy had taken off his tunic, but the yellow mae west was tied on like a wrinkled old pillow over the blue shirt with the crisp Windsor collar, the tight collar and the black tie smartly two-blocked.

The Blenheim did not fall apart in the dreadful racket of the takeoff, and Sandy's voice came through the intercom only seconds after the wheels banged up and stowed themselves away behind the engines.

"We're going on an anticlockwise tour of the eastern Midlands," said Pugh's wobbly intercom voice, "the heart of England. You should remember, though, that in the British Isles you can never be more than a hundred miles from the sea."

They cruised along, almost due east, at a wheezing 170 miles an hour. (Croft had noticed right away that he would have to stop thinking in knots, but that was easy enough.) The sun was already down behind them but it would not really be dark until about nine o'clock. Soon Croft saw an inlet coming up on the horizon and that broadened quickly into a wide bay.

"We call this the Wash," Pugh announced. "It's a deep wedge of the North Sea into the waist of England." He flew a short distance along the south shore of the Wash until he could point out the mouth of a river and a town. "There's the River Ouse and King's Lynn. Here we're just touching the wicket inside Norfolk to the east, then we'll cross from King's Lynn right over to the north side of the Wash. About thirty miles. I want to show you something." As an afterthought Pugh said, "Whenever you cross a coast in Britain, you should have definite clearance for it unless you are under control of a ground station. Even then, you should be prepared to fire flare colors of the day in case your radio is out. The armorers are charged to keep the right colors in the roof pistols." Pugh tapped the roof behind his head.

"What is all that for?" asked Croft.

"All that is to prevent the coastal guns from shooting you down. It's a drill the bods at the guns dearly love. Now we'll be making land again in a few minutes at a spit near Skegness and there is a structure you have to see."

A few miles north of the point of land, Pugh brought the Blenheim fairly close to a tall set of towers.

"That's one of the old Chain Home Low radar stations, range out to sea about twenty-five miles. There a long-range station further north, but we won't go up that far. Thought you might like to see this sort of thing. Part of history now, these old stations, aren't they?"

Croft was fascinated. Here were the famous antennas that guarded England in 1939. The long-range towers could see the *Luftwaffe* coming at a distance of a hundred miles. No building in Britain had a fraction the value of one of these ungainly towers. It was not unlikely that all the most valuable buildings in the land could have been bombed out of existence except for these antenna towers.

Pugh turned sharply southwest and followed pretty closely the upper shore of the Wash to Boston.

"St. Botolph's Town, they called it. Your Pilgrims started out for America here in 1607, but we, complete royal barstuds even then, clapped the poor sods right into the town jail. But John, I point out to you a nice landmark called The Stump, which is the distinctive tower of old St. Botolph's church." Pugh banked the Blenheim toward Croft's side, so he could see the single spire rising nearly three hundred feet out of the town. "This is the Witham River that Boston stands by. Should you ever be lost in this region, remember that the Witham goes right around in a semicircle to the north and winds up at Grantham and Spitalgate. So you can't really get lost inside the old Witham's friendly loop."

Flying northwest from Boston, with the meandering Witham River always in sight on the starboard side, the Blenheim brought them to Lincoln, about thirty miles from the sea. A trio of stone towers loomed out of the evening haze.

"Can't miss that one," said Pugh, "the Lincoln Cathedral. Started building that one in 1072 so that we'd have it as a fine beacon today. I'll turn a little west now and give you a look at something everyone has heard about."

Twenty miles beyond Lincoln, Pugh made a ninety-degree turn to a southerly course. "If we'd kept right on another twenty miles or so, we'd have hit Sheffield. And beyond Sheffield are the Peaks, the only mountains to speak of in this area, fifteen hundred to two thousand feet. But it's getting a bit late and I thought I'd take you right straight down here over the Sherwood Forest to Nottingham."

From the air, at least, Croft found Sherwood Forest disappointing. Pugh guessed what he was thinking, it seemed, for after about ten miles of it he said, "Even on the ground, I have to say, the forest is hardly up to its old self. It strings out from here to Nottingham in bits and pieces, none of them big enough to hide a starved fox."

Pugh didn't come straight in to Grantham and Spitalgate but took a short detour south of the town to a small village called Woolsthorpe. He had two sites in mind that Croft must see.

"Woolsthorpe," said Pugh, "was the home of the man who really had more to do with our profession than any other in history. Sir Isaac Newton, no less."

"What did Newton have to do with flying?"

"Gravity, John, he invented gravity. It is the one law, gravity, that I for one shall never knowingly break. And now, right here above Woolsthorpe is the home of Sandy Pugh. I live off the station, you know, and I do this with my wife and a new son, also named Brian, who is already fascinated by the sound of aircraft engines."

Croft had not thought he would have to hear about Sandy Pugh's private life. Certainly not while flying; it was irritating enough when a man went into these things, the snapshots and all, when he'd had a few drinks. They were flying at only a thousand feet. Pugh dropped down a couple of hundred feet, throttled the engines out of sync to make a horrible beat, and rocked the Blenheim from side to side pretty violently.

"There," Sandy said, "I've waked up old Brian for his supper and Violet will put my dinner on the stove for me. It'll take me about half an hour starting now to get back out there."

In Pugh's cottage near Woolsthorpe, Brian, Jr., did wake up, bawling. Violet Pugh did say that she had to feed the baby and make Sandy's dinner. She said this to Lieutenant Joseph Murdock, whose hairy body occupied two-thirds of her bed. Violet was enslaved, God help her, by the three weeks she had spent with this violent American. He abused her, verbally and physically. But when she could keep him from drinking, he was like a god.

"Joe!" said Violet, "didn't you hear that?" Murdock had not had a drink the whole afternoon. "He'll be here in thirty minutes."

"Okay, okay, Violet." Murdock rolled out of the bed and started dressing. "I'll go. It'll take you a good thirty minutes to look like a wife again. You'd better start practicing. Stop smiling like you've had a good screw or something. Look worried about the baby, about money."

At dinner, John Croft ate with Priest and Garland and learned about them, which was important. But his mind was occupied mainly with Sandy Pugh, and he didn't know why. Croft led them on to tell him about Pugh.

"We're finished up here," said Priest, "and we're going down to London tomorrow morning. You won't have any trouble with Pugh, because he likes you."

"You should know about Pugh," said Garland, who was the gloomy counterweight to Priest's optimism. "He is a complex man. He will tell you nothing about himself. But in 1940 he was flying these old Blenheims, he was one of the first night fighters. An English artillery shell, not a German one, shot off the back of his head but did not harm his brilliant mind. All that holds Pugh's brain in at the back of his head is a steel shell."

Murdock came into the mess dining room and sat next to Priest, facing Garland and Croft. He had a square, muscular face; his wiry hair and his thick eyebrows were black; he needed a shave badly and his jowls were blue-black; he was called Blackie Murdock. A civilian test pilot, Murdock had come into the Navy early in the war in the same capacity. Captain Parmenter had selected him for England from the peerless experimental division at NAS Patuxent River near Washington.

"John," said Priest, "you'd be interested to know that Blackie has been working from the beginning on the conversion program for the night fighter version of the Tigercat."

"Among other things," said Murdock. "Hell, we fly them all, good or bad. This damn Blenheim, though, is a complete waste of time. Just like Spitalgate, a waste of time."

Priest asked Croft if he thought Pugh would get him through the schedule by the weekend.

"I believe he will," said Croft. "He says the only thing he can't arrange is the weather. About four hours a day will do it by Saturday. Is he a stickler about this fifteen-hour thing?"

"Sandy Pugh was told to do what he could to get us prepared for Cranfield," Priest said, "but they left the details to him. He decided on fifteen hours and it won't be a quarter hour less. Sorry."

"I'm not complaining," said Croft, "just so I don't get held up here. Look, Sandy gave me this booklet to read tonight." He showed them the pamphlet-sized Pilot's Notes for the Bristol Blenheim Mark V Aeroplane, Air Publication 1530C. "Is this all he gave you people?" They all agreed that was it.

"It's all you need," said Murdock, "to fly the Blenheim. It runs on rubber bands, so just keep them wound up."

The next morning, Wednesday, Sandy Pugh told

Croft that he'd arranged for his first regular flight at eleven.

"I'm tied up all morning, John," said Pugh, "but you'll be in the best hands. You and I will fly together again either right after lunch or just before tea."

Croft returned the Pilot's Notes to Sandy. "I've gone through this, Sandy, and it says the Notes are only complementary to Pilot's Notes General"—Croft read from the cover—"A.P.2095, Air Ministry Order A93/43. Is that available on the station?"

"I'm sure it is, John, if you'll just check in the adjutant's office." Pugh was slightly puzzled.

"And Sandy, there's another item I always like to see before I handle a new airplane. In the Navy we call it the specifications and operating manual, and it may be the size of a small telephone book. Is such a thing available for the Blenheim?"

"Well now, that you might have to see the maintenance section people about." Pugh was mildly insulted. "I'll just say that I've been flying the Blenheim since it was new and if I ever saw such a manual, I've long forgotten it."

"No offense, Sandy," said Croft softly, "but I always study the manual, if you don't mind."

From his reading and his flying, Croft learned that RAF language was not all that bad, that it could be more descriptive or picturesque than some American counterparts. Cowl flaps did look more like "cooling gills"; landing gear was not so elegant as "undercarriage" or "undercart"; propeller was definitely less accurate than "airscrew." Power settings of the throttle, which Croft had always read as manifold pressure in inches-of-mercury, meant "boost" in pounds-per-square-inch to his British instructors. Pressure or boost, it was generally agreed that the dials ought to be metric on all Anglo-American instrument panels. What Croft liked best of all was the dignified British word for a button, a knob, a toggle or a switch; all these were translated out of the official publications as "tits." A tit was pressed, bashed, banged, noddled or tickled. A big tit, like the red button that feathered and stopped an airscrew in flight, was a "navel" and that was something to "pong" in an emergency.

By Saturday afternoon, Croft had seventeen hours in the Blenheim, including two night flights, but that turned out to be only a technical footnote to the brief Spitalgate interlude. What had happened to Croft in the four days he'd flown over the compact mosaic of the Midlands, alone or in the company of hospitable, urbane but deadly critics, was expressed by Sandy Pugh when he said goodbye to his American friend. Croft had simply thanked Pugh for taking so much time with him.

"John, it was a—no, it was *not* really a pleasure having you here! You were difficult, you were very hard on us. It will not be the same without you. But I have to say—call this Britannic revenge, if you will —that we have infected you, too. We think that you are already half-English."

Murdock had finished up on Saturday, too. He and Croft rode up to London in the same first-class compartment. It was during this confinement that Croft established a practice that would never change. He could have called Murdock "Joe" or "Blackie." Not "Murdock," for the older man was a full lieutenant. The lieutenant persisted in calling the jg "Croft." So John Croft always said "Mr. Murdock" no matter where they were, and that was an insult so correct that nothing could ever be done about it.

Saturday, June 17. It was precisely one week after Commander Dampier had talked to the prime minister in HMS *Kelvin* off the coast of Normandy. The PM had said to call "in about a week" and Dampier felt that he owed part of his long tenure in London to the fact that he always followed up his leads rather earlier than later. But Dampier was well aware that the casual attitude toward the flying bombs on June 13 had become, by June 17, a Cabinet-level crisis.

Dampier mentioned on the telephone HMS *Kelvin* and "Mr. P" but he did not talk to the prime minister. He was asked to wait, ten minutes as it turned out, and then they gave him another number. This was the private number of an Air Council member, Air Marshal Sir Frederick St. Martin Jerrold. Sir Frederick came on himself.

"Commander Dampier," said Sir Frederick, "I have a bare sketch of what you have in mind, but it seems to me that you should talk to our Air Vice-Marshal Swann." Jerrold gave Dampier yet another telephone number at Air Ministry. "You will undoubtedly find Swann preoccupied by these new threats, the buzzbombs, but he is definitely your man and he knows that you will be ringing him up."

The attaché called Swann immediately. His enthusiasm was damped at the outset by a cold voice, a remote and stubborn personality: "Commander," said Swann, "Sir Frederick told me you would call but I was not informed of any urgency. Could you possibly call me back in a week or so? My office is right now rather burdened with problems of the, ah, new weapons."

"Marshal Swann, I cannot claim any general urgency at this moment, certainly not in view of the flying bomb attack. But I do have to make some early inquiries about an idea that could be of the greatest importance to all of us. It would not take ten minutes of your time to decide whether my idea should be developed or dropped."

There was a long silence and then Swann said, "Commander Dampier, can you come over to the Air Ministry straightaway? I have commitments for the rest of the day and tomorrow that cannot be changed."

"I'll be there within thirty minutes," said Dampier.

Thirty minutes gave the attaché time to make a phone call to an English friend who provided a preliminary sketch of Air Vice-Marshal W. E. Korpo Swann, C.B., D.S.O., M.C., D.F.C., A.F.C. Swann was Controller of Special Operations, Air Defense of Great Britain, which was the new, unpopular name for Fighter Command. He was known as the Black Swann ever since his days as a fighter pilot in World War I, when he flew, among other well-known aircraft, a distinctive Sopwith Triplane that was all black but often seen by the people of London in the searchlights over their city. Not much was known about Swann's Special Operations branch.

Dampier's meeting with Swann—it lasted exactly ten minutes because the AVM kept a cooking timer with a loud bell on his desk for just such purposes—did not seem to go well. It went so badly, in fact, that the attaché never got beyond the arrangement to have his people assigned to operational squadrons when they finished the night OTU at Cranfield.

"I don't see much of a problem here, Commander," said the silver-haired Swann, whose black eyes and thick black eyebrows revealed a youthful impatience that was utterly discordant with the controlled manner. "Don't you think we could have settled this sort of thing over the telephone?"

The attaché offered a weak explanation, that he had some knowledge of the Flying Training Command but felt he should not even petition them in operational matters without proper authority. Early in the difficult conversation with Swann, Dampier had decided that the best he could hope for was a chance to develop his contact. When he left the Air Ministry on Saturday afternoon, he knew that the head of Special Operations was precisely the man he had hoped to meet.

Air Vice-Marshal Swann had precious little time to waste thinking about Dampier's trivial business. It was the fifth day of the buzzbomb barrage and the initial sense of relief that only a trickle of the loathsome weapons had come across the Channel on the first day had given way to terror, almost panic, that dominated London. Seventy-three bombs had fallen inside London on the third day; on the morning of the fourth day the Cabinet had held an emergency meeting with the Chiefs of the Staff. As a result of that meeting, which declared a crisis situation, Korpo Swann was to prepare an immediate reorganization plan for fighter aircraft defense. A hundred buzzbombs were now being launched in every twenty-four hours and the existing combination of fighters, guns and balloons was not stopping them. Ten thousand homes a day were being destroyed or damaged; each day nearly three hundred casualties were counted. Hundreds of people were homeless and they were pouring back into the underground to live, as they had during the blitz. Even if the rate of falling bombs did not increase, Swann knew that a massive evacuation of women and children, of the elderly and hospital patients would go into effect in the next few days. An ominous but indirect result of the bombing would be a serious diversion of air support from Normandy, where the foothold was less than two weeks old and by no means secure beyond all doubt.

Only seconds after Dampier left his office, Swann was on the phone to Anti-Aircraft Command headquarters, at the end of his patience trying to convince someone that a meeting next morning, Sunday, was important. Finally Swann said, "My dear colonel, your *personal* presence at this meeting is not of the slightest concern to me. Indeed, it might be better if you stayed away. All I am saying is that the Chiefs of the Staff have ordered a responsible officer of your command to attend this meeting. Nine o'clock, please, and thank you."

Swann placed the phone gently in its cradle. His fingers uncurled from the handpiece, which the heel of his hand pressed down once as a sword is pressed into the scabbard. "There," he whispered. All that was missing was wiping blood from a blade.

Matthew Dampier spent most of Saturday afternoon making a brief for Admiral Stark to present at a forthcoming Coastal Command Liaison Committee meeting. He then wrote two letters of the kind that he always typed out himself; no one in his office ever saw these letters, which made up a large part of his correspondence.

"Dear Clip," Dampier wrote to Captain Parmenter in Washington, "Thanks for the additional material on Croft. It arrived only yesterday and seems impressive, although I haven't had a chance to study it in detail. Today I met with an Air Vice-Marshal W. E. K. Swann, controller of Special Operations. I'm impressed with him but can't honestly say it was mutual. Anyway, there's no problem at all with our main objective. I was assured that our people can be assigned to squadrons (didn't discuss which ones) when they've gone through Cranfield. Seth Rothschild knows all about this, of course, but we'll hold off telling the others until we see how the training progresses. . . .

The second letter was addressed to Captain Ephraim Rothschild, USNR, commandant of NAS Barber's Point, the station on Oahu that housed NOCTU(Pac) to which Croft had been temporarily attached. "Dear Ephraim," this letter said, "The visit that Seth and I paid to Lady Saxe-Rowland several weeks ago has begun to bear fruit. I told you about the big meeting with a chairman in a ship. Well, I was put in touch today with Air Vice-Marshal W. E. K. Swann who heads Special Operations. He is stuffy but good. The squadron assignments are assured but it seemed the wrong time to bring up the other matter. We are having a bad time here with the flying bombs and Swann is right in the thick of that. I will keep after him. . . ." Ephraim Rothschild was Seth's older brother, one of the Navy's first naval aviators.

As Dampier was finishing the letter to Captain Rothschild, Murdock called from the railroad station to say that he and Croft were back from Spitalgate. Should they come over to the embassy or what? It was six thirty.

"No, Blackie," said Dampier, "I'll be leaving here in a few minutes. All of you are to be in my office at eleven tomorrow morning for a short meeting —and we'll have lunch somewhere, on me. Seth Rothschild said you should drop by his room at Claridge's, if you were in town by seven."

Murdock told Croft that he'd pass up Seth's invitation. Croft took a taxi to the Park Lane Hotel, where the clerk gave him his old room on the top floor. "Quite frankly, sir," the desk clerk said, "our upper floors, the prime rooms in ordinary times, have been rather empty since these bombs started coming over. I think you should know that."

Croft called Seth Rothschild and said he'd be over in fifteen minutes. "Bill McLaughlin is here," Rothschild told him.

In Seth Rothschild's suite at Claridge's, John Croft met the man who was to be his radar officer. Lieutenant Commander William McLaughlin was a Virginian, about four years older than Croft, a lawyer who had not yet practiced law. He spoke infrequently and then only slowly, but it was clear that his mind was very quick. Croft felt himself under intense scrutiny through the haze of smoke that came from McLaughlin's ever-present pipe. For nearly a month, McLaughlin had been getting himself ready to fly beside a total stranger. Now, here in Rothschild's room, in London, was the man in whose hands he would be placing his life.

Rothschild made a reservation for them at Kettner's, a restaurant in Soho. Their taxi could not enter Romilly Street, where Kettner's was, because a bomb had fallen and there were already police barricades and air raid wardens. There was that weird aura of the fresh bombsite, when the physical damage was still unknown, when the dead were still hidden with the screaming, moaning injured.

The flying bomb had hit the middle of the street, blasting out the fronts of all the shops. An air raid warden said that most casualties were probably out in the open, since these bombs exploded on contact and did not dig down into the London crust. Floodlights threw a grotesque pantomime of the rescue scene onto the smoke and dust and buildings of the area. Rothschild, Croft and McLaughlin walked the short distance to Kettner's. Their dinner was a somber affair, for a warden had told them that about ninety people had been killed by the bomb.

After Kettner's, John Croft said he wanted to take the underground back to his hotel. He had never seen the underground or the deep tubes. Here was the underworld of London. Every station was lined by triple-tiered bunks in which families slept or watched the trains. There were thousands and thousands of these homeless people. At Leicester Square station, Croft saw three Polish fliers enjoying the sight of a sixteen-year-old girl asleep with her thighs exposed. They grinned and spoke about her in a strange tongue, but just before they boarded Croft's train, one of the Poles covered the girl's legs with her faded quilt.

On Sunday morning, Croft was packing up again to go to Cranfield. His windows in the Park Lane were open; the sun filled his room and the day promised to be the loveliest he had ever seen in England. Zipping up the old parachute bag, he heard the hateful *burr* of a flying bomb coming straight across the parks, then the cutoff and silence, and then the explosion which deafened him for five minutes.

Croft went across Green Park to see what had happened. The bomb could not have struck a part of London that was more important. It had landed on Birdcage Walk, in the Guards Chapel of Wellington Barracks and it had killed eighty, seriously injured more than a hundred. The chapel was only four hundred yards from Buckingham Palace and it was not much farther from 10 Downing Street, the Houses of Parliament, the War Bunker, and the offices of British Intelligence. At the chapel, there was nothing but a flat area of brick rubble. But in the Guards Chapel remains, what sickened Croft was the red paste of brick dust, mortar and human blood that was spread around several acres of the heart of London.

5

RAF Cranfield

"Andabates."

The strange word was repeated by Flight Lieutenant Basil Smyth, boy-sized O-in-C of No. 1 Squadron, No. 51 Operational Training Unit (Night), RAF Cranfield. He scrawled the word dramatically on the chalkboard. The energetic pilot loved to lecture but he had none of the experienced lecturer's grace. He always emphasized his shortness by writing at the top of the board and he always held the chalk like a fountain pen so that it screeched and curdled the blood.

"If you had come into night fighting in 1940," said Smyth to the forty-eight men of No. 35 Course sitting before him, "you would have been *andabates*. These were Roman gladiators who were put on horses and given helmets without eyeholes. These blind horsemen fought each other to the death with great swords and other grisly weapons, and the citizens of Rome were amused."

Every month, Smyth greeted a new class at Cranfield, but this was the first that ever had Americans. Out in the room now were five American pilot-cum-navigator teams of the U.S. naval air arm—Smyth assumed that's what they called it—and the arrangements for them had been so last-minute that no one really knew much about them. The rest of the teams were transfers into night fighting from other branches of the Air Force and the composition was typical; mainly British, one Free French team, two Belgian teams, all with prior Ops experience.

". . . And then, in the late summer of 1940," continued Smyth, "you all know how everything came together with a complete system of *radar,* an American word for what we Britons had been calling RDF, radio direction-finding. Now we could 'see' the enemy at a hundred miles, we could put our night fighters right behind him, and then the night fighter could go in to a kill using his own airborne radar.

"About this time," said Smyth, "Sir John Salmond, Marshall of the Air Force, decided that night fighting was not quite like anything that had happened in the air before, and so he formed the Night Defense Committee that Churchill had asked for. It was decided that a night OTU be established—that was Cranfield —that special optical tests should be given to pilots for night work, that Fighter Command should have a permanent night Ops staff, and that radar should be supplemented by new navigational aids. That, gentlemen, is why you are here."

Croft had heard most of this before. He was the only night fighter in the class, although Peter Garland and two of the RAF types were experienced day fighter pilots. The English fighter pilots were recognized by their custom of keeping the top brass button of the tunic or battlejacket unbuttoned. In London, they said, these little informal signs of specialty were so widespread that the only way you could tell a *night* fighter pilot was by the fact that he wore only RAF wings. Night fighters were secret, anyway.

". . . So you gentlemen are highly selected," said Smyth, "but you must not expect to see your names in the newspapers, like regular fighter pilots. You will spend three months here at Cranfield. Grisly months. In the first month, with One Squadron, you will fly one day, go to ground school the next, and have every seventh day off. There will be no night flying in the first month! We will concentrate on instrument flying, navigation, and simulated night radar interceptions. In Two Squadron, you will do all of this over again at night, plus some freelance over searchlights to show how bad it once was." Smyth was telling the class how bad *he* had found it. "In Three Squadron, you will practice gunnery. Finally, in Four Squadron, you will learn to fly the de Havilland Mosquito." Smyth paused between "de Havilland" and "Mosquito."

The Mosquito! Among the British pilots, there was little doubt that most had signed up for night fighting in order to fly this legendary aircraft. So fast that nothing German could catch it; nothing faster in the Allied air forces. The most versatile aircraft ever built: unarmed bomber, day fighter, night fighter, intruder, fighter-bomber, torpedo-bomber, rocket-launcher, minelayer, photoreconnaissance spy, weather spy, and courier to Stockholm and Moscow.

"Some of you," said Smyth matter-of-factly, "will not pass all the way through. No shame attached to that. You will be happily reassigned. Some of you will find that the union of pilot and nav/rad does not seem to work, an intrinsic problem that we recognize by calling the unions, in the first place, 'marriages.' Here, too, we can rearrange things but it does slow each member of the team down."

Croft heard McLaughlin's nervous cough, stifled. Although the pilot had flown by himself from a carrier in the black Pacific nights, had operated his own radar and fired his own guns, he strongly supported the idea of a separate radar operator. Yet now, sitting in a classroom beside his own radar officer, Croft wondered what would happen to all the freedom a lone fighter pilot enjoyed when McLaughlin began to sit beside him in a cockpit.

Ground school began on the first afternoon. While the pilots learned about powerplants and airframes, the nav/rads attended radar refreshers. The teams came together for night vision, aircraft silhouette recognition and intelligence. All of this preparation was clearly preliminary to the first Event, which was the day that a pilot flew his own nav/rad in a Bristol Beaufighter. This occurred after about two weeks. It was a day of worry for all the nav/rads, from the moment they awoke.

McLaughlin jumped off the van and walked casually over to the big twin-engined Beaufighter, where Croft was lying with his hands under his head beneath a wing.

"Get in," said Croft.

In the Beaufighter, which was still used by some night fighter squadrons, the radar operator climbed into his office by a rear ladder that was far back from the cockpit. But the pilot had to climb another ladder into a cockpit that was almost a death trap in the event of a crash. Croft slithered into his seat and plugged into the intercom to talk to his nav/rad.

"Ready?" asked Croft. For this moment, he had read everything printed about the famous Beaufighter and he had flown the plane alone eleven times for a total of sixteen hours.

McLaughlin had never flown with a pilot like this one. They were airborne before he knew it. They flew for an hour or so, chasing clouds the way kids kicked tin cans. When the Beau was rolling over on its back or even flying upside down, McLaughlin was strangely comfortable. And when they finally landed, too soon for McLaughlin, that cold voice came to him through the intercom:

"That was bad, bad," said Croft, "so we'll go around again." McLaughlin felt the surge of power lifting him off the ground, without knowing exactly why they were doing it. They made the circuit again and landed for the second time, no better or worse than the first time, so far as the navigator could tell. He could barely hear Croft on the intercom whispering, "That's better," just before he turned the Beaufighter off the the landing path. As they taxied fast toward the No. 1 Squadron line, McLaughlin wondered what the episode meant.

The Royal Air Force took night vision training seriously. Croft was used to wearing the red goggles before a flight to preserve night vision, but that was all they'd ever done in VF(N)-1. Two weeks before night flying began at Cranfield, all crew members went into "training." A medical officer led off with a lecture on the physiology of vision.

"Your retinas actually contain two separate systems of light receptors called rods and cones," the MO said, "which are microscopic nerve endings leading directly into the brain, the retina being the only part of the brain that comes right out to the surface of the body. In daylight or bright light, we see with the cones. But as the light fades, we switch over to the less numerous rods, which are not so sensitive to color. Right at the back center of the retina, precisely where the cones are most numerous and day vision therefore most acute, the rods are absent. That is why, when you try to look directly at a star, you do not see it. Always, gentlemen, when you search for something in the black of night, I *implore* you not to look directly at it. You must scan, always scan!

"Each of you is born, really, with an ability to see at night that is basic and that we have thoroughly tested to our satisfaction under existing standards. Only two possibilities exist right now for improving night vision. One is the little vitamin A pill that you will start taking today and every day from now on. We do not know if this is really necessary to keep up the body's stores, but we do know that the complete absence of vitamin A will produce total night blindness. It will, by the way, produce other severe conditions. The second thing we can do is train you to see better at night. You will find out that our silly little exercises really do help."

The silly little exercises were ordinary games but they were played in semidarkness with white playing pieces: snooker, skittles and darts. In one of the hangars, the students played football—soccer to the Americans—with a white ball. Croft was not good at any of the games in daylight, nor was he interested in them, but there were many who noticed that he seemed to find a lost white football or a white dart on the floor more quickly than anyone.

It was the same in night recognition of aircraft silhouettes, which was taken much more seriously than the games. Lives would depend upon the accurate identification of enemy aircraft at night, and it was forbidden to fire guns without this visual confirmation, no matter what the radar said. The people at Cranfield had developed an ingenious silhouette box, in which a black model of an airplane could be moved into any position and also illuminated from any direction, at any desired level of light intensity. Here John Croft clearly had two advantages. In his lifetime, he had built models of nearly everything that had ever flown; there was no problem of recognition. As to seeing what had to be recognized, the silhouette box showed that Croft consistently saw the models at light levels far below what had ever been recorded on the Cranfield machine. The MO could not explain.

On July 8, three weeks after his first meeting with Air Vice-Marshal Swann, Commander Dampier returned to the Air Ministry under entirely different circumstances. This time he was invited to Swann's office personally by a spontaneous phone call.

It was the end of the worst week so far of the buzzbomb campaign. Dampier had the impression that the blind, impersonal nature of the weapons was having a far worse effect on the people of London than the blitz ever had. Fewer were killed but more were injured. More houses were destroyed, it seemed. The flying bombs exploded on contact, spreading their effects laterally without penetrating deeply. The women seemed to fear the buzzbomb especially for the injuries were horribly disfiguring, partly because of flying glass. Dampier had heard that another month would see half the windows of London destroyed and no replacements possible before winter.

Swann, of course, was swamped by the buzzbomb problem. "I tell you, Dampier," said Swann, "this damn thing could finish us if we don't find the proper defense. We quickly found that the fighters over the Channel had not enough warning and then they ran into conflict with the antiaircraft guns over Surrey and

Kent, which is Bomb Alley. Now we have put the guns on the coast, the fighters over a wide belt of land, and a larger balloon barrage just before London. We are still bringing down only about a third of the bombs that cross the coast."

"And what does that mean, sir, in absolute numbers?" asked Dampier.

Swann showed the first sign of relaxing: he began to stuff the crusty bowl of a large pipe with wads of black shag.

"Ah, Commander, it's very bad. This past week was the worst with about one-hundred twenty of the devil's toys a day plotted. Since the thirteenth of June, about twelve hundred have landed inside London. More than fifteen thousand homes a day are being destroyed—nearly a quarter of a million homes are gone to date. Thousands are homeless. The evacuation of women, children and old people will soon pass the million mark. Bad!"

"Marshal Swann," said Dampier, "I've heard that this dreadful attack is beginning to compromise the hold on Normandy, which is almost unthinkable at this point. What about that?"

"It is true, Commander Dampier. General Eisenhower has given CROSSBOW, which is the whole defensive plan against the V.1 flying bomb, a priority second only to the most urgent demands of battle in France. We are so far failing miserably in defense of England, but the assaults on the launching sites in the Pas-de-Calais are working well and that is how we will finally defeat this demonic business."

"Like all of us now, Marshal, I've seen the results of a few of the bombs too close for comfort. Sir, what are the figures on casualties?"

Swann looked down at his desk with troubled eyes, puffing hard on the pipe. Finally, he said, "Here it is, Dampier. We calculate ten thousand casualties so far, about three quarters the daily rate of the blitz. But, of course, the Germans are having a very cheap go this time, since the buzzbombs are completely expendable." Swann suddenly sat up in his chair and laid his pipe carefully in an ashtray made from an engine cylinder head. "Shall I tell you? Do you want to know how bad it really is, sir? We are both accustomed to keeping secrets, aren't we?"

"Yes," said Dampier. "And yes, I would like to know how bad it is." He was encouraged by Swann's sudden frankness.

"Right. Four days ago, Commander Dampier, the Chiefs of the Staff were asked to consider, for the first time, the use of poison gas as a retaliatory measure against the German population."

"Good God!"

"Yes, God indeed. What is more terrible, I think, is that they are also drawing plans for the use of bacteriological warfare. One agent called 'N,' I believe, is anthrax. Typhus is another possibility. It *is* a desperate situation but I am greatly anguished by two reactions in the high councils. First, I sense for the first time in this war a panic among heads that have earlier been quite cool. Second, I cannot personally condone these chemical and biological measures, it is simply not the British way. Considering other German secret weapons that are in store for us, however, I have nothing concrete to offer those who are now actually considering capitulation to Hitler as one alternative to the salvation of this island."

"Marshall Swann," said Dampier, "may I ask you some questions that could bear indirectly on what may be in your mind?"

"Of course."

"What I would most like to know is this. What is the RAF's capability now for striking a target in Germany that is measured in terms of a single room? Assume that I am generally aware of pinpoint raids on a certain shop in the middle of Krupp's or a design lab at the Zeiss optical works. I'm asking for more than that. Can you hit an automobile, a train, a given *room* in a building?"

Swann's onyx eyes were clearly searching Dampier's face for motive, while the interesting question was slowly processed by a cautious mind. "Yes, Commander, all of that can be done with a degree of certainty so high that one is better off to consider only what can go wrong. Let me give you some actual case histories that, ah, might shape the next question you are going to ask me." The stiff, older man did not exactly relax but he leaned forward and rested clasped hands on the edge of his desk, putting him a few inches closer to Dampier.

"In September of 1942, we learned in advance that Quisling was planning a Nazi party rally in Oslo on the twenty-fifth of the month. That morning we sent out a quartet of de Havilland Mosquitoes from Scotland across four hundred miles of the North Sea and the Skaggerak to Oslofjord. Under fierce attack by German fighters, our people roared into Oslo only twenty feet above the startled faces of unbelieving Norwegians, who were seen to be cheering and jumping about like madmen. Seconds later, right behind the rally plaza, Gestapo headquarters with its infamous torture chamber fell in ruins under the weight of its own dome . . . a weight we had carefully calculated to assist our bombs, which could not be so large or numerous as to injure Norwegians outside the building, you see. The operation itself was—"

"Magnificent!" exclaimed Dampier.

"—was not perfect. The *Luftwaffe* fighters harried our airplanes as long as they could keep up with them on the way out of Oslo, long enough to shoot one of the Mosquitoes down into a lake. And that is what went wrong in this case, although it had to happen sooner or later. We were by no means certain that the Mosquito wreckage could not be fished out of the lake and studied by the Germans. We learned much later that they succeeded in doing this and so the secret of this airplane was out. Still, we waited to reveal the fact—the Germans would not do this, of course, because it is always better to keep us guessing about what they know—to tell a very large audience about our Mosquito. This we did on the thirtieth of January, 1943, the tenth anniversary of Adolf Hitler's rise to power."

"I know about that," said Dampier, "but I didn't hear any of the radio broadcasts."

"Well, the Germans provided nearly all the wire-

less propaganda and advertising themselves." And now
Swann finally smiled, discreetly. "At eleven A.M., wireless listeners heard around the world the opening
speech of Marshal Göring cut right off the air after the
sound of many explosions. They got the Air Ministry
wireless station going again by four in the afternoon.
This time, the propaganda minister, Dr. Göbbels, had
barely cleared his throat when our bombs hit the mark
again! Twice in the same day, our Mosquitoes had
gone after the antennas. They got them, but I must
admit they did not have to be so careful in Berlin
about splashing up the place as was the case in Oslo.
It was quite a day for broadcasting—I'm sorry you
missed it. That night, our dear friend, the traitor
Lord Haw-Haw, seemed to have the last word in his
usual evening program from Berlin. He said, 'Britain
is now so desperate, she must build her air force of
wood!' Among the many advantages of the wooden
Mosquito, the Germans seem to forget that with so
little metal in it, it is very close to being a radar
'ghost.'"

"I'd never thought of that," said Dampier.

"A poor reflector of radar beams, wood." But
Swann was well into his story by now and even a
trifle enthusiastic. "The broadcasting was not really
over until nine P.M. when the BBC put on the crews
who made the trips to Berlin that day. There were, by
the way, only four Mossies in the morning raid and
six in the afternoon. I think it was quite thrilling,
frankly, for a laboring man to hear our chaps step
out of a Mossie, practically, and tell the man over his
evening pint in the pub what happened."

"I agree, Marshall. The Oslo raid and especially
the Berlin raid illustrate superb timing. Can you give
me an example where the space factor was a little
tighter? Like the size of a room?"

"The Hague. Yes, The Hague. About three
months ago, the Dutch underground called our attention to the Kleizkamp Art Galleries in The Hague.
This mansion was Gestapo Central for all of Holland.
Thousands of names, they said, were listed here for a
fresh program of persecution, torture and death. Now

the problem was that the only proper approach to this target was along a narrow allée to the five-story building and we had to hit the ground floor directly. My dear friend Wing Commander R. N. Bateson crossed the North Sea at nought feet with six Mosquitoes. At the Galleries, Bateson and his wingman slithered two bombs through the left ground floor windows. All the five-hundred-pound bombs were set for an eleven-second delay. The next pair of Mosquitoes attended the windows at the right. Then a fifth Mosquito slid its bomb through the double front door. At debriefing—I conducted this—Bateson said, 'By the time Numbers Five and Six came along, the Gestapo building just wasn't there.' And now, Commander Dampier"—Swann's expression was suddenly an odd mixture of humor and conspiracy—"you are going to ask me if, with proper location and timing, the RAF can go after a certain man in Germany and, ah, get him."

"Sir, that is exactly what I want to know." Dampier was certain by now that Swann was won, in spirit. It was just a matter of matching up capabilities.

"Dampier, I have to go back to 1942 now and tell you about a problem that obsessed me for a while. It will seem as if I am blowing my own horn but—but there you are. I became quite interested in one particular Nazi, Reinhard Heydrich. He was chief of the security police and deputy chief of the Gestapo, a monstrous mutant of the human race. One day, two of us set out for Warsaw, which is nine hundred miles from England, on a slim clue that the Hangman was riding a train at about the same time. As the train rolled into the Warsaw station, we came up the tracks behind it and we tore it right out of the station. But the Hangman, I'm sorry to say, had taken a later train from Berlin."

"What you're saying," Dampier interjected, "is that you can guarantee the place and the time but you cannot be responsible for the *content*."

"Exactly. The intelligence must give name, place and hour. It must be up to the minute. By the way, Dampier, my dear companion on that Warsaw bash, now dead, flew through some *Hausfrau's* laundry near Braunschweig, as I recall, and he landed in England with sixty feet of her clothesline and much of the poor woman's family wash draped over his wing. I continued to follow Heydrich's career. You may remember that he became the acting protector of Czechoslovakia and was assassinated by some Czechs who rolled British bombs under his auto. In reprisal for this marvelous act, the Germans wiped out the town of Lidice. Do you remember? I remember, sir."

"Of course, Marshal," said Dampier. He knew the name, Lidice, without recalling what it meant.

"On the first anniversary of Lidice, the tenth of June, 1943," said Swann, "I took four Mosquitoes into Prague, where I had learned there was to be an SS celebration of the Lidice massacre. We broke up this horrible remembrance and allowed the Czechs a few minutes or so of vicarious reprisal, bloody revenge, against their beastly captors." Now the serene black eyes were snapping indeed! "It was shortly after that trip, Commander, that I was promoted out of the flying ranks."

So it was at Prague that the Black Swann finally folded his wings, which had first fluttered before 1914. *Prague, the marshal's swan song,* thought Dampier. The attaché knew he was in the presence of a legend, but one whose light had been turned down. *I've seen this light before . . . it never dies out completely . . . John Croft is a young replica of this stern, formal air vice-marshal . . . I would like to introduce them to each other one day.*

"Marshal," said Dampier, "you may remember that fifteen months ago Admiral Yamamoto, chief of the Imperial Combined Fleet, was shot down, assassinated, by our air force while flying on a routine inspection tour in the Bismarck Archipelago. The background intelligence came through Admiral Stark's office from a source that you are undoubtedly aware of, and then it was forwarded to Admiral Nimitz in Hawaii. I've been told that this was probably the most perfect conjunction of intelligence and tactics that has ever been seen."

"The Yamamoto incident illustrates my two main points," said Swann. "Yes, the intelligence stolen from the Japanese was perfect, and for that very reason, the air tactics following could only fail by the worst possible toss of bad dice. Your own pilots who went out after Yamamoto that day would tell you the same thing. Come now, Commander Dampier, why don't you tell me that you now have a line on Mr. Adolf Hitler and that your prime question is, why don't we just see what can be done about it?"

Dampier was stunned. "That's it, Marshal," he said, "and I suddenly feel as if we've been beating around the bush too long."

"Not just this morning, Commander. For years, some of us in the RAF have dreamed of killing the *Führer*. I have told you what we can do. What can you add?" Swann's expression had hardened again.

"In our office, Admiral Stark's, we have an amazing new line on some 'friends' in Germany who have proved that they can keep track of Hitler every day, with almost no lapses. They have apparently been doing this for six months and no one has paid attention to them."

"If that is true," said Swann, "and I would want proof, then the Royal Air Force is at your disposal. The reason I seem to be prepared for you, Commander, is that apparently you have spoken to the prime minister. Maybe you will tell me about that some time. In any case, Air Marshal Jerrold told me that we should listen to you. That is why I called you."

"May I bring proof to you, Marshal? It will be a matter of days, a week at the most."

"Do, by all means. You are welcome here at any time." That was an entirely new ticket to the Air Ministry that Swann had written for Dampier. "I am *personally* interested in this, ah, question you are asking."

In the week of July 9, at Cranfield near the town of Bedford, No. 35 Course was finishing its month of day flying. The twenty-four crews had concentrated first on instruments, blind flying, using an ingenious sodium-light illumination that allowed an instructor to watch outside the cockpit while his student could see only the six dials of the blind-flying panel. Then the students went on to navigation by dead reckoning, radiobeams, radiobeacons, and the new, elegant radar-interrogator beacons—the ultimate in direction-finding and positioning. But most pilots were expected to fly straight-and-level without seeing the ground and to fly under the same conditions from point to point. In addition, night fighters had to find an enemy aircraft without seeing it and then shoot it out of the sky. The most important exercises at Cranfield, therefore, were ground-controlled interceptions, GCI, and gunnery. Some did not take these practice sessions seriously.

A GCI flight was an elaborate ritual, something like a bullfight, involving many performers. In reality, enemy aircraft would first be picked up at more than a hundred miles by long-range radar stations on the coast of England. The early-warning information would pass quickly through group and sector levels to the GCI station most likely to be involved, and this station would order up one or more night fighters. At this point, the GCI station would see on its radar scopes both the enemy and the "friendly," and it would try to bring the friendly close in behind the enemy.

Lieutenant Joseph Murdock and his nav/rad, Ensign Elliot Nicholas, were the first of the Americans to fly a daylight GCI practice under the control of the training station, FROGSPAWN. Nicholas was a serious graduate of the Pearl Harbor Radar School. He was overwhelmed by Murdock, who had told him, "Just leave everything up to me, kid, and we can't lose. You pass the info and I'll do the rest."

Daylight interceptions were easy, if the pilot cheated. When the GCI station, FROGSPAWN, brought Murdock's Beaufighter within a mile or so of the target aircraft, Nicholas would usually call "contact" and take over the interception on his own airborne radar. Then Nicholas would guide Murdock in for the last mile and the final simulated "visual" contact. But Murdock was an impatient man, who did not precisely follow his nav/rad's radar directions. Murdock could always see the target in daylight as Nicholas spoke to him, and it was easy for the pilot to warp the Beaufighter into a better position than the radar indications called for. Nicholas was pleased to think that he was learning fast. He was being cheated.

It was entirely different in Croft's Beaufighter. At the Ouston radar school, William McLaughlin had made a good name for himself as an operator, but some of his instructors had been impatient, like Murdock. So, when Croft followed McLaughlin's instructions to the letter—although the pilot could see the target escaping ahead of them—there were at first many failures and McLaughlin began to lose confidence in himself. Croft could say nothing. But gradually the firm policy of following only radar directions by McLaughlin led to the teamwork that Cranfield was trying to develop. Nicholas worshiped Murdock, who was cheating. McLaughlin hated Croft, who was not cheating at all. Croft was always looking ahead into the dark of night, when no one, neither the pilot nor the radar operator nor the GCI controller, could play games with each other.

Everyone was taking the vitamin A pills, eating the yellow vegetables at mealtime and playing the stupid games in the dark. There were arguments over these attempts to improve nocturnal vision but no one objected to the largesse of two eggs with every night-flying supper that the RAF served to every man who came out of a plane in the nighttime.

Escape & Evade was surely the most exotic class that Cranfield offered. The instructor was an old hand, a leathery major from the Belgian commandoes. He had an indefinable accent, since he spoke all the languages of Europe fluently.

"If you are shot down over Germany," the major told them, "it is not helpful to be British and it is hopeless to be American. Consider only the haircuts, gentlemen. The Englishman cuts his hair this way"— a head was grabbed in the first row and shown to the class—"which is close to the Continental way, but the American haircut, I'm sorry to say, is an automatic signal for capture. I've been told that ten of you in this

course are Americans. You perhaps should consider
this point on your next visit to the hairdressser, eh?

"To evade capture these days from Europe, much
less escape, you should be Belgian, Dutch, Danish,
Norwegian, Swedish, Czech, Polish—in that order.
Belgians are the chameleons of Europe."

In the middle of July, just before the night flying program began, the No. 35 Course students started
making visits to operational sites that were related to
night fighting, including several that night fighters
would work with. On the edge of Bedford, they saw
the handling of balloons, and on the windy day of this
visit, it was seen to be anything but a second-rater's
cushy job. The point of having balloon squadrons
around a city, they were told, was to keep enemy
raids up high where the day and night fighters could
get at them. It worked both ways: one of the worst
things that could happen to you was to blunder into a
garden of balloons, say at London, even with a working radio in your plane and a good radar fix on you.

More impressive than balloons was a distinguished
antiaircraft battery at Lowestoft, a coastal town in
East Anglia, the easternmost town in England. The
gunners wasted many shells for the airmen's amuse-
ment. Even in daylight the muzzle flash looked important. The noise was painful; the acrid smell of
cordite was never to be forgotten. The men from
Cranfield went away with the uneasy feeling that gunners were a nervous lot, anxious not to be left out of
the war. They were having a difficult time in the
southern batteries with the small, fast, erratic flying
bombs. Sixteen hundred coastal guns were deployed
against the bombs. Even with gun-laying radar and
proximity fuses in the shells, it was taking many thousands of rounds to bring down each of the doodlebugs.

Before freelance "candle" exercises could begin
in the air over searchlights, there had to be a night
visit to a searchlight regiment. While the students were
watching on the ground, a Cranfield instructor flew
over in a Beaufighter to be a target for the powerful
lights. These were, like the antiaircraft guns, also di-

rected by radar so that when the huge arc-lamps first snapped out their beams into the sky, there was a good chance that they would catch the target without hunting for it. To see twelve lights come on at once from a circular battery and cone the target, which seemed to be caught at the apex of a ghostly teepee, was more eerie than to see the firing of guns. There was a noise but it was the cracking-on of arcs, followed by a sizzling buzz. Pale blue smoke came out of the six-foot-wide lamps and drifted through the beams. All around was the antiseptic smell of ozone.

The most important site visit came when the No. 35 Course aircrews were nearly finished with the daytime practice GCI flights. As they became more experienced, the students noticed that their GCI station, FROGSPAWN, started putting women's voices on the radio among the more experienced male controllers' voices. These women were said to be students also, learning to assist the fighter-directors. Croft had rarely heard a female voice on the radio; it was a startling experience for him. The RAF crews were quite used to it and, indeed, the higher-pitched voices had a clarity that few male controllers could match.

FROGSPAWN was superficially disappointing, compared to the searchlights and guns. The raw kilowatts and megacandles of light were missing. The terrible explosive force of gunpowder and the authority of projectiles were absent. The combined sector-control and GCI station had a lonely, scientific appearance that was suggested even at a distance by the variety of elaborate antennas sitting on the roofs of some of the buildings. The most prominent antenna, a bedspring contraption, rotated slowly in a full circle: it was sweeping out a hundred miles of sky. Another bowl-shaped antenna was tilted at a forty-five-degree angle and moving slowly, as if it were following something. A third crescent-shaped contraption nodded rapidly and vertically from the horizon to the sky and back again as it rotated like the bedspring, for which it was measuring altitude. Yet all these devices could not entirely erase an air of poverty and transience about the station. Some of the buildings were really only shacks made of lath and tarpaper. FROGSPAWN had a shantytown appearance and it seemed to Croft that gypsies might be in command.

Inside some of the buildings there was very expensive equipment. All personnel spoke quietly, even whispered. Half of the people were uniformed women, mostly WAAF, who pushed markers around on large map tables like croupiers in a gambling hall, wrote backward with China pencils on Perspex panels through which other people could read correctly, or spoke into telephone headsets. These WAAF seemed to be working for others who watched large yellow-green radar screens or who sat up on a balcony around one room and looked down on the biggest map of all. Information from the biggest, round radar tubes, plan-position indicators or PPI's, was constantly transferred to the maps.

Some of the station personnel had been assigned to take the Cranfield visitors on a tour. Croft and McLaughlin were in a group of eight under the guidance of a WREN sublieutenant. She wore the trim black naval jacket with a double row of gold buttons. Narrow, wavy stripes of gold braid were on each sleeve. The WREN's white shirt had a stiff collar and thin, black four-in-hand tightly knotted, which choked her lightly and made her seem more formal than the men in her group would have wished. She was elegantly self-assured, perhaps because she was in the Navy talking to mere RAF types. She didn't notice the Americans at first, since the room was dimly lighted in favor of the radar operators.

"I am Sublieutenant Ince," said the young woman. She had an accent that Croft could not identify but he was certain that he had heard it on the VHF.

The Ince tour was conducted in a logical sequence that showed the guests how perfectly coordinated everything was at this station. The woman knew a lot about fighter-directing and she could field some pretty wild technical questions. She handled nontechnical matters rather well, too.

"Miss Ince," someone asked, "do we all sound pretty much alike up there to you?"

"Well," answered the WREN, suppressing a smile, "you do sound like men, after all, and you are all on our side. It would be nice, I think, to hear a woman's voice up there some time."

"Female fighter pilots?" There was much laughter.

"Ferry Command haven't found the women pilots of Air Transport Auxiliary wanting, have they?" asked Ince, raising her head so that the harsh light of a naked bulb in the hallway fell into her eyes. "They haven't found the aircraft *those* women can't handle nicely, have they?" Croft thought the eyes were a sort of olive-green, that color which changed so much with the lighting.

But women in combat! Again laughter.

"I do find," said Croft, moving out of the shadows, "that women's voices are much better for radio, much more distinct than men's." Only much later would Croft learn that Sublieutenant Ince had wanted to fly, to be an ATA ferry pilot, but those fine eyes were hopelessly nearsighted.

"That, at least, seems to be true," said Ince. The Cranfield men nodded in agreement, for the silent Croft had shown them how rude they were to the WREN.

When Ince announced that the tour was over, most of the men fell to examining some of the equipment they'd seen. Croft slipped out the door to go back and watch the plotters over their large sector map. The woman followed him.

"You are one of the Americans who clutter the channels lately, I know," said Ince, "but may I ask what that uniform means?"

"These are aviation greens," said Croft. "I'm in the Navy, too, Miss Ince."

"It's Rosemary Ince. Otherwise, you should say Sublieutenant."

"I see. How large an area does this sector actually cover?"

Rosemary ignored Croft's question, asking him instead, "And what is your name?"

"John Croft."

"You are a lieutenant?"

"Yes. Lieutenant junior grade, to tell the truth."

"You're in the, sort of, Fleet Air Arm?"

"Yes."

"I don't—what—how did the American Navy get into all this?"

"I'll have to think about that myself," said Croft. "But you, a WREN at a RAF GCI station?"

"There are three WRENs here, actually. I really can't tell you why exactly, but we are having a smashing time of it, since the RAF is so much nicer to us than our own stuffy service. Look, you do know, don't you, that I was joshing a moment ago about cluttering the airwaves? It has been rather exciting for us suddenly to have all these strange tongues coming out of the earphones."

"We sound that bad?" asked Croft.

"*You* are quite clear, honestly, certainly better than a Lancashireman. But there is one chap, I must say, who does mangle the King's—pardon—who mumbles English as if it were a throat disease. This pilot does not pronounce words correctly, much less distinctly. Once he told me to 'cut out this fol-de-*roy*.' Another time, he said I should 'disconcern' myself with his business and pay attention to my own radar 'scoops.' "

"That's Tarbox," said Croft. "Lieutenant Commander Archibald Tarbox. I'm sorry, but he's probably the best pilot we have. He's from Tennessee, the South. You'll have to get used to him. He has a good education, by our standards, but sometimes he even confuses me. Once he said to me, 'tête-à-tête this problem' and it was only later I knew he meant 'vis-à-vis.' "

"*Whush,*" said Rosemary, who had glanced at her watch, "it's after ten! They'll tear a stripe off me if I don't have you all out of here by ten thirty." She walked down the hall and clapped her hands. "Gentlemen," said Rosemary, "we must pack it up now, if you don't mind. We hope you enjoyed your visit. We should love to have you back at any time"—her eyes swept the group, lingering unnoticeably on Croft's face —"if you will just ring us up first. T'raa, all."

On the ride back to Cranfield, the bus was noisy for a while until the men began to fall asleep. McLaughlin was in his usual presleep period of hyperactivity. Croft was looking out the window into the darkness, grunting brief answers to Bill McLaughlin, waiting for him to shut up.

"That was quite a gal," said Bill, "that Ince. I noticed you were pretty well tuned in there. Any joy?"

"Don't be ridiculous," said Croft, "and please shut up."

"Well," said McLaughlin, yawning, "that's a real queen. A real . . . a queen." And then Bill McLaughlin's head fell sideways and he was asleep. *Thank God,* Croft thought. He watched through the window as the nameless farms and hamlets of Bedfordshire slipped by in the pale moonlight.

Queen, Bill had said. A curious coincidence, Croft thought, who was thinking of Rosemary Ince. Soundlessly, he tested the name:

Rosemary. Queen of Scots.

It sounded right. It fit her.

PART TWO

Ops

...A car owner should try driving a very fast car, with no lights and no brakes, on a dark night down a winding, unlit road behind another equally fast car with no lights driven by an armed desperado who is swerving violently and making unsignaled crash stops. Let the car driver then shut his eyes and keep them shut, and let him rely entirely on his passenger's instructions to keep him out of trouble; and at the same time he must keep closing in on the car he is chasing.

C. F. Rawnsley and Robert Wright
Night Fighter

6

The Assassin's Committee

During the night of July 20/21 the V.1 bombardment of London shifted into high gear. Everyone knew it, although no one could see it all. The city's professional prowlers especially—the bobbies, the air-raid wardens, the ambulance drivers, the taximen, the flower girls of Piccadilly Circus—saw on this night many more than ever before of the stuttering flames streaking across the sky, cringed at more heart-stopping cutouts, and heard or even felt more of the explosions. Of those directly in the path of the glass and brick shrapnel, nine hundred Londoners were maimed and more than two hundred died.

Even the wireless monitors who heard Adolf Hitler's personal broadcast at one A.M. did not relate the bizarre speech to the upsurge in flying bombs, although the *Führer*'s dilemma was recognized. He had to tell the Germans, and thus all others listening, that he was alive after an attempt to assassinate him with a bomb planted by Colonel the Count Klaus von Stauffenberg, who headed a "small clique of ambitious, dishonorable and criminally stupid officers . . . a very small gang of criminal elements who will now be ruthlessly exterminated." No stranger radio message had ever come out of Germany.

At ten thirty in the morning, Matthew Dampier received his second telephone call from Air Vice-Marshal Swann. The marshal's astonishing informality surprised Dampier more than the uncharacteristic agitation in the man's voice.

"Matthew! Korpo Swann here. You've seen the papers, I'm sure, you've got the news?"

"Hitler's broadcast? Yes, just now. I was about to call you."

"I've been in touch with a friend in Cambridge about it. He tells me that it will take a few days, perhaps a week, to collect all the gen on this affair. Would you like to meet this man? I've invited him to London to give us a sort of lecture on Adolf Hitler."

"At any time, Marshal . . . Korpo. One thing puzzles me. Do you—does your friend think that it was Hitler himself speaking on the radio? It's clear there was a bomb or else there would have been no broadcast. But what if the bastard *had* been killed? Wouldn't they put an actor on the air?"

"No, no! This was Hitler! The professor, my friend, has heard the recordings—he did not hear the broadcast itself—and he says it was Hitler."

"Fair enough, Korpo. Please call me, night or day."

"Will do, Matthew. Oh, by the way, you noticed the hotting-up of the chuff bombs last night? Nearly two hundred of them were launched, about twice the usual rate. The professor will have something to say about this, I think."

Two plus two, Dampier thought as he hung up the phone, *is almost always more than four.* Swann's sources were apparently of a higher order than Dampier's, but the two were already complementing each other. The attaché's sources were not placed to know about a bomb plot. But they would probably have known where the *Führer* was when the bomb went off at 12:41 on the afternoon of July 20. Dampier would find out.

While Adolf Hitler raved to the world on the ordinary wireless in the early morning of July 21, Sublieutenant

Rosemary Ince spoke quietly on VHF Channel D and played a deadly game with John Croft. The Scottish WREN was up for her first qualifying examination at FROGSPAWN, taking on the role of a fighter-controller in a ground-controlled interception. All the station's facilities were temporarily at her command as she bent tensely over the main control desk, the soft, green glow of the plan-position indicator tube accentuating the natural color of her eyes and the strain in her face.

The people at FROGSPAWN were drawn to Ince's problem for several reasons; those who were idle drifted onto the galleries and crowded around the plotting tables to watch. In the previous exercise, managed by one of the WAAF students, Croft's Beaufighter had been the target for Lieutenant Commander Tarbox. The Tarbox-Rothschild team was more precise and cautious, as befitted night fighters, than the Croft-McLaughlin team. Tarbox had made several perfect interceptions but had been unable to close in during his last one because of Croft's violent maneuvering. Peering out from his Perspex dome near the Beaufighter's tail, McLaughlin had seen the stalking shadow when it crossed a patch of water lit by the moon. It was hard for the FROGSPAWN technicians to take sides between the two: Tarbox was the controller's dream who followed instructions like a machine although his communications were difficult for Britons to understand; Croft spoke with a clarity that was almost English but he said little and his exercises were a bit vigorous for the training function. In the final analysis, what drew the personnel to this contest was not so much the expertise of closely matched American strangers as the fact that Rosemary Ince was known to be interested in the American pilot named Croft.

The WREN watched a dozen or so sweeps of the time-trace around the face of the PPI tube, to get hold of the problem and calm herself down. Like the second hand of a big clock, the thin, bright radius of light in each of its revolutions triggered two blips whose relative positions kept changing. One blip was

Ince's target. The other was her night fighter, Croft. When she had the picture, the WREN looked at the clock on the wall—it was 01.21 hours—and pressed her microphone button.

"Good morning, TADPOLE One-Six," said Rosemary, "this is FROGSPAWN. How do you hear me?"

"Loud and clear, FROGSPAWN," answered Croft. His voice came into the control room through a loudspeaker mounted on the ceiling.

"I have a customer for you, One-Six. He is on course two-six-zero above you, crossing right to left. Vector zero-seven-zero degrees and climb to angels ten."

"Wilco," said Croft.

The order to turn and climb came when Croft's Beaufighter was holding an orbit at 5000 feet just below a solid layer of cloud; no polygons of moonlight were now stenciled out below on the dark earth. FROGSPAWN depended on the pilots for local weather information, but Croft thought he would wait to tell them, her, about the solid cloud. As he made his turn and climbed on instruments into the directionless world of the cloud, Croft thought he would say something about it if he was not out of it by ten thousand feet.

Tarbox was in ecstasy, a state in which he talked to himself constantly. He was flying west at precisely 10,000 feet, right along the billowing cloudtop and in full moonlight. *It would be a crazy Croft, Archie,* Tarbox said to himself, *who would come out of the cloud down there and grab our tail, wouldn't it?*

"TADPOLE One-Six, turn hard port, *hard* port, to two-seven-zero. Continue standard climb. Your bogey is now two thousand feet above you."

"Wilco."

"One-Six, on your new course you will have the bogey almost directly above and pulling out ahead. When you reach angels ten, he will be about four miles in front on your port side."

"Roger," said Croft. He switched to intercom. "Bill, you heard that?"

"Yes, all set here." Back toward the Beau's tail

under his dome, McLaughlin faced aft with his eyes pressed into the rubber visor of his AI set. He faced the rear in order to keep watch—in real life—over the Beaufighter's stern when he was not buried in the radar. He felt the aircraft roll out of its steep turn onto a steady course and found a ghostly blip at the top of his scope.

"I think I've got him, John," said McLaughlin. "He's more than three miles ahead of you, thirty degrees above, and on your left. Tell them we've got it."

"FROGSPAWN," said Croft, "we've got a contact. Keep your eye on us, please." There was no need to worry her about the cloud. "Thank you."

Rosemary was terribly deflated by the abrupt dismissal from her problem. The chief controller, her examiner, said, "This is what it's all about, my dear, so shed no tears when your work is over quickly and they take it out of your hands. You've done quite well, Miss Ince."

"Take a sidestep port, John," said McLaughlin, "just to see if we're on his course."

Croft turned the Beaufighter sharply left, then right back on course.

"No, he's angling left," Bill said. "Turn port slowly." The miniature green caterpillar at the top of Bill's scope checked its leftward movement and began crawling back toward the right across the center line. "Hold this just a minute now, John . . . yeah, this is good . . . okay, *very* slowly port . . . keep coming, keep coming . . . there! you've got it. Mr. Croft, I give you Archibald Tarbox and Seth Rothschild dead ahead of you at exactly two miles, twenty degrees up. They are creeping away from us."

"All right, Bill," said Croft, "keep me at this range while I climb out of this stuff behind them." Bill felt the extra boost Croft gave the engines. "If I were Archie, I'd be boating right along the top of this cloud. I want to come out of it, though, before we go in any closer."

It was going to be a submarine attack after all, despite what Tarbox thought. Croft was going to take a periscope scan before making his next move. As his

Beau came up to 10,000 feet, the black envelope of cloud lit up, turned gray, and made a pearly shell around the night fighter just before it broke out into full moonlight. At the surface, the speed of the aircraft suddenly thrilled Croft as he raced through endless ridges of soft white vapor.

"Bill, we're out the top now"—McLaughlin's eyes were inside the visor, fixed on the scope—"so start bringing me in on them."

"Still two miles straight ahead." Several seconds passed. "We're closing slowly."

The moon was favorable, being slightly ahead of Tarbox's Beaufighter, so Croft climbed 500 feet. McLaughlin kept reporting on the decreasing range until he was giving it in yards.

"One thousand yards, John."

Croft was scanning the cloud surf ahead of him with the Ross night binoculars.

"Got them, Bill, they're clamped right down on the quilt. I'm going back down into it, so keep us back here at a thousand yards for a while."

Ten feet down in the cloud, Croft added full boost to catch up with his target. It took time but the attacker was certain that his target was flying half in and half out of the moonlit cloud surface.

"Range, Bill?"

"Eight hundred yards."

At 300 yards, Croft said, "Come out of the scope, Bill. Is that a Beaufighter up there?" The visual identification was the most important stage of the night fighter's attack and Croft made McLaughlin take it seriously.

"A Beaufighter," said Bill.

"Right. Now I want to go in and have some fun with them. Keep calling out the ranges until they're off your scope."

Croft watched the Beaufighter ahead come closer and closer, until McLaughlin said he couldn't see it any longer. The pilot switched on Channel D. "FROGSPAWN," he said. "I seem to have lost contact. Can you get us back on?"

Rosemary Ince was perplexed, for she had seen

her night fighter merge with the target. "TADPOLE One-Six, make your canary sing, please," she said. She was asking Croft to turn on his IFF—Identify Friend or Foe—which would put an electronic tag next to his blip on the PPI tube.

"My canary sings," said Croft, although he deliberately did not press the G-band button for his IFF.

"Sir," said Rosemary to her amused examiner, "One-Six is not coming through on his IFF."

"I think he's playing with you, Ince," said the smiling controller. "Watch and I'll interrogate Tarbox." He asked TADPOLE One-Fiver to turn on his IFF; immediately the PPI tube displayed the coded dots next to the fused blip that Rosemary had sudden doubts about. *Was* Tarbox alone in the blip? Had she somehow lost Croft?

None of the hushed conversations in the plotting room reached Croft, but suddenly his voice broke in on the loudspeaker as if he could hear them or read their minds. "This is One-Six, FROGSPAWN. Perhaps I should tell you that we are sitting here about twenty under the target."

Nasty bugger! Rosemary thought as she spoke calmly into her microphone: "Yes, One-Six, you can break off now and steer zero-seven-zero. Thank you for a lovely exercise this morning."

On July 28 at eight in the evening, Matthew Dampier met with Korpo Swann at the Air Ministry for the second time. This meeting was at Swann's invitation.

"Matthew," said the air marshal, "we are going to have a lecture by a Cambridge don no less, my friend Professor Jeremy Witcher. He said he'd be here at eight thirty."

"A lecture?" asked Dampier. "On what?"

"Hitler, mainly, I suspect. In any context, this will be a lecture such as you have never heard, I assure you. Jeremy does ramble, but he is one of our best historians, a perfect crown jewel straight out of Charlemagne's era."

"But a historian, Korpo! What does this have to do with, with our business?"

"You shall see, Matthew. We are military men and our judgments are always made under some senior's review. But these university sweats, like Witcher, have just that mentality that good intelligence—not necessarily *moral* intelligence, mind you—that intelligence of quality requires. The open mind, the rejection of authority, the supreme confidence in evidence."

"When you said a lecture on Hitler over the telephone, I somehow connected it to the July twenty affair, but you said something about the stepped-up buzzbombs, too."

"Both," said Swann. "They are connected. I'll let the professor give you the whole programme."

"How is the air defense going, though?" Dampier knew this was the marshal's main concern.

"We're making headway against the launching sites in France, definitely. Here at home, it is bad. It is bad in the sense that we have twenty-two squadrons committed to wasteful standing patrols, including nine squadrons of Mosquito night fighters. Still, about a third of the bombs are getting through to London, because of a higher launch rate. Do you know that one historical building a day has disappeared from this city since June twelfth? That would be close to fifty by now, wouldn't it?"

Dampier could only close his eyes and shake his head slowly from side to side.

"Yes, we think that more than six hundred thousand London houses are now damaged seriously or destroyed," said Swann.

Both men sat in silence. They heard someone padding down the hall outside, someone who might be wearing bedroom slippers. The footsteps stopped outside Swann's door.

"That's Jeremy," said Swann, jumping out of his chair like a child released from parental quarantine. "When Fate comes to your door in England, Matthew, he wears tennis shoes, not jack boots."

Swann opened the door, revealing a small man in a wrinkled sack of clothing that had not been seen in London since World War I. The insignificant person was caught in the act of knocking on Swann's door. His head tilted like a blackbird's, Professor Witcher's pale eyes suspiciously searched the air marshal's face through the circular windows of his steel-rimmed spectacles.

"Jeremy!" said Swann, "I knew it was you. Please come in, come in."

"Good evening, Marshal," snapped the agitated guest, who chose to stand at the threshold. To Dampier, he seemed preoccupied by events attending his arrival at Adastral House, for he kept glaring back up the hall. "I should have thought, sir," the old man said, "that Air Ministry were more used to visits after hours than seems to be the case. Perhaps you did not tell them, the fellows with the armbands, that I was coming."

"Professor," Swann exclaimed, "but I did! You were stopped by a sergeant?"

"A sergeant, yes sir, a-aa-and"——Witcher was angry and he stammered——"and a flying officer, I think. The thin stripe."

"Pilot officer, Jeremy," said Swann apologetically. "Won't you come in, though? Commander Matthew Dampier of the American Embassy has come over tonight to meet you."

Rumpled and unmollified, the ancient professor stood outside the door and glared now at Dampier. His baggage was a slim umbrella in the right hand and a grimy tan raincoat in the left. Swann gently took the umbrella arm and led the antique person from Cambridge into the office. Witcher, like a schoolboy, automatically took off his bowler as he stepped onto the marshal's Persian carpet. The top of the bowler, Dampier saw, was covered with years of dust.

"Professor Witcher," said Swann, "may I introduce Commander Matthew Dampier, the American naval attaché to London."

"*Air* attaché, Korpo," said Dampier.

"No matter, Commander," said Witcher. "I know you. You came to London in 1940, did you not?"

"I did."

"Yes, yes, I thought so." Witcher offered a fragile

hand to shake Dampier's; the attaché had the impression of briefly weighing a cluster of trembling pencils. "They told me about you," the professor said.

Witcher's cryptic remark annoyed Dampier because he could hardly back-query it without seeming anxious. He wondered who "they" might be. Meanwhile, the extraordinary visitor had somehow become distracted by the fine paneled ceiling of Swann's spacious office. The large head on a slender neck was bent back at a frightful angle so that the professor could look straight up over Dampier's head. Then the old man emitted several muted cackles—it was not clear whether the panels or some private joke amused him —and lowered his head abruptly, suggesting crankily to Swann that they get on with their business.

"I promised my daughter," said Witcher, "that I'd be by her flat without fail, without fail mind you, at ten o'clock latest. You know," he added wistfully, "I'm trying with not much success to have her leave these awful buzzbombs and come stay with me in Cambridge."

Air Vice-marshal Swann, always embarrassed by personal problems, made a quick offer: "We shall be delighted to have a driver take—"

"Not necessary, Marshal, thank you. But do let us proceed. Now exactly what was it you originally asked me to do? I remember it had to do with that Hitler broadcast of a sennight ago."

"Yes, Jeremy, that and a bit more." Glancing over at Dampier, Swann flicked his eloquent black brows in an expression of mock despair. "You'll remember we wanted to have whatever you could tell us about *all* attempts to assassinate Hitler. Knowing that your records are probably quite spotty here, still we would treasurer whatever you can give us."

"Hitler, Adolf Hitler! My dear Marshal, the record could hardly be called spotty. On the contrary, there may be rather more than you would want to hear." The professor was irritated as if an undergraduate had asked him what he knew about intrigue in the Holy Roman Empire.

Dampier, until now not much impressed by Professor Witcher, saw a new, fierce light in the faded eyes and he instinctively leaned forward in his chair.

"Let me see," said Witcher, squinting at the wall clock, "you should really have fair background on the political scene from about 1934 . . . no, that would take too long . . . there perhaps I can summarize . . . the so-called conspiracies? the plots? the plans? Heavens! it will take an hour to speak of actions alone. . . ."

It was unbelievable but true, and quite apparent to both Swann and Dampier, that Witcher had come up from Cambridge without a clue to his mission. He had forgotten his telephone conversation with Swann! And so they were apparently going to hear a lecture composed fresh from a remarkable mind that could read the inside of a hostile Germany but could hardly find its way from the Charing Cross station in the tube to Trafalgar Square.

"Gentlemen," said Witcher—it was to be a dazzling lecture for them!—"I simply must give you a picture in miniature of the present climate in Germany, so that you will better appreciate the action plans and especially the *actions* upon which I shall concentrate. Tonight there will be no time to give you more than a brief sketch on the larger history of conspiracy against the Third Reich. But I do want you to know what I mean by resistance, conspiracy and so-called grand plots so that you will better appreciate those plans and acts which finally came forth, upon which I shall concentrate. I suspect that is what you want me to do." Witcher sniffed disapprovingly.

"Is there a resistance movement in Germany, as we know it in Norway, say, or France? No, for three reasons. The Germans are not resistant to anything in Germany, except the present Allied bombing—nothing, absolutely nothing has ever united Germans more than this day and night bombing of their great cities. The Germans do not know or believe that their land is occupied by an evil spirit. Indeed, the last ten years have seemed to them the best years of their lives, perhaps even of their entire history. Finally, unlike a true resistance movement, there has been practically no assistance from outside Germany. All overtures to the Allies have been ignored.

"Is there a conspiracy, on the other hand? Yes, the record is quite clear on this. The two most important elements of a conspiracy, you know, are that it must be hidden from someone, usually from those against whom it is directed, and that if uncovered the conspirators face some kind of penalty. Well, we shall see just what the penalty in Germany today can be. It is good to be skeptical, gentlemen, but I tell you that the danger for conspirators in Germany is—we shall see!

"There seem to have been three strangely diverse groups of German conspirators. Most heterogeneous is the civilian element, often gathered into pathetic circles, salons and tea parties of intellectuals with vague goals. However, it must be said that these courageous men and women and, yes, university children, have shown the longest history of opposition, the highest motives generally, and the best connections to the outside world. Through Sweden, Switzerland, even the Vatican. Mostly ignored by the Allies, as I said. Marshal, your courier service to Stockholm and Moscow, however, is an exception that is greatly appreciated."

"Please, Jeremy," said Swann who was plainly miffed at the professor's disclosure. "Matthew, the professor is referring to a little service British Overseas Airways runs for us. Unarmed Mosquitoes with civil markings and all that. Rather dicey. I'll tell you about it sometime. But do go on, Jeremy."

"What was I talking about? Ah, yes, the conspirators. The Army, of course, was the most powerful if not the *only* force that could bear on the Reich itself, no matter what happened to the *Reichsführer*. But the conspicuous generals' conspiracy is greatly overblown. Their motives are suspect. The old generals only went into panic on the eve of a big operation. But when things were going nicely, there was little chaff from the generals. They were obsessed, by three unrealistic beliefs: that the Western Allies and Russia would openly have a falling-out; that Germany could buy a separate armistice with the west; and that they could retain all the occupied lands that they had already taken on the eastern front. Really!

"Now, the third element of the conspiracy was the *Abwehr* or secret service of the Armed Forces! Surely the most unlikely element but the best organized and most central one. Here the motives were most mysterious because of the nature of the *Abwehr* chief, Admiral Wilhelm Canaris. In any case, Hitler dissolved the secret service five months ago and transferred its functions to Himmler, who had been after Canaris and the entire *schwarze Kapelle* or Black Choir for years. The Black Choir was Himmler's name for the conspiracy in its totality. And now, since July twenty, Canaris himself has disappeared. Whether in prison or executed, we do not know."

"Excuse me, Jeremy," said Swann, "but I thought there had been a British plan to assassinate Canaris."

"There was. Someone in MI-6, little doubt who, has been protecting Canaris. Well, they can't help him now. By the way, Commander Dampier, you especially would appreciate the fact that the first plan to execute Adolf Hitler came in 1939 from our military attaché at Berlin. Yes, the attaché had a sniper with a telescopic rifle aimed at the Chancellory. This plan was rejected as unsportsmanlike. Probably a good thing, in retrospect, for Hitler would have died at that time as the greatest man in German history.

"But now it is time to go to 1943 and speak once more of the Army. The generals, you know, were sometimes prepared to arrest Hitler and several claimed that they were prepared to kill him. We may never know. In 1943 and 1944, it was the colonels and other junior officers who finally brought about all the actions I will speak of. The price they were willing to pay was almost certain death and even suicide. In all, we know of more than twenty *plans,* but I will restrict myself to the details of the last dozen actions."

"Twenty!" Dampier exclaimed. He sounded almost hurt to know there were so many.

"Ah, Commander, think of what we don't know. Even the plans would amaze you, if we had the time.

There was Ewald Löser, the chief officer of Krupps, no less, who was prepared to kill Hitler as long ago as 1937. Löser has just been arrested, we hear, a man whose managerial talent was several orders higher than that of Albert Speer. And at the beginning of this year, there was a double agent who was going back into Germany and he offered to execute Hitler without any fuss at all. It was rejected, I'm sorry to say."

"Is this the chap who came over here to bomb out the de Havilland Mosquito factory?" asked Swann.

"The same."

"On his arrival, Matthew, they grabbed this German agent, turned him around, built up a lovely fire and blast scene at de Havilland's factory at Hatfield, and had the agent send back all the details to his old masters. Absolutely wizard!"

"We must really be getting on, Marshal," said Witcher impatiently, taking another reading of the clock, "That is, if you want me to tell you about these later actions tonight. I have to leave in half an hour."

"By all means, Jeremy, sorry."

"Right, then, and now it is 1943. The campaign against Russia is going badly, the conspiracy is back in the oven again but with new cooks. The colonels. On one day in March, at the Smolensk headquarters of Hitler, four attempts were made to kill him. One, a panzer tank commander offered to mow down the whole Hitler party but his general vacillated. Two, a pair of conspirators planted a bomb in the general's office but withdrew it. Three, the same two put the bomb in the officers' mess but decided they could not kill their friends, understandably. Four, that night the weary bomb was finally installed in the transport plane taking Hitler back to his East Prussia headquarters at Rastenburg. The bomb never went off and was recovered by one of the conspirators at great peril.

"At this point it is important to speak about bombs, for all the near-successful acts depended on one or another bomb. It is interesting that the Smolensk bombs were a silent type supplied by the British. In these, a striker is held away from the firing cap by a slender wire. To activate these infernal machines, one

breaks an internal vial of acid which eats away the
wire at a rate determined mainly by the wire's diameter, and delays of several minutes to two hours are
available by a selection of wires. *But*—the acid erosion
of the wire is also dependent on temperature! This is
terribly important. We hear that when Hitler's airplane
flew out of Smolensk, the bomb had been placed in the
baggage bin and it apparently froze. So I am naturally
skeptical when I hear that the bomb came to earth
again and was disarmed. Why did the acid not go right
back to its deadly work again when it warmed up?
Curious.

"Later in 1943, the principle of suicide was
added to that of the personal bombing. There were
four successive overcoat attempts, and I should explain what this means. It all began when an officer,
who was to model new military uniforms for Hitler
personally, volunteered to conceal one or two bombs
in the pockets of a greatcoat. It would take such a
coat, you see, to hide these things. Well, the first time
there was temperature trouble again. The timing was
set for eight or ten minutes but the display took place
in an unheated building. The bomb slowed down and
Hitler left the scene.

"The second of these suicidal efforts failed because the uniform display was destroyed in a bombing
raid. The third failed because it was just before Christmas and Hitler decided to take a holiday at the
Berghof, his mountain aerie. And the fourth failed because of another air raid, this time because the *Führer*
did not show at all.

"By this time, it was apparent that Hitler's way of
life, the erratic schedules, demanded an assassin who
had perfect access to him. On July twenty last, we had
public admission by Hitler himself that just such a man
had almost got him by the throat. Colonel Klaus
Philip Maria, Count von Stauffenberg. This idealist,
blind in one eye, minus an arm and two fingers of the
remaining hand, turned up on Hitler's personal staff at
Rastenburg. Four times he tried to plant a bomb, we
hear, at the noon conferences. My skepticism here is
limited to one point: if all the generals were by now

personally searched and had to leave their sidearms at the door of a Hitler conference, how did anyone bring a bomb in a briefase into a conference room?

"In any case, something did happen and there was a terrific explosion at twelve forty-one on July twentieth. At first it was thought that a time bomb had been planted by the Todt construction workers, or a 155-millimeter artillery shell had found its mark, or that a Russian fighter-bomber had gotten through. Whatever did happen, it was finally *thought* that the *schwarze Kapelle* was responsible, and by this time there is no doubt that Stauffenberg is in charge, by nightfall, he was executed."

"Are you suggesting, Professor," Dampier asked, "that Stauffenberg did not plant a bomb?"

"I am suggesting nothing, Commander. There are all kinds of possibilities that I would like to tell you about. No one at Rastenburg believed that some *Luftwaffe* pilot might have come in and dropped a bomb or fired a rocket at the conference building, but that is a possibility, too—a good one. We have evidence of a *Luftwaffe* plot to kill Hitler from the air. It is not a bad idea, you know."

Dampier and Swann looked at each other. "Could you go into that a bit, Jeremy?" asked Swann.

"Five minutes, Marshal, that's all I have now. Well, why kill Hitler from the air? It is quite simple. The recent fiasco will dry up all approaches to the *Führer* from the ground. He no longer appears in public at all and he does not travel in autos or airplanes, only in trains. His schedules and itineraries are changed without warning. But Hitler does ride now mainly in Göring's trains, *Robinson* or *Asia,* so I would imagine the *Luftwaffe* would have to know the schedules. It seems to me that a *Luftwaffe* pilot could shoot up one of the trains and fly out to England. Of course, here the pilot would have to be killing hundreds of fellow Germans on the train. I don't know how this would fit."

"Besides," said Dampier, "it would take a tremendous blow to demolish a whole train." He had not thought of a train at all. "To hit part of a train would hardly be better than hitting a building where any room could hold your target."

"Exactly," Witcher said, "and now you are beginning to understand the problems of a political assassination. But I see by the clock that these are your problems and not mine. I am a historian, gentlemen, and if you go ahead with whatever you have in mind, I will probably hear about it. Maybe you will even tell me about it firsthand. But at this moment, my daughter is the one I am thinking about."

While the professor's footsteps were still fading away down the hall, Swann said to Dampier, "It's quite a dilemma, I think, for these boffins like Jeremy. He, at least, could say that he has had nothing to do with weapons, not even the development of radar. But he is convinced that he has been forced to use history as if it were a weapon."

"That's not too far from the truth, is it, Korpo? His specialty may be a more powerful weapon than the professor will admit."

"He did not get to a point that he mentioned to me on the telephone, Matthew. You will remember that those nights after the Hitler speech we had at least twice the number of buzzbombs coming over."

"I certainly do."

"Hitler ordered the extra push, personally. Jeremy says he has finally gone completely off his pivot, the *Führer*. Wholesale executions are underway now in Germany. All the secret weapons in store for us have been accelerated. Rockets, jet fighters and rocket fighters, remote-controlled flying bombs, heat-sensing missiles, sound-sensing torpedoes. There is a New York bomber—Hitler is apparently obsessed with carrying the war to America—which can fly to your country and back with a damaging bomb load. More to the point, says Jeremy, a submarine put out of Norway yesterday with an agent aboard who is to be landed in Maine, I think. This agent is the forerunner of *Seawolf*, a project to launch buzzbombs on New York from a flotilla of U-boats. The agent will be captured, I hope, but no one knows right now what will happen until he is properly interrogated."

"The professor may be more warlike than he will admit, Korpo," said Dampier.

"Yes."

7

Temporary Additional Duty

The marriage of John Croft and William McLaughlin was made in Washington and London, not in heaven, but it was in the heavens that some secret basis for an exceptional match was established.

The secrecy was natural: once those two hatches were pulled shut from inside a Beaufighter and as long as the transmitter switch was off, even the fighter-controllers knew only what their radar scopes and the occasional radio patter told them.

It was Jeannie Conboy, the Americans' WAAF housekeeper, who knew the most intimate details. She gleefully passed everything along to the other women, who were always greedy for any gossip on the Colonials, as they called the Americans.

"Lieutenant Croft, you know," said Conboy, "is incredibly sloppy!" Jeannie had already exhausted her Class A dossier on Croft—how he was a snob, a cruel man, probably an atheist, certainly a humorless clot—and was now picking away at the carcass. "*Sloppy!* I wish you could see his laundry problem. All he had to do, I told him, was put it in the sack I marked for him and I'd manage it. What does he do? He stuffs it all in a dresser drawer and I find it three weeks later. I tell you, these Yanks are *sinfully* rich!"

Yes, too rich, the women agreed, and their eyes shone.

"But you should see how mean this dreadful man is to his sweet nav/rad, Lieutenant Commander McLaughlin! You know how the lieutenant commander loves his pipes." McLaughlin had a dozen or so expensive pipes and he smoked them in a religious sequence that rested them; everyone knew about this. "Well, he also has a toothbrush for every day in the week. One morning I stumbled in on them and Lieutenant Croft had the whole kit of toothbrushes in his hand, shaking them at his navigator. 'Look at this mess,' he said, 'I suppose you learned this in kindergarten? Pink is Monday, blue is Tuesday? Jesus, Bill!' he said—yes, he curses too—'look at these brushes. So old and rotten, every bristle is worn down.' He threw the whole collection into the wastebin."

And what did McLaughlin do? the women asked.

"He fished the toothbrushes out of the bin and washed them off. He said, 'John, so help me, if you ever touch my toothbrushes, or my pipes, I'll ask to be relieved of my duty with you.' Croft spoke a nasty phrase, which I'll not repeat, and then he began to shave. He has not changed his razor blade, by the way, since he came here."

So no one, Jeannie Conboy least of all, could imagine why John Croft and Bill McLaughlin were a perfect union in the air. Like a bird, Croft was uncomfortable on the ground, and indeed he walked with a certain awkwardness, as a hawk or an eagle walks. McLaughlin was the wit of Cranfield but when he flew backwards in the Beau with Croft, when his eyes were in his radar visor, he was professional and very serious.

No. 35 Course at Cranfield, by the first week of August, was singular. Not one of the twenty-four crews had suffered more than the most trival of flying mishaps. No crew had withdrawn for incompatibility. Across all national boundaries, it was held to be a good omen when Peter Garland's navigator, Ensign Stephen Trice, announced his engagement to Miss

Laurie Berridge of Bedford. Faced with this authentic marriage, Garland said there could be no wedding until *he* decided to give Steve a divorce. "No bachelor's party, either," Peter decreed, "a divorce party."

On behalf of his staff and all seventy-odd men under training at Cranfield, the officer commanding No. 51 OTU accepted a blanket invitation to a party at Woburn Abbey, the Duke of Bedford's house. Part of the great house had been turned over to the WAAF as the residence of the women who were learning about fighter-control systems. Rosemary Ince lived in the Abbey and several weeks before the date of the party she began to wonder how she could decently discover if Croft were coming or not. She asked one of her WAAF friends, who went to the Cranfield tower every day for a while, to look into the matter of Croft; then she asked the WAAF not to do that at all. Several notes were written to other friends at Cranfield, including male officers; all were torn up.

Like her unfortunate fellow Scot, Mary Stuart, Rosemary Ince was strong willed except in crises of emotion, when hopeless indecision overcame her. She did nothing about Croft in the end and suffered for it every time she talked to him on the air. One of the FROGSPAWN women facetiously urged the WREN to break voice procedure just once and *order* the American to Woburn Abbey. Rosemary did nothing.

Air Vice-Marshal Swann and Commander Dampier held a panic conference the morning after Professor Witcher's visit to London. Both officers had been jolted out of a daydream, in which they had only a scheme, into a nightmare, until they had developed what Witcher called a *plan*.

"First of all, Matthew," said Swann gravely, "I realized that this is not at all like killing a Heydrich. Hitler, however evil, is a head of state. Overnight, I am suddenly very worried about highest-level effects of the RAF assassinating Hitler."

"Did you talk to Witcher again?" Dampier was a little suspicious of the mysterious professor.

"No, but we cannot press on without his help. I want to know what is going on in Germany after the assassination failure and I want to know the effects of a successful assassination at our hands. Effects on strategy of the war. Political effects, especially postwar. Naturally, I am most concerned about involving my own government."

"But Korpo, we would not be talking now if Churchill had not put us in touch, would we?"

"Ah, Matthew, the prime minister's enthusiasm, shall I tell you about that? It means we shall have all the help we need, no question, and that is what you are thinking about. I am thinking that *after* the fact there are only four possibilities. If we fail and are not found out, no matter. If we fail and are caught in the act by the Germans, we are cast adrift at home. If we succeed and happily end the war, to state the best case, the prime minister will step forth in his dancing pumps to take the bows. But Matthew! If we succeed and precipitate some monstrous deluge out of Germany, little matter that our heads will roll. What about our consciences, then, not to speak about the course of the war?"

To answer, Dampier had only to remain silent.

"So if you don't mind, Matthew, I really think we should arrange another visit with Jeremy Witcher and this time, if you can do it, go see him in Cambridge. Is that all right?"

"Of course."

"We have homework to do, then. Jeremy was not at all impressed with us last night. He is a professor, after all, and he hates students who waste his time. When we go to Cambridge, we must show the old man that we are not exactly cretins."

"Homework, Korpo. You mean develop a plan?"

"Can we do that without Witcher? I don't think so. No, but we have an excellent idea, and in my experience you can solve many of your tactical problems long before the strategy is worked out to the last dot. Intelligence, for example; the prime question being, where is Hitler?"

"Oh, I never told you, Korpo. When we met in July, I said I was getting top-caliber information from Hitler-watchers and you said you want proof."

"I haven't forgotten."

"Okay, proof. When you called to say that a bomb was planted on Hitler, I didn't know about the bomb and Witcher did. But at that moment, Korpo, I knew exactly where the bomb had to be planted and it took Witcher a week to find out. It was the East Prussia headquarters, the Wolf's Lair, in Rastenburg, as the professor said it was."

Swann was impressed. "I am quite happy with the quality of our intelligence, Matthew, and our— your idea. You see that we can go ahead, don't you, with almost routine planning for a number of contingencies? Cover stories for one thing, as Jeremy said. But the rest is pure tactics and, to be modest about it, you are in a good shop for that sort of thing."

"I know, Korpo. I've known that from the beginning. That's not my province. The decision I would like to make now concerns the disposition of my men. I would like to cut their training by one month and get them into squadrons that will satisfy Navy requirements *and* train them for what we have to do here. How many crews in all would be needed for what we have in mind?"

"Haven't the faintest, Matthew. One? Twenty? It depends on the target, you see."

"But you agree, don't you," Dampier asked anxiously, "that there will be an American crew?"

"Unquestionably. And a British crew. And after that, one for one."

"Do you have any squadrons in mind?"

"Give me a few days. I'm thinking of an outfit down in West Sussex. There's another wizard club up in Norfolk, at a station called Brevishall. . . ."

And still No. 35 Course was almost unique, untouched by misfortune and withal a bright, likeable lot in the opinion of the Cranfield stff.

On the night of August 2, Lieutenant Richard

Priest and his nav/rad, Ensign Thomas Squire, were assigned to a searchlight exercise with RAF Flight Lieutenant Cockcroft and his backseat man, Flying Officer Cobbden. The men were told they would see how it was when there was no radar. But that was not the real point of the exercise. They were also told that at least 45,000 searchlights waited for them in Germany and it was a good thing for a night fighter to know how it was to be caught in the candles.

Priest chased Cockcroft first and when he called "Candles, please," Cockcroft was pinned squarely in the beam of a radar-controlled master light. In milliseconds, eleven slave lights snapped on; the target was coned. Cockcroft was an ex-bomber pilot, though, and he squirmed away.

Then Cockcroft stalked Priest. It terrified Priest when he was first caught in the merciless lights. Twelve of them, 2 million candlepower each, converged on his cockpit and flooded it with pain, not light. The pain of staring at the sun. Priest did his best to escape but Cockcroft would easily have shot him down in real life. It was a lesson.

"Searchlights are not much," Croft told McLaughlin before their own candle exercise, "unless they paralyze you. We studied searchlights at NOCTU and I even spent a week flying an L-8 airborne searchlight. A fifty-million candlepower aerial flashlight. Funny. Once I flashed it on the outdoor movie at Barber's Point and they told me the picture didn't come back for five minutes. And once some poor pilot saw my beam, horizontal and not vertical like a searchlight is supposed to be. Poor devil thought he was out of his mind, banked to correct, and crashed into the ocean."

The searchlights could not handle the Croft-McLaughlin team. But only McLaughlin heard Croft on the intercom, laughing.

Seth Rothschild went up to London on the weekend, August 5. When he came back, he called a meeting; this had never happened before.

"We've got new temporary additional duty orders, my friends. Matt Dampier has arranged assignments for us to two operational squadrons starting one week from today. If there are no objections, Matt and I sorted it out like this. No. 68 Squadron is over on the Norfolk coast on buzzbomb patrols. I suggested that Murdock and Nicholas, Garland and Trice, and Croft and McLaughlin go to Six-Eight. No. 456 Squadron is Australian, flying intruder missions over the Continent. Priest and Squire and Tarbox and I are slated for 456. Is that really all right? I want to hear any objections from anyone. We should probably split up, two crews and three, but we can shift things around if anybody's unhappy."

There was great surprise but no objection.

"How much longer will we be here, Seth?" asked Steve Trice, who was now engaged to Laurie Berridge. "In England, I mean."

"Maybe six months, Steve, instead of three."

"Good, good," said Trice.

The women at FROGSPAWN quickly learned that the Americans would be gone from Cranfield before the Woburn Abbey party. They voted to move the date up by a fortnight and, for some reason, chose Rosemary Ince to make the new arrangements. Rosemary dutifully called Adjutant Drewry at Cranfield on the morning of August 7. After delivering the main message, Rosemary asked on an impulse if it were possible to speak to a Lieutenant Commander McLaughlin, one of the Americans.

"I'm sure the commander is asleep right now, Miss Ince," Drewry apologized, "but I'll leave a message for him."

At half past two in the afternoon, the strange but friendly voice of McLaughlin—a voice the WREN never heard on the radio—said "Hi" to Rosemary. Still she was petrified.

"Commander, I hope you remember me. I met you when you came to our station."

"Rosemary, how could I forget?"

"Well, sir, I have just told Flying Officer Drewry that our party has been forwarded to the twelfth, a Saturday. Does that seem unreasonable, sir?"

"Not at all, my dear. We're pretty flexible here."

"I was wondering about Lieutenant Croft, sir."

"Me too, Rosemary, often. What's your problem?"

"Sir, I—well, I was wondering if Lieutenant Croft, if he is a party man. I don't mean that either, I was—do you think, Commander, that the lieutenant will be coming to our party?"

McLaughlin laughed in those rich tones that made friends for him. "Rosemary, honey," he said, "if you want John Croft at your party, he will be there. *I* will be there and so will John. No problem."

Only three days were now allotted in Squadron Four to familiarize the Americans with the Mosquito. Croft flew by himself the first two days before he could take McLaughlin up. On the third day, they flew together a cross-country flight in daylight that Bill had worked out across the Irish Sea. The same night, they repeated the flight.

Bill learned that the French crew, Capitaine Duchard and his navigator, had drawn up a similar flight, except that the Frenchmen chose to fly their 600-mile circuit in a counterclockwise direction. Croft and McLaughlin were going clockwise. Both crews took off from Cranfield at about the same time and started timing over the center of Bedford.

It was a cloudless, almost windless night and remained so for the Americans through all but their last leg. In his last few Beaufighter flights with John, Bill had become more talkative and natural, perhaps because he sat out of sight, facing the tail. Now, sitting beside John for only the second time in the Mosquito, Bill was again inhibited. Watching the moon come up behind them as they approached Coventry and Birmingham, the navigator jotted down on his kneepad one of the questions he might have asked in the Beau. *Moon—why so big rising and setting?* he wrote. Back on the ground, he'd ask John, who knew all about these things. Wouldn't bother him now.

At Birmingham, they turned northwest to make the island of Anglesey right off the coast of Wales. The meteorology people had reported low cloud in that region, centered over the upper Cambrian Mountains. Flying over that range and just before turning at Anglesey onto the Irish Sea, Croft told Cranfield that he found almost total cloud cover capping the mountains. Snowdon's peak, at 3600 feet the sovereign of Welsh Mountains, was just visible through fleece that stopped at the coast. Presumably Duchard would be advised. He would be coming around the other way later.

Passage across the Irish Sea was mostly at deck level; Croft never missed a chance to fly low, which still bothered McLaughlin. Off their starboard wing now, the moon was much higher and its reflection followed them, a pale yellowish marker riding with them down on the finely frosted sea.

McLaughlin was pleased that their landfall in northern Ireland over the distinctive Strangford Lough was perfect in place and time. Four minutes later, there was a blacked-out city.

"Belfast!" shouted Bill.

"Hey, hey, I hear you," said Croft, pounding his right earphone. "That's where Belfast always is. Now, can you find us England again?"

Turning widely around the outskirts of Belfast, so as not to make the Irish nervous, Croft took up the southeasterly course for York that Bill gave him. This was the longest leg, nearly 200 miles, and they had to be at 3000 feet when they crossed the English coast. Halfway across the Sea was the Isle of Man; they slipped into Lancashire at Morecambe Bay. It was then that the Americans began hearing occasional voice transmissions from Duchard, who was probably south near the island of Anglesey. Croft reported directly to Duchard the weather he'd seen earlier over Snowdon.

"Merci, ah, thank you, Tadpole One-Seex, I 'ave already theese information. I am ten minutes from the Mount Snowden."

The Americans kept hearing the French chatter as they flew on to York. Finally, after an especially shrill *"Mon Dieu, mon Dieu,"* Croft spoke to them again:

"This *is* God, so for Christ's sake will you speak English or get off this channel? My son and I are working over here."

McLaughlin didn't think that was very funny. Somehow, he didn't think Duchard was just chatting with another French or Belgian pilot.

When their Mosquito landed at Cranfield at two A.M., Croft and McLaughlin learned that Captain Duchard's Beau had apparently slammed into the northwest face of Mount Snowdon. They had gone into the stuffed cloud that Croft had seen. The cause of the accident remained a mystery, which heightened the shock for everyone.

Croft had finally agreed to go the party at Woburn Abbey. He insisted on driving one of the jeeps, with McLaughlin, Tarbox, Rothschild and Nicholas as apprehensive passengers. Three navigators aboard, Croft remarked, and they got lost twice.

At nine thirty the jeep finally arrived at the Duke of Bedford's ancestral estate. More than once the Americans were startled by small bands of miniature white-spotted deer leaping across the gravel drive that wound through a cleared wood of magnificent black oaks and English elms. Several times the green eyes of a small animal, perhaps a fox, glowed in the jeep's headlights. It took ten minutes to make the transit from modern, wartime England back into the eighteenth century.

As they came up to the Abbey, there was barely enough light to outline against the sky the immense gray block of history. Only one small wing of the Abbey was lighted and Croft drove toward that part, where they could see the shadows of people. The rest of the dark Abbey seemed to look on this wing with disapproval.

Even the minor entrance hall was impressive. It was dominated by a chandelier twenty feet in diameter and thirty feet high, made of a thousand crystal prisms. Two curving stairways soared laterally to a mezzanine from which a straight course of stairs went on to the first floor. The hall floor was laid in a harlequin pattern of black and white marble rhomboids. The walls were faced in intricately carved, dark panels set between high columns of Italian pink porphyry.

Only a dozen people were in the hall and one of them was Basil Smyth, the diminutive skipper of No. 1 Squadron at Cranfield. Smyth held a pewter tankard and was talking to a striking WAAF.

"I say, chaps," Smyth greeted the Americans warmly, "how awfully decent of you to come! We've got a smasher going here, haven't we, Jane?" Jane Clough was introduced. "These people do speak English you'll notice, Jane, but you must listen closely."

Smyth and Clough led the way to the bar, a drawing room halfway up the wing, where guests were jammed up to the door. There was a table about thirty feet long tended by six RAF enlisted men. The room hummed at two levels: there was the low steady buzz of a hundred voices, half male, half female; there was the fainter shuffling of two hundred feet on the iron-hard floor. Out of one corner of the room came the brilliant sound of a hidden piano where twenty people were singing a French ballad. An outstanding voice, very bad, was leading:

> *Auprès de ma blonde,*
> *Qu il fait bon, fait bon, fait bon,*
> *Auprès de ma blonde,*
> *Qu il fait bon dormir.*

As the dreadful chorus finished, they raised their glasses to the pianist, who was Rosemary Ince. She saw John Croft and smiled at him, her face telling him that she was trapped at the keyboard, that this was not her idea at all.

Croft was tone-deaf so music and noise were the same to him. He whispered to Smyth that Peter Garland played all these songs that people sang over and over, jazz, boogie-woogie, anything. Then Croft made his first signal to Rosemary: *Can you get away from that piano?*

"It's good to see you again," said Rosemary, when Garland took over the playing. "He's very accomplished, isn't he?"

"That's what they tell me. But there you see the price of fame. They've forgotten you already, Rosemary."

"And a good thing, too. Would you like to see the Abbey?"

After a torch tour of part of the darkened Abbey, before they came back into the living part, Rosemary showed John a bedroom that may once have been for guests. A small notice near the bell-pull said *Ring for a mistress*. The bed was still made up in what looked like the original coverings.

"I've heard," Rosemary said, "that one of the dukes used to sleep here with a maid two hundred years ago."

"I wonder," mused John, "if that maid will be using her bed tonight."

Rosemary took John into a sort of greenhouse attached to the wing where the party was going on. Here, in this glass cage with its small trees and large ferns and white iron benches, they talked for hours. A full, cold moon was their light but John, curiously, would always think of it as the brightest day of his life.

They had to sort out their backgrounds for each other. Her father was a country doctor and his was an advertising man. Her mother was her father's nurse; his mother was dead. Rosemary had been engaged briefly to a RAF fighter pilot killed in the Battle of Britain; Croft was sorry for her although he had never been in love with anyone. Rosemary wanted to fly in the worst way but her eyesight kept her from being a ferry pilot. Croft told her she could probably do private flying if she got the right glasses and he would find a way to teach her.

If they had stayed in the glass cage, McLaughlin would have found them when it was time to go back to Cranfield. There was a general search and no one could find them anywhere. They had to take the jeeps back without Croft. He was back in the mess at breakfast, ready to drive to London. No one ever knew that a woman had driven him to the Cranfield gate in her Morris.

8

68 Squadron

RAF Brevishall sprawled over 2000 acres of flat, marshy farmland that East Anglian Saxons had claimed ten centuries earlier and that Englishmen had toiled to keep from the ravenous North Sea ever since. The old station out on the Norfolk Broads was only five miles from the coastal dunes and dikes. It was the smell of the sea, of the shoreline, that first greeted the four Americans who came to No. 68 Squadron on the evening of August 14.

Peter Garland had driven one of the jeeps down from London with Croft, McLaughlin and Nicholas, having spent only the day before, a Sunday, in London and most of that with Commander Campier. Tarbox, Rothschild, Priest and Squire took the other jeep south to 456 Squadron at RAF Ford in Sussex.

Steve Trice met the new arrivals at Brevishall when they came into the mess building. He had spent the weekend in Bedford with Laurie Berridge's family. Garland was SOPA, senior officer present ashore of the Brevishall Navy detachment; he angrily asked his navigator where Murdock was.

"Blackie said he'd try to get a bus from Grantham tonight," said Trice, "otherwise he'll come by train in the morning."

"Not good enough, damn him," said Garland. "It's one hell of a way to start off here. Who did you report to, Steve?"

"The adjutant, Flying Officer Spiller. He said no need to shuffle our papers until tomorrow. Spiller's in the lounge"—Trice led the way—"this is a working night for them, of course."

Five officers were having coffee in the lounge, listening to the BBC news. Two pilots and two with the nav/rad half-wing wore the short battle jacket. The fifth man, a giant F/O with great knobby cheekbones and the fierce jaw of a bony river pike, wore the standard uniform blouse, obviously old but carefully preserved like a policeman's. He had no wings but didn't need any; in his voice was the authority of a search warrant. It shattered the traditional after-dinner quiet hour like a traffic whistle, causing one of the pilots to duck slightly and cover his cup with his hand.

"Welcome, welcome to Brevishall, you all." McLaughlin, the Virginian, smiled. "I'm Jock Spiller, as Trice knows, and it's an honor to be the first.

"Our skipper, Wing Commander Adams-Ray, should be here shortly," said Spiller. "He's on the flying schedule tonight but he wanted to meet you all."

The mess lounge boasted a fireplace ten feet wide. From above the mantel, the painting of a magnificent tawny owl's head haunted the room. It had hypnotic amber eyes, perfectly round and childlike with centered pupils, sharply outlined in black and set in oval spectacles of soft, snowy down. *After a while*, Croft thought, *the bird's eyes would start turning up in your dreams*. In the official format of RAF squadron badges, the bird's head was centered in a gold ring bearing the number 68. A crown topped the ring and the ring rested on a scroll lettered *Vzdy připraven*.

"Is that a Polish motto?" Garland asked.

"No, Czech," answered Spiller. "Half our lads are Czechs. Can't pronounce it but it means 'Be prepared,' Ha, ha. Boy Scouts we are, you see, nothing more."

A ruggedly stout man in a battle jacket with three stripes on the shoulder loops came to the lounge entrance. About thirty, his thick auburn hair was parted in the middle and he looked older, Victorian. But most striking were the chalky facial pallor, as if he were ill or had been frightened permanently out of his wits, and the reddish guardsman's mustache that hid his mouth and gave his speech a ventriloquist quality.

"Gentlemen," announced Spiller, suddenly formal, "our commanding officer, Wing Commander Adams-Ray!"

"All right, Jocko, come off it." The CO's voice was deep and almost as strong as his adjutant's, but it was tired and unfocused, like voices that come from annunciator speakers in railroad stations. "All of you must call me Booster, please. Glad to have you, of course. Must fly tonight myself, early shift. Can we meet tomorrow, say lunchtime? I shall be here by half after twelve, is that all right?"

Adams-Ray excused himself at the door and disappeared, followed by a little white terrier, pug-faced-ugly and snuffling, scrambling and scratching after its master like a crab.

"Booster is under great strain," said Spiller, with concern for the Americans' feelings, "and you must not think he was being short with you. That's not his way. Fifteen years with the metropolitan police I was, and I saw some bloody fine leaders of men. None better than Vivian Adams-Ray."

Spiller introduced the RAF and Navy officers. The English crew was newly posted to Brevishall and hardly more at home than the Americans. Flight Lieutenant Karel Adeš—Spiller pronounced it *Odd*-esh— was the pilot who had covered his coffee cup when Spiller shouted. He had a *Czechoslovakia* patch at the left shoulder seam. He spoke English well but cautiously, with a deprecating series of smiles and shrugs. He was a chain-smoker, and when he held his cigarette it was always in that stiff, reversed manner peculiar to some eastern Europeans. Adeš had a hard face, almost cruel, with deep, natural creases chiseled down the cheeks. Blond hair fell over the left forehead, half-concealing a hard and pearly scar. Under the RAF wings on the light blue battle jacket was a row of four bright ribbons, two of them British. One of these was the ribbon of the rare Victoria Cross.

Drahomir Miloslav was Karel's fat and gentle navigator. He was even more self-effacing than his pilot, for his English was very bad.

"Karel is, what can I say, he is simply the squadron's prize," Spiller said, when the Czechs had gone. "After Cunningham and Braham, he is the RAF's best night fighter pilot. You saw his V.C. Few living men wear the Victoria Cross, you know. It's usually presented to mothers or widows."

Wing/Co Adams-Ray wasted no time putting his Americans into action. They were not matey souvenirs to him; he needed these men badly, to rest his people. If the Americans expected formal lectures and training in the rigorous manner of U.S. Navy fighting squadrons, they were disappointed. Booster ran a twenty-four-hour school at Brevishall, using the mess tables at breakfast, lunch, tea, dinner and night-flying suppers, the lounge in the afternoon and at eight, the bar at night, the dispersal huts down at the field, even the cricket field. There were never any lecturers.

At his first lunch with the Americans, Adams-Ray simply gathered Squadron Leader Monck of A-Flight and Squadron Leader Janacek of B-Flight and Karel Adeš as his leadoff team, his main faculty. The Wing/Co outlined his problems briefly:

"Fighter Command—sorry, we still must say Air Defense of Great Britain—Fighter Command have put us up here primarily because they think the flying bomb will have to start coming from Holland across the North Sea, as the launching sites are overrun in the Pas-de-Calais. Meanwhile, we still face the cross-Channel bomb, along with five other Mosquito squadrons for night and bad-weather patrolling plus fifteen day fighter squadrons. That's an expensive commitment to this bloody pilotless aircrft, considering the pressing need for fighters over the Continent.

"As to the bomb itself, Squadron Leader Monck

struggles with our tactics. Michael, could you give them the form?"

"Your V.1 doodlebug is perfectly witless," said Monck, dryly, "so it will not try to evade you. That is the only advantage you have. We've clocked them at two-fifty to four hundred miles per hour, faster rather than slower, so your speed margin will generally be slim. They're about half the size of a fighter and even in full daylight, when the tailflame is invisible, they're difficult to spot and hit. In the dark, the flame is easy to spot but almost impossible to range on."

"We've tried a simple photoelectric ranging-sighter but that wasn't too helpful," said Adams-Ray. "Your AI set is slightly handicapped, too, because the echoes bouncing back from the bomb are a bit weak."

"Twilight is the best time for hunting," Monck continued, "but the Germans know that, of course, so most of their launches are in erratic volleys at night or in ropey weather."

"Is it true that pilots have actually tipped the bomb's wing to tumble its gyro?" Croft asked.

"The hat tricks, yes," said Adams-Ray. "Karel, tell them how you've done it, will you?"

The shy Adeš took care to point out that he had not discovered the flipping game and had only done it twice. "Once I had a pretty slow one and the moon was bright. I came in from the side and flew with the bomb a minute . . . we were careful"—Miloslav was grinning as Adeš' hands moved slowly across the tablecloth—"and then I got my Mosquito's wingtip touching under the bomb's wingtip, so"—right thumb under the left—"and *poop!* my wing came up, the bomb turned left on its back, we turned right like hell, the bomb crashed." Karel's left hand slammed the table, palm up.

"Others have done this without contact," Monck added, "by making an air cushion to push up the bomb's wing. Karel doesn't think much of that."

"No," Adeš said, "it might be dangerous. Just a little mistake and the bomb's wing might not go up. It might fall down if the air . . . if you. . . ."

"Spoiled the airflow," said Croft, "the lift."

"Yes, Lieutenant, spoiled," said Adeš, with thanks only in the tone. Karel had a lot of English but not always quickly.

"Karel," said Janacek, "tell them about your other time."

"I had a slow bomb one night. I just pulled out in front, fifty feet maybe, and it turned over in my . . . slipstream and went down." Adeš was more pleased by the proper word, slipstream, than by his act. "This I have only done once, also, but it is the best way."

"So," said Garland, "it's usually a tail chase and the cannon, eh?" Peter Garland, fighter pilot, superb marksman, was not enchanted by the thought of ballroom dancing with a pilotless warhead, touching fingers with a stubby wing.

"Cannon, yes, but a tail chase is hopeless," said Adams-Ray, "unless your bomb is very slow. Your controller—we work under the famous Brookbridge station here—will try to put you well out in front and high. You have to dive absolutely full out, let the bomb overtake, then use least-angle deflection shooting. Suicide, practically, to fire closer than two hundred yards, though. As you might expect, Karel Adeš has broken this rule more than once and brought back toasted Mosquitoes."

Adeš blushed and shook his head. Croft, elbows braced on the table, hands cupping his chin, studied intently the Czech's face, a mask.

No. 68 Squadron wasted no time with anyone. Garland and Trice were assigned to Monck's A-Flight; Murdock and Nicholas, Croft and McLaughlin to Janacek's B-Flight. That night and the next belonged to A-Flight. Then B-Flight would have the duty while Monck's people stood down for forty-eight hours. And so on.

Captain Carlton Parmenter secretly believed in mental telepathy. Everyone in Op-33-H knew he was getting fidgety again toward the end of August, trying to think of an excuse to go to London. On August 24 he received a naval message from Commander Dampier, reporting only that his men were placed in the squadrons. While turning that all around for possibilities, Parmenter got a brief letter on August 25 from Dampier by officer-messenger mail:

> . . . So I think we'll have to talk face to face. Can you get away for a fast trip over here? The sooner the better.
>
> D

Sixteen hours later, Parmenter was in a Naval Air Transport four-engine Skymaster headed for Scotland. His "ulcer" had gone away. Halfway across the Atlantic, several fellow passengers noticed that the imperious captain's faint British accent was getting stronger.

The NATS transport landed at the Prestwick airbase on the west coast of Scotland, near Glasgow, just before dawn on Sunday, August 27. At about the same time, John Croft and Bill McLaughlin destroyed their third flying bomb over the town of Maidstone, Kent.

No. 68 Squadron shared the field at Brevishall with two day-fighter squadrons, whose Hawker Mark V Tempests were faster than any buzzbomb, faster than the Mosquito. But the Tempests had no radar. At night or in foul weather, the day-fighters lolled in bed. *The moon is up,* they'd say, *and man should not be dicing about.*

On their second night and second patrol with Six-Eight, Peter Garland and Steve Trice had shot down a flying bomb in Bomb Alley southeast of London. Between the coastal gunbelt and the London balloon barrage, the fighter patrol area was only forty miles deep. Bombs slipping past the guns gave a fighter pilot only five or six minutes to catch them.

Garland's success did not surprise Croft but inwardly he was depressed, McLaughlin could tell.

On the afternoon of their sixth patrol night, Croft and McLaughlin checked out their Mosquito and Mark X radar. It was a sacred RAF rule that the NFT, night-flying test, must be carried out in daylight by the

crew who would fly the craft that night. At five o'clock
they came down for tea. Croft went back to sleep; he
could do this until minutes before a flight, although he
usually began to stir around the time the sun disappeared. McLaughlin could only sleep *after* a night
flight, so he always had dinner, picked away at his
unending correspondence, or just visited around the
mess.

On August 27, they were airborne at two A.M.,
on a vector from Brookbridge down to the patrol
area. Twenty minutes later, McLaughlin had a diver on
his scope—the anti-buzzbomb effect was code-named
DIVER—and Croft saw the guns firing at it. He dove
from 7000 feet, keeping the flickering tailjet in sight
and turning on to its course and height, a mile ahead
of it. The flame began to pass them slowly. As it came
abreast of the Mosquito's cockpit, Croft glanced over
at the bomb and said to Bill, "The last time I saw
something without a pilot, it was a practice drone and
I shot it down—but the drone didn't make fire like
this." Then he dropped back and fired a short burst
with the four cannon, just to get the range. Unexpectedly, he hit the monster, which dropped its nose,
exploding when it struck the ground 3000 feet below.

They did it again at 02.48 hours. This time the
flying bomb blew up straight ahead of them and they
flew through the edge of the fireball, an orange chry-
santhemum. The heat of this one they felt in the cockpit.

An hour before dawn, they met the flying bomb
that led them into the London balloon field. It was
slower than the others; Croft took liberties. When Bill
found he was looking at the *inside* of the ramjet pipe,
he was sure that the flame had hypnotized John. Then
the cannons pounded at less than a hundred yards
and were still firing when the bomb ahead seemed to
stop as it blew up. The navigator heard a dreadful
hammering all over the Mosquito's shell as the evil
bomb wrapped them up for a second in its own fiery
death. The Mosquito seemed to be on fire itself;
Croft's left hand came off the throttles to grab his

hunting knife. He was wildly examining the cockpit. Then he slid the knife back into its sheath, saying they were probably all right.

But they had lost their antenna. They could talk to no one on the radio. No one could talk to them. And when Bill figured they had to be somewhere inside the balloon sector, the pilot and his navigator could hardly speak to each other.

"How deep is it?" Croft asked.

"Ten miles," said McLaughlin, "but maybe we've gone part-way through."

"So you want me to turn?"

"Good God, no! Maybe we're nearly through it."

"So shut up. I won't turn. I'll climb. You can probably see the balloons themselves on your AI, so keep looking. It can't take longer than a minute and a half."

The grimmest possible minute and a half. They were in a garden of 2000 slanting steel cables. The controllers could see their radar trace going through it.

"Relax, Bill, we're out now," said Croft.

McLaughlin had held his breath all the way and now he started shaking quietly.

Parmenter sat once more in the old office he loved more than his own, an iceless scotch-and-water in his hand, the treetops in Grosvenor Square just visible through the big window.

"Swann is on his way over, Clip," said Dampier.

"Fine. Now, Matthew, what is all this news you have for me?"

"You're up to date on the training from my letters, except that now I have all the OTU reports from Cranfield. Generally excellent. One problem may be Murdock."

"Blackie? Why, Matt, he was my best test pilot at Patuxent River. What's the matter?"

"The reports are a little cryptic and I'm not a flier. I want you and Swann to interpret the reports on Murdock. But the problem comes to me along other channels. Garland openly hates Murdock."

"Garland's good, a little hot-tempered perhaps,

but I don't know him as I know Murdock." Dampier had to smile, knowing Parmenter's total inability to judge people. "Of course, Blackie has a low boiling point, too."

"Croft completely ignores Murdock, Clip."

"Croft is very good but he even tried to ignore me, Matt."

"And that is *very* hard to do, Captain. Seth Rothschild says that Murdock is drinking pretty heavily. Did you know about that?"

"Heavily? I've seen Blackie plowed a few times. I've seen you plowed, Matt, and you've seen me."

"When Seth Rothschild says someone's drinking will have to be watched, I listen."

Parmenter looked troubled. "I see. Yes, you should listen to Seth."

"Okay, Clip, we can go on with this when you've seen the RAF reports. The next item is Garland."

"Good lord, Garland too?"

"Oh, this is happy news. On his second flight with Sixty-Eight Squadron, Peter got a flying bomb."

"Damn! That looks good, Matt."

"Yes. You know, Clip, since you sent me all the stuff on Croft, I'd come to think he would be the first. Garland or Croft, though I guess it's a toss-up."

"I'm surprised it wasn't Croft. I brought over more for you to read, Croft's training jacket. The most amazing record I've ever seen."

"Anyway, both groups seem well accepted by their squadrons. Now, Clip, put your drink down and fasten your safety belt."

Dampier was ready to break the big news. All that worried him was the Parmenter ego, vain as a French cardinal, which would assume that it had been too long kept in the dark.

"What Swann is really coming here for is—"

There was a knock at the door. A lieutenant came in with Air Vice-Marshal Swann, who immediately recognized Parmenter.

"Ah, Captain," said Swann, "when Matthew told me about you, I suspected my memory was correct. You were in the RAF before the war, weren't you?

We met when the first Eagle Squadron formed in 1940.
You're the chap who procured the first nuts and bolts
of our early radar for your Navy."

"Yes, Marshal," said the flattered Parmenter, "although Matt Dampier *procured* that precious gear. I
only delivered it to Washington."

Swann glared at Dampier, who laughed. "I'm just
a procurer, Korpo. Look, I've been giving the captain a rundown here and you said on the phone you
had something for both of us. What is it?"

"Absolutely wizard! Just before dawn this morning, your Lieutenant Croft and his navigator destroyed
three flying bombs thirty miles from this office."

"Three!" Dampier and Parmenter were in perfect synchrony, which amused Swann.

"Yes, a single patrol, not unique but rare. But
there was a near-tragic sequel. They flew through the
explosion of the third bomb. They, as well as their
helpless controllers, had a bloody awful two minutes
of it, for their Mosquito went straight through the balloons southeast of London."

"Jesus Christ! Korpo," Dampier exclaimed, "are
they okay?"

"Not a scratch. The Mossie is another matter.
Skin burned off, wood charred and all that. But your
men want to keep the Mosquito and, by heaven, their
CO is going to see what the fitters can do."

There was a long silence.

"When you came in, Korpo," said Dampier,
"Captain Parmenter and I were discussing our crews
and you should be in on that. But I was just at the
point of asking the captain's opinion"—Dampier was
preparing the Parmenter ego for surgery—"on our
little investigation. Why don't I go ahead and fill
him in? He may have the solution we're after."

Swann knew how Parmenter had to be handled
and he nodded innocently. He enjoyed the attaché's
approach.

Dampier swamped Parmenter with all the background that could be given, without saying that they
had already drawn up Hitler's death warrant in London. As the story unfolded, Parmenter's holder-ciga-

rette-and-lighter ritual went through four cycles. At the end, the handsome adolescent captain was on the edge of his chair, which was a cliff. To keep from falling off, he stood up.

"This is the most remarkable . . . the most unbelievable . . . the most seductive jewel of a war game that I've ever heard of!" said Parmenter. "Have you ever thought that you, that we must simply take advantage of this, this incredible structure? But I mean NOW! You are talking about Hitler, Hitler, Hitler!"

"A wolf hunts no mice, Captain," said the bland Swann. The Black Swann.

Dampier was only after the *we*. "You mean, Clip," he asked, "that you would approve sending our people out to assassinate Adolf Hitler?"

"If I were back in England, Matthew, I'd lead the goddamned mission!"

"All right," said Dampier, "where do we stand? If the target is Hitler's airplane, Korpo tells me there should be not less than two, uh, assassin crews. One of these crews will be American, the other British. There will be backup crews. So our problem is to line up the American crews, Clip. We have to start with Tarbox and Rothschild."

"No objection," said Parmenter, "but why?"

"Do you know Captain Ephraim Rothschild, Clip?"

"I've never met him."

"He is Seth's older brother. Ephraim has dreamed of killing Hitler since 1939. Through Seth, I was put in touch with Lady Camilla Saxe-Rowland, the newspaper publisher's widow. Polly Rowland spoke to the prime minister and I met the prime minister in a destroyer. Take it from me, Clip, the first American crew must have a Rothschild."

"I can see that," said Parmenter, "so you simply want to line up the rest."

"Yes. Priest and Squire are the next logical choice if only because they are already with 456 Squadron, flying into Europe where the act would occur."

"But Croft and Garland are the proven gunners, Matt, the fighter pilots."

"I know," the worried Dampier said, turning to Swann, "so can you think of a way, Korpo, to make Croft and Garland available? I wasn't thinking of them originally. All of our crews should have gone to 456 Squadron."

"That would have been impossible," said Swann, "but I think we can arrange to attach Six-Eight Squadron half-time to the Second Tactical Air Force. A number of other squadrons are on this sort of double duty. But gentlemen, aren't we playing draughts when the game is really chess? All the pieces look alike in draughts, all are interchangeable, but in chess you go for the king, don't you? His location is terribly important but that is *always* known. His movements are infrequent but in the end, to win, you have to know what his movements can be. Captain Parmenter, Matthew has told you that he has A-1 information on Hitler's location."

"Where he is inaccessible, at least to us," interjected Dampier.

"So we would like to think that when Hitler moves, he moves in a Focke-Wulf 200, his personal transport. But the fact is, railroad trains have come into the picture. You know it, Matthew!"

"I guess I've downplayed the idea of a train, Korpo, because I simply can't imagine how you go after one man in a train."

"Well, cheer up," the usually dour marshal said, "for Witcher has called me again. That's the professor Matthew mentioned, Captain Parmenter. Can you come to Cambridge with me on Tuesday, the twenty-eighth, Matthew? Jeremy says he will talk to us again."

"Absolutely."

"May I tag along?" asked Parmenter like a wistful small brother.

"By all means, Captain," Swann replied, "but Matthew and I had decided that we should wear civilian clothes to visit the professor. I know it seems childish but it is fairly important."

"Oh, I'll buy them!" blurted the enthusiastic Parmenter. "My regular tailor is right here in Regent Street. You know, this is almost like a holiday for me."

The air vice-marshal frowned, saying, "Yes, a holiday," as if the remark were quite out of order. "But that reminds me," he continued, "that Witcher said we can expect a lull any day now in the flying bomb assault on the city. That's not surprising so much as the professor's information on where the bombs will next come from."

"Not Holland?" Dampier asked.

"Holland surely, but as the Germans are pressed back, says Witcher, they will uncover some new tricks. But the first phase of the bombs is winding down and there will be a respite for London."

9

London: Entr'acte

September 8: a dreamy day of brilliant sun and almost hazeless sky, the perfect weather alone almost enough to bring the last of the wretched homeless out of the deepest tube. But it was not the weather that emptied the subway of its bombed-out gypsies by early afternoon, filling all the parks, bringing out the orators and costumed characters to Hyde Park Corner and restoring the normal queues. Londoners were feeling that a holiday should be declared this Friday because by noon they knew that the flying bombs had gone away.

On that happiest of days, Rosemary Ince and John Croft met in London, but not by some mysterious foresight. It was the first time their days-off cycles had coincided for more than a day at a time.

John met Rosemary's midafternoon train at the St. Pancras Station. To her it had seemed whimsical to wear a dress and a large hat and to let down her hair; in the end *she* had to find *him* on the station platform instead of the other way around; it did not exactly fit a daydream. He was looking for the severe uniform, the velvet tricorn, the blond hair smoothed back into a bun. The dress, of course—but of course!—he liked when she finally asked.

"But I can't wait to get to my hotel to put on that smashing war outfit again," she said.

"Your hotel, Rosemary? I've booked you at the Park Lane, where I stay."

"Sorry, cancel it. Even if you liked my dress, I'd stay at Brown's. All girls from good provincial families stay there because they watch over you. Mother knows I'm in London, you see, because I'm to pick up a gift she ordered for Father's birthday. They'll call and Andrew might even give a report to Father . . . look, it's too complicated. But I must go there with my things and freshen up a bit."

Brown's in Dover Street was only a few squares from the Park Lane. Old Andrew at the door, who wore dark plum livery brightened only by a magnificent waistcoat with horizontal scarlet and cream stripes, greeted Rosemary warmly, paternally, but was so suspicious of Croft that his new teeth clicked. Twice Andrew peered out of the dim entry hall into the positively dark bar-lounge where Croft waited; the pilot knew he was under close inspection. Rosemary was down quickly, still wearing the dress, and as they went out she promised Andrew she'd be in by twelve as usual. She smiled wickedly at Croft, who thought she was kidding. It was already four o'clock, one hour already gone of the weekend.

London had stunned Croft when he first saw it. He was coolly fond of New York, where his life had been spent, but he wanted to go after London aggressively as if he would never see it again. Rosemary knew the city well and said they had to walk on such a day or ride the red double-deckers or take the underground to see how much more there was to London than the Mayfair of his walking beat. From Bond Street Station to the end of the central line at Epping and back to the City showed Croft a little of the eastern suburbs. Then a quarter-trip around the circle line from Tower Hill to St. James's Park. It was only Friday; there was still Saturday and Sunday. They walked up between Green Park and St. James's Park past Buckingham Palace to Hyde Park Corner. Among all the speakers on the benches shouting at once about Home Rule, Free Caged Birds or Curfew for American Servicemen, Rosemary's favorite was an old fellow who for years had been trying to tell why they forced him to leave the Civil Service.

"Father showed him to me when I was a tiny girl and look, they still won't let him finish his story."

At twenty past six, Rosemary and John left Hyde Park Corner and started walking slowly down Piccadilly.

"I wish you had four days, like I do, Rosemary," said John.

"How did you cadge that?"

"This lull in the buzzbombs statred several days ago. No one knows what will happen. We may be out of work."

John didn't say that he'd shot down ten of the bombs and Wing/Co Adams-Ray thought he was a bit strung out. He wasn't but Bill was, with such a rough introduction to Ops flying. So the CO said four days; Bill went fishing.

18.20: In a dense wood between The Hague and the Hook of Holland, Batterie der Artillerie Abt. 485 rolled what looked like a thick dart out of a camouflaged hut. The 46-foot-long object rested upon a horizontal cradle on a Meiler six-wheel trolley, which started rolling toward a clearing a hundred meters away.

18.22: At the clearing, the transporter-erector trolley raised its burden to a vertical position, setting the four big tailfins gently on a four-legged frame resting on bare ground, so that the sharp nose pointed at the sky. Now the Meiler horizontal cradle had become a service tower running up along the side of the black and white checkered cylinder, whose diameter was nearly six feet.

It was too bad that such a day began to end with clouds hiding the sun and the return to haze that could seed fog later.

"Why is the sun so often red when it sets, especially in haze?" asked Rosemary.

"Take haze first. When sunlight, white light,

comes through vapor or smoke, it is scattered and the blue end of the spectrum is scattered most. So what gets through is yellowish, then orange, finally only red. But even when you can't see haze, as the sun sets its light comes through more and more of the atmosphere as it comes closer and closer to a grazing angle and finally a tangent to the earth's surface. Same thing, the blue is scattered first."

Rosemary already knew a John Croft that no one else knew. Bill, exorcised by the ordeal of flying with John, had learned that the pilot was not wooden, that he was only very private, that total privacy was his idea of democracy. But even Bill found John's humor a little warped, the gray eyes cold when people didn't measure up. Rosemary had always found John exceptionally witty, straightforward, talkative—"He is starting the fifth in a series of three lectures to me on aeronautics," she told her friends at FROGSPAWN— happy, healthy, fun-loving and very gentle with her. Everyone but Rosemary and Bill, then, either hated Croft or accepted him at a distance as a machine.

18.27: A slim mast swung up against the vertical object, bringing one end of a long, thick cable which was plugged in near the nose. The other end of the cable ran far back to an armored, boilerlike vehicle.

18.32: From inside the armored vehicle, the battalion commander started a thousand-horsepower pump out in his expensive machine on the platform. A mixture of ethyl alcohol and liquid oxygen went down into the combustion chamber.

They were looking at the side of a five-storied dwelling, all its flats exposed, floors sagging, beds and tables smashed, mattresses tossed about and ruptured, beam-ends and plumbing pipes jutting out crazily into space. It looked like a robber had pulled out all the drawers of a bureau.

"One of the worst things," said John reflectively, "is the way London's private parts are exposed. It's obscene, like seeing the intestines of a dead dog you got as a puppy. Especially when the damage is fresh like this. The older damage from the blitz is different, it almost has the grandeur of ancient ruins."

"Coventrated is what J. B. Priestley called it," remarked Rosemary.

18.33: It was ready. The service tower was lowered. Inside the armored control room, the firing button was pressed.

18.33.01: Ignition! *They had ignition! On a lengthening tail of flame out of a pancake cloud of steam, smoke and dust, the sluggish dart rose slowly at first.*

18.33.03: The strange aircraft was accelerating rapidly . . . five meters up . . . fifteen meters . . . fifty meters. Straight up it went until the tailflame was all the eye could see. Now it would be followed by optical telemetry until that failed, too. Then there would only be radar to follow the craft's course plus the radio signals it kept sending back.

They had come to St. James's Church near Piccadilly Circus. The church had stood alone now for three years. Its old neighbors on either side had left behind only piles of bricks and excavations full of utility conduits. The shell of St. James's was badly pocked but intact. Its tall windows had lost nearly all the stained glass. Most of the roof was gone; gable-beams jutted through like keel ribs of a ship capsized on the beach.

"One Sunday," John said, "I saw people here attending a regular service as if they still had a church."

It was gloomy inside St. James's. The sun was an hour gone, and to see traces of the fog along the littered aisle was eerie. They stood side by side before the bare altar, which was untouched by all the bombs the church had suffered. Rosemary unconsciously sought and clasped the pilot's hand.

"This is a Wren church, you know," she said.

"How nice to have your own official church."

"Christopher Wren, you silly!"

18.33.30: Six miles high and entering the stratosphere, the Roman candle had reached a velocity of 900 miles an hour. On command from the ground, it dropped its nose toward the west over the North Sea and continued climbing at an angle of forty-five degrees to the earth's surface. Its speed rose dramatically passing through successive sulfate and ozone layers.

18.34: A minute after ignition, the fuel was cut off and the flame burned out. Speed fell off from 4000 miles an hour but only slightly for there was no atmospheric friction. The machine was a dead projectile now except for its radio beep. Its climb came under natural forces, causing the nose to follow a parabolic arc. Radar in Holland was losing track while English radar was picking it up.

"Are you religious, Rosemary?"

"Not very. Births and deaths—perhaps not *all* weddings—these should be churched, don't you think?"

"I do."

"And don't you think a child should be exposed to churches as to anything else?"

He looked sharply at Rosemary but it was too dark to see her face.

"I do," he said.

18.34.30: What was now a massive artillery shell went through the noctilucent clouds and the meteorite dust-layer and the E-layer of the lower ionosphere and peaked at a height of sixty miles above the North Sea, more than halfway across to England. Starting down again, its velocity was 3780 miles per hour.

18.35: The sharp nose was pointed at London's center but the smallest change of forces could re-select any target within a circle of fifteen miles. The rocket struck a pensioners' home across the Thames from St. James's Church, demolishing it and drilling out a cavity in the earth forty feet deep and one hundred feet wide. And then it exploded.

John and Rosemary heard a powerful explosion across the river, then the sound of a great body whistling through the air, and then what seemed to be a sharp clap of thunder.

"Oh my God!" Rosemary screamed in terror, "they are back, they are back!"

Out in front of the church, John's face was raised to the sky. He seemed to sniff the air in the direction of the River Thames.

"That wasn't a buzzbomb, Rosemary, not even a

giant one. I don't know what it was, but it's not a buzz-bomb."

After the rocket exploded under the pensioners' home, the hole it left was twice as large as the impact hole. All of the old merchant sailors who lived there, eighty-five of them, were killed instantly, some of them simply vanishing.

Five minutes later, a second vengeance-rocket landed in Chiswick five miles west on the Thames.

Seventeen seconds after that, a third V.2 rocket hit way out in Epping.

Man had started that night to send against man his first missiles of space.

They saw *The Chocolate Soldier*, starring Ralph Richardson, at the Duke of York's Theatre, and then John took Rosemary to Quaglino's in Bury Street because she liked to dine by candlelight. Candles, she proclaimed, worked different magic for every woman but every woman seemed better for them. In Rosemary's case, it was the emerald eyes that shone so yellow-green.

It was after midnight when they got back to Brown's. The door was locked, and Andrew tore a strip off Rosemary before they even got into the lobby.

"Pay him no mind," Rosemary said as they sat down in the lounge to have a cordial. "I was saying that I don't know where they'll post me when I finish up at FROGSPAWN, but I'm Royal Navy property. You looked wise and said you had an idea. What could you possibly do?"

"Oh, talk to someone. Someone very powerful."

Rosemary made a skeptical face. "Look, here's what we must do when we go up. Here's the key to my room. You have to kiss me goodnight in the lobby, right in front of Andrew. He'll be furious and flustered, that's part of it. Then I'll say, 'Heavens, I've left my gloves in the lounge, Andrew.' He has a little vest torch he uses to find things in there, but I'll go with him. And you go up. That's all there is to it, and you were so worried." She was laughing at him.

"No, but it sounds to me like you've run this exercise before."

Rosemary stopped laughing and put her hand over John's on the table. "Never," she said, deadly serious, "it was never worth it before."

It worked. In the morning there would be no problem, for Andrew only came on at dinnertime. None of the others around the desk, Rosemary said, gave a damn. Only Andrew, bless him.

10

Trains and Bridges

In the predawn hour of September 17, seven flying bombs crossed the English coast from a new direction. Squadron Leader Janacek was on patrol and chased one of the bombs from a bad starting position. He chased it but was called off at the gunbelt before he could catch it. He saw the guns firing furiously at it and they missed. Then it was bracketed over land by searchlights for the Tempests, who had been pressed into night freelance defense. They failed to destroy Janacek's bomb, which flew on to London.

The next night, John Croft and Bill McLaughlin made the first of their two important September discoveries. No one seemed to wonder why all the daylight hours after Janacek's chase brought no more bombs. Only after dark did they start up again, about an hour after Croft and Adeš took their Mosquitoes out to the assigned patrol line. Thirty miles long, the line ran north-south across the new course of the flying bombs, which seemed to start anywhere between Rotterdam and the southern tip of Holland. While waiting, the Brookbridge GCI station, code name ARGUS, was running the two Mosquitoes through practice interceptions on each other as they flew back and forth on the monotonous patrol. Adeš was at

5000 feet, just under a solid cloud base that cut off all light below to the sea and wiped out the horizon. Below him 1000 feet and five miles back, Bill McLaughlin was just making contact on his AI:

"John," said Bill, "I've got Karel but something else is crossing east to west below him at only four miles."

"We'll go see—ARGUS, this is Cricket One-Niner, smacking north, going down, out."

The Brookbridge controller saw One-Nine disappear and he immediately put Two-Zero, Adeš, into a holding orbit.

Croft dove steadily. Bill's search radar got a clearer picture of what lay ahead. "Hold it," he said, "this thing is starting to climb. Turn left ten degrees and level off."

The turn had hardly started when Bill called out, "Throttle back! you're closing fast." Croft had no visual contact but the target suddenly helped by catching fire in a blinding flash. Then the pilot saw a familiar sight: the pulsing flame of a flying bomb! How had it started itself halfway across the North Sea? Bill had a confusing picture on the scope.

"My target has split, John, I've got twins here. One's going straight on west. The other's turning east and dropping fast. Tell me quick, which one?" Bill heard the answer go out on the air.

"ARGUS, Cricket One-Niner. You have a diver here at angels one-point-five, course two-six-zero. We are going after something else, out."

Brookbridge vectored Adeš after the bomb, while McLaughlin turned Croft onto the rapidly descending bogey. When they were down to 300 feet above the sea, Bill gave a range of 200 yards. Croft saw a twin-engine plane scuttling along slightly below them. He was boring in too fast and even cutting his throttle way back, he had to jink widely to the side and back again to keep from overshooting. His eyes never left the target; he was sure they could not see him.

"Take a look, Bill."

The first enemy aircraft Bill McLaughlin ever saw was only fifty yards ahead, slightly above. He felt exposed having a stern view of the ventral gun turret pointing back at them. The Mosquito had special louvered exhaust flame-shrouds, but on the other plane Bill could easily make out a set of quotation marks on the wings, the cherry red exhaust stacks and blue flames of the engines.

"A Heinkel One-Eleven, I think," Bill finally decided.

He must have been right about the old bomber for John started to destroy it. He leaned into the electric gunsight, aiming the Mossie at the left wingroot between engine and fuselage, where he knew there were fuel tanks—his right thumb mashed the control-column firing button. Only twenty rounds each from the four 20-millimeter cannon were fired. The Mosquito shook from the recoil like a sled hitting gravel. The Heinkel stood up on the other wing and headed for the surface of the water. There was no other place for the slow bomber to go. Its left engine was on fire.

John kept turning, turning after the Heinkel and when it flattened out he was ready to fire again. The other plane was so low, he had to depress the Mossie's nose to take aim. Now the wing of the Heinkel was blazing, lighting the water, showing that the propellers almost touched the surface.

John fired but something struck the Mosquito lightly just then, from below. He yanked the Mossie up quickly but not before the Heinkel's propellers chewed the water, throwing sheets of spray back over Croft's windscreen. The Mossie missed the Heinkel by a yard going over it, as it hit the water, bounced, hit again and stopped with its tail high. They watched the fire burn a few seconds and go out. It was a sad sight for Bill, who had mentally been flying in the other men's cockpit from the time they must have known they were trapped.

"ARGUS, this is One-Niner," John announced. "Splash one bandit, over."

"One-Niner, was it a diver, over?" It was Rosemary!

"Not a diver, ARGUS. Out."

Croft was prepared to resume his patrol but

Brookbridge steered them back to Brevishall. There they learned that Adeš and Miloslav had shot down the flying bomb. McLaughlin saw Croft examining the airscrews of their own Mossie.

"That thing that hit us," John said, "was the water. We wiped some paint off the propellers."

So, when Air Vice-Marshal Swann took Commander Dampier and Captain Parmenter to Cambridge, Professor Witcher had been wrong about the flying bombs, although he was dead-on about the rockets.

Swann flew them up to RAF Cambridge in a slow Miles Gemini twin-engine trainer he kept twelve miles north of London at Stapleford. Swann liked to fly. He let Parmenter drive the Gemini but not to take off or land. They put down at the high-security Meteorology Flight Station, and Swann quickly had them hopping for a car and driver to take them in to Cambridge.

Professor Witcher had an office at the back corner of the King's College library. In theory, his single window looked out on The Backs and the King's Bridge over the River Cam. But the window was blocked by piles of books, periodicals, reprints, newspapers and boxes of clippings. The tiny office had once been a pasting room and still looked like one. Captain Parmenter was appalled at the room, which looked slept in, and even more appalled by the man whose clothes also looked slept in. But Dampier noticed that Clip, who usually entered rooms offensively like a gladiator, was subdued and later even obsequious in the professor's domain.

The professor flapped a hand three times toward a sofa and two chairs, like a priest tossing a censer. He didn't seem to notice that his visitors had to slide things around to gain edges to sit on.

Smoking, of course, was out although Witcher never said so. It was awkward for them when Parmenter's cigarette holder and Swann's pipe automatically came out of their pockets. They glanced nervously around the room for a few seconds. Swann palmed his pipe as if he'd tried to pass a classroom note, then slipped the pipe back in his jacket. Parmenter acted as if he always held an unlighted cigarette in a silver holder, then coolly he separated these instruments of pleasure and put them out of sight.

"Well, it's good of you to come, Marshal, Commander Lamphier," said Witcher, as he collapsed in the desk chair, "and . . . umm . . . and that fellow, too. Good of you to come, indeed. First, I have to apologize for calling you all together here without explaining that we do not actually print the codebooks and cipher tables at Cambridge. That sort of scutwork is done by the Oxford University Press and—*huk-uk-uk!* —quite enough for them to do, I should think. No, our people work with the codes and ciphers themselves, and I should have told you that. But your trip is hardly wasted for we have found scores of errors in your raw data and—"

Swann gently interrupted, saying, "Excuse me, Jeremy, not codes, we are the ones who were quizzing you on Germany, Hitler, the July twenty plot."

"Are you sure?" Witcher gazed suspiciously at all of them. "But of course you are and now I remember. I said I had some new information on the V-weapons, didn't I?"

"That's it, that's it!" cried Swann, as if he were about to snap a photo of an inattentive, sleepy infant. At least Witcher wasted no time when his button was pushed.

"First, the bombs," he began. "We all know they are merely delayed until new launch sites are established in Holland. Now, London to Calais is only eighty-five miles, while London to the nearest point in Holland is a hundred and sixty miles, well beyond the range of the current bomb. We think that development of the new long-range flying bomb has been greatly accelerated, like all the retaliation weapons, since the Germans know that their tenure along the Straits of Dover is about to end.

"These long-range bombs can easily come from any part of the Netherlands or even nearby Germany. They are not different in principle from what we've already seen. Therefore, I think we shall have them straight from Holland by the middle of September.

"Now, the rockets. On July the tenth last, a German test rocket went off course and landed in Sweden. MI-6 literally bought the remains from the Swedes under the noses of German agents. Two of your courier Mosquitoes, thank you Marshal, flew up and brought the whole mess back. Not only did this rocket end all speculations, its state of perfection was such as to leave production capability as the only problem. There our calculations are reliable. It is trickier to gauge the German temper, how massive an impression they want to make on us. A steady trickle of rockets or a cloudburst? We don't know. But the rockets will start falling on London within a fortnight."

Dampier and Swann were speechless but not incredulous; Parmenter was both.

"You mean to say that a warhead rocket can reach London from, what, Holland? And be *aimed,* in the bargain?"

"With an error of fifteen miles, sir. The radius of London from Charing Cross is fifteen miles."

"May I ask, Jeremy," said Swann, "what you can tell us about official attitudes in Britain toward an assassination of Adolf Hitler that can be traced to an arm of our government."

"There is only one attitude in Britain, Marshal, and that is Winston Churchill's. You are asking me what I know about the prime minister. All right.

"I do not know him personally, never met him. He loves war, especially this war where he is largely in command. Well, many love war, don't they? But few have the inexhaustible energy and godlike will. the power, to play with a world war at all levels, touching as it were each aspect as a miser fingers his gold. A strange childlike quality—no, adolescence really—such a quality seems a part of these complex personalities. Why is this important to know? It is important because the prime minister, with all his power, remains a vicarious warrior. He wants to be in the outpost, on the bridge, in the cockpit with the brave young men. His record shows how he will personally support the wildest scheme if it has dash, a novel twist."

"Professor Witcher," the single-minded Dampier said, "I gather you were coming indirectly to Korpo's question."

"He asked a question? What was that, Marshal?"

"The attitude, Churchill's if you will, toward an Allied assassination of Hitler," Dampier quickly answered for Swann.

"That's better, you should be very specific. Well, what do we know? One of the first clues, happily, comes from my own experience." Witcher looked at each man in turn. "You know, I lived in Germany for forty years, off and on"—even Swann had not known that—"and had, perhaps still have, many friends there. Among them was the head of a magnificent family, Ewald von Kleist-Schmenzin. In thirty-eight, a year before the war, Kleist came to London on a dangerous mission for the *schwarze Kapelle*. He brought evidence of the coming takeover of Czechoslovakia and of a genuine conspiracy to overthrow Hitler. He gave proof that the *Abwehr* and the generals would arrest, if not kill, the *Führer*. Everyone ignored him but Churchill.

"Churchill was out of power, but he sat down and wrote a note for Kleist. I saw the note, gentlemen. And Kleist told me that Churchill looked him in the eye and said, 'Bring us your leader's head, Herr Kleist, and I guarantee you shall have what you want.' A Kleist would not lie. You will remember I told you about the bombs in the overcoat pockets to kill Hitler? Heinrich von Kleist, Ewald's son, was one of the men who faced death to carry such bombs.

"It is important that Churchill knows the Germans have no compunctions at all about killing *him*. They've tried. And they've tried to kill your president, too, Commander."

"The Germans? Roosevelt?" Dampier seemed surprised at this view through the wrong end of the telescope.

"Oh, yes, and that episode is much clearer than the Churchill affair. This plot was called Long-Jump, *langer Sprung."* Witcher seemed at home with German, even now. "It was Teheran. Six storm troopers of the SD or *Sicherheitsdienst,* security service, were planted to assassinate the president. The plot was discovered by the Russians. Stalin urged Roosevelt to move into the safety of the Russian compound, which he did. Now, of course, the British were sure there was a Russian plot, not to kill Roosevelt, but to capture his mind."

"And what about Churchill?" asked Swann.

"That was in June of forty-three. Churchill and Eden were returning to England from North Africa. Gestapo agents in Lisbon thought they saw the prime minister of England board a KLM DC-3 transport. Clearly, it was the Gestapo mentality to think that England, close to bankrupty, had to buy tickets at the window to ship its head of government about the world. So *Luftwaffe* night fighters were sent out from Spain or France. They shot the helpless airliner down and all thirteen passengers were lost." Witcher paused. "Including the actor Leslie Howard."

Parmenter, especially, was stunned for he was a movie addict and a Leslie Howard fan.

"Yes," continued Witcher, "the man who indeed bore a striking similarity to Churchill was, in fact, Howard's business manager. Howard, you see, had just completed a long propaganda tour in Spain and Portugal for the British Council, touting our documentaries and feature films, including his own, to offset Nazi propaganda. He had made one film on the Spitfire and another on . . . on———"

"Pimpernel Smith" was the name Parmenter supplied, "where he rescued victims of the Nazis. And remember, he was the star of *The Scarlet Pimpernel.* Isn't that curious?" Parmenter chuckled and asked the professor, "Leslie Howard wasn't by any chance a real spy, was he?"

"It's been mentioned," answered Witcher. "No, I believe the Germans went after Churchill and bollixed it up, as they've done before."

"Jeremy, do you think anyone in Germany will still try to assassinate Hitler?" asked Swann.

"Impossible, Marshal. All Germany has been under *Nacht und Nebel,* night and fog, since July. Thousands have already been executed in a horrible manner, strangling, hanging upon butchers' hooks. Whole families, such as the Stauffenbergs, have been wiped out, including children."

Swann pressed on. "What would happen if Hitler were killed and it leaked out that his death was the result of an Allied plot?"

"You would like chaos, collapse, popular uprising, is that it?" asked Witcher with a mocking smile. "Go back to what I told you in London. You, all of you, simply *must* be disabused of this strange idea that the German people are unhappy with their *Führer!* No one, not Churchill, not Roosevelt, not even Stalin who is perhaps more comparable to Hitler than the others —none has such a hold on the common man's mind, what's more his soul, as Adolf Hitler. Look, gentlemen, let me simplify by taking only the best and worst cases.

"In the best case, for us, Hitler's successor or successors come into conflict—that is almost a certainty—and fail to gain control of the country immediately. There could be a revival of the conspiracy, if any of the conspirators remains alive. A responsible and realistic plan for government would be presented to the Allies. If all the Allies accepted, the war could end right there, but the Russians will never listen and a unilateral surrender is impossible. But suppose anyway that the Germans, released from their evil masters, fearing the Russians as they do, flee wholesale to the west. Where do you suppose the postwar Russian border will then lie? That is the best case." Witcher smirked.

"And what is the worst case? Hitler is totally mad and so are all possible successors, but in a different way—they are crafty. They come quickly to terms with the Army and with the help of men like Speer, they reorder the insane priorities Hitler imposed on truly decisive secret weapons. Not the V.1 and V.2—the jet fighter, the even faster rocket fighter, air-to-air missiles, heat-sensing rockets, remote-controlled flying bombs, ground-to-air missiles. *Military* objectives would be pursued, not civilians. The war would be greatly prolonged and many times more costly. If the air were controlled quickly enough, the ground advance on Germany would grind to a halt. Germany would win a stalemate. If their resources still permitted, they would surely go for the checkmate."

Witcher's small office seemed designed to concentrate gloom. Even Dampier was hesitant when he finally spoke.

"I have one last question, Professor, but I'm almost certain of the answer."

"Don't ask then, Commander."

"I have to. Are you positive that Hitler travels only in trains now? Never airplanes?"

"Positive. Even in the trains, he has become more withdrawn. For example, he used to show himself at the windows wherever his train stopped. Now the shades of every coach are pulled down by the time his train rolls into a station."

"Do you have specifications on any of the trains he uses?"

"Oh, yes. Marshal Swann can call me any time if you find you must know more about specific trains in the Reich."

"Thank you, Professor," said Dampier.

"Now, Commander, may I ask you a question? Why do you insist on complicating things by all the high-level matters you queried me on? I am no strategist, don't even trust strategists. Nor am I a tactician, although these people usually know what they are doing. But it seems to me that there could be no assassination easier than one from the air to conceal from the enemy beforehand, and after the fact to claim as purely accidental. I mentioned the importance of a cover. You should think about that."

"We have not even reached the point of a cover, Jeremy," said Swann, "because we have nothing yet to put under it." He looked at Dampier gravely. "When we go back now, at least we can concentrate on trains. Perhaps we will decide to withdraw from the field."

"I hope you will not do that, Marshal." It was the most surprising statement that Witcher could have made. "Commander Dampier, if you are at all intimate with the prime minister, I would suggest that now would be a good time to have a chat with him."

On the flight back to London, Swann was delighted to have Parmenter fly the Gemini, so that he and Dampier could get down to discussing what Witcher had told them.

"What did he mean, Korpo, by saying I should try to see Churchill?"

"I don't know, Matthew, but I should do it without delay."

"I'll try. Well, there's no way around it, is there? It has to be a train." Dampier was very low.

"Yes." Swann took things in stride more easily than the air attaché. "So we will simply think about air attacks on trains, won't we? There is a lot of background on train counter-operations in Europe. We will have the best advice. I have no solution at this moment."

Croft and McLaughlin made their second September discovery at the end of the month. It was the germ of the solution that Dampier and Swann so desperately sought. But the discovery would not have been made if the air attaché had not asked Swann to have 68 Squadron attached half-time to the Second Tactical Air Force.

There was no relation at all between buzzbomb patrols and the work of the 2nd TAF. One day, Wing Commander Vivian Adams-Ray and his two flight commanders came back from TAF headquarters to brief 68 Squadron on their new assignment.

"Since well before D-Day," said the Wing/Co, "the job of the Second Tactical Air Force has been to do whatever will advance the Allied Expeditionary Force in Europe. We will work exclusively at night but you should know that this is a twenty-four-hour effort overall. Now let me chalk up the two types of work the TAF do."

Adams-Ray drew a line down the center of the board and wrote *Intruder* at the top left, *Ranger* at the right. He listed as he talked.

"The main difference between the two is that Intruders are sent to specific targets, while Rangers are freelance. Intruders are held at the ready, Rangers take off at predetermined times. Finally, Intruders maintain R/T contact with base, Rangers are silent. We are Rangers.

"As to targets. There is almost nothing TAF have not gone after. Aircraft in the air, on the ground, taking off, landing. Railroads—the trains, rail lines, marshaling yards, stations, maintenance and repair facilities. Highways, roads and motor transport. Communications centers, radar stations, searchlight and flak batteries. Factories. Military training schools. Flying-bomb ski sites and rocket launch platforms.

"Armament. In addition to our cannon, we may carry an assortment of bombs and rockets from time to time.

"If that doesn't cover it, drinks are on me come next July the hundredth. Any questions, gentlemen? English, please, no Australian, American or Bohemian dialects."

The squadron began at once to practice the most important art: contour flying. This was low-level, high-speed grazing over the crazy-quilted Norfolk countryside. Every available scrap of cover was used by the canny pilots: low hills, river troughs, rows of houses, long files of trees along straight stretches of road. The dangerous but exciting practice started in daylight during the usual night-flying tests. Then it began at night.

Norfolk was one thing, the Continent was another. It was difficult to prepare for the Continent until after the first Ops flight. The nav/rads studied all kinds of maps; the pilots read sheaves of combat reports. McLaughlin said he was learning French and German, just from reading the maps. Aircrews memorized the more important routes and landmarks.

Adams-Ray declared his crews ready on the tenth night of practice, September 19. That night, Karel Adeš started the squadron off by shooting down a Junkers 88 night fighter who was in his landing approach at the old Amsterdam airport, Schiphol, which had become a major night fighter base. Adeš also destroyed two aircraft on the ground.

Croft and McLaughlin saw no aircraft at first. They ran up a string of seven locomotives destroyed and two damaged. Bill McLaughlin, radar specialist, felt less useful than a fireman in the cab of a Diesel locomotive.

In the longest trip yet made by the squadron, Croft and McLaughlin were sent out on September 28 to patrol the Stendal night fighter station, fifty miles short of Berlin. There would be only twenty minutes in the target area.

Two minutes before their time was up, McLaughlin had the first indications on his scope. It turned out to be a Messerschmidt Bf110 coming home. Croft followed it into the landing pattern and shot it down in its final approach. They left Stendal right on time.

North of Hannover in Lower Saxony, skimming the treetops back to England, Croft saw a train making lots of steam toward a spindly steel-arch bridge that crossed a narrow stream. Hiding low out behind the hills and woods, he watched the progress of the steam and smoke until the time seemed right to turn the Mosquito in on a wide curve toward the bridge. The plan was to come up the stream and catch the engine out in the middle of the bridge. On a whim, he changed that.

Dropping back behind the train, Croft overtook it on the right side and began firing steadily on the engine when it was 200 yards from the bridgehead. The old four-wheeler sparked from the hail of 20-millimeter shells but nothing happened until the engine was almost into the portal of the bridge. Steam began to gush from the stack first and then the engine blew its kettle-shaped steam dome hundreds of feet in the air and split open along the top from the cab all the way forward to the smoke box. Derailing and twisting at a slight angle to the rails, the engine hit the bridge, ripping out the side-frames on both sides. It might have jammed and stopped in the bridge but thirty coal wagons were piling up behind it steadily. The bridge broke up, crashing down to the streambed with the engine and three wagons. On and on the wagons came; all but two poured through the gap and they did not because the stream was filled.

Many times Bill had found John silent but never speechless. The pilot circled three times around the jumbled dam he had built across the small river, shaking his head, mumbling to himself. Then he remembered that they were still in central Germany and there was not a round left in the cannon.

"On my first day in the Navy," John said, ten minutes later, "we were still civilians riding the Orange Blossom Special from New York to an Atlanta training base. Outside of Atlanta, a Yellow Peril biplane trainer with one head in it, a student, buzzed the hell out of us. I remember thinking, nothing that moves along the earth is as helpless as a train. Even a ship can change its course. But I never dreamed you could demolish a whole train with four small cannon—and a bridge."

"It looked to me," said Bill, "as if the train destroyed the bridge and committed suicide."

The next day Croft called Commander Dampier in London to thank him for arranging Rosemary Ince's posting to the Brookbridge GCI station. He mentioned the luck they'd had the night before at Stendal, incidentally describing the freak train-and-bridge affair. Dampier seemed to leave the phone, John thought.

"Listen, John," Dampier said in a recorded sort of voice, "could you come to London this afternoon? I'll call Adams-Ray and clear it."

11

Triple Crosses

October 1944 began for the naval air attaché as if
winter were not coming to England this year. October 1
was Matthew Beryl Dampier's birthday. In 1944 he
was thirty-eight years old, in perfect health, doing a
good job that he liked, working for an admiral he admired, living in his favorite city, practically living in
his country's most important embassy. As to background, that was about it, that was all that really
mattered, for the attaché was a plain man of few
needs.

He got a birthday card from his wife. She called
him Daddy. They had no children. She wrote from a
sanatorium in Maryland where she had lived for six
years. She would always live there, for her delicate
mind had split in her twenties and was most of the
time child-like.

There had never been a birthday like this one for
Dampier. Two days earlier, John Croft had come to
London at the commander's request and described
how the train just kept going down through the bridge.
Croft thought it was probably a rare stroke, since
locomotives rarely blow up like that under small can-
nonfire. He did feel that some kind of heavier armament aimed at the bridgehead itself while under the

weight of the engine might do the trick most of the time.

"I'll be trying five-inch wing-rockets when I go back," Croft said, "but would you check on something, Commander? At NOCTU I had a chance to fire two Navy rockets called Tiny Tim 11.75-inch AR, aerial rocket, equivalent to a naval rifle shell of the same diameter fired from a cruiser's gun. They may still be experimental but do you think there are any at our patrol plane bases in the United Kingdom?"

The 68 Squadron intelligence officer had given Croft a little general information on train operations in Europe, and McLaughlin had asked for all the detail maps he could get on bridges, but they would not show structure. Dampier said he'd flood them with such materials and anything else they wanted. He saw that John was interested in what he'd tried only once. Croft said he was learning that trains were more important than he thought.

The next day a nice thing happened, too. Croft came back for a social visit, bringing along the WREN that Air Vice-Marshal Swann's friends' associates' strings had somehow pulled up to the Brookbridge GCI station. She was a good-looking girl with striking green eyes, reserved and well-groomed, and Dampier was happy to impress her with a tour of the embassy, ending in a short visit with Admiral Stark. The old salt surprised the attaché by getting his scrambled-eggs cap and letting the WREN try it on. It was his idea and it was his idea, too, to perch her velvet tricorn on top of his white mane and cop a peak in the mirror.

Dampier thought Croft seemed livelier around the WREN. It was nice of them to come.

That was Saturday; Sunday was Dampier's birthday; Monday afternoon he got a call from the war bunker. The prime minister would see him the following Friday at ten P.M. sharp. What a weekend it was!

Matthew opened the top drawer at his right elbow and dropped his wife's card in with the illegible notes, nothing classified, that he'd been collecting since first meeting Swann.

At Brevishall, Wing Commander Adams-Ray attached no great significance to Air Ministry's request that John Croft be relieved temporarily of flying bomb patrols. He was a little piqued, that's all, since no one called to fill him in about what was going on. *Bugger them!* he thought and used his own judgment when Croft asked to be kept on the patrol schedule one out of four flying nights, offering to fly the patrol as an extra night, if necessary. Booster wouldn't permit extra flying but he gave in on the one patrol to John, who was actually bored with the dwindling trade in flying bombs. John had got Rosemary Ince to Brookbridge; he'd keep radio contact with her, by God!

When Korpo Swann called the next day, Booster's pique disappeared.

"I'm sure you were intrigued by Croft's train trick, Booster, as we were," said the soothing Black Swann. "We'll be sending along some bric-a-brac and some slide rule types from time to time. We want Croft to try out a few things. Clear the way for him, will you? You'll hear. 'Bye."

Booster understood. Loose talk sinks ships and all that. He'd been through this with Swann before.

But a *few* things!

Within a week, there had accumulated bits and pieces enough to add a new wing to the mess. The radar shack, mostly Canadians there, received a collection of odd cases out of which they greedily snatched the bare bones of a fine new Mark XV airborne radar, which even Adams-Ray had not yet seen. A Fleet Air Arm Fairey Firefly drilled in one day from Ford to deliver a U.S. Navy radio altimeter marked Naval Research Laboratory/RCA. The squadron leader who busted six trains in six minutes over France, Peter Panitz of the RAAF, flew his Mossie in one day to visit another Australian, chat with Croft and take him up for a spin, have tea and tootle off. Specialists began to queue up from such places as the Special Installation Unit at Defford and the Airplane and Armament Experimental Establishment at Boscombe Down; a train man visited from the London-Midlands-Scottish Railway. With the CO's help, Croft discouraged some of these people from wasting everybody's time. So far as the exotic boxed goods went, what seemed to please Croft most was delivered by a blue and gray four-engine U.S. Liberator bomber. A crane lowered two fourteen-foot pine coffins out of a side hatch. Someone handed Croft a ten-gallon paper drum of ice cream, a gift for the mess. They were all invited to stay a while but "Gotta go!" they said and were off.

Armorer Sergeant Snead took charge of the coffins and they were immediately opened. Tiny Tims, said Croft, proudly. No one had ever seen such rockets. White, round noses, straight green shafts, four rectangular green vanes. "Bloody clean-looking but vicious, ain't they," said Snead, when Croft asked him to hang on to the small rocket manual the Liberator man had passed out to him.

Commander Dampier left the Government Offices at midnight after two hours in the prime minister's war room. Swann had briefed him beforehand on what he knew about the man, mostly personal sidelights:

"If you feel nervous because you think you are staying too long, it means he likes you. Remember, he could flick you out with his cigar ashes.

"He may be wearing his rompers, which doesn't mean that you are an ill-favored guest. On the contrary, these he prefers to wear while roaming around his workspaces among working people, bouncing in on them. These are the people he likes best, I think.

"He may be dictating for a while after you arrive and that's fine. It will stop after a time. His document will be perfect and so will his memory of what *you've* said.

"At the Admiralty, when he was most recently First Lord, some of my friends used to call his conference room the 'capital W.C.' I'm sure he knew that. I don't know if that's done now that he's in the War Room.

"But watch him! He can make your head spin faster than a Catherine Wheel.

"Oh, and Matthew, a delightful thing you must

remember to tell him. It will help your case, our case. I only found out recently myself. When Geoffrey de Havilland bought Salisbury Hall for the Mosquito project, all the original design work was done there. Churchill's American mother lived at the Hall before World War I and young Winnie used to fish in the moat. One day he caught a fine big pike, which he mounted on the lavatory wall. It is said that frequent contemplation of that fish's graceful lines by the designers influenced the shape coming out on the Mosquito drawing board. Churchill will love that."

Dampier could hardly sleep, waiting until next morning to tell Swann about the meeting. When he was early, Swann's secretary asked him to wait in the marshal's office and she brought him tea.

"Korpo, we are in!"

"Tell me."

"To start with, we have a code name for our operation."

"Aha! The First Lord of contingency is at it again."

"The important thing, Korpo, is that we never came near discussing such a thing at Normandy. He's been thinking about this on his own. MACCABEE is the name."

"Pray, say again?"

"MACCABEE, the Hebrew for hammer, also applied to a small band of Jews once caught between the Greeks and the Ptolemies battling for Palestine. The Greeks knew they would have to kill all the Maccabees to wipe out their religion but, for twenty-five years, the Maccabees repeatedly defeated the Greeks. In 164 B.C., Jerusalem was recaptured by the Maccabees. They purged the Temple of idols and rededicated it to Jehovah. The Feast of Hanukkah commemorates this victory."

"How did he settle on this? The warlike ring of it?"

"More than that, I think. The Rothschilds. He knows Polly Saxe-Rowland intimately. I told him about Seth, who is Polly's cousin."

"Of course! She was a Rothschild."

"Now Korpo, the next most important thing is

that I think his interest in MACCABEE comes from a somewhat gloomy picture he has of Eisenhower's apparent willingness to let Berlin and Prague go to the Russians by default. To kill Hitler might be a sort of symbolic scoop. There is another bizarre twist that must be classified top secret but anyway he told me. Top gossip, maybe. Have you heard of the National Redoubt?"

"Never. What is that?"

"For about a month, Eisenhower's headquarters has been getting reports on a vast fortress in the Alps. Hitler and his henchmen are said to plan a withdrawal there, if necessary, to fight us off for a thousand years. Churchill thinks it's insane but he says the Supreme Headquarters is taking it so seriously, that their advance is being warped toward southern Germany."

"It sounds insane to me, Matthew, but then I just learned about it."

"Curiously enough, according to Churchill, the wildest part happens to be true. A large corps of elite commandos is being trained for the Redoubt, to creep out at night and infiltrate our troops. They are called Werewolves."

"The Redoubt rumor, I must say, fits something that Witcher passed on to me." Swann unlocked a drawer in his desk and took out an envelope stamped MOST SECRET, handing it to Dampier. "He even mentions a wolf."

Dampier read:

> ...A plan has apparently existed since D-Day to evacuate Hitler from Berlin, probably to Berchtesgaden or elsewhere in the Austrian Alps. He seems resistant; perhaps he is not afraid.
>
> Some years ago, I remember hearing that Hitler had the habit of whistling constantly a ditty from an American film cartoon, something about no need to fear the wolf. Don't know it myself, just thought it curious.

"What does he mean, Matthew?"

"Who knows what *he* means. The cartoon was *The Three Little Pigs*. The tune was 'Who's Afraid of the Big Bad Wolf.'"

Croft had learned a lot about trains. He was thinking they deserved the highest priority among air targets. To some extent, that was proven by the costly devastation of all rail facilities serving the Cherbourg Peninsula before and after D-Day. But a RAF analysis showed how wasteful of French lives the heavy bombers had been when used against bridges and fixed railroad targets; and they could not even hit a moving train. It was found that one bridge required 640 tons of bombs from the heavies. Even when a switch to fighter-bombers was ordered and only 200 tons per bridge were needed, the small planes had to fly a hundred sorties to do the job.

Croft knew what he had discovered. One plane with only four cannon had destroyed a bridge and an entire train. What would proper armament do?

The eight high-velocity wing rockets had not worked out. Neither had the six-inch Molins cannon, the equivalent of a destroyer's five-inch gun, which Croft fired from a borrowed Coastal Command Mosquito called the Tsetse. Both weapons tore up locomotives or blew them sideways off the tracks but hardly touched the bridges.

Croft waited to try his precious Tiny Tims until Captain Parmenter cabled that he'd found two more somewhere and was sending them over. One of the big rockets was fired in daylight against the concrete base of an abandoned coast artillery tower, the best simulation for a bridge pylon that could be found. The same night they went out to a bridge across the River Weser, south of Bremen, and waited for a train. The Tiny Tim whooshed out with a blinding flash and took away a concrete arch from under the locomotive. It was better than expected, considering that the small locomotive did little of the work.

It was at this time that Croft and McLaughlin acquired Leading Aircraftwoman Heather Stampford. Sergeant Snead had sponsored her, said he could get her if the Wing/Co approved. Snead was fascinated by Croft's armament-dabbling and thought he deserved a permanent aircraft chief of his own. One chilly afternoon in mid-October, Heather took charge of Croft's

Mossie and also Bill MacLaughlin. She took an instant dislike to Croft, however, because he looked her up and down coldly and said she'd be okay if she kept the Mosquito in better trim than she kept herself. Heather knew she wasn't the neatest but she was bright, dedicated and—she'd show him!

Commander Dampier received a letter from Captain Hamilton at NOCTU(Pac) on October 15. He didn't know Hamilton except by reputation: a tiger. Hamilton wrote:

> I was originally informed that the RAF training program for these officers would end in September. Now I learn they have been assigned to operational squadrons. Whose decision was this? About Croft and McLaughlin, let it be clear that they belong to NOCTU(Pac), which was finally allowed to nominate only one crew for England. These officers are urgently needed here and I would send a tracer on them, except that I feel you should have the opportunity to reflect on this informal communication. . . .

Dampier saw that the message was copied to Parmenter, who would take care of it. He dropped Hamilton's letter into his locked drawer—the one that would become the nightmare drawer.

November.

On the night of November 3/4 around three o'clock in the morning, Lieutenant Richard Priest and Ensign Thomas Squire disappeared over Germany. Croft and McLaughlin were there, without knowing it.

Priest, of 456 Squadron, had been sent from Ford on a high-level intruder mission to harass *Luftwaffe* night fighters at an assembly point over a radio beacon near Stendal, where Croft had shot down a Ju88. Croft was on freelance around Berlin, on the information that Tempelhof Airport was being used as an emergency night fighter landing field. Circling Tempelhof at treetop level and at a respectful distance, he had seen nothing when he had only ten minutes to remain on the scene.

Priest tailed an aircraft toward its landing at Stendal. His tail-warning radar suddenly told him he was being followed and he whipped around but not quickly enough: the bandit had disappeared. Priest circled Stendal, thinking that with only ten minutes left he would not waste them by climbing back up over the beacon. Squire announced a bogey on his scope and turned Priest in toward the field. Suddenly a light appeared behind the cockpit of an aircraft that was Squire's bogey; Priest could hardly believe it. He slid in behind the other plane and prepared to fire. The next thing Priest knew, he was dying. Squire was dead. Their Mosquito almost landed by itself at Stendal but it bounced hard and flipped over on its back without burning.

The big aircraft that had followed the Mosquito when it went after the lighted decoy circled Stendal once and started climbing west to hunt something else. It had two long engines and it was all silver, unpainted except for leopard-spot camouflage on all its top surfaces. Huge antlers, the radar antennas, bristled forward from the nose.

And behind the silver plane, Croft's homeward-bound Mosquito was getting ready to take its turn.

"I have a feeling we are followed, Marx," the German pilot said. "Have you anything on the Naxos?"

"Nothing," said the radar operator. But their tail-warning radar had just failed.

"Speak of the wolf, Marx, and he is not far," said the pilot. *Wenn man vom Wolfe spricht, ist er nicht weit.*

Croft fired. His cannon hardly spoke when their electrical connections failed and they stopped.

The *Luftwaffe* night fighter aircraft was, an *Uhu,* an Owl, and it was hit but not badly. At his base in south Germany, the pilot filled out a report on the English Mosquito he'd shot down. It was long, twenty-one parts:

20. *Damage to own machine by enemy action:* minor   21. *Other units operating (incl. Flak):* none

(signed) Robert Gabriel
Kommodoreoberst

Commander Dampier and Air Vice-Marshal Swann had finally drawn up the definitive plan for MAC-CABEE. In addition to millions of photographs of Europe that were available to them, Swann set up a special operation called MAPTRACK, the photorecon-naissance of rail lines leading out of Berlin that might be used by the *Führer*. Information from Witcher and from Dampier's observers inside Germany indicated that they should concentrate on the line from Berlin to Munich. Between Nuremberg and Munich, there was a bridge across the Danube at Donauwörth.

The crews were chosen. Croft would carry two to four Tiny Tims, depending on what Sergeant Snead could load in the Mossie, and Garland would cover him. From 456 Squadron, there would also be Tarbox and Rothschild plus Squadron Leader Anthony and his navigator. Croft complained that four Mossies were unnecessary, that two was the number.

At Brevishall, specialists began constructing sev-eral models in a large scale of key bridges and their terrain, including the most critical bridge at Donau-wörth.

On the night of November 9/10, Lieutenant Joseph Murdock and Lieutenant (jg) Elliot Nicholas disap-peared over Holland. Parmenter had just written Dam-pier to say that he had checked around at Patuxent River and, indeed, Murdock had a drinking problem. Garland told Croft that they should inform Violet Pugh about Murdock and return all her letters to her. Croft said the letters should be destroyed.

Four men were lost, if not dead, and Dampier had to say something to Washington, for they were technically on a training assignment. The six survivors told him that these accidents happened in training anywhere, that he should delay. He was not an aviator and he listened to them.

At Brevishall, Heather Stampford had become Mc-Laughlin's mistress—he was solidly married in Virginia —and a great trial to Croft. Such a trial that one day he decided he would have to straighten her out because she was really a good mechanic.

Heather was standing by the Mossie's ladder after an NFT, while Croft was fussing about something up in the cockpit.

"Get in, Stampford," the pilot growled, "and close the hatch."

Heather did as she was told. She had never flown before and suspected that she was about to do so.

Croft took her out over the Wash and circled back toward the cliffs. He turned the Mosquito upside down and still flew toward the cliffs. Heather's head was full of blood but the cliffs still loomed before her eyes. At the last minute, Croft pushed the stick forward and they climbed over the cliffs on their back. Then he rolled out and flew back to Brevishall with a quiet, quaking WAAF passenger.

"I fly this Mossie, Stampford," said Croft when they were on the ground, "and you have it the rest of the time. But don't think it was built for you to admire on the ground. It's a flying machine, do you understand?"

Sergeant Snead consoled Heather but he was frank.

"Don't mind 'im, Heather, luv. 'E's 'ard, yes, but 'e's the bloody Wooden Wolf, you see. We've got to humor 'im 'cause 'e's got dreadful things on 'is mind."

Peter Garland and Stephen Trice were shot down by English antiaircraft guns near Lowestoft on November 17 as they were coming back from Europe. There was a lot of flap about the signal flares they fired but no one really knew what happened. They were dead.

Their Mosquito had come down in a field near Extall. Croft went there with Adams-Ray at two o'clock in the morning. A hundred people were at the scene: police, RAF, civilians. A black night, threatening rain, cold, windy. Intensely white floodlights threw a harsh glare across an English farmer's fields. At the far end of one field was a broken Mosquito.

The Mosquito lay on the breast of a rise. It had burned—the skin of Croft's neck writhed. The fire had relaxed the airframe so that the aircraft hugged the ground closely. The Mosquito, Croft thought, was hiding and protecting the men he knew were inside. Then Croft smelled burned humans.

There was only one body, presumably Peter's from its position at the left of the scorched, shattered cockpit. The grotesque figure had been thrust violently forward and was pried with difficulty from the broken steering column and instrument panel. Both arms, rigid, were over the top of the panel, the left arm protruding through the shattered windscreen.

With its shaggy coat of torn and charred flying gear and flesh, the heat-swollen corpse resembled a gorilla. A gorilla caught scaling a wall. Croft and two enlisted men were at the top hatch, extricating Peter's body. One of Croft's unknown assistants slipped on the wet wing of the Mosquito and the body slipped out of their cold hands. It landed on its back with a dull smack, rocking back and forth. The fixed arms and legs reached skyward, as if warding off the gentle rain. A horrible thought flashed through Croft's numbed brain: *Peter doesn't look like an ape, he looks like an ebony Buddha fallen off its pedestal!*

The Mosquito's hatch was missing; Trice had evidently bailed out.

Next morning, Croft was going through the effects of both men for they had each named him for the dreadful task. He put the letters of Laurie Berridge to Steve Trice in a brown RAF envelope and addressed it to her in Bedford. Bill McLaughlin came in and said they'd found Steve's body in a schoolyard in Lowestoft.

Three days later, the funeral was held at the American Military Cemetery in Cambridge. Commander Dampier was there. More than half of 68 Squadron came. Laurie Berridge and her parents stood off from the rest until Bill McLaughlin went over and brought them to stand with the squadron. He had met Laurie only once, a frail, lovely girl who had hovered around Trice like a friendly vapor.

At the far end of the cemetery, a body of gravediggers was making a new, long trench. They were German prisoners of war. As the primitive sound of bugle taps died away, the rifle squad fired three volleys.

Immediately after that, the grave detail across the field began to raise an unearthly din with their shovels and picks. Four guards with automatic Brownings could not quiet them. Croft saw Karel Adeš step away from the burial party and run across the field. He was seen to speak to the Germans, who snapped to attention like iron filings in a magnetic field. They made no more noise.

Croft fell into step with Adeš walking out of the Cambridge cemetery. He asked what Karel had done to quiet the prisoners.

"I told them," said Karel, "that they would be quiet. I told them that if they were not respectful, they would be executed."

Nothing was more unlikely than a party in the Brevishall mess the night of the funeral. But factors were already at work to change the gloomy atmosphere of the place.

The weather over most of England was frightful; all flying was canceled. With both A-Flight and B-Flight on the ground at the same time, no one remembered ever seeing the mess so crowded after dinner or so depressed in spirit. Hardly anyone was talking and no one was laughing. The bar was having a record run.

Tarbox and Rothschild could not fly back to Ford and were in the drawing room with Adams-Ray, Dampier and McLaughlin, having coffee, listening to the eight o'clock news. Dampier had decided to cancel MACCABEE but had told no one yet, not even Air Vice-Marshal Swann. Six of his men were dead; Dampier was in shock.

It was when Stanley Holloway came on the radio with one of his famous monologues that Bill McLaughlin began to wonder where John Croft had gone . . .

I'll tell tha oov Magna Charter
As wair signed at barons' command,
On Runningmead Island in middle o'Thames
By King John, as wair known as "Lack Land."

. . . John loved Holloway and had even bought a small book of his ballads and scores. Once Rosemary Ince had played the mess piano while John tried to imitate the booming Lancashire dialect.

Surely no one thought the aloof John Croft would set off that night 68 Squadron's most historic bash. Even when he now and then drank his half-pint of mild draught, he was never moved to join in. But the night of the funeral found Croft silently drinking straight gin at the bar from eight to nine thirty. The party probably started when he disappeared from the mess.

Around ten o'clock, Bill McLaughlin was called to the phone. In a shrill voice reserved for catastrophes, an agitated Heather Stampford said that the lieutenant was prowling all around the dispersal area.

"Rotten drunk he is, Bill," the WAAF reported, "and howling for the moon. I came down to run up the Mossie, like he said, and found him marching around the ammunition shed, pounding on the door and walls. 'Let me out,' he says, 'get me out of here.' Bill, he was *outside* the shed! He's going to hurt himself but he won't listen to me. The sentry's watching him while I call you."

Wing/Co Adams-Ray took off in his RAF-blue Austin with McLaughlin, Dampier, Tarbox and Rothschild jammed in around him. Squadron Leader Monck sent Jock Spiller running for a van; a dozen of them piled in with Spiller, taking along their glasses and tankards of whiskey, bitter, shandys, black-and-tans. The party was public now.

John Croft stood ankle-deep in mud. With a bottle of gin in one hand, a glass in the other, he was holding the glass to K-for-King's chin.

"Won't drink, eh lady?" Croft was saying to the Mossie, "Well, try this!" He tossed a glassful of gin at the aircraft's nose. Then he saw his dumbstruck audience standing back with the sentry in a half-circle.

"Gentlemen," said Croft, his glass high, "I propose a toast . . . a toast to a bitch . . . a bitch toast . . . to K, to the de Havilland Mosquito."

Twenty solemn men stood at attention, most of them raising glasses full of rainwater. The rain was fierce. Bill McLaughlin was struck once more by the strange analogy between Croft and the Mosquito. Both of them looked clumsy on the ground: but in the air! In the air, the beautiful craft tucked its wheels away and, at the hand of its master, wrote music on the endless staffs of the sky.

They drove John Croft back to the mess. But two of them stayed down at dispersal, routing Sergeant Snead out of the sergeants' mess to set up a five-inch rocket to announce the party. So now the party had spread to the sergeants' mess.

Out on the airfield, Sergeant Snead fired off three rockets straight up. One of them came down in a neighboring farmer's well, sending him and his whole family into the village with news of an air raid. The second rocket landed across the field on the doorstep of the Tempest day-fighter squadrons' mess, an invitation to them to come to a party. The third rocket—and this was a mystery that Snead would live with for the rest of his life—the third rocket never came down at all.

Tarbox, who drank even less than Croft, was drunk. The squadron owl fascinated him and he had climbed up on the broad mantel to examine the owl's big eyes. Then he sat down on the mantel, swinging his legs. "Did you hear about the psychotic owl?" Tarbox asked the room at large. "He says 'Why? Why?' "

At two A.M. Squadron Leader Lawrence, chief fighter-director at Brookbridge, said he had to leave. Croft stood beside Lawrence's car, a soggy cigar in his left hand and a cigarette in the right—the pilot never smoked—waving the tobacco to the tune of "Frigging in the Rigging." As the car pulled away, Croft screamed out, "Watch that blind curve at the swamp" and fell headlong.

Some of the Tempest pilots had heard about the Wooden Wolf and now they were looking at him. He did not seem so forbidding close up.

"How did you choose night fighting, for God's sake?" one of them asked.

"I didn't," said Croft. "I joined the Navy because it was elite. Shit! Within two hours, I was on the ree-port, enough demerits to kick me out. I decided to survive because the Navy had planes I wanted to fly. I chose fighters because they were the best—and I got them. I chose carriers because not everyone can land on a ship—and I got them. I didn't choose night fighters, really, because a magician of a Navy commander talked me into it, but then I found that night fighters were even more exclusive than you are." The Tempest pilots grinned.

"And then there was the nervous owl," Tarbox said. "How, how? Where, where? When, when?"

At that moment, someone fired a Verey's flare down the chimney and it blew the log fire out into the drawing room. Tarbox jumped off the mantel and screamed as loud as ever he could.

Dr. McGillicuddy said that Archie Tarbox had a broken collarbone and he mixed up a batch of plaster of Paris on the spot to make a cast. Jock Spiller, the London bobby, fainted when the doc set Archie's slender bones. With extra plaster on his hands, the doc put Jock's good arm in a cast for fun.

"That's his right arm you've done, Paddy," said the Wing/Co.

"Sure and you're right, Booster. Well, he'll learn fast to write with the left. In a couple of weeks we'll take his little arm out of the cast with its withered muscles and we'll build him up again. No harm."

It was then that Commander Dampier told Croft, McLaughlin and Rothschild that he was calling MAC-CABEE off. They overrode him. Croft said he would have to fly the mission alone except for cover by his friend, Karel Adeš. "More than two planes, Commander," said Croft, "would be unnecessary and dangerous."

Seth Rothschild took a small gold Star of David on a slender chain from his neck. "My brother, Ephraim, gave this to me when I was small. Will you carry it, John? Archie and I can't do it. Will you be a Jew for a while and go after this monster? God bless you, you and Bill."

Bill McLaughlin cried. Croft took the star and held it up in his fist.

"I'll kill him, Seth," said Croft, "and I'll bring this silly trinket back with his blood, so help me."

On November 20, the night of the party, Adolf Hitler left the Wolf's Lair in East Prussia for the last time. He returned to Berlin. When Commander Dampier went back to London, he would learn that Hitler's next move would be a retreat from Berlin to the south. A retreat across the River Danube, at the Donauwörth bridge. There was no other way.

PART THREE

Operation MACCABEE

I have crossed out on the attached paper many
unsuitable names. Operations in which large
numbers of men may lose their lives ought not to
be described by code-words which imply a boast-
ful and overconfident sentiment . . . Proper names
are good in this . . . heroes of antiquity, figures
from Greek and Roman mythology, the con-
stellations and stars, famous racehorses, names
of British and American war heroes . . . Care
should be taken in all this process. An efficient
and successful administration manifests itself
equally in small as in great matters.

Winston S. Churchill

URGENT: TOP AND MOST SECRET

12

The Signal

"Hallo! Adams-Ray speaking."

The Air Ministry signal came in by scrambler phone on November 30 and it caught the Wing/Co wheels up after all. His opening boom was down ten decibels when the London caller rang off. But like a desk sergeant, he had automatically jotted down the time, 22.45. The pencil tip touched a number he'd put on the blotter three weeks earlier. The beefy fingers of his left hand curled toward the station phone. It was a Norwich number.

"If you call, Booster," Croft had said, "I'll be at the Ops block in half an hour."

That was the number the CO gave the station operator. He heard three rings. Each double buzz set off a muscular pull between his left eye and the corner of his mouth. By lifting up one half of the reddish, carefully grown guardsman's mustache, the tic was amplified and the unfortunate effect was that of a gull's broken wing. Around Brevishall, it was a well-known gauge of Vivian Adams-Ray's emotional state.

"Rosemary Ince here." It was a young voice, practiced in communication, faintly Scottish.

"Is Lieutenant Croft there, please?"

"He is." The woman's voice sounded as if she had

173

tilted the mouthpiece away. "Whom shall I say is calling?"

"This is Wing Commander Adams-Ray at Brevishall. The, ah——"

"I know. A moment, please."

It now seemed as if the phone at the other end of the line had been smothered in a pillow. The CO stared rigidly into the shadows beyond reach of his desk lamp, frowning.

A familiar voice, he thought.

After the NFT on K-for-King, John Croft had gone straightaway into Norwich for late tea at the Broadmoor with Rosemary. The WREN sublieutenant waved to catch his attention when he appeared at the entrance to the crowded dining room. He waved back, smiling in his embarrassed way, never taking his eyes off her, until he collided noisily with a loaded cart of sweets and savories. Rosemary laughed, notwithstanding that the genteel hum of the room was swept by waves of low crisis.

"Really," she asked John, when he had finally bowed his way from the scene of the accident, "how do you manage to fly right side up?"

"Bill McLaughlin takes care of everything."

An old gentleman across the dining room was basking harmlessly in the radiance of the trim, handsome blonde in the severe naval jacket and the elegant black velvet tricorn. In the overwhelming presence of his chalked and painted, finely wrinkled mate, it was not an easy pastime.

"Look at her, Eustace," said the man's wife, "didn't I tell you she'd be waiting for an American? That type have no pride, do they?"

"None, m'love," said the old fellow, his weak eyes glittering.

In spite of the rain, John and Rosemary had gone window-shopping. They had not reached her flat until seven o'clock. Rosemary said it would be hours until dinner, which she began to prepare on a wretched hotplate furnished with the flat.

"I haven't known many girls," said John, "—*any* girls—who cooked in the nude."

Rosemary's jacket, a thin, wavy, gold stripe on each cuff, hung upon a peg near the door. Her skirt was draped over the foot of the bed, a brass monstrosity capped at either end by barred frames like prison windows. On a chair and a cracked marble table were her shirt and tie, slip, brassiere and stockings. Croft rested on the bed, shooting hazelnuts into a wastebasket with Rosemary's garterbelt.

By ten thirty, they had long finished dinner and, for a shorter time, each other. They lay close together on the hard bed. In the cell-like room, the only light came through the high transom from a naked bulb outside in the hallway ceiling. An ancient alarm clock on the marble table ate time loudly, methodically, like the jaws of a senseless leaf-cutter. Rosemary felt her heartbeats mix with the clock's metallic rhythm: *lub-dub, lub-click, dub-twang, click-twang, click-twang.*

"I have a surprise for you, John," she whispered.

"I know. I found it weeks ago."

"Stop! I really have something you like."

"You bet. I worship it."

"Vulgar American!" Rosemary slapped his hand away and rolled off the bed. Laughing, she went to the bureau and opened her kit. From a nest of cotton, she removed and held up three eggs.

"See? I got these this morning for nothing."

"I can well understand. Why, a girl like you could go through life without any money at all, couldn't you? Maybe a little spare change for busses and the underground."

"*Will* you be serious! I thought you might like to have them for breakfast."

"Not your rations, Rose. You know we get extras for night flying. The RAF thinks eggs, carrots and vitamin A are good for your night vision."

"But these aren't my rations. They're—a friend who hates eggs gave them to me."

"Lawrence?"

Rosemary nodded. Squadron Leader Lawrence

was Rosemary's chief, the senior fighter-director officer at Brookbridge.

"He's in love with you, Rosemary. You shouldn't give all his presents to another man. Even if the other man is me."

"Lawrence is not in love with me! Why, he's all of forty years—"

The telephone rang. Rosemary dropped an egg. It smashed at her feet. She stared at the phone, until John sat up in the bed. Startled by the noisy springs, she lifted the receiver slowly.

"Rosemary Ince here." She had moved and was talking as if a drug were taking hold of her. Croft rested his chin on drawn-up knees, admiring the backs of her fine, long legs.

"He is . . . whom shall I say is calling?"

The telephone mouthpiece pressed firmly into a breast, Rosemary said, "It's your commanding officer, John." She did not turn until Croft had leaped over the foot of the bed and taken the phone. Then she retreated as if she had been whipped, to stand with her back against the door.

"Hello, Booster, this is John."

"Sorry about the intrusion, John. The show is on."

"I don't believe it! Well, I'm all set. Give me twenty minutes."

"Fine, there'll be a good hour or more. You have transport?"

Croft half turned toward Rosemary; a shiver nipped at the small of her back. "Yes."

"All right then, we'll be standing by. The others are out here. We're rounding them up."

As he hung up, Croft was absorbing the shock of something he had thought of for the first time while the CO was speaking. *Rosemary! In all the intricate planning, it had simply not occurred to him.*

"Well," he said, "they can't seem to get along without me. By the way, Rosie, I never asked if you were on duty tonight." He knew it didn't sound right. He almost never called her Rosie.

"In fact, I am on. After midnight. What did he want? You have to fly, don't you?"

"We have to stand by, at least. One of the A-Flight crews turned up sick." He didn't mind the lying but it was so useless now. His thoughtlessness was going to tear up five hours of her life.

"But you aren't on tonight, John! I should have thought they'd bags of spare crews on the station."

"Ordinarily. But there's been some kind of under-scheduling at Group." Rosemary wasn't all that familiar with RAF procedures.

John pulled on his shorts. Rosemary threw her mac around her bare shoulders and started out the door with her bag, toward the only w.c. on the floor. As the harsh hall light flooded the small bedroom, she looked back. Something about him, his shadow, reminded her of the shop window in Norwich that afternoon.

They had stopped to look at the same old pewter mugs that John was planning to buy. The sun had partially emerged; reflections from the wet pavement had blotted out the window display. John's image stood in the glass like a ghost. A ghost! Against her will, she had thought, *What if, one night, you do not come back to me?*

The Wing/Co was replacing his telephone when Jock Spiller stomped and shook his way noisily into the office. He slapped a soggy briefcase on the skipper's desk. He favored his "broken" arm.

"It's all there, Booster. I took a screw at the Met report, to see what lie they were putting out about this pre-bloody-cipitation. Says, mind you, says it'll dry up by midnight. Hah!" The red-faced Yorkshireman peeled off his soaked coat, which the rain had turned ultramarine from its regulation gray-blue.

"Let's hope, Jock. I'm concerned, you know, about the forecast *beyond* midnight. And further east."

"It's all there, all there. You've got every last executive order, too, for all of bloody England."

"Croft's on his way," the CO said. "I just called him. What about the others?"

"Right, Adeš and Miloslav are at the mess. Ten minutes, they said. McLaughlin left word at the mess he'd be at B-Flight. I'm off to find him now." But Spiller thought there might be time for a spot of hot tea. He paused. The skipper was sorting out signal flimsies and other papers from the briefcase.

"Oh," said Adams-Ray, looking up sharply, "they'll have some tea here for us by the time you get back."

The CO could see that it was going to be a big one tonight. Independent of MACCABEE but very helpful. From the Bomber Command orders, it appeared their first crews would go on the ready in about forty minutes. Poor devils! Like all experienced night fighters, Adams-Ray had seen too many of the big bombers end up as coffins. Seven good chaps, about fifteen Ops together on average, then the flaming funeral.

Lieutenant Croft had come boiling out of the hatch again that afternoon, following the NFT. Bill McLaughlin stood helplessly by, kicking one of the big tires.

"Stampford!" The pilot terrified her when he hissed like that, though his voice was so low that Heather could not have heard him from a yard further away. "According to the dials, the airscrews just twisted off the engines about ten miles out. What do you make of that?"

"Oh, Lieutenant, sir! Surely it's the indicators!"

"Yes, my dear, the rpm indicators. I don't really believe we pulled eight thousand rpm's, do you?" Croft's voice, not his face, was leering. The face was a reptile mask.

"Heavens no, sir! I'll take care of this, sir."

"And Stampford——"

"Yes sir! The pitch control mechanism. The engines."

"Thank you. Now, let me put it this way. I may wander down here after tea. If *anything* is out of line, if so much as the hatch door squeaks"——Croft reached

up and showed the WAAF that the door did squeak—
"I will set a fire under this kite and burn it. Do you
understand?"

As Croft marched stiffly to the perimeter road,
Bill McLaughlin smiled weakly at Heather. "He knows
its not your fault, honey, but find out what happened.
I'll see you later."

Heather skipped tea, to tackle the airscrew problem. It was getting so she spent sixteen hours a day
with the Mossie and the other eight worrying about it.
With some help, she found the trouble. They were still
working on it, two hours later, when the armorers arrived with the Tiny Tims.

"Green goods, lady," said Sergeant Snead. "Like
to try the leeks again?"

It was an old joke. The monster U.S. Navy rockets
vaguely resembled leeks. Eleven feet long and nearly
a foot in diameter, they had white noses, green shafts
and vanes. Snead's crew had put four of them in the
bomb bay every evening for a fortnight. If the lieutenant didn't fire them, the faithful sergeant took them
out in the morning. When Heather left them, they were
hoisting the first of the murderous beasts into the Mossie's belly.

After a hurried supper, the WAAF had pedaled
back through the driving rain. The armorers were gone.
Up in the cockpit, Sergeant Snead had left a note on the
control column, saying that he'd checked the emergency
flare colors of the day in the overhead pistol. Heather
raised the pilot's seat pan as high as it would go, to
accommodate her short, stout body. She could put it
back precisely where the lieutenant wanted it. She
started the run-up of the port engine.

The lieutenant had left standing orders that he
wanted the engines checked every hour after the NFT.
Heather would also test the generator and electrical
systems, including all lights, hydraulic pressures, instrument vacuum, heating, engine cooling gills and
flaps. And, of course, the blasted pitch controls!

Waiting for proper cylinder temperatures, Heather
surveyed her cockpit with pride. A charwoman oc-

cupying the executive chair in the wee hours, she amused herself with an old game. She always took the part of the lieutenant.

"All right, Bill," she said, looking over at the empty seat to her right, "I see this one now."

Heather switched on the electric gunsight. She squinted through the red pattern hanging in space before the slanted glass plate.

"Keep him in the scope . . . ranges, please . . . okay, five hundred yards . . . bang on, we're holding nice and steady . . . see him, Bill? . . . right under him now."

The WAAF eased back on the stick and tapped the rudder pedals, almost out of her reach.

"It's a bloody one-eleven!"

She pressed the gunbutton on the control grip.

"Chung-a-chung-a-chung-a-chung-a-chung-chung-CHUNG!"

Her body shook with each imagined round. Heather liked the sound and power of cannon. But they had long ago taken out all the cannon to make room for the rockets.

"There he goes, Bill . . . splash one Heinkel! . . . shall we pack it up?" Heather glanced knowingly at the empty seat. "Can't wait to get back to your little Waafie, can you?"

Heather ran the port engine up to 2000 rpm. By that time, Bill McLaughlin was on the ladder, reaching across the cockpit to tickle her ankle. Ten minutes later, she joined him in the unlighted ammunition shack.

An icy formality had settled into the tiny Morris with the Scottish plates. It was confirmed and intensified by fierce rain beating the windows and condensed vapor clouding the glass inside.

"Are you coming back to Norwich from Brevishall or going straight out to Brookbridge?" asked John. The idiot secrecy of MACCABEE tormented him. He toyed with the idea of an innocent phrase that would tell her. . . .

"Brookbridge, of course," snapped Rosemary. "I have to be there before twelve, you know."

John was convinced that Rosemary's shortcut would get them hopelessly lost. He was stubborn on that point, until the car came around a bend in the unfamiliar road. Without comment, Rosemary flicked her hand toward the flat, murky expanse of the airfield.

After passing the Brevishall sentries, Rosemary asked if John wanted to go to the mess, his quarters, or the B-Flight dispersal.

"Ops," he said. "Do you know where that is?"

For an answer, the WREN executed a smart, almost vicious turnabout on the main road. She always drove with maximum concentration, hands high on the wheel. Her skirt was thrown back to the hips. Not an hour ago, those great long legs had gripped John as if to strangle him. When she drove or shopped or read a newspaper, he almost forgot that she loved like an animal.

Rosemary brought the Morris to a jolting stop in front of the Ops block. She folded her arms across the stop of the wheel.

"Well, Lieutenant?"

He was thinking that she would be at Brookbridge long before he was airborne. It depressed him so that he could not speak. Instead, he opened the door and went around to her side of the car. She had got out and was standing to meet him. He clasped her tightly, kissing her face blindly.

"Rose, I love you."

Rosemary shook her head, splashing rain from the rolled brim of her hat into his face. Croft looked up into the invisible sky. He knocked her hat off and they laughed as he picked it up and wiped it off with his sleeve.

"I don't think anyone will be flying out of England tonight," he said. It was a stupid remark, no better than an incantation. "But I guess you have to get back in that car and report for duty. I'll see you at the flat in the morning, okay?" She nodded dumbly, as he hugged her and opened the car door.

"Will you say it once more?" She had rolled down the window.

"What?"

"That you love me. I don't know what made you say it now but it doesn't matter. I'll think about it all morning."

"Well, I do. You've known it all along."

"No. Just say it, please."

"I love you."

She rolled up the window. The little car leaped away from the curb and disappeared in the rain.

Except for a policeman's instinct, Jock Spiller would have barged right into the ammunition shack. A woman was whispering. He stopped at the threshold.

"Are you there, Mac?" he called. Only Jock called McLaughlin "Mac."

"Is that you, Jock?"

"Right. The skipper wants all of you up in his office, soon as possible. Sorry, Mac."

The adjutant was startled by McLaughlin's sudden appearance at the door.

"Let's go," the American said. "We may have to fly in this stuff but I damn sure wouldn't walk through it. I'll ride with you."

The Czechs and Bill McLaughlin were in the Wing/Co's office when Croft arrived. Karel Adeš was smiling blandly, as always, holding the perpetual cigarette in his stiff, reversed manner. He squinted from time to time, inhaling the smoke deeply.

"Gentlemen!" The Wing/Co came back into his office and closed the door. "I have now had two signals from Air Ministry. At this moment, Hitler's train is moving with all speed some thirty miles below Berlin. Pending further reports, it seems you would want to depart in about one hour. That will give you your thirty minutes on the target site. Have you had a chance to look this bumpf over?" The CO waved his pipe toward the contents of the briefcase.

"Yes, Wing Commander," said Adeš. "We did not find here the latest weather. This"—he held up a pink flimsy—"is an hour old."

"Karel, a Met flight is due back about the time you will be taking off. If you have gone before his data are in, they will be encoded to you en route. Also, a photorec pilot from 1409 Flight will be bringing back his pictures in the next hour. His information may be of value to you."

"Skipper," asked McLaughlin, "what are the highlights of the big operation? Frankfurt?"

"Yes, Bill, Frankfurt and a bit more. The main force, about nine hundred bombers, will be on stage between Holland and Frankfurt from 0200 to 0400. Your strike should come off roughly in the middle of the Frankfurt raid. Meanwhile, there will be a dozen or so small siren raids all over north Germany, around the clock. The Fast Night Striking Force will put on a special show at Berlin. And you will see here that the *Oboe* people will be handling your relay communications. Please be sure to check the proper channels."

"What are these objects near the bridge, Booster?" asked Croft. He was holding several photoprints. "We haven't seen them, have we?"

"No, John, they came in a few hours ago. P.R. have not interpreted them fully. To take the dimmest view, they are saying we should consider them to be flak barges."

"I'm not surprised," said Croft. "Photorec still claims no flak emplacements on the bridge itself?"

"Emphatically. That comes from ground agents' reports, as well as aerial pictures. We've sent urgent requests to have agents look into these spots you see on the river. I hope we'll know more about them within the hour."

"Very strange," said Croft, "a bridge like this without guns." He loathed flak, especially the unpredicted kind.

"Draho and I will have binoculars," said Bill McLaughlin. "At the worst, we'll have a chance to scan them from a distance before they open fire on us."

"Have you chaps had any last-minute thoughts on the—the protocol of the, ah, last step?" Adams-Ray knew that this, paradoxically, was almost beyond planning. It was a matter of hunches rather than tactics.

"Ah, Booster," said Croft, "the big chop!" He and Adeš exchanged knowing glances. "We've come back to the old scheme. Karel will blast in high from the east side of the bridge, while we stooge down the river low from the west." He laughed. "That may change again when we get there."

Adams-Ray nodded sympathetically. "Well, lads" —he glanced at his watch—"it's past the time for lessons. I'll be on hand here to pass the latest gen."

"Booster," Croft asked, "where's the key to the model?" He had to speak privately to Adams-Ray about Rosemary.

"Here is the key," said Karel. "I went there after supper. Everything was good-looking and peaceful." The Czech handed Croft a small slab of wood with a big key attached.

Adams-Ray was standing at his window, sizing up the weather. "Better take my car, John," he said, turning, "or you'll get soaked." The message in Croft's eyes was immediately apparent. "Here, let me show you where it's parked." He followed the American into the hallway.

"Some kind of a bind, John?"

"You know Lawrence at Brookbridge pretty well, don't you?" Croft explained Rosemary's situation; how she was going to see something she wouldn't understand at all. "Maybe you can bail her out, Booster," he said.

"You know I'll do my best," said the Wing/Co. "It'll be sticky. Lawrence will have fits over my interest in the girl. Sublieutenant Rosemary Ince, you say?" His facial twitch came on again. The girl on the telephone!

The abandoned air-raid shelter felt like a butcher's cold-storage room. Croft's hand slid across the damp wall to the switch and turned on the overhead lights.

An elaborate display was spread over a table, thirty feet long and ten feet wide, resting a yard off the floor on a framework. A shining river coursed up the center of the structure. Near one end, an old-fashioned bridge spanned the river perpendicularly. Its middle cantilever section extended without support between triple-arched, stone bridgeheads on the banks.

The scale of the model gave a standing man an effective altitude of 500 feet. Other heights between 100 and 1600 feet—there was a ten-foot ceiling—were achieved from a traveling, adjustable platform, which was suspended between rolling trucks on either side of the table. Most of the river surface was laid in removable squares, so that almost any desired surface-level view of the bridge was also accessible to an observer kneeling on the floor below the table.

Few experts who took part in building the scene had even the faintest idea what it was. None knew what it was for. Among the twenty-odd Britons there had been carpenters, plasterers, artists, draftsmen, machinists, toolmakers and electricians. Also a cake decorator, a landscape architect, a designer of golf courses from Scotland and two railroad buffs. The rail modelers may have had the best clue: they built from scratch a small train of ten pieces, including a German Pacific engine and two strange gun wagons.

Road Research Laboratory types from Teddington had drawn the plans. They knew they were replicating a Bavarian rectangle, about one mile long and one-third mile wide. The river was the Danube. The bridge crossed near Donauwörth.

From an ingenious electrical panel, Croft could dial in almost any conditions of moon and cloud. He knelt at the lower end of the table, to peer through an optical device. It had been designed with the bridge, the Mosquito, and the Tiny Tim rockets in mind. The pilot advanced the control of a variable transformer. From a cleft in the mountains at the left, the north, rolled a marvelous little train. It was *Asia*. . . .

". . . This is the closest we will get to Czechoslovakia," said Engineer Nowarra. *Asia* was climbing steadily into the mountainous Thuringian forest. Czechoslovakia pressed a thin fingertip into Germany here, not more than ten miles from the track.

Fireman Bauer could not see beyond ten meters from his side of *Asia*'s cab. The snow turned the black trunks of the forest into a gray-striped wall. The fireman's first Berlin–Munich run had been a maze of landmarks, timechecks and estimates, flowing continuously out of the engineer's head.

"When do we get to Nuremberg?" asked Bauer.

"Ninety minutes, at this rate," said Nowarra. "We have a ten-minute stop there."

Bauer leaned over and saw that they were holding about eighty-five kilometers an hour upgrade. He liked to make calculations in his head, but he didn't trust them.

"When do we get to Munich?" he asked.

"Allowing for Nuremberg," said Nowarra, "about a quarter over three hours." Then the engineer gave a startled cry, as the fireman felt a light thump from the front of the locomotive.

"What the devil was that?" exclaimed Bauer.

"I don't know—we hit something. I saw its eyes in the beams. Probably a deer."

A few seconds later, Bauer saw Nowarra lean far out his window, looking down and back toward something in the snow. "It just fell off," said the engineer, "a big wolf."

The Bedford lorry stopped at Ops to pick up the two crews at five minutes to twelve. Adams-Ray had found no chance to speak with Croft about the WREN. He rode over to B-Flight with them, where they would change into flight gear. Croft was pulling things out of his locker when he noticed the Wing/Co standing beside him. The skipper's twitch was very bad. His voice was unnaturally weak.

"No luck, John. Lawrence thought it would not do to send Miss Ince off the station without reason. Especially since they were already one hand short tonight. He had her working at the scopes before I called. I was in no position to explain, as you know." The Wing/Co's eyes were asking the American to understand.

"Thanks, Booster," said Croft.

"Even so," Adams-Ray blurted emotionally, "I shall call Lawrence and order her out of there, if you say so."

"No, she's not a fool. It's too late to fix it now."

The lorry dropped the crews at the parking pans like registered mail. Heather greeted Croft as if he had not insulted her mortally after the NFT. "The aircraft is ready, sir," she said. "Your helmet is on the steering column." She smiled secretly at McLaughlin.

Croft climbed the ladder and crept through the hatch to the left side of the cockpit. Heather had arranged everything; it was like taking the chair in a dentist's office. McLaughlin poked his head up, after kissing Heather quickly. The pilot was attaching himself to the Mossie: the parachute, safety harness, oxygen tube, radio cord.

Heather walked out in front of the port engine. The battery cart was in place ready to fire off the engines electrically. She switched on one of her Lucite torches and, pointing at the engine, rotated it in a small circle. Croft pressed the starter button and let the Merlin come to an idle at 1200 rpm. They repeated the ritual for the starboard engine. Croft called the tower, to check his radio.

"FERRULE, this is Cricket One-Niner. How do you read me? Over."

"Cricket One-Niner, we hear you five by five. Please call again when ready. Out."

Croft heard Karel speak to the tower. After turning the engines up to test magnetoes and flaps, he waved to Heather. With the cherry-colored torches, she directed the Mossie out of its resting place. Bill strained for a last glimpse of the WAAF over Croft's shoulder, through the port windows. He could not see her waving as they rumbled away. "God bless," she murmured.

Adeš moved out next from his parking spot, to follow Croft at a distance of thirty yards. It amused him, the way the American taxied the Mosquito as if it were a racing car. He thought Croft was the perfect weapon, hard as a cutting tool of tungsten steel. "Draho," exulted Karel, "think of what we are going to do!"

At the downwind end of the flarepath, Croft turned into the wind and held the brakes. Each engine was again run up to full power, to clear them and recheck the mags. When he had also set the trim tabs, mixture control, propeller pitch, supercharger and engine gills for takeoff, he pressed the microphone button.

"FERRULE, this is Cricket One-Niner requesting takeoff clearance. Over."

"One-Niner, you are clear. Please call us when you are airborne. Out." A green Aldis light winked several times out of the tower.

Croft gunned the Merlins, turning the Mosquito up the path between the blue lights. When the wheels were barely unstuck from the ground, he flipped up the undercarriage lever and called the tower in the climbaway. They gave him a heading to the coast and an altitude, at which he should report on channel D to ARGUS. That was the Brookbridge fighter control station on the marshes between Lowestoft and Great Yarmouth.

"ARGUS, this is Cricket One-Niner at angels five, approaching the edge, over."

"Good morning, One-Niner, this is ARGUS." It was Rosemary. "Welcome to our range. Vector oh-niner five, please, to angels ten. Over." The radio always brought back the faint Scottish curl to her voice, which Croft no longer noticed when he spoke to her on the ground.

"Wilco, ARGUS. One-Niner out."

Crossing the coast over Lowestoft, Croft heard Karel introduce himself to ARGUS in his self-effacing manner. He said "Cree-kett Two-Zayro." The Czech thought his radio voice, the accent, was a liability. But according to Rosemary, Karel's deep, mournful tones thrilled the women at Brookbridge.

"You have a picture," she explained, "of this civilized Genghis Khan preparing to rape you."

Like a pair of sharks rising from the ocean floor, the Mosquitoes climbed to precise locations over the North Sea. As if exchanging sentry duty with them, two other Mosquitoes dropped down toward England from very high altitudes and from different directions.

The more northerly machine was still recording meteorological information along a track that had started over Berlin. The pilot and his observer had taken off their oxygen masks when they had come down to 15,000 feet, to have a snack of chocolate and sultanas. In the second Mosquito, three big cameras had automatically snapped photoflash pictures of Germany in a wide swath from the Danube to the Ruhr. These aircraft were unarmed, except for their complex instruments.

Over the sea, the moonless sky was void of ordinary clouds. For a brief moment, the photoreconnaissance plane descended through an invisible stratum, which pulled a long, double streamer of condensed moisture contrails out behind its engines. The white streak resembled frosting from a pastry tube. To the north, there was a delicate mother-of-pearl formation, suggesting an aurora to the inexperienced eye. But these rare clouds, like the contrails, were also bodies of moisture, moving at hundreds of miles an hour, fifteen or more miles above the surface of the earth.

ARGUS directed Croft and Adeš to opposite ends of a forty-mile line running north and south, halfway between London and Holland. From a point forty miles east of Felixstowe, Croft flew south on the first leg. Starting seventy miles east of the Thames Estuary, Adeš flew north. ARGUS was prepared to divert the night fighters from this patrol line down onto Heinkel 111's, which were now coming low over the sea to launch buzzbombs toward England.

Halfway through the second leg, Croft gave the signal to Adeš over the privileged channel, F. The American held an orbit until the Czech crew had picked him up, first on their radar and then visually. Both Mosquitoes dove steeply toward sea level, to begin the business of MACCABEE.

Squadron Leader Lawrence, at Brookbridge, was just learning that he could not raise the Cricket patrol, when he heard Sublieutenant Ince gasp. Monitoring the azimuth scope, she was gripping the arms of her chair, pushing back and staring in horror at the glass.

"What is it, Ince?" Still speaking softly into his headset, Lawrence had come over behind the girl.

"Sir! This can't be real!" Rosemary twisted round to see the FDO's calm face, to be told it was an instrument failure. "I'm losing them completely. Look!"

The yellow-green blips were leaving tracks down the face of her scope.

"I don't know, Rosemary." Lawrence had a midair collision in mind; he was not going to put her off with lies. "It looks very bad. Be prepared for the worst."

Rosemary barely heard the chief's dogged voice, then, calling every few seconds. He continued at that pace for twenty minutes, although everyone in the room knew that they had disappeared from the screens in less than thirty seconds. Lawrence went on calling every few minutes until dawn, about one hour after the last drop of petrol would have been sucked through the engines.

As Brookbridge's scheduled aircraft landed through the early morning hours, the station personnel began going off duty in small, sad clusters. Lawrence felt deeply his responsibility to say something to Rosemary, somehow. When they were finally alone, he could say nothing. It took all his courage to leave without speaking. He did not have the heart to turn off the radars she was still watching.

As the hidden sun traced a phantom horizon in the east, Rosemary spoke at last to the flickering screens.

"John," she cried, addressing the stupid, cataractous eyes as if they were alive, "John, what has happened to you?"

The only answer was an occasional spike of noise in the sea return at the bottom of the electronic rasters.

13

Penetration, Holland

When the blips fell from the Brookbridge radars, it was the metamorphosis of MACCABEE.

At 400 miles an hour, Croft eased the whistling Mosquito out of its long dive. Karel Adeš trailed slightly below, to the right. The needles of their barometric altimeters, unreliable now, trembled around the hundred-foot mark. Croft continued dropping, but very slowly.

The moonless surface of the water was difficult to fix, except for the breaking of occasional white water into patches of lather. From the length and straightness of streaks scudding directly across the invisible waves, McLaughlin estimated a steady wind force of fifteen knots out of the northeast.

Adeš, his own cockpit less than a dozen feet above the North Sea, saw the fan-shaped wake generated on the water by the slim shadow ahead. Croft's propeller blades skimmed a yard or two above the waves. Turning the radio altimeter to zero, he set its flasher—a trio of yellow, green and red jewel lights— to monitor fifty feet exactly. Bringing the Mossie up to that height, he watched the lights for a moment and then throttled back to a steady 230 miles an hour, the speed chosen to launch the Tiny Tim rockets.

"Let's see the Dambuster lights, Bill," said Croft. On the tinny intercom, the emotionless voice sounded like a bad wire recording.

McLaughlin unstrapped himself, folded the seat down and lay on the deck. He peered forward under his radar scopes into the crowded nose space, where a specially fitted window gave him a view downward. Flipping a switch, he watched the beams of two powerful yellow lights from the wingtips skip erratically across the choppy water, like playful, luminous fish. The beams were angled to converge fifty feet below the center of the Mossie's keel. Croft flew under McLaughlin's instructions until they had the fused spot dancing along the surface.

They had called it the Dambuster system because Guy Gibson of 617 Squadron had used the simple altitude-keeper to deliver the complicated, rotating *Upkeep* bombs at the Möhne, Eder and Sorpe dams. McLaughlin had cleverly solved, for the Tiny Tim rockets, the critical problem of the aircraft's attitude, its fore-and-aft tilt relative to speed and trim. Looking down toward the water through a free-swinging, vertical sight, the navigator told Croft where the fused spot of light was in the sight, as the pilot made small changes of throttle and trim-tab. *If they were selling the device,* Croft had once remarked, *they could hardly charge half a quid for it.* Bill had jury-rigged the sight out of spare parts. It was infallible, working by gravity alone. When the spot of light on the water was centered in the crosshairs, Croft made the sophisticated electronic altimeter agree with his navigator's crude gadget.

"Seven minutes to the beach, John." Croft grunted.

McLaughlin was back in his seat, the red penlight casting little red circles on the special strip maps. Below his windows, the hypnotizing blur of the etched sea fascinated him. McLaughlin had heard about sensory deprivation; that might explain his stupid feeling of security. The sea. Low and safe from radar. Droning engines, beating faintly out of sync. The fainter humming of the solid airframe. A soft red glow: the penlight, the circles, the instrument panel. An overheated, cramped cockpit. Even Croft's grim silence was reassuring.

What are you doing here, McLaughlin? You're a fucking lawyer! Safe from radar, so you hit the mast of a ship or a flock of birds. You'd freeze to death in five minutes down there. You're soft and harmless, you love women. You hate pain, you're William McLaughlin, man! What in God's name are you doing in this airplane?

The nav/rad's thoughts were terminated by a definite break in the elusive horizon. He'd been here before.

"It's the West Schelde, John."

The Americans could see land now on both sides of the estuary's mouth, five miles wide. A large Allied convoy was moving up toward Antwerp. The flooded island of Walcheren, once a shallow salver edged by massive dunes and heavily fortified, looked like the ruins of a child's sand castle. RAF bombers had blasted a huge gap through the dyke at Westkapelle. The inrushing sea, with the help of British and Canadian troops, had taken Walcheren on November 4.

At the narrow throat of the Schelde, between Flushing and Breskens, the prominent windmill still stood on the low cliff on the south shore. Its arms were broken now, so that it resembled a swastika more than a Maltese cross. The guns of Fort Frederik Hendrik were silenced.

"I make it 0051," said McLaughlin, as they flew by the marker windmill, "and your course to Verdun is one-five-zero." He felt the Mosquito turn gently. The number 15 slid under the index of the gyrocompass. "Thirty-five minutes."

"Any checkpoints on the way?" asked Croft.

"Ghent, Charleroi, Brussels. Brussels will be fifteen miles north."

They were only in Holland two minutes.

The leading elements of Bomber Command's main force were assembling over thirty airfields in Lincolnshire and Yorkshire when the MACCABEE Mosquitoes came down to sea level. The loose stream of 900 four-engined heavies—first-rate Lancasters, obsolescent Stirlings, obsolete Halifaxes—would grow over more than an hour until it was about 170 miles long. Despite strict orders to pack the stream, height bands would be ignored and the width would spread to fifteen miles.

Twenty-four earth-colored Lancasters of No. 100 Group, the famed Pathfinder Force, labored clumsily upward over the Wash toward the assembly point at Great Yarmouth, a hundred miles to the southeast. Upon the elite PFF squadron, commanded and led by Wing Commander Hector Timmins, rested the central responsibility of marking the target accurately, with *Oboe*'s help, and dropping the first bombs.

The PFF leader twisted his pelvis into a more comfortable position under the seatbelt and began his famous intercom "rounds." The six in his crew, he felt, liked to have this intimate contact. Had he been a ship's captain, instead of the skipper of a tubeful of bulkheads, beams, struts, control rods, oxygen tubes, ammunition magazines and runways, wires and cables, Timmins would have strolled the decks to show himself before the battle. By some dispensation from Air Ministry, the wing commander was in the middle of his fourth tour in bombers. Since he should rightly have died about halfway through the second tour, he was a good luck piece to all who flew with him or in the sky near him.

"Pilot to rear gunner," said Timmins into his oxygen mask microphone, "are you with us, old son?" He never varied the order of calling them; they would have been troubled. Sixty feet back from the cabin, the tail gunner sat in his cold, drafty turret. It was his task, if the night fighters came, to destroy them while providing an "accurate and unimpassioned commentary" to the pilot.

"Pilot to mid-upper gunner. . . ." The second active gun position was on top of the fuselage. A nose turret was never manned except on low-altitude missions; a ventral turret was not fitted in Timmins' machine. "Both you chaps, remember," the pilot said, "no firing over the Wash. You can test when we leave

Yarmouth." The two air gunners constantly exercised their servo-driven turrets and gunmounts, to keep the hydraulic fluid and the lubrication from freezing and to maintain some control over taut nerves.

The remaining four crew members shared the cabin with Timmins.

"Pilot to navigator. . . ." At a portside table, the navigator sat directly behind the pilot's armored seat, tracking the course by dead reckoning, mainly, with help from several electronic black boxes. Celestial fixes were hardly ever taken through the cabin astrodome.

"Pilot to wireless operator. . . ." The radioman was surrounded by his W/T and R/T equipment at the after end of the navigator's table, monitoring all voice and key transmissions and radiobeacon bearings. He was the official timekeeper and, for emergencies, was also a trained air gunner.

"Pilot to bomb-aimer. . . ." Only in the final run-up to the target was the bomb-aimer required to be at his station in the Lancaster's Perspex chin. At other times, he assisted the navigator.

Timmins never made a formal call to the flight engineer, who sat on a collapsible seat at the pilot's right shoulder. From his own instrument panel on the starboard wall, he managed the engines constantly and was Timmins' right hand at takeoff and landing. Theoretically, the flight engineer could land the Lancaster if the pilot were incapacitated. RAF bombers carried no copilots.

PFF eliteness was marked in curious ways. Timmins and every man in his crew proudly wore a brass badge on the left breast pocket. It was the same badge all RAF air crew noncoms wore over their sleeve chevrons. If that was an obscure economy, more obscure was the PFF privilege of flying sixty trips in a full tour of duty, not the usual thirty.

From bases at Gransden Lodge, Oakington, Downham Market, Woodhall Spa and Little Staughton, the Fast Night Striking Force had committed ninety Mosquitoes to the night's Berlin Express. Two waves of the No. 8 Group squadrons were scheduled to bomb the German capitol, with an interval of two hours. For the round trip of four hours, each Mosquito carried two fifty-gallon slipper tanks on its wings. In every bomb bay was a 4000-pound boiler-shaped, high-explosive "cookie," which Bomber Command had once believed could not be carried by the small fighter-bomber.

Sixteen aircraft, the Marker squadron that would lay down the target flares at Berlin for the first wave of sixty, roared in a low, wide circle around the airfield at Woodhall Spa, awaiting the takeoff of its last two Mossies. One of these was rolling halfway along the flarepath, holding ground to the last moment for maximum speed. It was the approved technique for dragging a cookie aloft, to minimize the awful hazard of engine failure.

The pilot and navigator of the last Mosquito, new replacements to the squadron, watched from the downwind takeoff point. They saw the other airplane, almost at the far side of the airfield, take the air briefly, bounce down again and then swerve up as if the right wing had caught a giant crab in the wind. The starboard engine *had* failed! At a height of only five feet, the doomed Mosquito carried away a section of the perimeter fence with its undercart. It plowed only twenty yards of the wood before the bomb exploded in a ball of white fire. The shockwave rocked the replacement crew in their cockpit across the field and rattled china in the sergeants' mess.

Holy mother of God! The Irish navigator felt his pilot push the throttles forward for their own takeoff run. *We're mad, insane!* He was thinking like a civilian in a commercial transport who had seen the plane ahead go up in flames. As they flashed straight over the fiery scene at the edge of the station, he saw the rescue and fire vehicles crawling out from the Ops block.

The Marker squadron, minus one, climbed fast out of England to gain height in smooth, clear air. It was bad form and not a little dangerous to wobble through cumulonimbus clouds with the heavy cookies.

It was also safer to be as high as possible at the coastal night fighter belts, although the long-range German radar, *Freya,* would pick them up that much sooner.

"I can feel *Freya* tickling the old gonads right now, Sam," the Marker leader said to his nav/rad. "Her fingers are long and bloody cold."

At eight minutes to one, a young woman nursing her wakeful infant in a Yarmouth cottage felt and heard the first bombers. A certain window always buzzed and rattled when they passed directly overhead. Wing Commander Timmins signaled for a minor course correction as they left the coast at 10,000 feet, climbing. He aimed his formation toward a point between Haarlem and The Hague. The mother heard the muffled *put-put-put* of 132 machine guns far out over the water, then a short period of silence, then the growing sound of more bombers.

Ten minutes later, a quartet of *Oboe* Mosquitoes from Bourn airfield set out across the North Sea from the town of Wrentham, seventeen miles south of Great Yarmouth. The fast "musical Mossies" were assigned to outdistance the PFF bombers into Holland, then turn down in a remarkably precise maneuver and meet them at Nijmegen. In all, twenty *Oboe* crews would, at different times, ply their rare skills over Germany this night.

At Little Snoring, Squadron Leader "Butter" Taffey hung up the wall phone of a *Serrate* squadron's smoke-filled ready hut. "Time, gentlemen," said Taffey, as if he were closing down his old dad's pub in Manchester. The hawk-faced O-in-C of A-Flight waited patiently until the childish whistles, obscenities and scraping of chairs had stopped. Fingering the rolled neck of his thick, grimy white pullover he spoke again in a low voice.

"Group have just told me that our charges are ten minutes away from the assembly point at Yarmouth. Leaving now, I should think we'd have a comfortable twenty-minute wait for them at Nijmegen."

Taffey's red goggles, which preserved his night vision, made the faces of his squadron mates soft, flat and infantile. A few, who were not wearing the special goggles themselves, seemed to have eyes as dead as black buttons pushed deeply into their faces. The peculiar lack of visual definition in the room augmented the stifling atmosphere of secrecy in which the *Serrate* unit carried out its critical assignments for the Bomber Command Support Group.

My work is so secret, I don't know what I'm doing myself. It was a squadron legend that this old saw had first appeared in the world as a hand-printed sign on the desk that "Butter" Taffey had inherited from his dead predecessor. It had achieved the status of a motto, although the official words on the squadron badge were *Jacta est alea*—The die is cast.

An excessive lot of homework was required to keep up with all the latest "electrickery" crammed into the Mark XIX Mosquitoes. Their hottest item was the new American ASH radar, generating an unbelievable frequency of 10,000 megacycles and requiring very skillful operators. Taffey's boys had taped it up in five months of practice. The backward-looking Mark VI *Monica* was also familiar. But tonight they had two big surprises for the *Luftwaffe*, never before carried on Ops. There was the Mark IV version of *Serrate*, the squadron's characteristic instrument, which homed on the enemy's own SN-2 search beams. *Perfectos* Mark II was the least-known quantity, designed to pick up the radiations of *Naxos*, the German equivalent of British and American IFF, a pulse for "identification, friend or foe."

"Ten bob says none of the *Perfectos* work, Butter," one of the nav/rads sang out. He was emptying the contents of his pockets onto a locker shelf, from which he retrieved a good luck piece: a radar cable fitting from a crashed Mosquito.

"The *what?*" asked Taffey, in mock horror. "You pull my leg, sir! Did I hear you say *Perfectos?*"

"That's a Yank cigar, isn't it?" someone asked.

"No, you effing sprog, a bloody invisible condom!"

"There's no such thing as *Perfectos*, sod! It's all

an RCM myth, you know." Radar Countermeasures, Foulsham.

"Well, make that a quid, then," said the nav/rad. "If it's a myth, it won't work even better." Slamming his locker door, he added in a burlesque Lancashire dialect, " 'Ands oop, all oo's for puttin' breeze oop bludy Saxons!"

Laughing at the good-natured jester laureate, the crews went out to man their twelve Mossies. Like *Oboe*, they would beat the slow bomber stream to Nijmegen. But then the artful *Serrate* teams were to infiltrate the defenseless formations of heavies and set up a running ambush for the German night fighters.

The intense activity on the English tactical airwaves on the afternoon of November 30 had not gone unnoticed in the Reich. Wireless operators of the long-range radio intercept service tuned in on a crescendo of unintelligible bird chirps and whistles, the *dit-dah* conversations of British W/T during NFT's of the RAF bombers. By sunset, radio intercept issued an estimate of not less than 700 aircraft. During the long, silent interlude before midnight, the coastal radar system patiently watched England.

At intervals of twenty-five kilometers along the Dutch coast and out on the Frisian Islands were Germany's most expert ground radar teams: *Dolphin, Lion, Tiger, Polar Bear, Salt Herring* and *Jaguar* in the northern chain; *Robin Redbreast, Beaver, Butterfly, Sea Eagle* and *Gorilla* to the south. But an unparalleled string of first contacts and kills made by a coastal station north of Haarlem had earned it the unusual name, *Göring*.

Göring's personnel lived and worked in barracks and huts near a miniature castle behind the dyke. From this picturesque nucleus, they maintained a compound of antennas and apparatus as forbidding and ungainly as prehistoric monsters. *Freya*, a Goliath's bedspring, swept the North Sea as far as England from a commanding position on the dyke. By the inflexible laws of radiation, *Freya* sacrificed accuracy for great range; she played only the openings of the game. Down on the beach in front of the dyke were the two *Würzburg* bowls, twenty-three-foot facsimiles of electrical household heaters, with only half the range of *Freya*. One of the *Würzburgs* always followed an enemy bomber, while its companion guided a night fighter to make the kill.

All the radar stations in Holland reported by landline to 3 Division headquarters at Deelen, a monolithic, sunken blockhouse where a hundred men and women performed the many mysterious rites of a paper battle. These were the brokers of electronic warfare.

The focus of all activity was the enormous battle room, called the "cinema" or "opera house." Cool, semidark, efficient. The sovereign element here was a frosted glass map of northern Europe, twenty meters wide and half again as high, standing like a screen before the main floor. The front rows of the "orchestra" were occupied by many ground control officers and their assistants. Immediately behind and above them was the command platform, dominated at front and center by the division commander. The *Nachtjagdführer* was flanked by his two operations officers and the senior liaison people for intelligence, signals, meteorology and civil defense. Two additional banks behind the top brass were filled by those in direct telephone communication with fighter units, the *Horizont* flak network, radar and searchlight control, and the air raid warning service. More than a score of *Luftwaffe Helferinnen* with telephone headsets sat in a high gallery over the command level. These young women spoke to the radar stations; each had a special projector to flash a spot of light representing the position of a night fighter onto the great map. A larger number of women, similarly equipped, were behind the glass to throw up spots and numerical data for the target bombers.

It was 01.55 hours.

"*Göring* reports a contact at extreme range, sir," said a *Telefonhelferin* to her sector control officer. The handsome young *Leutnant* had taken a stretch from his desk to have a closer look at the new girl; he was standing behind her. "They want to talk. I've put them on your phone."

The long-range *Freya* near Haarlem had stopped the monotonous side-to-side oscillation. The big antenna held a fix toward Yarmouth, like a hound at the point. Skewered in its beam were the Pathfinders, ninety miles away.

"Get it on the board!" barked the *Leutnant*. Before he was back at his desk, a cluster of lighted numerals had appeared in grid square Bernhard-Friedrich Three. BF3 was 145 kilometers across the sea from Haarlem.

The sector control officer spoke to *Göring* briefly, then reported to the *Nachtjagdführer* on the same phone. The night fighter commander had fifteen minutes before *Göring's* short-range equipment would give accurate figures. He directed an assistant to inform the *Flugwachtkommando* in Berlin, who had supreme mastery of the entire German defense. *Fluko* would set up a continuous analysis of the night's battle. From availability charts flanking the glass map, the commander drew up an early assembly order and passed it to another assistant. Phones began to ring at the coastal night fighter bases near Gilze-Rijen, Schiphol, Bergen-am-Zee and Leeuwarden.

The lighted replica of the PFF squadron marched steadily across the glass from grid to grid. New lights came on in other squares.

North of Bayreuth, a milky plume of steam on the treetops marked a hidden train to a low-flying Ju88 night fighter, which had come northwest over the mountains from Regensburg.

"You wouldn't find me riding a German train these nights," said the pilot to his observer. "No wonder the Tommies have strangled our transport. I would forbid all trains which were not electrified."

"That would pretty well eliminate travel through these mountains," said the observer.

"All right, then, I'd allow diesels, too. At least their smoke isn't white. Look, we could smash that little toy there, if we wanted to." The pilot tipped the nose of the Junkers toward the moving white feather below them, grinning at his observer.

An 88-millimeter gun in the leading flak car behind *Asia*'s locomotive followed the sound of the Ju88 overhead.

"Here, dreamer," said an off-duty gunner, passing a cup of scalding coffee to his companion. "What makes you think you could hit that phantom?"

"I hear we'll soon have the *Zaubergerät*"—the magic tool—"to hit these targets blind."

"Don't hold your breath."

"It could win the war! The finance minister said they could bomb every city off the map, if he could still transport between all the ruins."

"Drink your coffee. Be glad you're out of the war zone."

In the *Reichsmarschall*'s coach behind the flak car, the valet finished preparations for a master who might not return from the conference coach before the train was in Munich. Upon a bed gimbaled against the thrust and rock of the fast train, he had turned down the blue counterpane, half concealing a meter-wide *Luftwaffe* eagle embroidered in gold thread. Göring's garish Chinese pajamas, pink silk with chartreuse and lavender tracery, were laid out beside a silver brocade dressing robe edged at the neck, sleeves and hem with gray fox. The favorite cognac sparkled amber in a crystal decanter beside the bed, its surface tilting gently with the train's motion. The valet was repelled by the lacquered black box beside the cognac; it held a syringe full of the latest opiate prescribed by one of the doctors for the night tremors. A "needle woman" always accompanied the Iron One in *Asia*.

Two *Luftwaffe* colonels and a captain, the development officer from the Rechlin proving ground, watched the last of several films they had been reviewing for the *Reichsmarschall* in the second coach, the cinema salon.

"There will be one shot here," said the captain, "of the R4M rockets firing from the Messerschmitt 262 against American Fortresses. I would hope the *Führer* might see it."

"Not if the Iron One can help it," said the thin younger colonel, bitterly. "How would Hermann explain that the jet seems to be acting like a fighter? Remember, the *Führer* has abolished the concept of defense. Thus, the world's first jet fighter is a 'blitz *bomber*,' gentlemen."

Several smooth, clear scenes on the screen showed volleys of rockets, twenty-four in a single blast, flaming out from the camera lens toward pilotless drones, which were blown out of the sky. Then came sequences which were jerky and grainy; gun cameras had photographed these in actual combat. In the most spectacular action, a tight box of eight Flying Fortresses disintegrated in an evil oily vapor.

"Ironic!" mused the older colonel, a pilot. "He's put the jets under wraps and we have plenty of fuel for them. They could still win the war. But the regular bensin—you've heard, of course, that Speer has been ordered to hold it up for a big counteroffensive. Over there." The pilot waved toward the windows at the right side of the car, the west.

"Where?" the captain asked. "Are we supposed to know?"

"Of course not," the grinning colonel said. "It will be through the Ardennes."

There were no proper sleeping accommodations for most of *Asia*'s passengers. It was inevitable that a full-scale party would develop in the operations car at the center of the train. In the sixth year of the war, in a rigid system that committed lies to its own archives, gossip was the only satisfying informational transaction.

"Is it true," a general's aide asked of the *Reichsmarschall's* nurse, "that this is the *Führer*'s last trip out of Berlin?"

"Within two weeks," a rival aide interrupted, "the seat of government will be the Obersalzburg. There, the *Führer* has said, we shall defy the world for a thousand years."

Alpenfestung, the National Redoubt. It shaped a major part of Allied strategy, this twenty thousand square miles in the Alps.

Some of the gossip was more reliable.

"I wonder if he knows that Rundstedt will not even attend the meeting in Berlin tomorrow," said a major general to the coach's ranking officer, *General-leutnant* Friedrich von Kreilsheim, deputy chief of signals.

"Where did you hear that?"

Kreilsheim's wide face and perpetual smile, his bushy hair parted in the center, the heavy-rimmed and tinted spectacles, and a habit of wiping his mouth with both hands, suggested the secret name his people gave him: *Waschbär*. The raccoon, the bear that washes its face.

"Myself, Herr *Generalleutnant,* I have just come from Rundstedt's headquarters. He strongly opposes the Ardennes operation, will send only Blumentritt to the meeting. Model, Manteuffel, they are also opposed but will hardly change Keitel and Jodl."

"I suppose not," said Kreilsheim. He was unconcerned about the Ardennes right now. His problem was his wife, who had fallen in love with a night fighter pilot, a boy who had spent his career making training films in Berlin. A *Leutnant* Barth. The general waited to see if the lad's recent posting to Holland would solve the affair.

"Perhaps, Herr *Generalleutnant,*" said the major general, "you could speak about this to the *Reichsmar-schall*. I think the *Führer* should know that the field generals are opposed to the plan for the Ardennes."

"What?" Kreilsheim was far away. "Oh, yes, of course I will. Do you really think the *Führer* cares about them?"

"I do. I think he cares so much that he will back this train up to Berlin and flog the generals."

"Perhaps." Kreilsheim yawned, tapping the back of his hand against his mouth. "The meeting is when?"

"Tomorrow."

A black, twin-engined Ju88R circled widely over the sea, sixty-five kilometers from The Hague, at a height of 7000 meters. *Leutnant* Barth was the first of the coastal night fighters to arrive on his station. He was a green spot of light on the *Göring* controller's glass Seeburg table. The English Pathfinders' spot was red.

"Achtung, Natter-Sechs!" Barth's Squadron Two of *Nachtjagdgeschwader* One was Viper; he was Nr. 6. "Information: wait ten minutes, ten minutes. We have a target for you."

Barth and his radar operator chafed at the delay. The experienced observer was not so eager as the two new replacements to 2/NJG1. Barth was the observer's third pilot in nine months, the other two having abandoned him when they were killed by enemy nightfighters. Twice he had managed to get out safely by parachute and become "available" for reassignment. To the observer's surprise, *Leutnant* Barth had shown promise; he had that indefinable *Kraft* of all the great ones. But they would have to get rid of the radar operator. He was hopeless.

I Division now had the outlines of the main force, whose lead elements were halfway across the North Sea. The *Nachtjagdführer* at Deelen had positioned his fighters only in accord with current information, resisting the fatal instinct to make predictions. He knew that there were components of the battle, invisible to him, which could change its shape at any time. At irregular intervals, lone Mosquitoes slipped out of England toward specific night fighter bases in the Reich or the twenty-odd fighter assembly points known to the RAF. These were the dangerous, freelance Intruders and Rangers.

Göring vectored Barth's Ju88 onto the Pathfinders. The radarman was all set for their first contact on his long-range SN-2, which could find the target at a distance slightly greater than the Junker's altitude. The Lichtenstein was warmed up, ready for the close-in kill.

The exultant Barth leaned forward to check his Revi gunsight. The observer, who sat beside the pilot, felt the Junkers buck horribly. Barth's head and a large segment of the round canopy ahead were blown away by a sledgehammer from the rear.

In the rear seat, with his back to the pilot, the radar operator's left leg was explosively amputated.

Something hard, sharp, hot but oddly painless destroyed his pelvis between the legs. The man's hands clawed up and back for the armor plate, to hold himself out of the mess he was making. Then he relaxed and died. The Ju88's starboard wing was buckling; fire was eating the junction of the wing stub and engine.

The observer's hand slid over the gushing stump of the pilot's neck, before he realized that Barth had been decapitated. "The third time!" he said, his horror suppressed by the icy calm of self-preservation. As he left the lower hatch, the fire out on the wing blotted out his mental picture of the freezing sea. The blazing engine twisted away with the outer wing section still attached. The observer's parachute opened beautifully and wrapped itself around the falling engine.

Flying Officer Thring stopped the clanging of his four 20-millimeter cannons to see if the fire in the Ju-88's starboard engine was taking hold. When the wing and engine fell away, the Ranger pilot said to his nav/rad, "That should do it, Bobby." Neither crew member saw the parachute, which skirled briefly in the wind, like a woman's petticoat. In a lazy, wide spiral, the Mosquito followed the German craft down to confirm its death in the sea.

After their two minutes in Holland the course of the MACCABEE Mosquitoes across Belgium converged with the Allied front line; they would not cross into enemy territory until they saw the Rhine. The moon was rising. It was bright enough to see a Belgian village now and then rushing up and disappearing under the wings.

14

Opposition

At dusk on November 30, Heidelberg floated over invisible meadows on the south bank of the Neckar. The somber mirage was caused by an amber streak of fading sunlight splashed across the medieval town's tallest roofs and church spires, as ground fog pressing up from the river formed a gray moat around the foundations. A towering line of snow clouds, iron-colored and unevenly rusted by the filtered twilight, advanced toward the old city from the northeast.

The *Uhu* emerged like a coppery spark from dense mist trapped beneath the flat cloud base. Anyone looking up from the streets of Heidelberg might have had that impression of the distant Owl, whose cold aluminum was polished and unpainted except for leopard-spot camouflage over all the top surfaces and for the *Luftwaffe* markings. Only the sun's rays gave a reflected warmth to the growing image of the rare and graceful night fighter.

Kommodoreoberst Robert Gabriel framed Heidelberg in the center of his antlers, the great forward array of radar antennas jutting from the egg-shaped nose, and started his descent.

The *Kommodore*, who had survived almost nightly warfare for more than five of his twenty-eight years, returned from Berlin to his command in south Germany. Upon the Knight's Cross at his throat, he wore the new Oakleaves and Diamonds which the *Führer* had personally awarded only twice before to pilots of the night fighter force.

In the western sky, only a narrow band of muddy purple light marked the horizon when the Heinkel Owl crossed the Neckar between Heidelberg and Mannheim, near its junction with the Rhine. Gabriel followed the east bank of the Rhine upstream toward the Speyer-Bruchsal airfield where his group, *Nachtjagdgeschwader* Eight of the Seventh Fighter Division, was based. Turning up his red panel lights, he made first radio contact with Flying Control:

"Achtung! Vintner! Here is Beaujolais One, north at five kilometers, height three hundred meters. Condition Three lights, please, when I start my final approach." The minimal lighting order, a foil against waiting intruders, required constant demonstration for it was considered hazardous by some of the younger pilots.

"Victor, Victor, Beaujolais One, and welcome! You are clear to land on the lighted path, nineteen . . . one-nine . . . in the direction of the upwind beacon."

Control's voice was routinely monotone, as if the group commander's return after four days were not being announced on several tower telephones as someone pushed the circuit breakers lighting the runway. A double row of orange lights pierced the almost invisible haze, below and ahead of the Owl at forty-five degrees to its course.

"Damn, Vintner, DOUSE THOSE LIGHTS! I want Condition *Three* when I am in my final approach . . . do you hear me?"

Leutnant Rudi Anderian, in the rear of the large cockpit nacelle, nervously pressed his forehead against the canopy to see the ground. The young radar operator sat back to back with his pilot, facing the Owl's twin tail. *Bookends, Rudi, that's what we are,* the *Kommodore* always said, *just a pair of aerial bookends.* The orange field lights had been extinguished but Rudi saw something else. A large trapezoid of white light fanned out over a hangar apron; several motor vehicles were creeping about with pale mainbeams probing the ground like short feelers. Gabriel would—

"*Mosquitoes,* Vintner!" shouted Gabriel, as the big night fighter rolled down to the right, throwing Anderian sidewise against his straps. The Owl flashed its leopard-spotted back at horrified watchers in the tower, crossed the swamps, came to the Rhine before Rudi began to think again. There had been no ticks from the *Naxos,* the *Flensburg* was on; the instruments had given no warning. He heard the pistons hiss below his feet as they charged the four cannons and held his breath against the malignant bursts and recoils.

It was all over in thirty seconds. Gabriel did not fire a single round. The Owl banked out widely over the river and turned back to the airfield. Rudi felt the engines shudder as they were throttled back and passed quickly through their rough ranges. Less than a meter to either side of the observer's head the propellers screamed down into low pitch, sweeping out their vicious arcs toward him like buzzsaws. Electric motors hummed, landing flaps cranked down, pods below the engines opened like clamshells. The mainwheels dropped heavily; the double nosewheel thumped lightly seconds later. In total darkness, Anderian's disorientation threw him into utter dependence on Gabriel's supernatural composure.

"Vintner, this is Beaujolais One. Let me have the lights now, please." The *Kommodore* spoke calmly to the tower as if he were stating the play to them in a friendly game of skat.

A white beacon appeared at the landing point; a red shone dimly at the intersection of the two runways. Anderian gripped the sides of the seat pan, pressing his helmet hard against the armored back; every landing was a shameful crisis for him.

At some distance from the crowd that had gathered in front of the hangars, Gabriel's chief machinist, *Feldwebel* Theodore Bockelmann, cocked his bullet-shaped head and opened his mouth to hear better his wailing Daimler-Benz 603's. The Owl bored in through low, shifting planes of vapor steaming up from the swamps. Sparks plumed from the exhausts as the throttles were chopped to ground the heavy machine smoothly. Nodding lightly on its nosewheel as Gabriel braked hard to meet the intersection, the craft became a ponderous crustacean blindly probing its antenna toward the idle runway marked by the red light. Double cowlings on each engine top opened upward. (The action always reminded Anderian of fat sea lions on their backs, spreading their clumsy flippers.) The engines were cleared with quick blasts and cut off rudely, as Gabriel wheeled around and halted near the edge of the apron. Both field lights were extinguished.

The harsh glare of a command car's headbeams blinded Anderian as he dropped out of the hatch below his seat. He could barely make out several other vehicles standing behind the car. A number of bicycles lay on the ground; others were still arriving. It was quite a gathering, thought Rudi, even for the *Kommodore*. The report of a British night fighter had undoubtedly attracted most of the spectators. Some were there simply because their awesome *Experte* had been away from Speyer-Bruchsal for four days. All might secretly want to see if he wore the new Oakleaves and Diamonds, the "cauliflower-and-cutglass" to his Knight's Cross, for which the *Führer* had called him to Berlin.

Gabriel's familiar fur-topped flying boots hung for an instant at the exit before his heavily suited, compact body dropped to the frozen ground. The left leg buckled at the knee with a harsh metallic rattle, causing several bystanders, even Anderian, to move protectively toward the pilot. With an oddly aggressive smile, the *Kommodore* smacked the offending joint into place with the heel of a gloved hand. Both legs were amputed right above the knees. The proud, athletic figure was supported upon unique prosthetic limbs, special gifts of a grateful Reich. (It had been weeks after Anderian's arrival on NJG8 when he had learned that the *Kommodore*'s "cavalry stance" was not just another of the impossible eccentricities.)

Oberleutnant Just, the pompous *Geschwaderadjutant*, bounced forward with a delicate flourish of ridiculous fat legs, virtually an effeminate two-step. The heels snapped closed, the stubby right hand flared up and out like a dainty salad fork. Just, they said, would take three days to wind down if you stole his key.

"Herr Kommodoreoberst," whined the adjutant, "you had us worried, being so late from Berlin. And then the Mosquito! We had no sign here of———"

"Oberleutnant," said Gabriel smoothly, ignoring the prescribed salute, "you will have your driver turn off those lights." The *Kommodore* waited with hands at his hips like an irritated *danseur* until the beams disappeared. "Thank you. The Mosquito, yes. Perhaps the Englishman saw our flarepath as I did, all twelve hundred meters of it. Also, the floods from the repair hangar. *Also,* the vehicles running about with shine-throwers blazing." The fat adjutant sagged. "Really, Just, I think you and I should review the principles of aerial security. Tonight. Will you be so good, then, as to remain on call? Perhaps I shall be free to speak with you by midnight."

Gabriel seemed deaf to the adjutant's desperate acknowledgments, having noticed Major Lorenz standing quietly near his staff car behind the crowd of fascinated young officers. It had surprised Rudi to see the cold, inaccessible *Gruppenkommandeur* in the large welcome committee. He looked exceptionally grim tonight, this dark major with fierce black brows.

"Good evening, Herr *Kommandeur,"* said Gabriel. The two senior officers were known to be old friends —Gabriel the teacher, Lorenz the pupil. Night fighters from the beginning, they were almost never heard to address each other casually. It was accepted, among the leading, surviving crews, that this formidable and deadly pair had a right to maintain a certain tone for the benefit of the endless series of young replacements. "Will you wait for me a moment, Major? I should like to chat in your office before dining."

Lorenz silently tapped the broken peak of his shapeless cap.

Gabriel talked briefly with the junior officers, who had been shocked and not a little pleased at the ruthless censure of the adjutant. The *Kommodore* had removed his helmet—the clipped, damp hair on the perfectly round head was indeterminately blond or white—and accepted a cigar from one of his timid admirers. They followed him like *Kindergärtner* as he pointedly moved away from the Owl before allowing someone to light him up. It seemed odd to Rudi that his pilot kept evading the Mosquito business in a mysterious manner.

Feldwebel Bockelmann was all the while planted like a gravestone ten meters away from the officer cluster. Gabriel eventually excused himself graciously from the fawning aircrews. "Well, Teddi," the smiling *Kommodore* asked his rawhide-faced mechanic, "what seems to be the problem?"

"I don't know. I heard there was some kind of emergency."

"No, dear *Feldwebel,* not an emergency at all! However, both my engines have been pretty hot, up to Berlin and back. Not critical, except in the landing approach and, of course, while taxiing. What do you think? Engine cooling gills?"

"Not likely. Major Lorenz has started having the same trouble. We did not put the automatic gills in his Owl."

Gabriel and Lorenz flew the pair of Heinkel 219's belonging to NJG8, which was routinely equipped with Junkers 88's. Bockelmann had practically built each *Uhu* from parts secretly gathered by the *Kommodore;* there were no more than eight of these "phantoms" without registry numbers in the entire *Luftwaffe.* Germany's only specific aircraft answer to the Mosquito was, for purely political reasons, out of favor with *Reichsluftministerium.*

"I suspect," added Bockelmann pointedly, "that *your* problem is the damn bensin we've been getting to feed these monsters lately."

Gabriel had indeed thought of it for he was extremely sensitive on the point of fuel supply for the *Geschwader.* But the trip to Berlin had finally revealed what controlled the desperate shortage of bensin.

"In any case, Theo, this Owl has not seen a good

mechanic in four days. I deliver her into your competent hands. We may need her again tonight."

Bockelmann's stiff nod and bearish grunt were typical. He snapped out orders to his men to have the Heinkel yoked up behind a tow wagon. As Gabriel and Anderian walked toward Lorenz's auto, the *Kommodore* looked back affectionately to see her follow the wagon like a gentle idiot child, her head pulled down by the heavy yoke bars. Even if he had not been preoccupied, Rudi would hardly have wasted a glance at the hated aircraft; he was glad to be safely away from "it."

"Herr *Kommodore,* about the night fighter," said the radar officer, hesitantly, "I had no indications at all, sir. My apparatus was on always and working."

Gabriel's wild laughter had the faint ring of madness.

"Rudi, there was no night fighter. We were playing a little game with *Oberleutnant* Just. But come, Major Lorenz will drop you at the mess. I will meet with you sometime after dinner."

It was uncomfortably chilly in the *Gruppenkommandeur*'s small, inhospitable office. A perfectly adequate oil stove stood in one corner, unlighted. Gabriel only opened his fur-lined leather coat without removing it.

"Next to me, Paul, you are probably the *Luftwaffe*'s worst administrator, but you have certainly learned some of the tricks." The *Kommodore* laughed as he sat down jerkily in one of two identical camp chairs, demonstrating for Lorenz the extreme wobble of its spindly legs. "These are worse than my own pins! I'm beginning to believe you really do trim off the legs of these chairs to discourage loungers. That's what they all say, you know."

"Do they!" Lorenz, who did not smoke, saw Gabriel's cigar and pulled out an ashtray he kept hidden in a desk drawer.

"I'm afraid so, Paul. By the way, I've just learned what they call you. Me and Just, too. It will amuse you. I am the Fearless Leader, you are the Fearsome Leader and Just is the Fearful Leader. *Furchtlos, furchtbar, furchtsam!* Isn't that marvelous?"

Lorenz was not amused. "Herr *Kommodore*," he said, "I am very sorry about the breach of lighting security out there tonight." Lorenz rarely broke the old habit of using the colonel's courtesy title.

"Now listen, Paul, that is something we must not have to worry about! These details belong with the staff. Just means well, I think, and he will learn a lesson tonight. Was I too harsh with him, do you think?" The question was obviously academic, for Gabriel quickly added, "—we can't have an adjutant who is *too* fearful."

"No, he's a stuffy bastard. I'm for getting rid of him." Lorenz wasted no further time on the adjutant. His voice became tainted with suspicion. "What *about* the intruder, *Kommodore?*"

"You have guessed correctly, Paul—there was none. I thought it would do no harm to shake the station up a bit, since it looked like a Tivoli on opening night. Besides, I don't often come back from a trip without some kind of horror story, do I?"

It was true, although Lorenz had to shake his head disapprovingly. Gabriel was so far beyond conceit that his powerful ego had reverted to a charming, almost childish simplicity. Only three night fighters had received the Oakleaves with Swords and Diamonds; two were Gabriel's close friends. Lent, of NJG₃, had died in October with 102 kills at night. Schnaufer, of NJG₄, was approaching 120. Gabriel himself had predicted that Major the Prince zu Sayn-Wittgenstein, *Kommodore* of NJG₂, would beat them all, but the Prince had died in January with 83. Only two weeks ago, Gabriel had passed the century mark himself.

"Speaking of horror, Paul, you would cut your throat if you worked in Berlin these days." Gabriel drew a finger across an exceptionally large larynx, unconsciously drawing attention to the new embellishments of his Knight's Cross.

"Did he present that to you himself?" Lorenz asked, with genuine curiosity.

"He did. Also said he wrote the citation personally. I'll show it to you sometime. He seems to enjoy these affairs, spent about two hours with me. I must say he rambles a great deal, although he was very gracious. You can't be sure if he is telling you about definite plans, secrets, ideas or wild dreams. I learned one very important thing, which will greatly affect our lives. The *Führer* wants to split the Allied front in the Ardennes region of Belgium. His objective is to retake Antwerp, which he says is the key to Anglo-American supply. The balance of supply from now on, he thinks, will be the story of the war."

"When is this supposed to start?"

"He mentioned no dates. 'In the immediate future,' he said. We of the seventh division are deeply involved. After the morning ceremony at the *Reichskanzlei*, the *Führer* said that Göring would give me the necessary details. I spent most of the afternoon with the Iron One at RLM. Let's start with your map." Gabriel lurched up awkwardly from his chair toward one of Lorenz's large wall charts. "Look. Here the Seventh stands practically naked. Three Division got out of Metz only a week before the city was taken on the twenty-fifth. It is now less than one hundred kilometers to the nearest part of the front southwest. Göring says we must expect orders at any time to close down Speyer-Bruchsal and move, probably east to Schweinfurt or Schleissheim."

Lorenz shook his head sternly. "They cannot cross the Rhine in the south within six months. I do not even think they are interested in forcing the issue down here."

"Maybe not. But I remind you that it is *Armégruppe* Patton which stands across the river there before Strasbourg. In any case, Göring tells me that he has ordered *Oberkommando der Luftwaffe* to work out a reorganization of the southern divisions. OKL have suggested to him that Three Division be dissolved and split between Five and Seven and that a new corps be created for the entire south. The *Reichsmarschall* wants me to command that new corps. I would be promoted lieutenant general."

"*Sieg Heil,* Robi, to jump a rank!" Instinctively using Gabriel's first name, Lorenz also fell back on night fighter radio slang for a kill.

"But Paul, the other consequence is that the *Führer* will order me to stop combat flying. I will refuse, of course. It will be quite a problem for them."

It was not a Prussian threat; Lorenz knew that his commanding officer was serious. A problem for them, not him.

"All personal considerations aside, Paul, I consider the new corps under discussion to be the end of organized night fighting."

"Politics?" Like all old night fighters, Lorenz had long experience with the political vulnerability of his speciality.

"Not exactly. It is the mission of the corps, not the reorganization, that disturbs me. Starting with the opening of the Ardennes offensive, whenever that occurs, we will provide all air-to-ground support at night, plus heavy contributions to *daylight* ground support, plus our regular night operations against the bombers. We will carry out our new duties under tactical control of the Army! I will also mention that selected members of the new night fighter corps will be charged with leading novice fighter wings against American Fortresses."

"The Amis will join the English in night terror raids?"

"No, Paul, listen to what I am telling you. The current deficit in day fighter pilots is appalling. Therefore, the fighter wings I speak of will literally be composed of half-trained fledglings. They will be taught just enough to take off, fly, shoot—after a fashion—and perhaps land again. They will learn nothing else. No navigation or blind flying and precious little air discipline. We will lead these poor devils. Perhaps it *is* time to stop flying, after all."

Major Lorenz brought the *Kommodore* up to date on prospects for their operations that night and on the weather.

"I will be at the mess for the next hour now, Paul. I could eat a horse, I am so hungry. For all we know"—Gabriel had to make one of his painful jokes

—"that is precisely what our mess has been serving us, old cavalry mounts, if not the saddles as well. Tonight, I want to start off with me, you and Birk, in that order. After that, I leave the schedule to you and *der Arzt*." To the physician, Birk.

Günther Birk, *I/Staffelkapitän,* was a young physician whose phenomenal skill in the art of night fighting had long erased what small lifesaving gains he had made in a brief medical practice in Lübeck during the first year of the war. No one knew why he had become a pilot or, indeed, how he had escaped military consignment in his major profession. Birk himself would only admit to being the last of his line in Germany who still made regular calls at night.

Rudi Anderian jogged rapidly along the tree-shrouded back road to the operations area after his hasty evening meal. A gentle powder of snow sifted through the tangle of black branches and crazy-quilt netting of camouflage that covered the nine Ju88's of 2/*Staffel,* lined up like sable lizards along both sides of the road section. *How ugly they were, the Junkers, their engines bandaged in bile-colored tarpaulins, their multipaneled cockpit canopies bulging above the bull snouts like exposed, glistening brains.*

Since childhood, the young radar officer had driven himself to run, both literally and figuratively. In the physical sense, he was convinced that his lifelong and rigid program of calisthenics had compensated for the early history of a weak heart. This the *Luftwaffe* examiners had not wholly accepted, for medically the striving *Leutnant* was still provisional aircrew.

A stiff wind blew in from the field. As a shortcut to Flying Control, Rudi opened the personnel door in one of the huge, rolling armored curtain doors of the repair hangar and stepped into Bockelmann's world.

It was a vast gymnasium of silver-painted girders, traveling chainhoists, rubber-wheeled inspection platforms, airplanes in all stages of dissection. Unshielded bulbs cast a steady glare down from fifty overhead reflectors; sputtering bluish welding arcs threw grotesque, magnified caricatures of men and machines in all directions. The rich, soft smell of oil and the sensual pungency of high-octane aviation fuel hung in the dangerously starved air. Crude language, laughter and the occasional ring of expensive tools on cold cement echoed offensively in Rudi's ears, as he crossed to the other side of the hangar, unnoticed in the shadow of a balcony along one wall. He passed behind a line of unattended aircraft: Major Lorenz's Owl, a Ju88, two small staff planes. Bockelmann himself and his black gang crawled over the *Kommodore*'s Owl like sooty maggots.

In the Control operations room, Rudi barely greeted the pilot duty officer, *Leutnant* Helm of 3/ *Staffel*. He knew the man only slightly as a coarse, insensitive contemporary whose total motivation was split between women and the coveted *Ritterkreuz,* the Knight's Cross.

"Christ! Anderian, what brings you down here at this hour? Are we under attack?"

"The *Kommodore* has ordered me to prepare a tactical preview for him. Under the fuel emergency, which you are well aware of, he will provide no more than six aircraft if we are called tonight."

"Six, you say?" mused the pilot, shrewdly calculating his chances of flying. They were borderline, he felt, *if* they were called after midnight when his control duty ended. Helm watched Anderian for a moment, who was self-consciously copying data from a large slateboard filling the wall behind the counter separating him and the pilot. The radar officer sensed that he would be harassed.

"There's no doubt we'll be called, Anderian," said Helm, "and that means the *Kommodore,* Lorenz and Birk, at least, and *in-that-order,* as he always says. So. You will fly surely. Your first Ops, isn't it?"

"Yes." Rudi's face reddened. Men behaved like Helm only in war films.

"Scared?"

"No, concerned." One must lie to a pig.

But there was no answer as yet to Helm's basic question. Forcing himself to copy the last of the weather information onto his pad under Helm's probing eyes,

Rudi knew that the answer might well be only hours away. As if the room pressure suddenly rose, choking him, he stiffly announced that he was going outside for some fresh air. Helm would later recall that he had seen men move like that when they were about to be seasick.

Anderian strode rapidly away from Control, gulping the cold, damp air. His pounding heart was almost stopped by an awesome flash of lightning. As it lit up the inside of the massive cloud cover above Speyer-Bruchsal, Rudi's vision held the frozen image of a cave roof, endless and terrifying. A more experienced airman than Anderian would have questioned a display of lightning under the prevailing atmospheric conditions. And there was no thunder.

On his runback from Munich to England, the PRU Mosquito pilot cursed the ten-tenths cloudtop he had just filmed from 20,000 feet over the Rhine. His forward, vertical and oblique Fairchild cameras had thrown their shutters across the wasted emulsions in synchrony with the aircraft's forward speed, at the one-tenth second, 700,000-candlepower peak of the sixth of his twelve M.46 photoflashes.

At 01.55 hours on December 1, Division asked for three NJG8 defenders in the lower Ruhr. There were definite confirmations on the formations over East Anglia and Lincolnshire. The duty officer who had replaced Helm at midnight put out calls for the *Kommodore* and others whose names headed the list. Gabriel and Lorenz were on instant ready, followed by Birk and Veltjens on alert.

"You have a takeoff of 02.20 earliest, sir," the *Kommodore* was told when he responded by telephone from Adjutant Just's office.

"Thank you, clerk. Please tell *Staffelkapitän* Birk that he may update the schedule to suit himself. I will be there in five minutes. You have called *Leutnant* Anderian?"

"The *Leutnant* is already here, sir."

Gabriel realized that his new radar officer would naturally have spent the evening in the alert shack. He wondered if Anderian suspected that he, Gabriel, knew of the young man's terrible fears. The *Kommodore* missed his old observer, Marx, very much, of course. But by a favorable coincidence—Gabriel was incurably superstitious—the great Marx had never overcome his own terror of combat flying.

Control was jammed with curious or ambitious crew members when Gabriel arrived. Lorenz and Birk had already gone out to their machines. The flight board had been changed: Veltjens of 3/*Staffel* had replaced Birk and was up on instant ready with his squadron mate, Essner; Bollweber and Heinrich of 2/*Staffel* were on alert. Gabriel immediately saw that Helm had been loudly proclaiming injustice, as usual, although he was remarkably subdued before the *Geschwader* commander. Gabriel filed a mental note to speak subtly to Birk about this Helm fellow. Birk and even Lorenz were not so acutely tuned as they might be to the signs of rare excellence in a man, especially one so insufferable as Helm.

Gabriel and Anderian walked out to the Owl in silence. Rudi tapped the snow from his boots as he climbed the ladder into the cockpit shell. The pilot began his ritual inspection of the big night fighter, as Bockelmann came up from the tail with the rudder locks in his hand, wheezing deeply in the bitter night air. Gabriel had almost never found fault with the Owl at flight time but he liked to impress the newer members of Bockelmann's flock. He knew that the chief himself appreciated the pressure on his men.

"Good evening, *Feldwebel*—morning, I should say."

"It *was* the fuel, of course, Herr *Kommodore*." The chief's custom of carrying on conversations over several days would simply never change. "Nothing wrong with this *Uhu*. Nothing wrong with those cooling gills or anything else."

"*Um-m.* Well, Theo, I appreciate your trouble." The *Kommodore* guessed that Bockelmann's people had torn both engines down almost completely during the early part of the night. He made a show then, for the benefit of the young machinists watching from a distance, of examining closely the starboard wheels. "Surely, *Feldwebel*," he asked in a loud voice, "this is not a hydraulic leak, is it?"

Bockelmann kneeled close to his commander and tasted what his fingers picked up from an oleo strut. "Only water," he said, glaring sternly back toward his men.

The *Kommodore* grasped the hatch ladder and pulled himself up into the belly of the Owl. When his head appeared at the front canopy, a young *Funker* was ready with orange torches in his hands. Five minutes after starting the engines, his cockpit check completed, the *Kommodore* signaled the torchman. Hand signals directed the Owl out of its revetment onto the taxiway, which the sweepers had cleared of snow. Rumbling along near one edge to keep his bearings, Gabriel called the tower. Anderian imagined the tower men spilling their coffee in a rush to answer. It always sounded as if the *Kommodore* were trying to be polite with distant cousins.

"Good morning, Vintner, this is Beaujolais One. I am going to runway two-seven. When I am ready to take off, I shall flash my lights. Give me the field lights then but turn them off the instant I am off the ground. Is that clear?"

"Good morning, One, we see you. Yes, all clear! Moselle One and Chablis One have departed. We are standing by."

At the end of the runway, Gabriel locked the brakes and ran up his engines. Rudi heard the startling *blip-blip* of the double magnetoes on each side. The flaps hummed down partway. The Owl was gunned forward, turning out to the runway center in slow motion. Before the radar operator was aware that his pilot had flashed his own lights, the throttles were pushed full forward and the Owl was surging madly up the middle of the flarepath. As it rocked lightly several times, tapping its wheels upon leaving the runway, the field lights disappeared. As the nosewheel and main carriage came into their housings, Gabriel pulled around in a climbing turn to the north and once more addressed the tower. They gave him course and altitude to Norseman, a control grid northeast of Cologne. As Rudi jotted down the local time, 02.21, Gabriel called him on the intercom.

"All set, Rudi? Oxygen? *Naxos? Flensburg?*"

"Yes, *Kommodore.*"

"All right, then. Good luck! When the time comes, I want you to forget about me and run the whole show. We are not setting any records, understand?"

"Yes, *Kommodore.*"

Unlike the Tommies and Amis, German crews logged flights but not flying hours. December 1 marked Robert Gabriel's 1758th operational takeoff in defense of the Third Reich.

Shortly after the third Owl left Speyer-Bruchsal, the pair of Mosquitoes from Brevishall made a forty-five-degree turn to the east at Verdun.

"Can you see them, Bill?" asked Croft, as he watched the magnetic compass stabilize and compared it with the gyrocompass.

McLaughlin's face was pressed against the Perspex.

"Yes, I saw them when we crossed a patch of water or ice. They're below us, John, about two hundred yards back."

"Below!" The radioaltimeter was flickering around the hundred-foot mark. "Those crazy Czechs will kill themselves, probably on a church steeple."

Bill McLaughlin kept watching the Mosquito dogging their track. *God help us,* he thought, *if Karel were a German and that airplane was stalking us!*

Croft peered across the Mossie's smooth nose into the darkness of France. He felt lonely, even with Bill at his side and Karel close behind. *What if the intelligence was bad? Was there or was there not flak at the bridge? The train could stop or be delayed for a dozen reasons. Fog can develop in minutes. They were all crazy to give serious thought to this joke.* Croft pictured the PM, whom he'd never seen, dusting ashes from the cigar onto the war maps. "Too bad about those chaps," the prime minister was saying.

The train *Asia* went through the Bayreuth station as if all rules of way were suspended. Indeed, they had been suspended and Engineer Nowarra pretended that they had told him why.

"I suppose you have guessed, Bauer, that we are pulling an important passenger."

"The *Führer?*" asked the fireman, bluntly.

"Would I tell you if I knew?"

Knowing how hopelessly dull Bauer really was, what irritated Nowarra most was his own effort to make a simple fireman aware of the distance between the two seats in this important cab. Bauer did not even have enough intelligence to imagine that the driver of Göring's best train was fully briefed on every itinerary.

They were coming now into the best part of the Reich, Bavaria. Only ten minutes behind schedule at twenty minutes after two. Bauer would soon have a look at the real Germany. The fireman was *plattdeutsch*, poor fellow, and this was his first trip out of the north.

Winston Churchill was overtired and cranky. His physician had ordered him to bed and General Ismay had been summoned. There was a fresh signal in the PM's hand, received at 01.20 by scrambler telephone from Air Ministry.

"Ismay," said Churchill, waving the salmon flimsy, "this tells me that MACCABEE has been launched. How can I sleep while these brave idiots stooge about in the hinterland?"

"Prime Minister, sir," the general replied, "there is nothing you can do, as usual."

"How right you are, Ismay. I shall have a small brandy, then, and totter off to bed. Good night, Ismay."

Churchill sat on his bed in the house at Chequers, gazing eastward through the leaded windows. He raised the brandy glass.

"Good luck, lads," said the prime minister. "Get the bastard for us."

15

Collision at the Rhine

At half past two on the morning of December 1,
Deutschlandsender started broadcasting the hateful
ticking of a clock that would continue until the
raid's end. Now the *dicker Hund*, the fat dog of a
bomber stream, spanned the North Sea. As its tail still
rose from England, its Pathfinder head touched the
Dutch coast sixteen kilometers above The Hague.
While the alert was spreading eastward to successive
zones in Holland and Germany, the national radio
would stop the clock in the *Rundfunkhaus* only for priority reports on progress of the terror raiders.

Wing Commander Timmins, Pathfinder, could
not afford to think of himself as a terror raider. Bomber Command issued reluctant doctrine on cowardice
and moral turpitude, faced daily by medical officers
and chaplains. Is it instructive that there never was a
directive on the biology of bombing? On the possibility that a Pathfinder would come back one night
saying, "I've just set a wizard firestorm at Hamburg"
—as Timmins had in 1943—"and was wondering,
you know, about the *people*." Was it more paralyzing
than cowardice to think like a bombing victim? Was
the shocking insensitivity of Timmins his defense

against personal danger that had no precedent or modern equal?

A calculating WAAF in the Command's records section had taken an interest in Hector Timmins. The young woman was charged with the daily, preliminary reductions of raw casualty data on their way into sanitized tables and graphs for the high war councils. In the name of the Crown, the flesh and blood she purged from the archives in her eager youth would snap her own mind in middle life. Even as a statistical curio, the WAAF noted, this Timmins was remarkable. During the night of November 30/December 1, the man was to fly his thirtieth mission in a fourth Ops tour! At the current rate of 5 percent attrition, the chance of survival to that point was less than the probability of a meteor striking the earth. Rightly, the wind-commander should have gone for a Burton during his fifty-first trip, near the end of the first PFF long tour. He had to have seen some 1900 squadron mates fall from the sky beside him. The WAAF whistled softly as she replaced the Timmins file. Twenty-nine years old, he was. With the name Hector, they would be calling him "Timmy," surely. Unmarried. She wondered if he was good-looking. Only a grimy crust of mucilage remained where the photo had fallen out.

Timmins could smell the night fighters. He worried incessantly about the rear and had stationed Flight Lieutenant Grimble, a keen old hand in F-Freddie, back there to take the brunt of it. But the zed end was not where the trouble started.

In the relatively safe middle of the twenty-four PFF Lancasters, Pilot Officer Turleigh was out on his third Ops flight with a sprog crew. The upcoming Dutch coast meant flak to Turleigh; he feared flak more than all the night fighters in the German air force. He dreamed about jagged, crystallized shards of steel slicing through the Lanc's thin shell, tearing up the seat pack, scooping out the contents of his pelvis. For this reason, the pilot had scrounged a square foot of scrap armorplate to sandwich between his seat cushion and chute. Turleigh's green crew thought no worse of that than of the less practical dolls and snapshots and crucifixes that many in the bombers carried to ward off death. But the six men were terrified by the habit their leader had formed of climbing slowly out of a tight Pathfinder formation.

Major Heino Meister, *Gruppenkommandeur* of II/NJG.1 out of Bergen-zur-Zee, had been brought by *Seeadler* right onto the Pathfinders as they crossed high over the beach. Coastal flak was always muzzled in the presence of night fighters, who were currently destroying two bombers for every one brought down by the guns.

"Watch this, now," the Sea Eagle controller said to his small audience, *"die Schaflaus* will dog them in and out, back to England, if necessary."

From his grim style of attachment to a bomber stream, Meister was known to controllers as the Tick. Reputedly the smallest pilot in the *Luftwaffe,* Meister was also a colorless, pigheaded crank. Sheer doggedness had earned him a good reputation. A dash of aggressiveness would have put him in the class of Lent, Streib, Schnaufer, Gabriel and the two fighting princes.

"I have them, Major!" screamed Meister's excitable radarman. His new FuG.218 *Neptun* had picked up the extreme-range contact only a second after Sea Eagle's last steering order. "Distance, seven thousand meters . . . above you, two hundred . . . COLLISION COURSE! . . . Rolf, *schnell!"* Right, quick!

"Easy, Lang, easy!" said the phlegmatic Meister, "you will have an adrenal crisis." The major made short work of the radarman's triumph. "A good eye can see their silhouettes at two kilometers, their exhausts at three. There! Do you see? Lang? Albrecht?" The radarman and the observer saw the Pathfinders and nodded obediently. Meister droned on: ". . . And the poor devils in those bombers cannot see us against the ground beyond a hundred meters." The pilot announced his visual contact to Sea Eagle in the traditional words of the medieval duellist—*"Kesselpauken! Kesselpauken!"*—kettledrums, kettledrums.

The velvet-black Ju88 skidded around behind

the oncoming enemy formation. It fishtailed lazily into a stable position under the dull, earth-colored bellies of Timmins' three trailing Lancasters. In these final stages, Meister's idle companions endured unintelligible monologues:

"*Ja-hah,* hold it right there, please . . . good, good . . . off those throttles with hands, English shithead! . . . easy, easy, easy. . . ."

At last the '88 stopped right below Grimble's bomber, the steadiest one, and rose smoothly like an electric hospital lift. Perched on his special cushion, the tiny major showed the alarming closeup to his crewmen as if he were about to make the Y-incision on a morgue cadaver.

"See the wing roundels, English, yes? . . . those vertical fins, like Zulu shields leaning against the stabilizer . . . that rear gunner cannot see us to, ha, to save his life, can he?"

Meister switched on his special roof-mounted gunsight. He would dispatch this one with *schräge Musik.* Twin MG.151 20-millimeter cannons mounted in the upper fuselage were thrust upward and forward at an angle of seventy degrees; they resembled a pair of tilted clarinets. Firing almost vertically at engines and wing tanks, one avoided all the mess of flying through bomber debris. "Jazz" or "slant" music had naturally spread through the night fighter force with the speed of *Gonorrhöe.*

The major's victim-elect made a vicious, telepathic downbreak to the right. Its exhaust flames were stripped from the reflector sight like a rejected lantern slide.

Uncanny! Meister blinked and shrugged. He calmly shifted aim to the next Lancaster, which drove on in blind ignorance at the left.

"I have a pigeon here, Major, a crazy fellow climbing right out the top," Lang whispered hoarsely. It was comical the way all night fighter crews whispered.

"*Danke*, Lang, I see him. But keep him in the beam."

This time the standard quartet of cannons was charged, firing forward from a belly tray. Meister expected a chase from the way this fool started. *"Nyech!* what an idiot," the pilot snorted, with a trial squint through the Revi sight. He had to stretch to get his eye up to the luminous ring floating over the instruments.

There was no chase at all. Few tail gunners ever saw a German night fighter and lived to tell what it was like. The *Luftwaffe* considered the great Lancaster to be practically unarmed. Once marked by a German pilot of only average ability, the heavy bomber with an unexceptional crew was doomed.

"Horrido!" was Meister's announcement to Sea Eagle that he was about to fire.

"Sieg heil! Sieg heil!" the major quickly added, hauling the Ju88 upward with all his strength to escape what he sensed was coming. He had fired a long burst at the port engines and had been unable to resist carrying over to the big fuselage.

Timmins recognized the reflection of the terrible green flash. The flight engineer turned with a smothered cry to look directly at the expanding fireball above them. As the burning Lancaster began to lag, checked by its own explosion, it became a multicolored teardrop fed by its marker flares, incendiaries, photoflashes, oxygen, oil and petrol, dripping long streamers, all turning orange before they burned out. The main fire blew apart in a second, brighter flash—it was Turleigh's 8000 pound bomb—which formed a fountain of satellites. Most were quickly snuffed, these burning parts of the dissevered bomber; some traced out graceful, fragile streamers like spider legs groping for a footing on the dark earth.

"Turleigh or Parke," said Timmins, after a long pause. His own Lancaster had pressed on through it all as if it were riding on rails. "They were carrying the greens."

"Right, Timmy, Turleigh, I think." The flight engineer's words were barely intelligible. His oxygen mask was slimy inside with sweat; he pulled the gray rubber mold forward and blew into it. Acid from his stomach bit the bottom of his throat.

The tactical airwaves had hardly come alive at twenty minutes to three, when landline traffic in Holland and western Germany was already saturated. At the center of his web in Berlin, Fluko had to make his analysis from a cyclone of code and plaintext, much of it premature or exaggerated or even self-serving. This much was clear:

The main force, a thousand heavy bombers, was on a course to the upper Ruhr. They could turn. Still, Fluko believed that Happy Valley, as the English called it, was to be the primary target.

A second force, size unknown, was halfway across the North Sea on a high track toward Berlin. These were undoubtedly the familiar Mosquitoes of the Berlin Express.

A hundred *Luftwaffe* night fighters were airborne, exhausting the resources of III Division at Deelen in Holland and II Division at Stade on the lower Elbe. Another hundred from the south and southeast as far as Regensburg were being ordered to a line along the west flank of the Ruhr, slanting across the Reich into Denmark.

The status of every defensive unit in the land was known to Fluko, from the radar stations to the smallest city fire sections.

High-level Intruders had already engaged the first German night fighters patrolling off the Dutch coast. One Ju88 had already gone off the air and vanished from the radars as he had prepared to open the attack on the bombers. Six low-level Intruders were punching through the coastal flak belts at widely separated sites, and four Ranger Mosquitoes had gone out from Hartford Bridge to wait for the Berlin group of night fighters who would be taking off soon after the Fast Night Striking Force.

Oboe aircraft of 8 Group faced extremely tight schedules throughout the night. These were the "musical Mosquitoes" that would mark all major targets, genuine and bogus, with complex flares dropped at the command of an ingenious finding system. The first *Oboe* quartet, which had taken off from Wrentham at 01.02, was about to make a critical turn south at Appeldoorn, on the precision course over Arnhem to Nijmegen.

Squadron Leader Taffey's *Serrate* squadron had tapped the wicket at Nijmegen and turned back to pick up the incoming bombers. As the twelve Mosquitoes spaced out smartly to enter the stream, the leading crews began to pick up their first microwave reflections from the Pathfinders. Taffey saw an inauspicious glow on the horizon, which only an overloaded bomber could produce. To his radar operator, whose head was in the scope, Butter said, "The first poor bugger's gone for a Burton, I'm afraid." This bugger was Turleigh of the Pathfinders.

High over the East Frisian chain of islands, which dot the North Sea coastline from Holland to Schleswig-Holstein, the spoof bombers were preparing to open their sideshow over northwestern Germany. "Siren raids" were designed to draw Fluko's attention away from the main arena. A notoriously excitable radar station on the comma-shaped isle of Borkum had sent a frantic Telex to Fluko: "50–100 aircraft, 10,000 meters, 500 km/hr, course 089." That was a heading to Bremerhaven. There were only twelve Mosquitoes in that first section.

Nearly halfway along their straight leg from Verdun to Strasbourg, the MACCABEE Mosquitoes were a pair of ephemeral dragonflies, skimming the unfamiliar terrain. Three hands above a now hazy horizon in the east, the gibbous moon wore a complete silver halo, telling of invisible ice clouds above 30,000 feet.

"An interesting stretch of the tour," said McLaughlin cheerily, "want to hear about it?" He was bent over the spiral-bound strip maps he'd worked so hard on. They were overmarked in the hieroglyphics with the colored pencils; the red penlite turned everything gray. "All right, then, when we cross the Moselle in a minute or two, Metz should be ten miles north, downriver, that is—to our left—and Nancy fifteen miles south. If Metz is on the right and Nancy on the left, then I suggest——"

"Come on, come on," growled Croft.

"Okay! Christ, aren't you interested in the scenery? In fact, we'll cross the river at Pont-à-Mousson. A very distinctive bridge."

"Which you have seen many times, of course."

"No, captain, I have a picture of it here. And twenty miles down the road, we have the charming village of Château-Salins."

"You will recognize this village from your childhood vacations on the Continent?"

"No—no. You're jumping ahead of me again, Mr. Croft, sir. Château-Salins, as it happens, is at the intersection of two major roads. A third road cuts across and makes a neat triangle south of the town. That's how navigators keep from going crazy, like pilots, you see."

"This weather is too good to last," said Croft gloomily, scanning the void over the port wing. "Hey! What are those flashes? Can't be lightning."

"I'll bet that's Metz. There are still some holdouts in the city, even though they took it a week ago. That's Irwin's Fifth Division."

"Irwin who?"

"Oh, Jesus! *General* Irwin of the Third Army."

"When can we get a fresh met report?"

McLaughlin could never hand down a decision regarding time before consulting both his watch and the panel chronometer. "If *Oboe* doesn't call us by the time we hit the Rhine, we can call them. If a German answers, we hang up."

They were entering the pocket that Patton's Third Army had carved out of the German line, almost down to the Rhine at Strasbourg. Hundreds of men in the rear supply areas had moments of terror when the two friendly shadows roared low overhead. A nervous gunner in a light armored vehicle opened up briefly with a machine gun.

"Was that someone *shooting* at us, for God's sake?" asked McLaughlin, in true outrage. They had only seen the flashes, heard nothing.

"I think so," said Croft.

"Son of a bitch! That's something we never thought of. I can see the headlines."

"There'll be no headlines on this job, friend!"

Kommodore Gabriel reported to Norseman that he was approaching Cologne. He had followed the Rhine all the way up from Speyer-Bruchsal.

"Beaujolais One," answered Norseman, "steer three-one-null, climb at maximum rate to eight thousand meters. It is a red alert here."

"Not much time to wait, Rudi," said Gabriel, pushing forward on the throttles. "Excellent fellow, this controller. He says little, he never exaggerates."

"We are in luck tonight, my friends," the Norseman controller announced to his assistants. He had worked with Gabriel from time to time, since the Kammhuber Line was first organized. "Gabriel, Lorenz and Birk! That's half the night fighter force right there. Now you will see the textbook thrown away. It will be like spying on the secrets of great lovers."

A *Helferin* up on the narrow platform before the data board giggled. The controller glowered at her but he smiled as he bent over his Seeburg plotting table.

The "Cat" at Dover ordered its first *Oboe* Mosquito turned at thirty-two minutes past one. From Harderwijk on the Zuider Zee, Flying Officer Britton-Dippy took up the precision course, a shallow arc that would intersect Nijmegen fifty-five miles to the south. His Polish observer, Flight Lieutenant Cybulski, tuned the A.R.5513 sharply so that they both heard that piercing, steady tone in the earphones that vaguely resembled the haunting sound of a cold oboe. The least drift would cause them to hear slow dots on the left or slow dashes on the right. While giving the crew this information, the airborne equipment also stepped the pulses up and re-radiated them back to the Cat and to another station, the "Mouse" at Cromer, a hundred miles up the coast from Dover. Cat kept the aircraft at a constant radius from the Dover transmitter. Mouse followed the Mosquito along its slightly curved track.

"Two minutes to go," said Cybulski, who always followed the run-up with an ancient stopwatch. It was unnecessary to do so, but the Pole always had about nine minutes to kill on the arc.

Clearly, on a proper course, at a fixed airspeed and altitude, an object of known ballistics could be dropped from an airplane right onto any spot in Europe. They could flick the pigeon poop off Eros' wings in Piccadilly from 36,000 feet. Britton-Dippy flew fussily on the steady tone at precisely 30,000 feet and at exactly 300 miles an hour indicated. If there was not a trace of slip or skid in his gentle curve, which would pitch the load wide, why wouldn't it always be a piece of cake?

There were the winds.

Once the load had fallen, it was at the mercy of the winds. Met reports were not up to the minute. Fortunately, the Cat and Mouse together could tell exactly how the wind blew by comparing Britton-Dippy's faithful indicated airspeed with his true groundspeed, as shown on their instruments.

"Here we go," said Cybulski, "nine minutes and thirty."

In the earphones came the suddenly high-pitched warning letters, abcd, .__ __··· __·__· __··

Then a series of fast dashes, __ __ __ __ __ __ __ __ __ __ __ __, and a series of fast dots, ...

When the dots stopped, Cybulski pressed the red tit on his panel. The big flare canisters tumbled out of the bomb bay and fell toward Nijmegen. A barometric mechanism opened them at 800 feet, releasing a cluster of sixty yellow candles, each under a tiny parachute. These drifted differently from the heavy canister but that, too, was already in the calculations. The hissing, smoking cluster sagged and spread at the bottom as it fell, the reason Germans called the target indicators Christmas trees.

The yellow TI's cascaded onto the ground, to burn fiercely for another four minutes. They were impossible to imitate and difficult to extinguish. The second, third and fourth Mossies augmented the fire at three-minute intervals. They were prepared to change colors at the last minute or to lay the TI's above an unexpected blanket of cloud, if so ordered by their leader. In Britton-Dippy's flight, the last two Mossies flew on to the southeast instead of returning to England. They had a mysterious assignment to establish a radio relay station high over middle Germany.

Wing-Commander Timmins saw the yellows break out from a distance of thirty miles. He spoke to his entire squadron for the first time that night. "Backers-up, prepare to drop your markers." An unfortunate slip, that, with Turleigh gone. Parke alone would be dropping his greens as the last *Oboe* yellows were burning out. The color change signaled the arrival of the first bombers at the turning point. Others in the long stream that followed would augment the green datum marker at Nijmegen from time to time.

The Fresnel spotlights and wax pencils on Fluko's glass map confirmed his hunch. The Pathfinders were turning down the Rhine valley toward the Ruhr.

Luftwaffe night fighters raced up the Rhine to meet the bombers.

Serrate Mosquitoes laced themselves into the slow bomber stream. Squadron Leader Taffey and his observer thumped hard across a fresh slipstream, made by Major Meister's Ju88. The major had abandoned the alerted, disciplined Pathfinders to find easier game among stragglers in the huge main force.

At the port city of Wilhelmshaven, the siren tours began with a massive drop of red spot fires, changing to white. No bombs fell at Wilhelmshaven. The first wave of twelve spoof bombers roared straight on across the Jade Bay and bombed Bremerhaven, without marker flares, four minutes later, from a low altitude. Sixty-four bombs struck the city centrum: there were thirty-two 500 pound HE's and sixteen incendiary tins of the same weight. The tins burst open as they fell, each spawning a hundred phosphorus sticks.

Wilhelmshaven was to remain on alert for the rest of the night. Bremerhaven estimated that about eighty bombers had somehow compressed their attack into less than two minutes, starting a fire so intense that there would be no personnel or equipment to handle a second episode of any kind.

Fluko's second thoughts on the enemy plan were still in flux, when Hamburg reported (quickly and accurately, as usual) that both marker flares and bombs were falling from a flight of sixteen Mosquitoes, probably the beginning of a major attack. The Hamburg group then turned up immediately for the submarine pens at Kiel. A third force arrived on the northern scene, feinting with green and white flares on Bremen, then dropping its bombs on Wilhelmshaven. Fighter Division II at Stade screamed for night fighters from Berlin, to replace what had been sent to the Ruhr. By that time, all the spoof raiders had disappeared. It was to be perfectly quiet in the north for about forty minutes.

Asia had easily made up her lost time well above Nuremberg. The cyclops headlamp of the thundering Pacific drilled a deep and endless funnel into the snow. Engineer Nowarra imagined the lines of soft flakes streaming over the cab to be fascicles of impenetrable tracer flak, through which he drove fearlessly. He was irritated by the trainmaster's unexpected call on the cab telephone.

"Orders, Nowarra," said the *Schaffner*. "Reduce your speed and watch for our pilot train. It waits for us in the forest twenty kilometers above Nuremberg. They are putting out signal flares. You are to drive down beside them, head-to-tail, understand?"

"What the hell is this, Gottbaum? We are right back on time. We are due in Nuremberg at two fifty-one."

"Please, Nowarra, no shit from you. I can put Göring on, if you like. We will follow the rest of the schedule as planned. I will call you again."

"What is it?" asked Bauer, as the engineer slammed the telephone back into its hooks.

"How should I know? Maybe the *Reichsmarschall* has to take a piss under the trees. Keep your eyes open for stop flares."

"They must have been busy on the radiotelephone back there."

"Not at all, Bauer, not at all. These people hear Voices, didn't you know that?"

As Nowarra trimmed *Asia*'s speed, he tested the steam brakes cautiously. Ice on the tracks, under the snow. They were crossing a high, wide plateau, unprotected from the howling wind. The force of the wind became apparent as the train slowed and the hypnotic funnel of snow in the beam of the headlamp broke down into a confusion of whorls and eddies.

Five minutes after the train plunged into the gothic shelter of the forest, Bauer saw a cherry flare far ahead beside the track. He was soon waving to the strangers in the other cab, as *Asia* rumbled past them and matched its length against the shorter pilot train.

"That's strange," said Bauer, "their loko is hooked up at the north end, facing the rear. Are they going to *push* it into Nuremberg?"

"Oh, you stupid Bauer! Don't you know that a loko pulls in both directions? They're recalling the pilot train to Berlin, that's all." Nowarra hoped he was right about this. They wouldn't have shifted the engine if it were simply a breakdown. They hadn't turned the engine around, either because the table at Nuremberg wasn't working or, more likely, there wasn't time.

"They've turned off all the lights back there." Bauer was leaning far out his window; something was going on between the trains. "We're making too much steam to see anything."

"Don't worry about it. They're watching trains copulate, something you don't see every day. Well, we still stop at Nuremberg and we terminate at Munich."

"Remember, we *must* pick up water at Nuremberg."

"We will, Herr Bauer, we will. No schnapps, though, until this black crocodile is in the shed at Munich."

The engineer's jibe was malicious. Bauer was a

young alcoholic. The fireman opened the big firebox doors and stabbed the dormant coalbed repeatedly with a long iron. Firelight lapped his face. Not once looking over at the engineer, Bauer slammed the doors shut and climbed back into his high seat. The men waited in awkward silence. Ten minutes passed in the forest.

Lorraine and Moselle behind them, Croft and Adeš were now deep into the Third Army's bulging salient. As Croft twisted a petrol cock to change his tanks, he saw McLaughlin peering through the dark Perspex, his gloved hands forming a light shield.

"Keep your eye out for Strasbourg on the left, John. We're coming up to the Rhine. Just a few miles west of the city, I think, everyone speaks German."

"Nun, Erdemann, was für ein Prädikament!"

So spoke *Kandidat* Heinrich Erdemann aloud to himself. Thirty miles east of the advancing Mosquitoes, the boy was also looking for Strasbourg. He was alone and nearly frozen in the open front cockpit of the pretty white He50 biplane. Not over an hour earlier, Erdemann had taken off from his training base at Tübingen, with his instructor, for a last examination before the young pilot's first night solo. Now he was lost somewhere over the Black Forest. Keeping north of west, he would surely find the Rhine. Going slightly north would also steer him well away from the dreaded high Feld Berg (4900 meters) and place Strasbourg south, if he missed the city on his arrival at the river. Grimly, Erdemann believed he would recognize Strasbourg at night, if he could see it at all when he got there. Then the course from Strasbourg to Tübingen was precisely 090 degrees. With all that knowledge in his head, it was still a predicament if one had only to consider the fuel remaining.

If Erdemann were to survive the war and eventually develop a sense of humor, he would probably look back on this horrible night as a classic comedy.

The tyrant-instructor had started by saying, "All right, Erdemann, you're as well prepared as ever you'll be. Take me down, let me off, and try to keep yourself alive for thirty minutes. Thirty minutes! Fly at three hundred meters. Stay within ten kilometers of Tübingen."

The infallible instructor had then pointed down at the airfield, Erdemann nodding obediently. He took off alone and landed twenty-nine minutes later at his Tübingen base. They were furious at him!

"Dear Erdemann, idiot," they said, "you have set your instructor down at the Stuttgart night fighter satellite! How, in God's name, how?"

Erdemann recalled that the airfield *had* seemed unfamiliar but he had never flown before at night. And the instructor had *ordered* him to land there. They sent him off again to retrieve the *Leutnant* from Stuttgart, saying that the *Leutnant* was by now a raving maniac.

Whether *Kandidat* Erdemann feared more the instructor's wrath or a crash in the Black Forest, there was no possibility of comedy or humor in his situation. He had not found Stuttgart where it was supposed to be; the instructor was still waiting. Now there was some doubt that he would find Tübingen again.

"There it is, there's Strasbourg," said McLaughlin. "Your course is zero-eight-five to—to the bridge."

Perhaps the slight hesitation in McLaughlin's voice had caused Croft to glance over and back quickly. It was disturbing to Bill, after all this time and intimacy, as the Mosquito rolled gently into the last turn they would make before the target, that he might never know whether John was bursting inside to kill Adolf Hitler or calculating the fuel they might have to use up waiting for the train. (In fact, neither. Croft was thinking of his disastrous solo flight at Atlanta, when he had almost flown into the Piedmont Mountains.)

Karel Adeš saw Strasbourg two miles off his port wing, shortly before he followed Croft into the turn. He grinned and punched Miloslav with his elbow.

"Draho," said Karel, "now we go in to kill this fellow. How long is that?"

"To Donauwörth is twenty-five minutes. But we

wait for him there, I don't know how long. That is
where it will go wrong. I know something will go
wrong."

"Oh, Draho, you are such a gloomy farmer! You
should be sitting up there with John. *That* would be the
happy pair! I would have old Bill back here with me.
We would laugh and sing right up the *Führer*'s ass, I
will bet you."

Kandidat Erdemann found the Rhine and
promptly broke one of the strictest rules in his training
command. No student was allowed to fly below 300
meters in the Württemberg region, except in the vicin-
ity of airfields when it was the intention to land.
Erdemann descended as rapidly as he dared along the
east bank of the Rhine, so that he could see landmarks
on the black ground below. What terrified him now
was that the pale moon was spending more and more
time behind thickening clouds. When he was already
down to fifty meters, he could barely see the broad
river itself.

Far out ahead of Croft, a jet-dead patch caught
his restless eye. He sucked in his breath, as the patch
turned gray and then white. As he instinctively
whipped the Mosquito violently to the right, the thing
went by a wingspan away.

"We nearly bought it," said Croft, "that was a
plane."

There was a blinding flash and a faint thump almost directly below them.

"Gunfire again?" asked McLaughlin.

"I don't think so, Bill. Call Karel." Croft's voice
was thick. He banked the Mosquito tightly to circle the
fire on the ground. The wind turned it into a huge
exclamation mark running east and west.

Before McLaughlin had called a dozen times,
Croft told him to give up and make a record of the
time and location. He said that Karel had flown into
the ground, trying to avoid whatever it was that had
nearly hit them first.

"What are you going to do, John?" Bill temporarily deferred all the questions about Karel Adeš
and Drahomir Miloslav.

"We'll keep going. It'll take a few minutes to think out any changes we have to make on the way. You do the same. We may have to abort this thing."

McLaughlin immediately thought of a few minor modifications that he would offer. His own mind was made up but he wanted Croft to speak first.

"Yes, we'll keep going," said Croft. "If there's flak at the bridge, we won't have the Czechs to break it up. I don't like that, personally. But if we don't smash the bridge with the big rockets, it wouldn't matter whether the Czechs were with us or not. They could only go after the train with their wing rockets and that wouldn't be enough."

"Yes, I agree."

McLaughlin was appalled at the way Croft said "the Czechs." He had never called them that after he'd met them the first time. "Karel was a Czech, John. Draho was actually a Slovak."

"A Slovak, was he?" Croft held the control grip with his left hand. He had slipped the glove off his right hand. He was flexing the fingers methodically.

Kandidat Erdemann had not seen the first Mosquito slash by his left wing, nor was he aware that the second had dived sharply to escape the wheels of the pretty white biplane. When the fire bloomed on the ground, Erdemann was convinced it was flak—he had never seen gunfire, day or night—and he climbed right back to a height of three hundred meters. He never saw Strasbourg. He flew on into the Allied territory of Lorraine, since he was now reading the compass backward.

It was the coldest winter Europe had seen in thirty years.

16

Operation at the Danube

"Helga Forstmann, you are a *whore!* You will come to a bad end."

Her father's words—lately there was almost nothing he had not called her—haunted Helga's mind and what little conscience she was said to have. But that was only on her "bad" nights when she hurried back to Papa's hut. One of Helga's saddest discoveries, as she left childhood, was that the Forstmann home was, in fact, a hut. And now it leaned forlornly for support against the slope of a hill near the peak of the Taunus Mountain.

A line from the center of Frankfurt, twenty-five kilometers away, through Homburg at the eastern foot of the Taunus, would continue to the north through countless map points, including the disintegrating roof of the Forstmann home. Then the line would transect towns and cities unknown to Helga—Altenkirchen, Düsseldorf in the Ruhr, Goch at the tip of the North Rhineland. Helga had never even heard of Nijmegen in Holland, but here the line would make an important bend, as a thousand navigators of the Royal Air Force had drawn it.

Helga Forstmann would mark the way to Frankfurt.

Helga had thanked most of the soldiers who had given her the ride from Homburg in their lorry by kissing them innocently enough. They liked her because she teased them with fine style, for a country girl, rather suggestively and without discrimination. But Helga Forstmann had a not unusual code for an eighteen-year-old woman: she could love deeply only one man at a time. That man had been in the lorry, the last one to let go of her hand when she had jumped down into the snow. Sepp Hemer had laughed the loudest when she almost disappeared in a big drift. Helga had never, never confused Sepp with innocent kisses.

". . . A miserable little whore, Helga Forstmann, and you will come to sleep with the Devil!"

Sepp Hemer, the Devil. It was almost a certainty that Joseph Hemer had got her pregnant. If that were true, one good thing would happen: Helga would have to leave her father forever. She would leave him whether Sepp wanted to marry her or not.

As soon as the lorry was out of sight, Helga turned to the immediate problem of finding the path to the top of the mountain. She had no watch. She only knew that it was past two o'clock in the morning. For two hours already, she had been eighteen years old. The soldiers had arranged the birthday party for her in Homburg, although Sepp had been the ringleader. As she looked up the moonlit slope, covered with virgin snow a meter deep, all the bright and pleasant memories of the evening turned into miserable little bats, which fluttered out of her head to hang themselves one by one in the dark eaves of her father's mind.

The wretched road was completely hidden by the snow. It was hard work to push upward through the stuff and the footing was wicked. Helga's boot slipped off a teetering stone. She fell forward, under the snow again, cursing.

At 02.32, the Cat at Dover started to light up the target aiming point, fifteen miles out in the country northwest of Frankfurt. This time, the electronic tether had brought the *Oboe* Mosquitoes south on a gentle curve starting near Marburg. Mouse initiated the sequence of semimusical tones which ended when the first Mosquito was in a carefully plotted position at an altitude of 29,000 feet. When the complex package from the bomb bay had fallen nearly six miles and burst open, a crimson pyrotechnic fountain marked the official opening of the siege at Frankfurt.

Helga's head was down as she climbed wearily out of the trough her body had made in the dense snow. It was a trivial fall, she was not injured. Why, why the blinding red light in her eyes? It was so bright, that everything around her looked flat like newspaper photos.

". . . I promise you, Helga, you will burn in hell!"

The girl looked up. She was in a giant birdcage of red fire streamers, a crackling, hissing canopy which shed tortuous worms of oily smoke as it settled down over her. The unbearable heat enveloping Helga caused her finally to run. Or try to run, so far as the deep, bloody snow would allow. Perhaps it was significant that she turned down the slope, directly away from her father's house, although the direction no longer mattered. The flaming mixture of cotton, rubber, benzene and phosphorus from the 2300 pound Pink Pansy, dripping blobs of molten slime, was beginning to strike the snow in an irregular circle several hundred yards across. It would burn there for ten or fifteen minutes after Helga Forstmann had practically disappeared. Even her own father, if he came out to look and did not simply believe she had run away, would have the first impression of Helga's body as the grotesquely charred remnant of a tree formation.

For Robert Gabriel, it seemed at first to be one of those nights when everything worked like a Swedish machine. The Norseman controller had put them onto the bomber stream over the Rhine, about thirty-five kilometers above Duisberg. Gabriel had an early hunch that the target was not going to be in the Ruhr.

"Green and yellow marker flares, Rudi," the *Kommodore* had said to his observer, when they were just south of Goch. "I think they are fakes."

"Yes, Herr *Kommodore*." Anderian readily accepted the idea that an *Experte* could tell which flares were false.

Gabriel had slightly rearranged his metal legs on the rudder pedals and slid his bottom around on the hard seat, as if to get a better purchase on the big Owl. He charged the cannons, firing a very short test burst.

"All prepared, Rudi?"

"Yes, *Kommodore*."

Shortly afterward, they had gone into the bomber stream. A minute later, Rudi had brought them in solidly on a contact, a Lancaster.

Gabriel did not use the popular *schräge Musik*. It was a matter of honor with the *Kommodore* to take his chances, boring in relentlessly from the rear, slightly below his quarry, a few degrees to the side for minimum deflection. He knew the anatomy of enemy aircraft to the last stitch of rivets and saw no profit in sparing English crews to make his own job a little safer.

The *Kommodore* killed the pilot by firing between the stabilizer and top of the left wing root. Part of the cockpit roof was blown out and back over the Owl's wingtip. When the tail gunner's tracers opened up on the empty sky at the right and slewed around like a wavy fan toward the night fighter, Gabriel's shells folded the man into the ruins of his elaborate turret as one would mix the filling and pastry of a cream tart.

"Congratulations, Rudi! Do you want to see what happens to your first kill?"

There wasn't much to see. Only two parachutes were counted, leaving the doomed parent like naked white newborns. The Lancaster's great wings rotated slowly in the last moment before plunging vertically into the ground. The fire that the men in the Owl waited to confirm in the final crash was no more than the flare of a match.

"All right, Rudi?"

"Quite all right, *Kommodore*." Anderian was nauseated.

They were again in level flight, surrounded by

darkness. Anderian refused to believe that one could faint from fright, yet the *Kommodore*'s voice seemed to rouse him from a dream. The tone was not anxious, telling Rudi that the bizarre lapse may have gone undetected.

The *Naxos-Z* tail-warning set lit up. Its faint ticking in the headphones warned pilot and observer that they were caught in the beam of an English search radar.

"Where, Rudi, *where?*" Gabriel waited for Rudi's bearing from the small rotating antenna. He already knew that the hunter was at extreme range from the rate and faintness of the sound in the phones.

"Nearly straight back, *Kommodore*. He seems to be turning in from the left."

"Get set to pick him up when I turn. I will try to outrun to the right and turn back to the left."

Gabriel would concentrate on outreading the enemy observer at his own tubes, if possible, on making the man's image of the Owl as confusing as a master card trick.

Rudi felt the Owl surge forward, engines shrieking in a wild cadence he had never heard before. The *Kommodore* had rammed his throttles past the MW.50 stops on the quadrants, injecting methanol into the carburetors for a temporary 25 percent power increase. The ticking in the earphones faded.

"Damn it, Butter, I'm losing them!" The *Serrate* leader's nav/rad willed the Mossie forward, rocking his torso back and forth like a desperate oarsman. "Can't you get this bloody kite cracking?"

"Sorry, old man, she's tootling along at top boost now," said Squadron Leader Taffey. "What's the *Perfectos* gen?"

"So, Rudi, we can outrun this Tommy"—*thank God, thank God!* the observer whispered—"if we have to," said Gabriel, "but let's give him a bit of fight first." He cut off the alcohol to the engines and turned ninety degrees to the left. "When I turn back again, be ready to pick them up immediately."

"Yes, he's got his IFF on, Butter." *Perfectos* caught the emissions identifying the Owl as "friend" to radar stations and other German night fighters. "Let's try a hard left, ninety."

Gabriel completed his timed reversal, and a miniature sausage crept in at the left of Rudi's SN-2 screen. The observer quickly warned his pilot that the enemy aircraft closed dangerously fast.

"Now he's looking straight at us on his SN-2, Butter. I don't have him yet on the main gear." The English Mark IV *Serrate* receiver was activated by those very 90-megacycle radiations that Anderian used to find the Mosquito.

Measure, countermeasure, counter-countermeasure. On May 9, 1943, a defecting crew had delivered to the RAF a Ju88R-1, complete with the latest short-range Lichtenstein C.1. *The compromised radar system was then first jammed at Hamburg by foil strips of "window" cut to half the 35-centimeter wavelength of* Li C.1. *The* Luftwaffe *quickly recovered and improved its position with long-range* Lichtenstein SN-2. *On July 13, 1944, a Ju88G-1 bearing SN-2 landed in Britain by mistake. It was repainted in RAF colors, registered as TP190 and called simply "P." Among others, Taffey and his nav/rad flew and studied P, whose capture was cleverly hidden from the* Luftwaffe.

"Left *fast, Kommodore!* Turn . . . turn . . . keep turning! He's below us, two hundred meters. He's still turning with us."

"I've got him, Butter, I've got him on the *ASH!* Turn hard left . . . left . . . left. Six hundred feet above you. Oh, oh Christ, he's *gone!*"

Gabriel had broken the circle by pulling the Owl straight up, almost to a stall, falling off to his right, and flipping over again to the left—a metal-wrenching S in three dimensions. Rudi was stunned to find any indication whatever on the SN-2.

"He—he's going straight away from you, *Kommodore*. We're gaining very slightly." The *Kommodore* was diving shallowly to come out below the other craft.

"They're coming up behind us, about a thousand yards back," announced Taffey's observer. This time, the rear-looking *Monica* Mark VI had seen the Owl overtaking the Mosquito. Taffey counted off a few seconds and turned 180 degrees.

After only two more cycles of stalemate with his ingenious adversary, *Kommodore* Gabriel had figured it all out. He snapped off the friend-foe switch and gave new instructions to Anderian.

"Shut everything down, Rudi—*Naxos, Flensburg*, both *Lichtensteins*. We're practically giving ourselves to them. Now, use your *Li* sets only to keep a finger on them, or when I ask for a reading. I want to go in on their beam, about a hundred meters below them."

It was a difficult approach and Gabriel couldn't shut off the Owl itself. These fellows had both front and rear search apparatus, that was clear, but maybe he could squeeze in sidewise. Rudi was quite good.

After several false starts, when the Tommy turned into them, Gabriel began to realize that the range and search angle of the SN-2 were superior to what the English equipment offered. He asked Rudi to bring him in from extreme range. "If I can get just one visual, Rudi," the *Kommodore* promised, "I will never lose it."

It worked so well that the *Kommodore* remarked to his observer, "I believe they think we have run away."

No matter how the Mosquito twisted, it was never able to break free of the Owl, which ran below like a pilotfish. The *Kommodore,* if not Rudi, repeatedly saw his shell bursts striking off pieces of the wings and fuselage. The twisting and turning stopped shortly after a fire was seen in the port engine nacelle. The nacelle doors suddenly opened and the big landing gear dropped down. When the long, jutting engine fell off with its airscrew still spinning, Gabriel drew away to the side. *For the good God's sake, Herr Kommodore!* Anderian pleaded silently, *why don't you leave them alone?*

With one engine working, with its port wing dragging badly, the Mosquito flew on and even seemed to be trying mild evasive action. Gabriel came back into a firing position and pounded shell after shell into the starboard engine without significant effect. In utter disbelief, he paused again. At that moment, the Mosquito rolled slowly over onto its back and dived straight toward the earth. It was a *Luftwaffe* requirement to observe the crash.

"Done, Rudi!" said the *Kommodore*. "That's your Mosquito."

No, no, I won't have it! was the angry, soundless reply. *That is the last murder, Kommodore, I swear it!*

Ten uniformed men at the almost deserted Nuremberg station boarded *Asia* when the train arrived at six minutes before three in the morning. Engineer Nowarra then eased *Asia* out of the vaulted, smoke-grimed shed to a siding in the floodlit section of the snowbound yard. No one left the train while they took on water. Only three of the Nuremberg delegation, an army signals major and two junior officers in the black-and-silver of the SS, left the train when *Schaffner* Gottbaum signaled the cab to proceed.

Nowarra was still taking up slack between the cars, the big drivers were barely turning, when a yardman overtook the three officers. He had been greasing the locomotive; a pressure gun was in his right hand. The gun fell out of the oiler's grasp as he tripped on purpose and sprawled flat in the snow. To this question, the signals major answered by picking up the gun and handing it to the oiler. The oiler was asking the major if Hitler was aboard *Asia* and the major was saying yes.

A few kilometers south of the station, a civilian munitions transport was parked at the side of the empty highway. Two men were discussing a motor ailment, while one of them worked with a spanner down near the crankcase. They stopped a moment to watch *Asia* roll by, the engine snorting powerfully but still moving slowly. The oiler from the station rode by on his cycle and stopped near the transport to look in on the difficult motor. After a brief conversation, the transport driver walked to the rear of the munitions vehicle and reached for something under the tightly strapped tarpaulins.

As the cyclist left the ammunition carrier, he heard it start up behind him. It passed him and was soon out of sight, soon catching up with *Asia,* to follow her as far as possible on her way down to the Danube. Two VHF radio sets were sending scrambled signals from the back of the transport to the *Oboe* crews who were equipped to hear. Explosives were set, should danger threaten the driver and his mechanic.

The third Mosquito from Flying Officer Britten-Dippy's *Oboe* flight at Nijmegen received the garbled ground signals from the German truck, while orbiting at 35,000 feet over the Eder River near Kassel. After automatic relay to England, where unscrambling took place, the primary signals plus new weather data were retransmitted from a paper tape to the *Oboe* aircraft.

Seventeen minutes after Karel Adeš and Draho Miloslav had gone down, the red lights on two identical VHF sets in Croft's Mosquito began blinking.

"Go ahead, John," said Bill McLaughlin, shutting off one set and flipping a covered switch on the other. "MACCABEE Relay, this is MACCABEE One, over."

"MACCABEE One, we have a message for you. How do you read us?"

"We hear you five by five, Relay. What is the message?"

"MACCABEE One, the message is: 'The temple doors are open.' I will repeat: 'The temple doors are open.' Acknowledge, please."

"MACCABEE Relay, we understand. *The temple doors are open.* How will we find the oranges, over?"

"Yes, MACCABEE One, we have the latest on oranges for you. Blanket is eight-tenths. Mattress at angels one, quilt at angels five. Pillow, five miles at angels zero. That is all we have for you, over."

"Thank you, Relay. MACCABEE One, out."

The weather they would find at the bridge was not that much different from what they had run into below Stuttgart: 80 percent cloud cover rising from 1000 to 5000 feet, visibility five miles.

"Willie," said the *Oboe* pilot, "did you hear that voice? That's a bloody Yank we're working for! I wonder what he's up to."

" 'E's doin' me no good, I'll tell you." The observer was fighting severe gas cramps in the unpressurized cabin, brought on by a double serving of turnips and Brussels sprouts. "Can we go home now?"

The lights went dead on the special VHF set in Croft's Mosquito. Fascinated by the entire transaction, McLaughlin said, "Someday I'd like to track down all the characters in this affair. That message must have quite a history." He reset the covered switch on the VHF set.

Fifty-nine Mosquitoes of the Fast Night Striking Force came in to Berlin right on time, three minutes before the first bombs would fall on Frankfurt. A desperate throng of night fighters from Stendal formed a long, defensive line across the three "tracks" regularly used by the FNSF. The line was almost totally bypassed, vertically. Only two *Luftwaffe* planes could reach 40,000 feet where the Berlin Express traveled. Even those two Ha-Ha fighters—whose engines drew a limited supply of extra oxygen from shots of nitrous oxide, laughing gas—could not cope with the great speed of the Mosquitoes when they started the shallow dive toward the capital city.

A heavy storm over Berlin had moved south, leaving broken trails of cloud. On a weaving path down through clear channels, the FNSF leader prepared to drop his bomb and lay flares for his big pack on the concentrated target area. Bombing would start at the giant flak towers near the *Tiergarten*, the zoo's west corner. With a normal spread of bombs—nearly

120 tons in units of 4000 pounds, a unit every five seconds (on average)—they could hope to strike the Propaganda Ministry, ministries for Army, Navy and Air, SS and Gestapo headquarters, and the Chancellery itself. Also the Swiss Legation, Swedish Embassy and Hotel Adlon, unavoidably.

"Look at that," said the Marker Leader.

A rectangular patch of fire had broken out in open country near the River Havel's junction with the northwest edge of Berlin. It was clearly a German diversion.

"They never give up, do they?" The navigator chortled with scorn.

"No—and for such bright bastards, I don't know why they're too stupid to make good copies of anything. Especially, I suppose, a bombed area."

A full-scale replica of Berlin afire had been built out in the countryside, complete with flares, smoke, searchlights, flak, incendiaries and clockwork explosions. The German decoy was not only geometrically perfect, it burned with uniform intensity. To the Englishmen, the elaborate fraud resembled the ragged, sprawling, sparkling target of real bombs as a rack of votary candles resembled a forest fire out of control.

"I don't think," said the Leader, pressing his bomb release, "that our people will be confused, do you?"

The ugly, blunt cookie fell from its crutch gear into a trajectory precisely along *Kurfürstendamm*, which led to the two flak towers. Like a frightened stallion, the lightened Mossie reared upward. The bomb struck close to one of the giant towers, whose dangerous streams of tracer, lazy at first, raced terminally past the bomber's windows in a meteorite shower. Parachute flares, mixed yellow and green, had broken out with the single bomb. They settled slowly over the smoke and dust tossed up by the high explosive.

Circling back low, watching his companions come down by twos and threes, the Leader surveyed this city whose outlines were now more familiar to him than his own London. "You know," he said, "we're just shifting the same old rubble back and forth across the Zoo Garden night after night. A bit discouraging, what?"

"I'm still standing that fortnight of drinks," said the Navigator Leader, "for the bloke who finally prangs the chariot on the Brandenburg Gate. You'll do it yet, old man."

There were more than 400 searchlights in the array at Berlin. Through an incredible administrative error, these lights were not activated until the last FNSF Mosquito had built up two minutes outside the city limits. There was not a single RAF casualty in the raid. Not a single Berliner was injured or killed. A zoo lion named Empress gave birth prematurely to male cubs, both dead.

At Frankfurt, time wound rapidly down to zero, 03.36. Radio silence over Germany was officially broken by the Master Bomber at zero minus ten:

"Marker Leader, this is the controller. What is your position, please? Over."

"We are ten miles north of target center at twenty thousand. Only nine of us now, Master Bomber. Marker Six went u/s with a bad glycol leak right after takeoff."

"Thank you, Marker Leader. I am going down now to have a look about."

The Master Bomber's Mosquito dove from 15,000 feet over the center of the well blacked-out city. At 1000 feet, it leveled out and crossed back over the River Main from the south. Although the marking point was a distinctive configuration in the central railroad yards, the Master Bomber had first to find a bridge. With a cathedral near one end and a narrow island hugging the shore under the opposite bridgehead, the bridge pointed directly at the marking point. The rail yards were shrouded in darkness but ice and snow on the Main outlined the bridge as if it were a strip of draughting tape.

"Come down, come down, Marker Leader," said the Master Bomber, when he had crossed the city once at top speed, a thousand feet above the ground, and was sweeping widely back to the north. "I make cloud base at three thousand, well broken up, haze not too bad."

Oddly, they had drawn no flak. Not a searchlight had stabbed out at them.

"Link Aircraft: this is the Master Bomber over target center. How do you hear me, please—Link One?"

"Link One here. Loud and clear."

Link One was in Timmins' PFF squadron; Two and Three were further back in the main force. Plain speech was to be used throughout the raid, if possible, with the Links acting as relays for the Master Bomber, putting his voice into W/T if R/T failed or was jammed. Links kept in touch with Group back in England, to pass on prime orders and Met changes. Only prime orders, "mission canceled" or "recall," were encoded. No acknowledgements were given to the Master Bomber, except for the order "go home."

As the Master Bomber climbed to a middle height of 10,000 feet for an average view of the scene he was setting, the Marker Leader led his eight Mosquitoes down through wide lacunae in the layers of cloud. Hunting out the landmarks his group had to light up, the M/L quickly decided to split his force.

"Leader to Marker Force: Two, Three, Four and Seven—stay down here and drop your loads right after me. All others keep away for the time being. With the cloud buildup, I'll need you later."

"Good show, Marker Leader," cut in the Master Bomber, "I didn't like the looks of that cloud either. We'll be repositioning the Check aircraft when they arrive, I think."

There were four Check Lancasters among the earliest Main Force squadrons, whose assignment was to assess target visibility from several height bands.

"From Marker Leader: *tally-ho!*"

Starting at 2500 feet, the leader's Mosquito descended briskly to 900 feet and released a finned 1000 pound cylinder. There was a brilliant white flash from the bomb bay, a burst of red fire from the falling canister. The Mosquito roared across the main switching yard of the Frankfurt terminal.

"Marker Two, tally-ho!"

The second Mosquito repeated the leader's run, with minor aiming corrections. He had seen that the initial drop, a red spot fire, had fallen a hundred yards beyond the prominent signal tower at the terminal's choke point. His own red spot broke out as the Leader's camera flashed for the fourth time.

"Marker Leader, Two here. Yours was a bit long. I have corrected."

"I see that, Two. Okay, Markers Three and Four —aim at the near spot, the *near* spot."

Three complied precisely. The aiming point began boiling properly.

Marker Four disappeared in a scarlet puff, blown up by the red spot fire in his bomb bay. The flares were set to open and ignite at a barometric pressure corresponding to 700 feet. Concentrating on an accurate drop, the fourth pilot had gone below the limiting altitude. His brainless pyrotechnic tore the Mosquito apart. Directly beneath the explosion, a small locomotive chuffed energetically out of a spur with several goods wagons in two. Upturned faces on the short train reflected the red death falling upon them.

It was T-minus-four.

The Master Bomber saw the searchlights, a hundred or more, suddenly form a magic fence of silver pickets over the western approaches to Frankfurt. He had wondered about the strange delay; it seemed as if a single hand had desperately broken orders and thrown a master switch to all the lights at once. From the way the unleashed beams swept their sky sectors in slow and stately patterns, the controller noted, no targets had yet been fixed by the master radars.

"Controller to Estate Car Force: you may queue up now and bomb on the red TI's." The Master Bomber was satisfied with the target's readiness. "Checkplane One, when you have finished your run, will you circle over the way in and give me your opinion of the visibility? We have broken clag all over the target right now but I fear it will consolidate."

"This is the Marker Leader, Master. What can we do for you now?"

"Marker Leader, I should like to keep the two chaps with cancellation yellows. The rest of you can pack it up and go home. Good show!"

"Thank you, and I acknowledge *go home*. All right, Markers Niner and Tenner, stay on the target, will you? All other Markers, go home, go home, without delay."

The sound of laughter came back with one of the acknowledgments—*Without delay, without delay, and live to fight another day!*

A B–17 flying ferret on loan to Bomber Command picked up the first public announcement of the Frankfurt raid, although the reason for the outrageous delay was never discovered. The Flying Fortress, an aerial intelligence center packed with electronics to monitor all radio and radar traffic, kept an "entertainment channel" open to the German civilian network. At 03.30, zero-minus-six, the *Deutschlandsender* clock stopped.

"*Achtung! Achtung! Achtung!* A large raider force comes up to the town limits of *Füchsin*"—Vixen, the code name for Frankfurt—"from the northwest. All citizens will immediately go to their cellars or assigned public shelters. Stragglers will be arrested by the police. Crimes committed during air raids are punished by summary death sentences in the People's Courts. The following city officials will report by telephone to. . . ."

Major Meister's mood was foul. After the first Lancaster blew up in his face, nothing had worked right. A small piece of Alclad from the bomber had starred a canopy pane right in front of the pilot's face; it was difficult for the short man to see. Something large had raked through one of the SN-2 antlers on the right side of the Junkers' nose and wedged itself in the angle between wing root and fuselage. Albrecht, the observer, identified the large object as the body, or a good part of the body, of a man. Albrecht and Lang were obviously depressed by the discovery and Meister was brutally contemptuous of them. Then Lang's *Neptun* began to fail.

"Most sensible pilots would give up at this point," said Meister, scornfully. That was true.

Instead of quitting, the major had followed the bombers almost to Frankfurt. He was practically blind, except for occasional spurts from the fading *Neptun*. He began shouting at the helpless Lang. Albrecht, thinking of the half-corpse on their wing, gagged and vomited on the major's right leg. Even so, it was only the dwindling fuel supply that forced the mulish *Kommandeur* to turn back to Bergen-zur-Zee.

"Cheer up, comrades," said Meister, imagining his absolute control over the spiritual temper of his cockpit. "We will refuel and trap these bastards on their way out again. Of course, with that bent antenna and"—the major forced a terrible grin and glanced quickly at the miserable Albrecht—"the stink in this cockpit, I may have to take over someone's '88." Frowning, he added dismally, "If any are available."

Thirty minutes later, Heino Meister crossed over the beacon near Bergen-zur-Zee and prepared to come straight in for his landing. He was tight on fuel. As the wheels and flaps were going down, the *Naxos* started ticking faintly.

"Mosquitoes, *Kommandeur!*" shouted Lang.

"Shit!"

"Danger, Sea-Star Two, this is *Atlantis* calling. We think there are intruders in the area. Please delay your landing."

"You *think*, Atlantis? I am very sorry, my tanks are dry. Light both ends of the landing path when I am below twenty meters. Cut off the lights when I am grounded."

"Sea-Star Two——"

"I am coming in."

The *Naxos* was loud in the earphones. As the Junkers descended over the dark sea, it flushed an invisible flock of seagulls off one of the rock jetties. A disoriented bird was smashed into the corpse on the wing. Three blue lights appeared in a line across the downwind end of the runway. Meister flattened his descent.

In the tower, they could hear the warbling en-

gines drag the Junkers into a sudden stall. Lines of
orange hyphens and commas flickered over the water,
past the swastika on the black fin. Meister's airplane
mushed steeply to the ground, struck tail first, burst
both tires. Still, skidding straight forward, it seemed
momentarily that the '88 would recover nicely. One
observer later said that a "giant match appeared to
strike along the landing path" and the night fighter began to burn. It came to rest ten meters short of the
guard fence and burned beyond control for five minutes without exploding.

There were none at Bergen-zur-Zee who could
honestly claim to feel deeply the loss of the *Gruppenkommandeur*. *Feldwebel* Lang was liked by all; his
death with Meister was the real tragedy. *Unteroffizier*
Albrecht was new, extremely shy and virtually unknown. The most durable and mysterious aspect of the
accident was the discovery of remnants of *four* bodies
in the wreckage. And the feathers seemed out of place
until it was agreed that they had come from one of
the *Kommandeur's* seat pillows.

Down through the Ruhr's dead center the Pathfinders
had come, through the ocher fog-smoke which was the
ugly monument to the Reich's industry. The filthy haze,
Wing Commander Timmins noted, was thickened by
cold moisture in the direction of Frankfurt. They would
find towering cloudbanks in their path long before
reaching the city.

Three times in the Ruhr, while passing Duisberg,
Düsseldorf and Wuppertal, the Pathfinders had seen
false marker flares go down, stirring the furious re-
sponse of local flak batteries. It was a grim certainty
that the reception at disciplined Frankfurt would reach
intolerably lethal levels.

When Timmins identified Helga Forstmann's pyre
on the mountain peak, it resembled a rose-tinted cameo
with irregular black patches in the center and a twin-
kling glaze of yellow at the edges, where the fires fed
on sparse trees. The marker badly needed replenish-
ment.

"All right, now, here's the initial point coming

up," was Timmins' R/T warning. "Let's close up from here on in. Z-Zebra, heave the red marker when you're all set."

Timmins' own bomb aimer had already taken his station in the Perspex nose, as all his counterparts in the other Lancasters were doing. They would have about five minutes to get set for the bomb drop at Frankfurt, from the moment Zebra's Pansy stoked up the traffic signal for the Main Force.

Zebra's bomb doors were opening when the first red marker at the target cast a dull glow against broken clouds over the center of Frankfurt, fifteen miles away. Timmins thought he could make out two or three more flares at intervals of about five seconds. Two minutes past the initial datum on the Taunus mountaintop, the wing commander's bomb aimer was ready to guide the Lancaster in its dangerous minutes of undeviating flight.

". . . Queue up now and bomb on the red TI's."

The bomb aimer had an undistorted view of Frankfurt through the flat glass set into the soft Perspex chin, which was scratched and grazed beyond all optical value. Timmins' old Lanc had no remote controls for the aimer; he had to direct the run by verbal orders to his pilot. But Timmy Timmins was better than a machine. He worked with his man like the chap's own fingers.

"Steady, Skipper, steady . . . left a bit . . . left. Bang on if we just hold this now."

Under radar direction, two searchlight units swept brilliant wands toward the Pathfinders, which were coming in on a line astern. They would all first be caught in the lights, then two or three would go down before the synchronized, automatic-firing guns. Later arrivals in the Main Force would have a decidedly better chance as the target lost discipline and organization. Timmins' crews faced the immediate prospect of flying steadily through a fresh Frankfurt system of heavy guns, firing from four successive ranks up to the city limits. Preset time fuses in the 88- and 105-millimeter HE shells built a concentrated box barrage in the air space through which the bombers must finally fly in the critical moment before releasing bombs.

Suddenly the searchlight beams, which were beginning to finger the Pathfinders, wandered crazily out of control. One of the *Mandrel* Lancs—there were two in Timmins' squadron—had connected with the Horizont searchlight-directing radar. Producing broadband interference much like that of unshielded auto ignition, the *Mandrel* temporarily wiped out the searchlights.

"Thirty seconds, Timmy," the bomb aimer announced. His eye on the altimeter and airspeed repeaters, the Mickey Mouse release in his right hand, the aimer was suddenly thrown hard against his Mark IV bombsight. He cut his forehead against a sharp edge of the optometrist's contraption.

The Lancaster was only bruised by a near-miss. Although the guns were radar-directed, they needed only altitude information which would not change on the bombing run-up. Quickly resetting his drift ring, the aimer watched the Lancaster crab against a strong wind along his calculated path to the red flare pools. His cross-hairs intersected the flares perfectly. He snapped the release in a dart-tossing motion of his whole arm.

"Bombs gone, Skipper!"

By the welcome leap the old bomber made when her four-ton blast bomb and the incendiary load of equal weight dropped from the slips, she expressed perfectly the desire of all aboard to get up and out. Seconds later, the photoflash canister burst over the rail yard to give the F24 camera light for its assessment picture. Every two minutes, on average, a squadron like Timmins' would add eighty more tons of carefully planned fireworks. Half the loads were incendiary, in short phosphorus sticks, long phosphorus cans, or tins of 350 to 1000 pounds packed with 4 pound magnesium hexagons. The other half was in blockbusters of 4000 or 8000 pounds, whose blasts created the draft to feed the incendiaries and threaten the firefighters. Five percent of the high-explosive loads were set to bury themselves and go off at irregular intervals up to eight o'clock in the morning. The raid itself would last about fifty minutes.

McLaughlin found the silent tension in the Mosquito's cockpit unbearable. It made him nervous, the way an unanswered telephone would. The analogy was pertinent because, on several occasions, he had come back to a hotel room to find Croft reading or watching London traffic under blasts from the phone bell that could tear paper from the walls.

"Where's the sanitation tube in this airplane?" asked McLaughlin.

"The what?" It was as if Bill had merely asked about the recognition signal pistol. "Oh, the manual calls it the sanitation tube, yes. It's under my seat."

"May I have it, please?"

Croft reached down and unclipped a six-inch funnel of metal attached to a rubber tube.

"Have you ever used one of these," asked Bill.

"Only once." Croft's laugh, deep in enemy territory, defused the cockpit atmosphere. "I ferried a Corsair from Jacksonville to Norfolk on top of three cups of coffee. I had to use the tube somewhere off North Carolina. When I landed at Norfolk, they said I seemed to have a fuel leak. I didn't argue, I just walked away fast."

"What happened?"

"There was no connection between the funnel and the blowout. Three cups of processed coffee were sloshing around the bottom of the Corsair."

McLaughlin's teddy bear, chute straps and Sutton harness caused no end of trouble with the relief tube but his good nature was restored by the sound of Croft's voice.

Both men saw the Danube at the same time. It bore no resemblance to a river. The snow that covered the low hills dipped into the shallow valley and lay unbroken upon what looked like a wide, unused *Autobahn.*

"Frozen solid!" said McLaughlin.

The sight of the Danube energized the navigator as if he had made landfall on a rare Pacific island. For minutes past, he had had nothing to do. Once more the maps began to rustle, the flashlight danced.

"Okay," said Bill, "my maps aren't exactly *National Geographic* for the region but we can't be more than ten miles from the bridge.

"Downstream or upstream?"

"You son of a bitch! Just keep driving, I'll watch the road signs."

The mountains on either side rose sharply as they flew east. There was a mild sensation of entrapment. The smooth surface of the river became increasingly broken by tumbled ice floes, masses of crates covered by white canvas.

"There it is," said Bill, "that's the bridge!"

They had come around a real bend in a real river but the scene was an unexpected shock to Croft. As in a dream, he found the Donauwörth bridge toylike. But the incredible accuracy of the Brevishall model also gave the illusion that the operation would be ridiculously simple.

One after another, complications were discovered.

They made a first pass low along the south bank. McLaughlin frantically gathered information through his binoculars that no Y-service could provide.

"I don't see any flak barges."

"Good," said Croft. "Those dark objects in the photos were piles of ice. Or shadows of ice."

"Yes, but that ice is stacked up against the bridge like a Roman ruin. What will that do?"

"I have no idea. It won't help."

"If there are flak nests on the bridge, I can't see them," continued McLaughlin. But the navigator gasped as the Mosquito crossed the south axis of the bridge. "Jesus, there's a train standing on the bridge!"

"What?"

"Yes, there are two tracks on the bridge, right? On the east track I see eight cars. One of them is a flat car with what could be a long gun mounted on it."

Croft cursed. "Do you know what that is? That's a 128-millimeter gun, the rail-mounted type. That's very bad news."

"And what about the Dambuster lights on this

rough ice, John. It's like the Grand Canyon down there."

"We didn't think of that either, did we? I don't know, I just don't know."

"Want to take another look?"

"The hell with it! We've got to go up and find that damn train. What's the heading for our first leg?"

"Zero eight zero. Just follow the river and I'll tell you when we're coming to Regensburg."

They were marking time now for *Asia.* After eight minutes of silence, McLaughlin's voice was strangely subdued: "Turn to three-two-zero. Next turn in eleven minutes. That brings us fifteen miles south of Nuremberg and about twelve miles east of the tracks. The train should be thereabouts."

It seemed unnatural to both men that they should hold the Mosquito back, which could find the train so quickly.

They had turned from the Danube only ten miles short of the Regensburg night fighter station. A trio of Ju88's passed above them. The emergency enveloping the upper Reich was now so desperate that squadrons in southeast Germany and even Austria were being summoned up into the action.

All below the low-flying Mosquito was white. A mountain blotted out the face of the moon to their left, although a soft light made weak, helpful shadows on the ground. The altimeter showed a steady loss of altitude as the Mosquito, flying right over the treetops, followed the terrain to the lower level near the city of Nuremberg.

"Time, John. Two-two-zero is the heading. That's right back to the bridge."

"Okay. Where's the bloody train?"

Croft angled the Mosquito to the right of the course Bill had given him. They could throw some time away, finding *Asia,* and still beat her to the bridge.

Far away, across a wide, dished, treeless plain of snow, a plume of smoke trailed north close to the earth.

"That's *Asia,*" said Croft. "She's doing fifty-sixty miles an hour. Should I go back to the bridge or go around behind her and watch from the west?" They

had tried to figure out all the contingencies. But here
was *Asia* herself.

"Why don't you keep her in sight as long as you
can, John?"

"I think you're right."

Croft flew well behind the train and swept around
widely to the far, western side. He dawdled the Mosquito in and out for occasional close looks. He broke
away when it seemed that he could get back to the
Danube in time to meet the train again at the bridge.
That was a decision that had always remained vague in
the planning. Planning and instinct are incompatible.

Back over the north bank of the Danube, the
Mosquito orbited at an altitude that would just give
them a look at the train's smoke. McLaughlin was busy
with the binoculars.

"I'll be damned," the navigator said. "Do you
know what that flak gun on the flat car is? It's some
kind of Maypole or flagpole. It has a stripe running
around it and a wreath with a swastika at one end.
There's not a sign of life on that damned bridge."

"There's the train," said Croft. "Get those lights
on."

From their wide orbit, the Dambuster lights traced
a dim circle on the snow and ice of the river. Croft
turned the special ranging sight on and leaned forward.

Asia seemed to crawl onto the bridgehead, causing Croft to think he had miscalculated her speed badly. But it couldn't make that much difference. When the
engine was halfway between the bridgehead and first
pier, the pilot pressed the button on his control; the
first Tiny Tim rushed forth below the fuselage. It was
then a matter of firing the remaining three rockets: the
second at the first pier and the third and fourth at the
second pier.

Bill McLaughlin had held his breath like a man
under water. When the second pier disintegrated, he
blew up with it.

"Christ! Christ! Will you *look* at that damn
bridge!"

It was the train that Croft watched. Her engines,
and first three cars disappeared with the bridge. The

remaining cars plunged into the river, a fall of nearly a hundred feet.

McLaughlin was pounding Croft's head and shoulders.

"If you'll let up a minute, Bill, and turn on that VHF, we can report this thing to the authorities."

While Bill fiddled with the radio, Croft took one long look at the broken bridge, then set the Mosquito on a climb toward Frankfurt. When the duplicate red lights flashed, the pilot pressed his microphone button. The restricted channel was guarded by a fresh *Oboe* crew.

"MACCABEE Relay, this is MACCABEE One. Do you hear me, over?"

"MACCABEE One, you are loud and clear. What is the message?"

"Relay, the message is—" Croft turned quickly to his navigator. "What the hell were we supposed to tell them, Bill?"

"The temple is restored, you clot!"

"Relay, the message is: The temple is restored."

"MACCABEE One, we will tell them 'The temple is restored.' Anything else?"

"That is all, Relay. This is MACCABEE One, out."

"T'raa, MACCABEE One."

17

Duel at Frankfurt

"Bombs falling now at *Füchsin!* . . . it is forbidden to leave the shelters except on direct orders . . . ready all sand and water stores . . . anti-incendiary squads will begin recruiting citizen-helpers . . . *Führebefehl Nr.35* is in effect and the message is: 'A baker's dozen, a baker's dozen.' "—for the first time in the Reich, a special squad would publicly execute thirteen random Germans at the raid's end—"The Propoganda minister reminds us that we have another opportunity to grind the enemy against the steel of Germany. *Sieg Heil!*"

First, Wilhelmshaven, Bremen and Bremerhaven. Then forty minutes of quiet. Then Berlin and simultaneous spoof raids at Kiel, Erfurt, Münster, Dortmund, Essen, Hannover and Hamburg. All the while, it was to be Frankfurt.

The opening at Frankfurt was orderly, for Wing Commander Timmins' Pathfinders dropped the initial salvoes onto bright pools of red through a fairly clean sky. There were scattered clouds and a winter mist but no moon and, strangely, no flak over the main railyards at target center. They'd had a fright when the disciplined searchlights came on all at once, but then the lights had gone crazy. From a height of 20,000 feet, the men in the bombers saw only the giant-stepping mushrooms running up the central tracks. They had faith, they knew the photoflash snaps would prove, at assessment, to be "interesting" or "not without merit," in the usual words of Timmins. One of the unearthly-flat shots would prove that an eight-driver locomotive had reared straight up on its smokebox, spreading a dense sauce of steam over the picked ribs of its twisted track. At high magnification, one of the assessors would solve the problem of the "clock figure."

"Look here," the assessor would say, "I believe this is a 12.8-centimeter railroad gun (the minute hand) lying across its carriage (the hour hand). These dozen men (the numerals) were blown out in a perfect circle as they were activating the gun. Incredible!" The clock was stopped at 03.40, four minutes after T-zero. And *that* was truly incredible.

Color was missing from the black and white photos. Also sound and smell. Also closeups.

Six minutes after Timmins had wheeled his large group sharply away to the welcome dark southwest of Frankfurt—"There's the half of it, Skipper, can we *please* pull our finger out right now?"—the familiar deterioration of the target site began. Three squadrons directly behind the Pathfinders started up the tons of dust and smoke that nourished an incipient fog to make a stable, filthy haze. Visibility fell rapidly as the haze rose, filling elaborate channels in the cloud labyrinth. (Yet in the conspiracy peculiar to debriefing, the chaos of Frankfurt would be tidied for the records. Squadron intelligence officers, who rarely saw a bombing, and weary, adrenalized crews would compromise on a civilized summary that would satisfy the main thrust of British history.)

"Estate Car Force, this is the controller: you are already beginning to fall back. Let's not have that tonight, chaps, we've made a bloody good start here!" The Master Bomber was an expert at projecting anguish. "Bomb right on those reds, will you?"

The Master Bomber's Mosquito raced across the brilliant arena of the railroad yard, out over the surrounding dark rooftops, under constant fire from the deadly, bright-colored 37-millimeter flak. He was a powerful presence. He spoke anxiously against the natural tendency of terrified bombers to creep back and back from the aiming point.

"Master Bomber, this is Check One at angels twenty. We have difficulty seeing the target. You have a dreadful haze down there. Your clouds are building up."

"Do we need the sky markers, Check One, over?"

"Not yet, not that bad yet."

"Right-o, Check One, thank you. Attention, all Estate Car Force: let's try dropping from two thousand feet below your assigned height bands. Repeat, bomb two thousand feet lower if you are not already in your runs. Who is my Check aircraft below twenty thousand, will you come in, please?"

"Check Two here at angels fifteen, over."

"How do you see it, Check Two?"

Six squadrons, nearly two hundred bombers, had by now crossed over the target center.

"Fairly well here, Master. Getting ropy though."

Thousands of incendiary sticks were falling. The liquid, maplike sparkle they made on ground structures were filtered by their own smoke and the dust, removing a sense of the heat that turned sand into glass, that caramelized and charred human flesh.

"Check Two, thank you. Link One, will you please send the following home:

TARGET SUCCESSFULLY ATTACKED ON PRIMARY PLAN STOP WEATHER CONDITIONS FALLING RAPIDLY STOP SKY MARKERS MUST ARRIVE HERE IN TEN MINUTES STOP AND OUT."

Startling white photoflashes repeatedly silvered the dark clouds, throwing generations of flickering shadows onto a gray, bleached city. The monstrous cloud of incendiaries and smoke spread, drifted, settled. An ammunition store near the rail yard went up, an orange hemisphere laced in black and pierced by flying spines of white hot shrapnel. One mile from the aiming point, jettisoned bombs ignited a gas main. The *fssk!*

of an electrical transformer was distinctively violet-green. *Leichenfinger,* the hated cadaver-fingers of flak tracer, strobed fanwise across the marbled sky, stretching sluggishly for victims that the impatient Würzburgs had marked with the speed of light. A decrepit Halifax was straddled and caught by a cone of searchlights. Two lines of white smoke streamed back from the starboard engines, as a tiny string of black pills fell into the light from the bomb bay. The illuminated craft rolled slowly onto its side and curved down to its doom. Out of curiosity, the searchlights followed until someone ordered them back to work.

Four old Heinkel 111's fanned out over the mean top of the lowest cloud layer, dropping lanes of green-tinged white flares. A school of Ju88 night fighters freelanced across the pillowed high shooting ground to pick up dull outlines of the bombers against the lighted clouds. As the last of the candles on their miniature parachutes sank into the wet clouds, several searchlight regiments received orders to produce *Mattscheibe* for the night fighters. The 200-centimeter lights were defocused and swept slowly across the cloud base, producing a frosted-glass effect. An inexperienced night fighter pulled up to shoot at his own shadow and spun down to his death.

"Markers, this is the Master Bomber. My petrol is low, I must leave the target. Can you stay?"

Marker Nine thought he could manage another five or ten minutes. Ten said he was about finished.

"Right, Marker Nine, I will call for sky markers before I go. Will you look after them, please? Perhaps you could drop your remaining yellow on target center. Tell your blokes they have done a fine job here tonight."

Staffelkapitän Dr. Günther Birk of 1/NJG8 had gone down into the cauldron to find the Master of Ceremonies. Birk's horrified observer looked back at the radarman and tapped his own helmet, mouthing the word "Crackers!" The doctor, who had no living relatives, looked after the health of ten women in a Frankfurt brothel. In effect, the women had adopted the lonely, violent man and had partially tamed him.

Birk found the well-lighted Mosquito, skillfully weaving through the dense flak fields on its last sweep across the city. With precious speed gathered from his steep dive, the German night fighter overtook the important enemy and started long deflection firing before he was in a good position. No one was more surprised than Birk when the Mosquito stalled and spun.

"We struck the pilot!" Birk screamed, his whole body shaking violently. This alarmed his crewmen more than the thick bundles and puffs of flak whipping around their cabin.

The Mosquito crashed within the city limits, untouched earlier by nearly half an hour's exposure to the wildest groundfire that anyone had ever seen. The same 20-millimeter pompoms and 37-millimeter low flak cut Birk's Ju88 into pieces of scrap so small that much of it fell on Frankfurt like the last dry leaves of winter.

It was an airport traffic controller's nightmare, the ten-mile, forty-five-degree sector west of Frankfurt-am-Main. Here the bomber stream was most condensed, running up and turning out again. At any moment, more than 300 aircraft, six in every square mile, filled the airspace to an altitude of four miles. Lancasters, Halifaxes and Stirlings came into the critical angle, many of them limping, smoking, burning, exploding, while faster craft on both sides fought back and forth across the backbone of the sluggish, seemingly endless stream. The nerveless, cold nonweavers (Wing Commander Timmins the paragon of this rare strain) were far outnumbered by the weavers. Some corkscrewed continuously from Lincolnshire to Frankfurt and back in complicated patterns that were almost patentable. Some climbed slowly and steadily, others descended. En route there was fraying and widening; at the target there was drift, overshoot and fallback.

Except over the brightest area of the battle, few men ever saw either friendlies or enemies between the takeoff and the blessed touchdown. Yet it was a common, breathtaking experience to bump and rock across a fresh slipstream, that invisible track which could wrench the control column from a strong pilot's hands and suspend the vital functions of all his crew. The ultimate horror of a midair swipe or head-on collision, or a direct hit by the heaviest shells could hardly be imagined but one or another of these catastrophes was vividly displayed with statistical regularity.

Bomber Command was very touchy on the subject of bomb jettisoning or aborting of a mission. At the least, it was foolish to carry out these actions without airtight explanations, for either was sufficient to nullify the trip no matter how close the crew had come to the dropping point. What Bomber Command liked was boyish high spirits. The dropping of trash on the enemy, for example. In addition to their pay loads, many of the crews delivered private collections of the city on Frankfurt: beer bottles, of course; English soil and rocks; bricks and cinder blocks; cartridge cases of all calibers; newspapers and pornographic booklets; metal scraps and shavings; paper bags full of water (and sometimes urine or feces). Jolly good!

"Testing, testing, testing, testing: one—two—three—four—five—four—three—two—one. Testing, testing, testing, testing, testing. . . ."

No voice in any language could have been so abrasive and monotonous as that of "Oor Wullie," the Airborne Cigar of 101 Squadron, Ludford Magna. The powerful, multichannel electronic jammer, a modified Lancaster with three large spar aerials and a special radio operator, was a little late. It began to broadcast nonsense.

". . . Weather changes as of 0245 follow, code Victoria double A-Able: william george george unit victor *slant* iota unit x-ray tare baker *slant* fox william charlie love love *slant* zed king harry mabel victor"—thirty-two five-letter groups followed—"I will repeat, code Victoria Able-Able: william, george. . . ." Oor Wullie confused the Germans.

Even the code designation was trivial, being the name of a girl the radioman had met the night before. The utterly meaningless message was intercepted by Air Intelligence Regiment 351 of *Funkaufklärungsdienst,* the 10,000 man Radio Reconnaissance Service.

Oor Wullie would have been famous in the RAF if the broadcasts were made on Allied channels and if there had not been great secrecy on the *Corona* jamming program. But the hated voice—actually a dozen voices, live and gramophone- or wire-recorded, male and female, direct from the Lancaster or relayed from England—was well known in Germany. There was always a basic program, with wide latitude for the contingencies of battle. Oor Wullie most enjoyed the sometimes hilarious three-way conversations with controllers and night fighters:

"Moselle One, turn slowly right, the target will be two hundred meters above you." A controller between Mainz and Frankfurt had worked himself into a sweat with Major Paul Lorenz from Speyer-Bruchsal. The pair had discovered the presence of *Serrate* in the bomber stream and had agreed to go after them instead of the docile bombers.

"Correction, Moselle One: turn slowly left, left!" The counterorder from Oor Wullie was in perfect German.

"What the hell——?" Lorenz shouted.

"Yes, what are you doing? Clear this waveband, *we* are working Moselle One. Repeat, Moselle One, turn *right,* HARD now!"

"That is correct, *left, left!*" said Oor Wullie.

"Damn, Moselle, we have lost him! We must start again, please ignore this jammer. Level up, fly course null-nine-null, that is null-nine——"

"—Nine." Oor Wullie blended smoothly with the controller, imitating him perfectly.

"Is that null-nine-nine?"

The exasperated Lorenz was not immediately enlightened, for a terrible roar suddenly came into his earphones. Purely by chance, a wireless operator in the main force tuned into the major's waveband and activated a less sophisticated jamming device than Oor Wullie's. It was called *Tinsel,* a simple microphone mounted in one of the port engine compartments. NOISE!

Right after he had done his bit at Frankfurt,

Timmins' bomb-aimer had come back up into the cabin behind the cockpit, desperate for the company of the navigator and wireless operator.

"The bomb-bay doors never closed," they told him.

"I'll have a look," said the bomb aimer. He doubted he could do anything but it would keep him busy.

For twelve minutes, as far as Timmins knew, his Lanc flew alone as if the war had gone away. Even his own squadron had straggled and lost him. Their peril, of course. It was so quiet out here that the tail-gunner stopped exercising his turret and guns. They were frozen in less than a minute. Exhausted and very cold —the outside air temperature was—45 degrees Centigrade—the normally bright tail-gunner was fascinated by the length of the icicle he had grown on his oxygen mask.

A.M. Pamphlet 165. Icicles. In very cold weather the moisture from the breath may freeze in the region of the mushroom breaking-out valve . . . it is important to break up the ice with the finger and thumb at repeated intervals and not to indulge in competitions to see who can grow the longest icicles (see Figure 88). As the icicles increase in length obstruction to breathing out occurs, the efficiency of the oxygen system is much impaired and the risk of frostbite increased.

The tail-gunner had often called his mates back to witness the champion icicles he could grow on the way home. Tonight he had brought a vacuum bottle along. He was going to take this beauty all the way back to England.

There was nothing to be done about the bomb-bay doors and the aimer knew it. He rested briefly at the head of the runway to the rear turret. A cannon shell slammed through the left edge of the runway tearing up nearly half the diamond decking over the rear of the open bay. The aimer, thoroughly dazed and with a shattered leg, scrambled blindly forward toward the dim lights up in the cabin. Timmins had started his famous corkscrew and the Lancaster brutally tossed the bomb-aimer out through the broken deck. He would have been caught by the bomb-bay doors, if they had been closed.

Both the navigator and the wireless operator heard their friend's shouted word: "Shit!"

"And he didn't have his chute with," said the navigator, disapprovingly. "How many times have you heard me tell the little bastard about that?" The two men huddled over their small table, watching Timmins and the flight engineer fighting for all their lives.

"Timmy will bring us through, all right," prayed the wireless operator, who was the baby of the crew. He'd been out with them only three times and he talked about the skipper as if he'd seen the old man walk on the water. Yet the young operator's jaw was trembling in fear and the navigator reached over to grip his shoulder. A second, a third explosion rushed forward through the fuselage tunnel. The wireless operator was hurled against the flight engineer on the right side.

"Get the hell off my back!" said the engineer, his eyes watching Timmins' movements. He pushed the lad away without looking.

"But he's dead," whispered the navigator.

Maybe he isn't. The navigator was dragging the boy to the rest bunk in the wing bay when the flames boiled up, back between the runway ammunition boxes. Wrenching a fire extinguisher from the nearest bulkhead, the man pushed himself toward the fire like a fiddler crab, protecting his face with the metal tank. The flares, the flares! He remembered that they had not tossed all their flares out of the chutes.

The extinguisher sputtered and quit.

"Goddamn those people, I'll put them all on a charge!" the navigator said. He threw the defective cylinder out through the holes in the deck. He tried to pull another extinguisher out of its clamps. The bloody thing stuck and his hands were burned but he finally pulled it away. Spraying the contents into the fire, he found that the hot extinguisher was making no headway. Unable to reach the mid-upper gunner or tail-gunner, who were aft of the fire, the navigator turned to the flight engineer for help. The Lanc stood up on its tail at precisely the wrong moment, sliding the navigator backward along the oily diamondplate. Not even the mid-gunner could hear the screams of the man clawing desperately at the jagged edges of the flooring. Leaving most of his hands and the flesh of his arms on the metal, the navigator was wrapped into the flames.

The mid-upper gunner had known they were badly hit but the draft of the bomb-bay fortunately sucked the fire down and away from the narrowing tail section, which ran below his feet back to the fire doors protecting the tail-gunner. A line of tracers slashed under the tailplane into that section. The mid-gunner fired wildly back into the void between the oval fins. His taboo track, an interrupter gear which kept his own guns away from after parts of the Lancaster, was at the same time struck by one of the night fighter's shells.

"We have stopped the tail-gunner, Rudi," said *Kommodore* Gabriel.

He was wrong about that, having misread the mid-upper's shooting *through* the tail structure. The mid-gunner had killed his own tail-gunner, who had been unconscious for several minutes, starved of oxygen. He would have died soon anyway.

"We have a fire going in the belly," Gabriel added, "and now I will start on the engines." He was embarrassed and faintly insulted by the Lancaster's superior twisting and turning.

Down near Munich, the Seven Division headquarters at Schleissheim had made a tenuous connection between the confirmed destruction of an "official" train on the Donauwörth bridge and a persistent *Kurier* speeding up into the Frankfurt area. One of those alerted was the *Midas* controller at Mainz. Gabriel's spot on the controller's plot was quickly identified as in the best position for the problem. Even had he not been so favorably located, they might have tried to use the *Kommodore* anyway.

"Beaujolais One, this is *Midas*. Order: break contact immediately and fly one-three-five. We hope to intercept an important *Kurier*."

"*Midas*, sorry, I am——"

"*Order,* Beaujolais One! This is on the highest authority."

Gabriel was tempted to make one more pass at the stricken Lancaster but decided he had not really earned that, anyway. He turned the Owl onto the new southeast course they had given him.

Wing Commander Timmins was suddenly aware that his tail-gunner had stopped firing, then the night fighter had stopped, too. He began calling both gunners on the intercom. The flight engineer saw the bloody mess of the wireless operator behind him for the first time. He had no idea where those buggers, the navigator and bomb-aimer, had gone, until he saw that the damn fools had left the armored doors between the cabin and center section open. Then, through those doors, he saw the fire.

"Timmy, Timmy, we're burning!"

"Ah, I can't get either of them on the wire," said Timmins. "Will you have a look back there?" He seemed to have misunderstood his flight engineer.

The engineer was back in seconds, almost unable to speak. He grasped the skipper's helmet and stammered into his ear. "The two are gone, Timmy. Can't get to the others. Best get out of this!"

"Are you mad?" With a scornful flash of his black eyes, Timmins checked the Lancaster's altitude and switched on the automatic pilot. "Here," was all he said, "George is on. You just sit here and watch him."

The pilot yanked a hand extinguisher from the cabin wall and another from behind the engineer's seat. Dropping them into the bay between the mainspars, he surveyed the fire before climbing through to the center section. His first impression was that the poor engineer had been right. But if he could not properly account for four members of his crew, Timmins would sit in the kite and burn.

He quickly analyzed the fire's behavior. It seemed strictly limited to the after end of the bomb-bay. The extinguishers would do no good because the foam would blow out as fast as the flames. If he could en-

large the gaps in the decking, perhaps it would blow
the fire out. Failing that, he would bang the bomb-bay
doors; if they closed, they might snuff the flames out.
He wrenched a fire-ax down and attacked the seams
of the decking.

It would never do. The pilot slipped as he threw
all his weight into a last, blind stroke. The ax slid
through his grip. Its heavy head bounced soundlessly
against something, not metal, down in the bay and
the huge doors cracked fully inward and closed. Timmins assumed that the fire, obviously never threatening the flares, had been suffocated. (An idiot had temporarily stuffed a large, rolled tarpaulin up behind the
crutches in the bay, wedging against the door micro-
switches. The stiff cloth had then been soaked by high
octane fuel trickling all the way back from the
bomber's nave. The heavy ax knocked both problems
out into the slipstream.)

There were no immediate clues to explain the
loss of the navigator and bomb-aimer. Even more trou-
bling was the absence of the mid-upper gunner from
his intact turret. *He has evidently departed via the
main access door,* thought Timmins. *Well, he must
have had good reason.*

Opening next the small folding doors protecting
the rear turret, the wing commander was relieved to
see his second gunner still there. Obviously wounded.
The turret was angled forty-five degrees to port, the
guns trailed downward. A "dead-man's gear" was
supposed to allow centering of the turret from outside;
it was totally u/s. The gunner was sealed off. But the
skipper felt he had encouraged his man, seen the lad
nod, shift his position slightly, wave his hand weakly.
All the movements were caused by stiff whipping of
the tail, as the flight engineer took the Lanc off and
back on auto-pilot.

The engineer gladly relinquished the pilot's seat.
They were dangerously low on petrol, he thought,
suggesting damaged fuel lines, probably in the cross-
feed between the wings.

"All right," said Timmins after minutes at the
controls, "I can't promise we'll not go down in the sea.

I'm advising that you bail out in about five minutes when we're safely over the middle of Holland."

The flight engineer was prepared to dally, although he really wanted an order to jump. He had never endured a night like this.

"What are you going to do, Skipper?"

"I'll be coming right after, never fear. So that's an order, just for the records."

When Timmins gave the word, the engineer squeezed his commander's knee wordlessly and went forward to drop out of the bomb-aimer's compartment. Timmins, who had not the slightest intention of leaving his trapped, helpless tail-gunner, was annoyed by the frigid blast now coming from the open hatch forward of his legs. *Should have asked the blighter to go out the main door*.

Timmins leaned out all his mixtures on the four engines as far as he dared. Airscrew pitches were reset for the longest possible descent. He was fairly comfortable about his course to the Dutch coast. There he would hope to find a familiar rock or two that would set him on the best crossing to the Woodbridge facility. With his petrol low and a wounded man aboard, there would be no time to waste stooging about the East Suffolk countryside.

Midas introduced *Kommodoreoberst* Gabriel to the Wooden Wolf at 04.08. The control station near Mainz, sweeping through an 80 kilometer radius, had just picked up the *Kurier* on a course of 308 degrees.

"Attention! Beaujolais One, this is *Midas*. He is flying almost reciprocal to you, three thousand meters high, climbing, forty kilometers away. Hold your present course, speed and height."

Gabriel's *Höhenmesser* said 6500 meters. Halfway between Mainz and Heidelberg, he was close to the Rhine where the Neckar joined. And with Speyer-Bruchsal not far beyond that, Rudi Anderian prayed for the problem to fall apart or the fuel to run out. Rudi's sets were on standby. So were his intestines. Hardly recovered from Frankfurt, they coiled under his diaphragm like vipers.

The chief *Midas* controller had taken over the interception, transferring his assistants with their red and green spots to a reserve Seeburg table. One of the girls subtly kept the table clear of a steady drizzle of ashes from the chief's cigar. All of them were in awe of this man who really could not carry on a decent conversation outside the plotting room. He was very fat and he was shy in daylight. Even in *Luftwaffe* parade uniform, he looked like an Italian prisoner.

"Maybe he is sloppy," said the prim *Helferin* so compulsive about the ashes, "because there is nothing in that big head but these numbers."

He dropped ashes, he smelled, he was flatulent and he belched by radio all over the middle Rhineland. But no one questioned his cunning and they'd never seen him fully occupied. Even now, he could not keep his big nose out of problems at the other tables. He had never been off the ground in his life, yet through his scopes he *saw* the German sky and the German aviators moving fluently through it as the old Beethoven must have heard his music.

"Well, what do we actually know?" The major started thinking aloud, drawing in his brighter helpers. "They close at a thousand kilometers an hour. Two or three minutes for our first move. Will the target make any drastic changes? Stephan? Gisela? Heidi?"

"No, Major," said Stephan, firmly. He was the plotter, the divider-straightedge-sliderule pusher. "He is on a course for East Anglia. If he did come from the Danube or beyond, he has a real fuel problem."

"Correct, Stephan. If he *does* continue like this, though, what else do we know?"

Stephan placed a meter stick along the *Kurier*'s track so that it extended through Gisela's red spot. "He will pass almost directly over our station."

"And that will be very exciting for us, won't it? Gisela, you are the red spot. Stephan says you are very nearly on a diameter of our command circle. Why is that so bad for you and very good for us?"

"Because you will have me in your beam for the longest time, sir."

"Of course. Now we agree that the *Kurier*'s projected plot is the best possible case. What if the red spot does *not* hold what he has. Heidi?"

"Yes, Major! He could turn. On the one hand, he could turn to the right. On the other hand——"

"Stop, stop!" Heidi only tried to be so methodical because she thought it was the controller's way. "Would you rather see him turn left or right? This is not an easy question, Heidi."

The girl was flustered and she forgot to use all the evidence on the table. It was even clearer from the glowing green phosphor of the big search radar screens.

"Gisela?"

"Stephan?"

In England, they had received the Master Bomber's message saying that the raid had started well. Seventeen bombers had so far turned back short of Frankfurt: the Blighty boomerangs. One of these crews went down in the sea near Holland. Another got out of a burning Stirling over Saarbrücken; they could be prisoners. The other fifteen at least were not heroes. A few might be cowards.

"If you don't believe me, God damn it," said a tail-gunner at Leighford, "why don't you hop aboard next trip and see for yourself!" The intelligence officer was highly offended. He brought the cheeky liar up on a charge.

"There, there, Billings," said another IO at Nottingham, "we're not accusing you of anything. We know about the flak at Frankfurt." They simply had to cross-check Billings' story because the pilot had now turned back three times in a row. And he was only a flight-sergeant in an all-noncom crew. This IO could be dangerous with enlisted men.

"Ah-hah, our bad penny," said a WAAF rigger in the parachute loft at Pentland, as she checked in a flight-engineer's chute. Turning the pack around and over with exaggerated care, she asked how many bullets he thought they would find.

"You *bloody* effing bitch, you! Do you know, you're the only female I'd want to see on aircrew? I'd like to be there when you muck up your sticky drawers, filthy hag! Why, you'd shit all over the GEE-beams, you would!" As they dragged the engineer away from the counter, the cool girl made a rude gesture. "God save England," she quipped. Lord, how she loathed a coward!

Wing Commander Timmins had traded off altitude for airspeed during the run across the North Sea, stretching out his precious fuel. Red fuel-gauge warning lights were beginning to flicker. He was flying just under the cloud wedge that had been thickening from the time he'd seen its shelf at the border between Germany and Holland. He had crossed the sea under the downward press of the front. Ten miles from the Suffolk coast, there was the fog.

"The hell with it," said Timmins, calmly. He pressed the panic button for Woodbridge.

"The *hell* with it!" the pilot said, loudly. "I'm tired. I'm bloody tired! I'm going to occupy a desk and masturbate old Harris to death with his own figures."

Timmins announced himself to Woodbridge and asked them for FIDO. The fog was as thick as gray mucus but he kept coming down into it.

FIDO—Fog Investigation and Dispersal—was a heroic effort to save lives. Aircrew were constantly impressed with the system's expense. It was not all that good. The warm, coffee-drinking, wingless creatures at Woodbridge began to question Timmins' credentials.

"Turn the bloody thing on, Woodbridge," said Timmins, "or I'll spread this kite right through your bloody sergeant's mess, *do you hear me?*"

Someone recognized his name, perhaps, or else they really thought this chap would lay them out in parade rows. He sounded so awful.

Woodbridge technicians turned some valves in a pipeline, releasing a burning mixture of petrol and crude oil into the vast perimeter of Woodbridge, a rectangle two miles long and more than one-eighth mile wide. By a massive condensation of vapor droplets, the fog was hollowed out to form a ghostly cavern. Inside, the visibility was raised from a hundred feet to more than a mile. At a distance, as Timmins felt his way in on instructions from the Woodbridge caravan, the glare seemed to come from a long floodlit stadium. Crossing quickly through a region where the luminous fog threatened to blind him, the spent pilot found the magic field stretching out to the vanishing point before him.

A pipe! sighed Timmins, as he gentled the old Lanc down to the turf. He rolled past a crashed Halifax, around which they had set warning flares. *That's what I'd do with you, you old pross!*—he addressed his own bomber affectionately—*if our poor gunner wasn't stuck back there in your faithless arse.*

The single operation took four minutes. It cost the United Kingdom about one hundred pounds sterling, mainly for 2900 Imperial gallons of fuel. Woodbridge Control noted that the wing commander was Number 1057 among those who had so far made use of FIDO.

"Sir," said the flying officer who had ridden out with the van, "you understand that we must clear the airfield for other casualties." They were already pressing Timmins to allow his Lanc to be towed away.

"Where is your ambulance for my gunner? I called about this, you know, on my way in."

A leviathan tractor with towing gear and a Cole crane rumbled up out of the fog.

"No, no, I'm sorry," Timmins shouted, striding back to the tail of his Lancaster. "Perhaps you did not understand me. He is badly hurt in there and the aircraft cannot be moved until we have cut him out, you see. Then you can blow this ruddy kite from here to Air Council, for all I care."

Airframe artificers began sawing into the wrecked turret. They avoided the oxygen torches because of petrol trickling down from the bomb-bay. For the same reason, the wing commander had not lit a cigarette in his lips. Timmins waited anxiously to see his tail-gunner, the only other man who'd stuck out the whole trip with him.

Midas made the first mistake. Unavoidable, but a serious error nevertheless.

When the controller decided to turn Gabriel over

the *Kurier* slowly, they had just begun to lose the *Kommodore* in high cloud. The *Kommodore*'s signal was being swamped by heavy returns from a stationary storm in *Midas'* southeast quadrant.

"Beaujolais One," the controller said, "identify yourself in the Greek language, please."

Rudi Anderian activated *Naxos-Z*, to put an electron asterisk at their position on the *Midas* screens. He (and *Midas*) quickly learned that the instrument was not working.

"Beaujolais One, make a tight left turn. We must confirm your location."

Gabriel's Owl made the orbit. Its radar spot at Mainz also "orbited." A routine procedure but in this instance a mistake.

"Good, Beaujolais One, we have you. Steer left to three hundred degrees, come down at your lowest rate of descent."

It was a course to overtake the *Kurier*. Fortunately, it would take the *Kommodore* away from the storm.

McLaughlin had been in the hood all the way up from the Danube. Croft was going to join the bomber stream near Frankfurt and go back to England with them. Using the Mark XV to avoid collision, Bill had so far picked up nothing.

"I think we're being watched, John," said Bill. "I have a bogey up there, orbiting. Level off and turn slow, very slow, to port."

It worked.

"Beaujolais One, turn hard left, ninety degrees! The *Kurier* stops climbing, he is going to the west."

The *Midas* controller's mind was like a microfilm machine, even to the point of working best in dim light. On instant recall were a thousand cathode-tube images and their sky analogs. Several of these stored graphics now told the major that the problem was about to fall out of his hands.

"Yes, he turns when we turn," said McLaughlin. "Want to keep an eye on him?"

"Hell no, we don't have the fuel for that. I'm sorry, Bill, we have to go down where it's dark and safe."

Down to the floor of the radar ocean, where the most powerful microwaves were impotent. McLaughlin shuddered, sighed, put his wizard Mark XV on standby, reached for his maps.

"Beaujolais One, EMERGENCY!" screamed *Midas*. "The *Kurier* dives! His heading is two-seven-five. We will track you as long as possible. Stay on this waveband. Good luck!"

Midas was dismissed.

Gabriel slammed his yoke forward. Falling through 6000 meters, surely he could get the heavy Owl below the Mosquito, where Rudi's *Apparat* would work. But a cunning *Kurier* who twisted going down would wipe out the Midas heading.

From north of Heidelberg, Croft turned west across the Rhine. Now it was the plan to run out low through the Rhine valley, since a hundred-mile width of mountain country cut them off from the Belgian flat. But at 8000 feet, they slanted steeply into thunderheads of the storm that had worried *Midas*. An enormous electrostatic machine, its edges and base were alive with energy. Air turbulence buffeted the Mosquito, almost whipping the controls from the pilot's grip.

"Quick, what's the highest ground to the west here?" asked Croft.

"Donners Berg, about twenty-two hundred feet. We're not going to miss it by much."

"That does it. I'm flattening out at four thousand. Give me a vector home."

"Three-three-five."

Thick, frayed cables of lightning blazed repeatedly across fissures in the clouds. St. Elmo's fire sheared around the nose radome and over the leading edges of the wings like phosphorescent plankton in a destroyer's bow waves. Blue circles glowed at the propeller tips shedding tubes of spiral gauze back around the engines. Croft warned McLaughlin to keep his eyes in the hood. Bright violet streamers cascaded up across the windscreen to fuse in plastic figures, which were ripped away over the cockpit roof. Croft tried to watch only his instruments; he was nearly blinded and felt physically threatened by the display.

Deeper in the wet clouds, the electrical show was quenched.

The Owl dove so much faster than the Mosquito that it was missed by McLaughlin's rear-looking *Perfectos*. Forced to level out by the mountains, Gabriel was unaware of his favorable position.

"We can't hope to pick them up, Rudi."

"No, no, *Kommodore*, I have them! It's perfect. They are almost straight ahead of you at eight hundred meters and three hundred above. Turn left five degrees."

"Yes, Rudi." Gabriel was astonished and pleased. To himself he said, *you're quite a sparker!* Anderian heard it on the intercom, smiled grimly.

"We'll lose them if they go lower," Anderian continued. "I have bad echoes from these mountains. The clouds are damping me out."

"The damn Li antlers are wet, Rudi, that's part of the trouble." Moisture grew goblins on the big front toasting forks; it was not well understood. The English could keep their smaller antennas dry in neat housings.

Gabriel coaxed the Owl to close faster and followed his observer's instructions to climb slowly. As the signals improved, Anderian guided the *Kommodore* closer to this target than he had ever dared to do in practice. There was no frame of reference at all outside the cockpit. The pilot kept an eye on his panel as he peered ahead and up into the unlighted cloud. Only the dials would save him from vertigo.

"Rudi, I can't see them yet. This stuff is like black steam."

In the Mosquito, McLaughlin's discovery was like an icy draft from the tail. It caused a tingling of hairs on the back of his neck. He spoke hoarsely.

"I've got something on *Perfectos*, John. It's at dead center back there, about five hundred yards and slightly below us."

"Gaining?"

"Very slowly."

"He can't see us yet, so just——"

But they broke out of the clouds. The rough ground was itself invisible but snow reflected a subtle light.

"Hard right, John!—*go, go!*" Statistically, a right turn was slightly less to be expected than a left turn because most pilots were righthanded.

But Gabriel saw them. *Der Uhu schreit, Rudi!* The Owl screams, he said, switching alcohol into his engines for the second time that night. Anderian was thrown into his straps as the Heinkel leaped forward into a tight turn. His eyes on the enemy, Gabriel fought to cut inside them. The Owl staggered, wings nearly vertical.

You'll not get back in that cloud, English!

Gabriel fired all six cannons, not even trying to use the Revi sight. A fine mist amplified the bright muzzle flashes; the tracers curled back too short. Pounding recoils bucked the Owl into a stall so that it could not close the circular chase.

"Don't lose them, Rudi, for God's sake! I can't see them, I can't see them."

"Keep turning, *Kommodore*, they go all the way around—and down."

"I can't see them."

Croft had no intention of hiding, having made visual contact with the earth again. McLaughlin would prefer the clouds and his magic scopes but the earth restored his pilot's confidence. Besides, there was something strange about this Ju88; it was very fast. To simply run away—they could not stand and fight without guns—might not be enough.

"From where you picked this bogey up, Bill, how far west do you think we went?"

Time and distance were practically interchangeable to them. "About eight minutes," Bill answered.

"Forty-five miles. Look, if we backtrack just a little toward Frankfurt, won't we get right out of these mountains on the Rhine again? I want to sneak out along the river."

"Okay, okay," McLaughlin said gloomily. His red light shimmied over a map. "Steer zero-one-five."

Damn, he thought, *here we go into a winding match at zero feet! Jinking through the hills at night. Powerlines. Flak towers. Chimneys. Some Hausfrau's clothesline. I wonder what the Germans call a winding match.*

The two machines, tandem wasps, raced over the mountains and then the hills.

"They seem to be going for Frankfurt again, *Kommodore*," said the puzzled Anderian, "but they're not climbing."

His target seemed to feel its way down. Gabriel followed the observer's instructions meticulously, disappointed and not entirely comfortable with what was happening. The enemy was out of his visual range.

"Aha! Yes, my dear Rudi, I see what he wants to do, this clever fellow. He wants to slip out along the Rhine at *Ritterkreuz* height. We'll see about that, *Tommy!*"

For the third time, the engines were abused by long draughts of methanol, as Gabriel tried to catch his target before it had descended too far. The lives of his engines were shortened every time by the poison alcohol for, as Bockelmann always told the *Kommodore,* they were only human.

"He's gaining slightly now, John."

Croft already had full normal boost on. Now he pushed his throttles right through the CLIMB stop, set the supercharger on AUTO, upped his turns to 3000 rpm, pulled the boost CUTOUT. These were full COMBAT conditions and there was no fuel injection for more power.

"Still gaining, he is."

"Getting cracking, you fucking tart!" Croft bobbed against his straps as if the Mossie were a racing sled. He was worried. No Junkers 88 he knew about could catch the slowest Mosquito.

They came to a river.

"If this isn't the Rhine, I'm sorry," said Croft, banking sharply to the west again. Dawn was more than an hour away, yet there was a forecast of the light all around the sky. The clinging mist no longer seemed so solid on the river banks.

"He's still riding back there like a tow sleeve," said Bill.

"Jesus! All right, I'm chopping the speed way down." Croft estimated the visibility. "Sing out when he's in to five hundred yards."

When McLaughlin marked 500, Croft took off more throttle. As the airspeed needle touched 190, he dropped the undercarriage, then the flaps. He sidestepped the Mosquito briefly, starting the wheels up at the same time.

There was no way to slow the Owl that quickly. Gabriel could not get below, for the Mosquito was nearly boating on the river. He could not turn widely enough in the river's trough on either side to weave and stay behind. He horsed the Owl straight up, cursing.

Less than a hundred yards behind the Heinkel now, Croft mimicked every move. He exulted in this; it was almost a sport.

"I'll be damned if this baby doesn't have a twin tail! It's *not* an eighty-eight. Bill, take a look with the glasses."

McLaughlin grabbed the Ross binoculars. "I've got him, John . . . Lord, what a monster!"

The Owl shimmered, so close, so optically big that Bill could only see a third of it at a time. The hazy image danced to the Mosquito's vibrations. It was a no-color dark; it had the faint gleam of antique pewter.

"Look at the rear of the engines, Bill. Do they stick way out behind the wings?"

"Not at all, nothing."

That ruled out the Bf110, which was too slow anyway, and those Arados that no one had ever seen in action.

"Now, the tip of the tail. Does it come out behind the stabilizer like a sting?"

"No."

So much for the Dornier 217. Except for the old Messerchmitt 110, Croft had seen none of the five night fighters he was thinking about. He had only studied small black models, silhouettes, a few photographs. "This is a Heinkel 219," he said. "I think they call it the Owl."

What did he know about an Owl? It was built just to catch Mosquitoes at night. He knew a lot about the Owl.

"Bill, we can't outrun or outclimb him and we don't have the gas anyway. I don't think he's in a panic, do you? So before he figures out we can't shoot, I'll try to have him make a big mistake."

There was no point in spelling it out for Bill. It was a frightening plan, especially when you weren't in the driver's seat. What was critical right now about the Owl was its very high wing loading, more than half again as much as the Mosquito's. Croft was going to kill them, if possible, with the German earth.

Anderian reported that the target had pulled out in front again. He shuddered to think that they had been below him all the while.

"I see him, Rudi, and that's his mistake. I think he must be out of ammunition, maybe even unarmed." Gabriel was the first to admit the English could shoot. "He'll never get behind us again, I promise you." That was true, although not for the *Kommodore*'s reasons.

McLaughlin had loosened his harness to twist partway around, since he could still see the Owl through the binoculars. Croft's hands and feet seemed tied to his controls, working them hard. A weaver, Bill imagined, running a loom to spin a deadly net. With the glasses, Bill would feed him as much fiber as he could gather.

"Bill, I'd strap up if I were you." The pilot's voice had that flat tone.

As he flew along the great river, Croft watched closely the dim shores parting back on either side. At a point where the river turned sharply, the centrifugal flow of ages had worn out a shallow bay from one rocky bank. Here Croft bored right in toward the low cliff. Waiting as long as his nerve could stand it, he hauled the Mosquito only far enough up to graze the cliff's cutting edge.

Rudi Anderian felt the Owl mush through the air like a hangar door. His thin neck buckled, his head sagged like a cannonball. His eyeballs dragged like gold spheres the surgeons used in enucleated sockets. Even the *Kommodore* was badly shaken; they had nearly smashed the cliff! He had a very dangerous enemy here, possibly suicidal. The Owl was much too heavy for this business. But what other way to hold a firing position, with the enemy glued to the Rhine? *My* Rhine!

When he had once more been tricked into a narrow ravine by the damned Mosquito, Gabriel decided *he* was the suicidal one. The *Kommodore* never panicked; nothing forced him to keep on. But he was a realist: perhaps the Englishman simply had the better night vision. And he was a fatalist: the fuel warning lights had blinked a few times and he had a very high temperature on one of his engines. So he began to fire the cannons. One of the Mosquito's engines burst into flames, trailing an orange streamer for a few seconds.

When he felt the strikes, Croft thought he was plowing through treetops, at first. Then he punched one of the big red buttons to feather his port engine and a smaller button to set off the Graviner fire extinguisher on that side. There was a strange cloud of dust or smoke in the cabin.

"Okay, Bill?"

There was no answer . . . Croft was trimming to counteract the dead engine's drag . . . at least there was no coherent answer. Bill seemed to say *Mother!* . . . over and over . . . *Mother* . . . *Mother*. . . . The navigator leaned far forward in his straps, his chin down on his chest. Croft knew he was dead as surely as if he'd examined the man. But he would have no reason to imagine that Bill had been saying *Heather* . . . *Heather* . . . *Heather*. . . .

So Bill was dead. One engine out. No guns. Fuel running out fast. Croft decided to ram his tormenter.

Gabriel was no barbarian himself and he never seriously took the English for barbarians, either. But here he had a Mosquito with one engine, probably unarmed, and it was *he* who suddenly felt trapped. They were in the flat country of Belgium now. A hidden moon and a sun just rising somewhere in the Ukraine gave only the illumination that would draw a faint line between earth and sky. Gabriel felt trapped because it had pulled up right in front of him and they had missed each other by only ten meters.

The shadow came at him again, for he had naturally scissored with it. He heard the single engine scream over his head in a Doppler crescendo. Closer it was this time, at 1500 kilometers an hour.

"For God's sake, Rudi, can't you help me?"

"*Kommodore . . . Kommodore. . . .*"

Gabriel could hardly hear his observer, who was trying to say that he'd been shot in the left shoulder. He was not shot but his arm and chest burned, he seemed to be swallowing his tongue, the noise in his ears was twisting the top of his head off. As he tore away the oxygen mask, Rudi's heart fibrillated, sloshing blood without purpose back and forth in the chambers and great vessel roots. And so he died, as his parents once thought he would. The heart was weak from childhood.

When Gabriel had scissored for the fourth time, he lost his nerve but still not his good sense. The English maniac could not block withdrawal. He turned the Owl away when the Mosquito turned back for the fifth time. The red fuel warning lights were on steadily. Gabriel reached down to switch tanks. One overstrained engine coughed; the other suddenly seized and stopped with a terrible grinding of metal. The Owl struck a low hill, bounced up in a shallow arc, came down again and slewed. The outer left wing section was torn away, causing the massive aircraft to tumble and cartwheel, to burst into flames. Burning parts, ever smaller, were shed like a line of road flares until there was nothing left.

Croft saw it all. Feeling neither curiosity nor a sense of victory, he turned west again, this time climbing slowly. *If they just leave us alone now. . . .*

Bill McLaughlin seemed to take up more space now than he ever had when he was alive. He slumped to the left, crowding the pilot. He dominated the cockpit like—like a silent passenger, which disturbed Croft most of all. The lamb's wool of the torn jacket was exposed all over the back. It was set stiffly in a gel of still-moist blood. There was a jagged hole in the sheet of armor protecting the navigator's seat behind. What had killed Bill was a direct hit on that armorplate.

Five miles ahead of the Mosquito, a crippled Halifax could not hold its height band on the run out of Frankfurt. A port outer engine was stopped; the port inner and starboard outer were smoking badly. The undercart was damaged so that one wheel hung halfway down. That would give them a bad time, if they ever got home at all. The pilot fought vainly to salvage what altitude he had.

Croft was exhausted. He could hardly be blamed for what happened.

The airscrew of the good engine stitched a perfect line of checkmarks into the bomber's lower fuselage from the tail almost to the nose. The glancing blows did no real harm to the Halifax, although they must have sounded to the crew like cannon or machine gun shells. Damage to the Mosquito was not serious, either, but it was very critical. Only a few inches of each propeller tip were curled; thrust was diminished and the engine was set to vibrating. The wheel of the Halifax had rolled across the canopy roof, smashing it down against the pilot's head.

Croft awoke with a sense of calm and well-being that he had never known. There was no pain. He seemed to know exactly what had to be done. Clearly, the first thing was to save Bill. They would never make it with the engine shaking like that. He punched the big disk on Bill's Sutton harness. The four straps were free. Then he tugged the wire that jettisoned the main exit hatch below Bill's feet. He kicked the small door, flipping it out into the slipstream like a poker chip. Wind howled into the cabin, blowing the navigator's maps against the roof. Croft trimmed the Mosquito to fly hands-off, though always losing altitude, so that he could cut Bill's seat straps and tie them together in a length of six or seven feet. Not much. He attached the free end to Bill's parachute release grip. It was difficult getting the stout, unconscious navigator, with his fat flying kit, out the door. Croft pushed the legs through first. He used his foot to get the rest out. They were over Holland. The worst would be a prison camp for Bill. He had a fifty-fifty chance of falling into Allied territory. Croft knew the ripcord line was very short. . . .

McLaughlin's body bounced against the fuselage halfway back to the tail. It was slapped and pounded against the thick plywood by the slipstream. The Sutton webbing from the hatch was tied to the proper grip but it was also tied to a chest strap. The chute never had a chance of opening.

Croft had worked slowly and carefully. But slowly most of all. He had planned to jump after his navigator but he had run out of Holland. Already out on the North Sea, he calmly prepared to ditch. As a Navy pilot, he had never understood the RAF's fear of the sea.

Air Pamphlet 2019C, Pilot's Notes (2nd ed.).— *(i) The aircraft has been successfully ditched by day but, whenever possible, bail out rather than ditch.*

No, that's out of the question. I'm too low. How long do you think I'd last in that water?

(ii) When ditching, jettison roof panel but keep entrance door closed.

The entrance door went out with Bill. The roof is crushed, the panel is jammed.

(iii) Lower flaps 25°.

Yes, I was about to do that.

(iv) If one engine has failed, the final approach should be made without engine.

Right! Sorry, I was brought up on one engine. Croft chuckled. He had the idea that his British friends were watching. Friends, but very critical.

Twenty feet above the water—he used the powerful landing lights for the first time—Croft cut the engine. The Mosquito hit hard but straight, bouncing once. A rather good landing; the pilot was pleased. But how stupid to forget the lower exit hatch! Here he shipped gallons of water. There'd be no time to work on the crash panel in the roof. Croft decided that he could not afford to panic.

He jerked the tabs on his mae west. Carbon dioxide bulged the limp cloth into a yellow pouter's breast. He checked the one-cell flashlight pinned to the mae west. It worked but it wasn't very bright. What else? Croft triggered the pistol in the roof and fired three flare colors of the night: yellow—yellow—green. He watched the green burn out high above the water.

By now, the cold salt water was halfway up to Croft's knees. Its weight had tilted the Mosquito slightly nose down. The pilot unbuckled his straps and put his feet up on the seat. The only sounds or motions came from the water. There was a gentle swell, which rocked the Mosquito, rolling the water inside to slap the bulkheads rhythmically. Croft was confident that the flow would stop, that the wings would then keep him afloat.

Croft had almost forgotten Rothschild's little gold Star of David. It caught his eye, swinging from the gunsight, when he idly flicked on the flashlight. He unhooked the slender chain from the sight and dropped the charm into an inner pocket. There was nothing more to do. Croft waited to be rescued. From time to time, he snapped on and off one of the many familiar switches in his cockpit, to keep busy.

Eleven minutes after the water landing, the Wooden Wolf slipped under the surface of the North Sea, ten miles off the mouth of the West Schelde.

And the air crackled, only a minute or two after that, with the sound of bastard German:

Thus will we hurl our enemies, poison tools of world Jewry, back from the sacred German soil—again and again and again. My iron will decrees this. No one can replace me, I say in all modesty, though assassins will try. The fate of the Reich depends only on me. Time will show that these vile attacks on us are but the brown stains of seaweed on the stone of our thousand-year fortress. I tell you, my people, we must learn the power of hate. To hate! And hate! And once again, to hate!

It was a wire recording. High over Frankfurt, the Airborne Cigar radio operator jammed all night fighter bands with old speeches of the *Führer*. The *Corona* people had found, quite by accident, that no English gibberish, no electronic screeching, so confused the German as a second or a third hearing of what the *Führer* had told them all when they were young.

Epilogue

"Assassination has never changed the history of
the world."

Disraeli

Leading Aircraftwoman Heather Stampford always
swore she could hear the thrumming of her Merlins
when they were still ten miles away on a cold, clear
night. Closer, they would growl and finally roar as
the sleek, shadowy form of the Mossie streaked across
the airfield at only a hundred feet, making a victory
roll if they'd had luck and if the pilot could see any
horizon at all. Lieutenant Croft was the only one
Heather knew of who slow-rolled at a hundred feet at
night. Then the Mossie would come back around to
land, skimming the fence by inches. Croft would turn
out of his landing run fast, as always, and drive the
Mossie toward her red torches in a wide arc. She
would slash a torch across her breast and hear the
engines race and die. The sudden quiet of that moment
was the goal of Heather's profession.

Bill McLaughlin would pop out of the hatch first,
jerking his clumsy helmet off. The damp hair would
stand out all over his big head. "Hi, Heather," he
would say, "what've you been up to?"

On the morning of December 1, it had turned
warm and Brevishall was enshrouded in fog. At three
A.M., Heather was out alone with her torches, waiting.
The engines would be muted by the fog, damped like

funeral drums, and several times the rolls and ruffles Heather heard were tricks the fog played on her keen hearing and her imagination.

Sergeant Snead joined Heather at four o'clock. Yes, he agreed, they *are* late. Impossibly late! said Heather. At four thirty, with the Lucite tips of her wands touching her trembling lips, Heather cried, "Oh Sam, Sam, something awful has happened!" The gruff old sergeant held her in his arms and gently stroked her hair with his rough fingers. *She's right,* Sam was thinking, *soomthing 'as 'appened.*

Sublieutenant Rosemary Ince got up from the chair where she'd been sitting at the Brookbridge radar screens and threw open the door of the mobile GCI caravan. Soft dawn sunlight filled the caravan with rose shadows. (Why is the sun so red, John?) She looked across the lonely dunes and the gentle surf of the North Sea where he had disappeared.

The WREN tried to blot out the next half hour, to concentrate only on getting back to their flat in Norwich where he had said he'd meet her. The spires of Norwich Cathedral drew her Morris toward the flat she shared with John Croft. From the high spire of the Cathedral, you could see on a rare, clear day the old town's other forty-nine churches and 300 public houses. One church a week but nearly every day a pub, as they say. But *they* didn't say that, it was John who told her that. He knew a lot about England. Not very much about Scotland.

Of all days, her mind screaming in pain and hiding what was yet to come, this morning Rosemary had to drive the Morris right over a constable's cycle on the outskirts of Norwich. She flattened it and the constable came out of a telephone booth with his eyes blazing. He took one look at her troubled green eyes, though, and said the damned cycle wasn't worth a square farthing anyhow. "King'll buy me another," he said. Rosemary thanked him and drove on. And on. And on.

She hardly knew how she got to the flat. And how could she go in? That prison of a flat . . . how could she go back to it? Unless, if by magic, he was there. . . .

The prime minister had finally gone to bed with a signal flimsy in his hand, saying *The temple is restored.* He had finished off his brandy and stubbed out his cigar at three thirty and they heard him snoring, happy. At seven, they had to wake the old man again and only General Ismay could carry in such dreadful news. The prime minister read the new signal and Ismay had to watch that noble face crumble, see the pale, sentimental eyes fill with tears.

Churchill roared from the bed for a pad. *Pray let me have,* he wrote, *on a single sheet, please, a full account of this event. By noon, latest.*

By the evening of December 1, Commander Matthew Dampier knew that his career in the Navy was compromised; for all practical purposes, it was ended. It would be a grim ending for Dampier loved the Navy, which was his family.

First, there were the two sets of orders that would be the heart of the inquiry and, if it followed, the court-martial. Alone, these orders would hang Dampier. He had issued the first set of orders, attaching ten men to ComNavEu, to Admiral Stark. It would seem that he had something special for these men to do and that he was cutting out the influence of Washington and all other commands west. But this first set of orders came when Priest and Squire and Murdock and Nicholas and Garland and Trice were killed in a period of two weeks. Dampier had decided to call off MACCABEE; Rothschild, Tarbox, Croft and McLaughlin had talked him out of that.

The second set of orders was initiated in Washington. Dampier understood that Clip Parmenter could no longer cover for London. These orders, dated November 25, directed the ten officers in England to report to the Chief of Naval Operations in Washington. On November 30, having lost six men, Dampier had allowed two more to carry out a secret mission that would itself be a major part of the inquiry.

Civilians, especially lawyers, find it hard to understand that orders are the heart of military law and that almost nothing supersedes them.

There was much more than orders. Captain Hamilton of NOCTU(Pac) had issued a tracer on Croft and McLaughlin. Dampier had letters from the Naval Aircraft Factory (Special Devices), Massachusetts Institute of Technology, Electronics School at NAS Vero Beach, Pearl Harbor Radar School—all asking for news of their people. Air Vice-Marshal Swann, sympathetic as he was, told Dampier that there would have to be a RAF inquiry into the deaths of Garland and Trice because they had been shot down by guns of the Anti-Aircraft Command.

Matthew Dampier seemed to accept his personal ruin as some kind of penance. There were only two questions in his mind. Most important was, what has happened to Croft and McLaughlin and the Czechs? Next, he wanted to know if they had gone out fruitlessly against an empty target. Had Hitler ever been in that train, *Asia?*

The second question was more easily answered, although it took three weeks. On December 16, the Germans launched a surprise offensive through the Ardennes region of Belgium and it became the Battle of the Bulge.

Yes, Hitler had been in *Asia.* But at two twenty in the morning of December 1, when *Asia* was twenty minutes north of Nuremberg, a message to the *Führer* was received in the train. This message caused the *Führer* and his main party to transfer to the pilot train in the forest above Nuremberg and ride back to Berlin. On December 2, in Berlin, Hitler held a seven-hour conference in the Reich Chancellery, in which he confronted and overwhelmed his field generals who were almost unanimously opposed to the Ardennes operation. It would gain them at least two months, said Hitler, and it would split the British from the Americans, while offering a possibility of the recapture of Antwerp, the most important port in Europe.

What about Croft and McLaughlin and Adeš and Miloslav? That was what Dampier really wanted to know and it took thirty years to find out. This book is only part of the answer, although it is complete as far as facts are concerned. How these facts were established is a story in itself but, unfortunately, a story that cannot be revealed at this time.

ABOUT THE AUTHOR

JOHN KELLY was a nightfighting pilot in the U.S. Navy and the RAF during World War II, and has been a medical school professor of anatomy and pathology and a biochemical research investigator in the field of cell biology. He lives in Westchester County, New York, with his wife and children.